SAINT

SIERRA SIMONE

Cover image: Stevan Reyes
Cover model: Zachary Ledrew
Cover design: Hang Le
Interior layout: Caitlin Greer

For Erica Russikoff.

Content Warning

The main character of this book has a history of depression, and his past experience with suicidal ideation before his diagnosis is described in Chapter Forty-Seven. This chapter can be skipped, and its meaning inferred from the rest of the story.

This book also contains brief mentions of sexual abuse of a child by a Catholic priest and a sister's death by suicide. The abuse and death take place before the events of the story.

Set me as a seal upon your heart,
as a seal upon your arm;

For Love is strong as Death,
longing is fierce as Sheol.

Its arrows are arrows of fire,
flames of the divine.

Deep waters cannot quench love,
nor rivers sweep it away.

Song of Songs, 8:6-7

PROLOGUE

The air is crushed sage and lavender, and a naked monk is singing in front of me.

He's sitting so that I can see his lips move against the warm summer air as he sings. So that I can see the bite mark I left on his hip not an hour before.

Naked, bitten, well-fucked.

Praying.

And he's praying with his whole body too, his lungs working, his ribs and back expanding and contracting, his face lifting to a sky so clear and blue it looks like the sky in a dream.

He thinks I'm taking notes for the article I'm supposed to be writing, but I'm not, I'm not. Instead, I'm noting the sweat running between his shoulder blades and down the muscle-banked valley of his spine to the dimples at the small of his back.

I'm noting the rich melody of his voice as he sings psalms in plainsong, the tones low and stirring as he sings them under

1

the rustling trees of this Provençal mountain.

I'm noting the scruff on his carved jaw, the brush of his long eyelashes over his sun-flushed cheeks, the working of his throat as he sings songs thousands of years old. The hair on his thighs as he sits cross-legged with his breviary in his lap. The careful trail of his blunt fingertip over the verses on the page.

Five years ago, this same man never prayed, never even stayed still for more than a few minutes at a time. Aiden Bell was all play, all energy—frisky, kinky, frenetic, kinetic. He was exhilarating and exhausting. He thrilled and thrummed through me like a drug, making every moment blurry and sharp all at once, and the crash was always worth the high.

Almost always, anyway.

I loved him.

I still love him.

He looks over at me after he finishes a psalm and smiles. "Come," he says, and I go, taking my notebook with me like it's a breviary of my own. And then as I join him on the blanket spread over the soft, dry grass, he drags me into his lap with an easy strength. In his past life as a chaotic millionaire, he had a playboy's body—lean muscles, a corrugated stomach, mouthwatering lines from his hip to his dick. But after five years of monastery labor, he's brawny and broad, big-shouldered and big-thighed, and even though I'm tall and older than him by five years, he pulls me to him like I'm a doll, nestling my ass against his groin.

He stirs and thickens against me, but he doesn't do anything about it. Instead, he wraps his arms around me and resumes singing his psalms low in my ear. His chest rises and falls behind me, the song vibrating through his body and into mine.

I close my eyes and listen. I close my eyes and feel.

There's no instruction manual for falling in love with your best friend's little brother. And there's no manual for falling back in love with him when he's a monk.

There's only the aching knowledge that you yourself are a kind of momentary prayer, uttered with reverence, spoken softly into the air, and then finished with a gentle and loving *selah*.

KANSAS

CHAPTER ONE

In the hermitage, I dream of him again.

This dream is slow and almost painful in its sweetness. We are on a plane holding hands, and he is scolding me for getting extra rental insurance for a car we've hired at our destination. I respond by scraping the pads of his fingers with my teeth until his scolds slip into shivers. We can't bear to wait to touch each other until we get to our hotel later that day, but the cabin is full, and first-class seats aren't convenient for under-the-airplane-blanket relief…

*What if…*he murmurs to me.

And it feels like the plane will never land, and maybe it never should, because at least if I'm here, then he's here with me, and if we're together, then that means I never left—

And then I wake up.

I'm sweating and my heart is racing and the sheets are slick with spilled semen. And my God, it's like losing him all over again when I dream about him like this. All fucking over again.

I sit up and scrub my hair, miserable with myself.

Four years and six months. Four years and six months of choosing this life, of finding a purpose beyond making money and chasing the next hit of dopamine. Of living close to the god who found me on the floor of my farmhouse one night, the god who'd found me when the tether holding me to life itself was gossamer-thin.

It's also been four years and six months of clawing myself free from a love I swear I still feel in my guts and in my marrow.

It's been four years and six months of trying to let Elijah Iverson go.

CHAPTER TWO

Silence, if you didn't already know, is a lie.

For example, I am currently in a hermitage in the woods, on the last day of a two-week silent retreat. My monastic brothers are two miles away, and there is nothing and nobody anywhere near me. It should be the definition of silence. It should be a vacuum of sound, a bubble of pure, undisturbed stillness.

And yet.

My breath is sawing in and out of my body. A storm-laden wind is yanking impatiently at the trees. Beyond them, just past the edge of my vision, a creek is rushing, glutted with recent rain. And from two miles away, I hear the faint toll of the bells from the church.

No, there is no silence here. Not in the truest sense of the word. And yet, it's somehow the utter opposite of noise.

I came from a world of noise. Of phones ringing, laptops humming, fingers tapping on iPad screens. Of cars and planes and clinking glasses of airport beer. Of voices—arguing, negotiating, cajoling. Of myself—loud and giddy and wild.

But there is only one common phone here, shared by all of us, and only a handful of computers and cell phones, used specifically for abbey business. There is beer, but it's drunk with pleasure, not desperation, and there is no negotiation, no wheeling and dealing, no hustling.

The silence here is birdsong and creeksong and wind in the trees. It's singing, praying, chanting, the ringing of bells and the drone of the organ. The whirr of tractors going up to the barley fields, the chirr and ruffle of the printing machines. The clink of rosary beads and the whisper of Bible pages and the echoes of music from places unseen.

It's the sound of Brother Patrick's life, not Aiden Bell's.

I drop my ax and wipe my forehead with my forearm, listening to the bells tolling for lauds. Normally, I would do what I've done every day for the past two weeks and say my daily office on my own, and then resume clearing the deadfall around the hermitage and turning the fallen trees into usable lumber to be hauled off to Brother Andrew's woodshed. But I'm still shaken from my dream, and I feel at loose ends with myself.

I'm worried that if I stay here alone, my thoughts will go back to him.

I lift my eyes to the hills.

I have just enough time to wash up and trot the two miles to the church before lauds begin, and I make it to the sanctuary just in time to bow towards the altar and slip into my choir stall before the first prayer is sung. The smell of incense is heavy in the air, but I still catch the scent of fresh wood and damp dirt on myself, even though I'd stopped by my cell to shuck my clothes and pull on a fresh habit to wear.

I hope I'll escape notice, but I know it's impossible. While the pews for lay visitors face the altar, the choir stalls in the chancel face each other instead. So when I look up, the first thing I see is not the altar or the crucifix behind it, but my former novice master Father Harry glaring at me. Glaring because I am unexpected or late, I'm not sure. It could be merely that he's never liked me. Not when I was a postulant, not now when I'm less than a year away from making my solemn vows.

But when I look across the aisle at my mentor, Brother Connor, and at Abbot Jerome, they both look like they're trying not to smile. And then I see Brother Titus and Brother Thomas giving me twin grins, and I relax a little. I haven't been late to lauds since I was a novitiate, and I've worked hard to scrub away all traces of Aiden Bell. Aiden Bell who was always late, always scrambling, always putting out his own fires.

Brother Patrick does none of that.

Brother Patrick is on time for everything. Brother Patrick rarely speaks and even more rarely laughs. He is responsible and hardworking and serious. He oversees the monastery's accounting, he helps wherever he's needed, and he's never a burden on anybody.

Brother Patrick isn't late for lauds, and he certainly doesn't come in his sheets dreaming of his ex-boyfriend.

My fingers tighten briefly around my breviary as I remember nipping at Dream-Elijah's fingers. My body tightens too, pressure coming from the cage I'd hurriedly locked around myself before I came here.

How will I make it through another year of missing him? Through *forty* more?

But Mount Sergius provides the answer, as it always does. My fellow brothers move into the first psalm, and the singing forces my breath to keep moving in and out. Forces my eyes across the page, forces my mouth to move, my lungs to expand and contract. Song fills the air just as the morning sunlight does, consoling in its timelessness. The sun has always been here, and so it seems, has the song. It's the Divine Office which grounds me: the prayer with our breath and muscle and bone.

After some more psalms, canticles, and prayers to St. Catherine of Siena—it's her feast today—lauds ends, and I close the breviary feeling better, feeling less restless and tight. Less itchy inside myself.

But I'm still a little unsettled. I came here to leave my past life behind, I came here to live entirely for God, but Elijah keeps blooming in me, and I can't seem to stop him.

I can't stop the tender shoots and slender, seeking roots of him, and I am his garden, his soil, his place, and it would be wonderful if I wasn't supposed to be the garden of my god instead.

Since I'm already here at the abbey, I eat breakfast with the others. We observe the Grand Silence until after our morning meal, and so the refectory is filled only with the slow clank of coffee mugs and the rustling of habits on the floor. No talking at all.

I've grown to like the sound of my voice less and less over the years—and I used to be the asshole who dragged friends and clients to karaoke bars at the end of a long night without a shred of contrition. I used to fill up entire meetings with bullshit, jokes, gossip, proposals, pitches, apologies, promises. I used to talk so much that Sean would hang up on me sometimes, so much that my mother started wearing headphones when she drove me to basketball practice because I wouldn't shut up about why Kansas City deserved a pro team.

One of the things I craved when I came here was to learn how to be quiet, so that I could listen to the same voice that brought me here. I wanted to be purified and refined like metal, all my dross burned away, and I wanted to burn it away by any means possible. Prayer, routine, labor, isolation, anything—anything at all, just burn the old Aiden away.

I finish breakfast before everyone else and take care of my dishes as quickly as I can. As suddenly as I decided I needed the company of my brothers, I decide I can't bear anything but solitude right now.

Those tendrils of Elijah are still twisting around my ankles and twining up my throat, and I don't know whether I need to pray or chop wood about it, but whatever I need to do, it's not here, it's not with other people around. This is between me and God.

But when I leave the refectory, I see Brother Connor waiting for me, his hands folded together and his lips creased in a kind smile. "Brother Patrick," he says warmly. "Will you walk with me?"

CHAPTER THREE

Even though all I want to do is to go swing an ax until I can't move anymore, I nod and fall into step next to him as he begins walking.

Brother Connor could ask me to scrub the cow shit off the barn walls and I'd agree, because I trust him completely. He's a short, slender white man with a snowy mustache and bright blue eyes, well into his sixties but with the energy and strength of a man half that age. Before he came to Mount Sergius in the eighties, he owned a karate school, and most days, he can be spotted under the large oak tree near the graveyard, practicing his old forms under its shady branches.

"I know you are silent today, so there's no need to respond to my rambling," Brother Connor tells me.

It's a courtesy, because there isn't a "you broke your vow of silence" jail at the abbey or anything. In fact, there are no vows of silence at Catholic monasteries at all, at least not in the permanent sense. There are periods of silence throughout the day, and brothers and visitors often take temporary vows of silence to induce greater introspection and contemplation—as I have been doing for the last two weeks—but there is no total surrender of words.

The only silences that are enforced—mainly by frowning and mild scolding (for severe infractions)—are the Grand Silence between compline and breakfast, silence at meals, and in the chapels where monks and visitors alike go for prayer. Still, though, I appreciate Brother Connor's courtesy. It's important for me to honor my promises to myself—even if they only matter to myself.

Especially if they only matter to myself.

Like, for example, the promise to have God and God alone as the sole object of my devotion.

"The abbot would like to see you," Brother Connor says as we walk from the refectory under a covered walkway toward the building that houses our various offices and the welcome center. Visitors are already beginning to mill about the cloister, sitting on the green, grassy garth or on the many wooden benches. "And I hope you don't mind, but I asked for the privilege of being with you while he speaks to you. I think you'll be very excited by what he has to say, and I wanted to see my Brother Lumberjack smile for once."

He says the last part in a teasing voice. All the brothers here are assigned work according to their strengths, and with my background in finance, my work has been primarily of a QuickBooks and Excel nature. But my other strengths are quite literally strengths, and so the abbot has designated me the official grunt of Mount Sergius. I heave plastic tubs of hops in the brewhouse, I lug around reams of paper in the printing house, and when I'm at the hermitage, which is less frequently than I would like, I'm tasked with chopping up the deadfall and bringing it to Brother Andrew, who is our resident carpenter. And the years of labor have left their imprint. While I've always been tall and wide-shouldered, there'd never been any doubt that my muscles came from solely a gym, but now...

Well, now I'm built like a lumberjack. And given that I haven't shaved in a week, I probably look like one too.

"And if you don't mind me saying so," Brother Connor says as I rub self-consciously at the thick stubble on my jaw, "you seem like you could use a smile today."

I'm grateful for my shield of silence right now, because I worry if I start talking, the old version of myself will take over and I'll never stop. I'm worried that I'll trap my friend in this walkway and make him listen to me describe the precise arch of Elijah's eyebrows and the low, rough notes of his voice.

So instead of speaking, I give a slow nod of assent.

Yes.

Maybe I could use a smile. God knows I don't get to see Elijah's anymore.

But I do feel better as we walk through the spaces of the abbey. The windows are open in every building we walk through, letting in the humid spring air and a stiff breeze intent on ruffling every paper in the building. It smells like coffee, grass, and something unique to Mount Sergius. Like incense and old paper and name-brand clothing starch.

It smells like life, like living. Like being alive.

And as it does every day when I remember why I'm here, the gratitude comes. I'm grateful that I'm here; I'm grateful to God and this place and even to the version of myself who came here.

I'm grateful and I'm content. And contentment is enough, despite the occasional wet dream.

"Memories aren't meant to be torments, Brother Patrick," Brother Connor says in a too-casual voice, the one that means he's guessed what I'm thinking about. "They are gifts."

Gifts, my ass, I want to say. But I don't. Brother Connor knows what I left behind when I came here. He knows *whom* I left behind. Everyone does, because I didn't want it to be a secret that I was bisexual. No more a secret than the late wives of the widowed brothers, no more a secret than the fondly remembered girlfriends and teenage sweethearts. I wasn't coming back into the Catholic fold because I felt shame about whom I liked to take to bed or whom I let into my heart.

I came here for God. I came here to stay alive.

Anyway, looking back, I can't help but think God led me to Mount Sergius for a reason, because the abbot understood me completely when I explained my stance to him, and then introduced me to Brother Connor, who eventually told me about the man he'd left behind to come here almost forty years ago, and who listened with the understanding of the fellow broken-hearted when I told him about Elijah.

Only Father Harry has been what I'd braced for: cold stares, pointed Leviticus readings at mealtimes, et cetera. I could've guarded against it better if he hadn't also been my novice master, but after the fifth meeting with him silkily suggesting that my soul was in mortal danger if I didn't repent of my lust for men, I went to the abbot and asked for help. That was when my spiritual development was given over to Brother Connor instead. It was an unusual arrangement, but monasteries are their own little worlds, somewhat removed from the ultramontane politics that stifles parishes and dioceses, and so Abbot Jerome was able to do as he saw fit. And then when the year was up, the post of novice master was given over to Father Matteo and Father Harry was put in charge of ordering giant rolls of toilet paper and industrial-sized bags of coffee and other such supplies.

Brother Connor seems to sense my inner disagreement with his words of wisdom, and his eyes twinkle as he pats me on the shoulder. "*Gifts*, Brother Patrick," he says again. "Because of what they can teach us."

My memories aren't teaching me anything other than how to hide stained sheets like a teenager, but I don't say that, of course, because I don't say anything at all. Temporary vow of silence and all that.

Abbot Jerome is already sitting behind his desk when we get to his office, the ubiquitous breeze blowing through the room and an audiobook playing from some unknown source. It's in French, and Brother Connor asks, "Proust again?" as we sit down in the sturdy wooden chairs set across from the abbatial desk. Brother Andrew made them years ago, and I'm grateful for them now, because the arms are set back far enough that I can sit with my thighs apart, which is more comfortable with the cage. Funny how I've forgotten how to move and sit with it on when it was a near-constant companion for me in my early days at the monastery. But in the last two years, I've needed it less and less.

Well, until last night, that is.

"I'm on to Camus now," the abbot says, looking up from the papers on his desk to us. "Vivre, c'est faire vivre l'absurde, and so forth. Hello, Brother Patrick."

The abbot looks like no one more than he looks like Friar Tuck from the cartoon *Robin Hood*, except he doesn't have a tonsure. And he isn't a badger, obviously. He's short and round, with fair skin, bushy eyebrows, and silver hair. His nose is as prodigious as his chin isn't, and his scoldings are as common as his smiles. He spends most of his free time writing about a very, very dead person named Gregory of Nyssa.

We sell his books in the gift shop. They have a lot of footnotes.

I nod my hello at the abbot, and he pushes something across his desk—scattering pens and what looks suspiciously like spilled Tic Tacs to the side as he does.

"I'm aware that you're silent today," the abbot says as I reach forward to take the packet of papers he's offering. "So I'm not expecting you to respond immediately to what you're about to look at. But I wanted you to have the chance to think about it while you're alone at the hermitage tonight. This, I believe, will require much discernment."

Paper-clipped to the top of the packet are three glossy

pictures. In them, rocky cliffs jut against a dark and cold-looking sea; a simple medieval church sits among austere hills with a crop of weathered gravestones around it; a small stone structure—*cottage* seems a generous term, perhaps *hut* is better—perches at the edge of the cliff, missing its doors and windows and roof. The sky is dark and coffered with clouds, and sea mist hangs in the air. The grass around the cottage seems nearly flattened with wind.

It looks like the end of the world. The absolute end of the world, and someone's built a monastery there.

My soul gives a sharp and silent cry at the sight of it.

"St. Columba's Monastery," the abbot says softly. When I look up, he's watching me closely. "A Trappist monastery on the west coast of Ireland."

Trappist.

Mount Sergius is a Benedictine abbey, meaning we follow the Rule of St. Benedict, who was the first person to lay out an actual plan for how clumps of people could live and work and pray in the same place without descending into spiritual chaos or unredeemable smelliness. But five hundred years after St. Benedict wrote out his plan, a group of monks decided nobody was following the plan hard enough and moved to a swamp and spent the rest of their lives in a sort of austerity-off with each other. Until eventually they turned the marsh into viable farmland and everyone remembered that it was nice to eat and rest and wear shoes once in a while, and by a few hundred years later, the Cistercians weren't much more austere than the Benedictines they'd broken off from. So then, another group of monks broke off from *them* and went hardcore austerity. Barely any food, constant work, silence, penitence, isolation— the whole thing. For a while, they even lived without a roof over their heads. Literally.

They are called Trappists. And aside from the Carthusians—who are like the antisocial Silent Bobs of Christian monasticism—the Trappists are the most dedicated to a life of prayer and contemplation of all the monastic orders.

I look back down at the desolate landscape in the pictures.

"You'll see some information about St. Columba's below the pictures, and underneath the St. Columba pile, there are more monasteries. All Trappist."

I flip through the papers quietly, quickly. Even though I used to be the definition of a hard-partying business bro, I was actually pretty good at my job, and part of that job was being able to accurately skim and metabolize information while people stared at you from across a table. And so I see that indeed, all the monasteries are Trappist. Two are here in America—the famous Mepkin and the even more famous Gethsemani—and the rest are scattered between France, Belgium, and Italy. They all have pictures as well, and I glimpse sun-soaked stone arches, cheerful gardens, and a fairy-tale forest before I stack all the papers as they were.

From the top of the stack, the lonely cliffs of St. Columba's stare up at me, beckoning me. I can practically smell the sea and hear the gusting wind. I can imagine my muscles aching, and my soul singing. Cleansed of everything but love for my eternal bridegroom, because in a place like that, there would be nothing left. There would be only sea and sky and God.

The breeze is tousling the abbot's eyebrows as he studies me.

"I know you have been craving more, Brother Patrick. More silence, more solitude, more work. More prayer. And I have deliberated some time about the papers you have in your hands, because I have seen this passion in young men before. They crave more, they desire to be burned down to the bone with devotion, and more often than not, it leads to an irrecoverable consumption. They don't burn down, they burn out. And they either leave or they become listless and untethered, and struggle to find peace in a community again."

I look down at my hands, rough and calloused with amateur forestry. To be *burned to the bone with devotion* is my entire dream right now, my sole vision for my future.

I want to be holy and whole. I want my heart and body to be God's in total, all of it burned up on his altar.

I look down at the picture of St. Columba's again.

"On the other hand," the abbot continues, "there are other men I see come through here, with your drive and your relentless seeking. They go on to do great things, and to lead lives that I can only call saintlike. But they must find a place that fits them. This is the trouble with the monastic life, you see— you must be able to find an entire life in a single place. You must be able to find the deepest corners of your own soul in one chosen fold of the world, and I sometimes wonder if eastern Kansas is that chosen fold for you. I sometimes wonder if the Benedictines are the right order for you. And so to that point…"

Next to me, Brother Connor adjusts his hands in his lap. From any other person, the gesture would mean nothing. But from Brother Connor, it means he's roiling with excitement.

The abbot smiles at Brother Connor and then at me. "And so I have permission *and* the funds to send you to three of these monastic houses to see if one of them might be a good fit."

Brother Connor jumps in. "Officially, this would be a research trip on behalf of our brewery, so you would tour the breweries at each monastery and engage in some mild corporate espionage while you were there."

"Ethical corporate espionage," the abbot says. "You know, *Christian* corporate espionage. Be holy about it and stuff."

"But the research is only the justification for sending you, not the real reason," Brother Connor says. "You are the real reason. Your future is the real reason. And our hope is that you'll find the answers you're seeking on this trip."

Even if I weren't silent today, I still wouldn't know what to say. These kinds of trips are extremely rare for mere brothers like me, especially trips outside the order and outside the *country*. Do I want to spend a trip drinking beer and seeking holy ground? Yes, of course, but I also feel a profound uncertainty. An unworthiness and a cutting doubt.

I don't deserve this gift.

"I am so excited for you," Brother Connor says, touching my hand where it rests on the St. Columba paperwork. "But I also know what we're discussing. If you take this trip and ultimately decide to join a new order..."

The flinch at the realization is instinctive. If I join a new order, then I will never see Brother Connor again after I leave. Or Abbot Jerome or Brothers Thomas, Titus, and Andrew. I will never see my woods again or my troublesome creek.

We will write emails to each other, I'm sure of it, but we will no longer sing together or pray together or walk together under the trees. These men have become my family, and I would have to leave them behind. And for what? For some formless need I can barely express even to myself?

"Now, St. Columba's in particular is a hard life," the abbot begins, leaning back in his chair. "But their prior is looking for—well, he used the word *sturdy*—and there's no one sturdier than my Brother Lumberjack. Ah, yes, Brother Thomas, what is it?"

I turn to see Brother Thomas and Brother Titus crowding at the door, their shoulders heaving like they sprinted into the building.

"Brother Patrick has a visitor," Brother Titus pants. "In the south cloister. Waiting."

"I see the Lord is using his favorite tool to teach today—interruptions," says the abbot dryly. "Very well, then. I assume you informed this visitor that Brother Patrick will be silent today?"

"We did," Brother Thomas pipes up. "He said that's okay." *He.*

I stand, my interest piqued. There's only four *he*s who would visit me at present—my three brothers and my father. I wonder if Sean has brought a baby from his growing baby pile for me to hold while he updates me on the family gossip. My ordinary, human heart warms at the thought.

"Brother Patrick," the abbot says before I leave, "you have time to decide about the trip and which monasteries you'd like to visit. Three weeks before we'd have to finalize arrangements. And Brother Connor and I will be here any time you'd like to talk about it."

I give both men a grateful nod, hoping they can see my humble thanks in my body since I cannot express it in words. And holding the information about the Trappist monasteries tight, I follow Brother Titus and Brother Thomas out of the office building and through the warren of covered walkways that leads to the south cloister, where my visitor awaits.

The young monks hover at the entryway into the cloistered garden, curious, and I can't blame them. Not much happens here that's worthy of remarking upon, and sometimes visitors turn out to be fairly interesting people—prominent Catholics or artists or visitors from other countries. But they're going to be disappointed when they realize it's just an asshole named Sean.

Except I finally see who is waiting for me on the other side of the fountain, and it's *not* Sean. It's not any of my brothers, and it's not my father.

It's the most beautiful man I've ever seen, with his arm slung along the back of the bench, and his long legs sprawled everywhere, like a bored king on his throne. His eyebrow is lifted ever so slightly, as if I'm the riddle here, as if I'm the anomaly in an otherwise seamlessly ordered world.

I forget how to breathe.

I forget how to think.

"Hello, Aiden," says Elijah.

CHAPTER FOUR

The fountain in the middle of the cloister spills happily under the encroaching clouds, although it's not as lovely as the sound of my creek down by the hermitage.

It's not as lovely as the sound of my name in Elijah's low, throaty voice.

I manage to drag in a breath, and another, and then another. It's difficult with him in front of me, with those dark eyes watching me, but somehow my body remembers. It remembers how to inhale and exhale, and to think that there was a time when I could nap naked around this man, when I could prop my feet in his lap and fuss for a foot massage, when I could flick cereal at him across the table because he wasn't paying enough attention to me…

The thought that there was ever a time when I wasn't frozen and shell-shocked just to be looking at him is an impossible one.

He doesn't stand, but he slowly straightens up, his arm

coming off the back of the bench and his hands lacing together in his lap. The fast-chasing clouds send shadows across the warm brown skin of his face and hands, briefly darkening his eyes before the sun returns again, brighter than before.

So much about him is different from when I last saw him. His face is leaner, setting off those sky-high cheekbones, and now there's mouthwatering stubble dark against his jaw, a jaw which used to be zealously clean-shaven. And that's not even to mention what he's wearing: a cream-colored Henley, pale blue shorts, and low-top sneakers. Years ago, he wouldn't have even gone out for condoms without wearing at least two dry-clean-only items of clothing, and now he's here looking like he just got back from a vacation. A good one. To Disney or wine country or something.

Some things haven't changed, however. That subtly cleft chin, that perfectly arched eyebrow as he observes me, those whiskey-colored eyes glittering from underneath thick lashes. A mouth so perfectly sculpted in the geometry of its upper peaks and the curve of the lower lip that it's worthy of worship.

The studied coolness of his expression.

The deliberate grace of his self-possession.

It might be that alone—the chilly, handsome gravity of him—that sends blood futilely rushing to my cock, but there is also the rest of him to contend with. Like the strangely erotic sight of his ankles above the low collars of his shoes. The stillness of those elegant hands in his lap.

I, of course, still know the truth about those hands, about the man they belong to. I know that under all that poise and coolness is a searing, trembling heat.

Am I being punished for my dream? Am I being tempted as some kind of test?

How can he be *here*? *Now*? When it's been nearly five years since I left him standing in a gravel driveway with a crumpled tie in one hand and the key to my house in the other?

"Aiden," Elijah says again, and then he frowns a little. "No, sorry. Brother Patrick now. Right?"

I make some stupid gesture that's like half nod and then half wave of my hand, trying to indicate that it's okay, that I go by both. My religious name is like a spiritual robe—I've put it on to wear for the rest of my life, but I've put it on over the top of everything else. I am still Aiden Bell underneath it. Even when I don't want to be.

I force myself to step forward, to come to the bench and sit at the very end, like I would with any other visitor. Although no other visitor would have my flesh straining against the metal currently caging my sex.

How funny to think this cage began as something playful and sexy—chastity as *kink*, chastity for *fun*—and for the past four years, I've worn it to suppress the very urges that inspired us to buy it in the first place. Although sometimes, in the deepest reaches of night, I wonder if I wore the cage so much in those early days because it reminded me of him. Because it felt like him touching my body, even if it was by proxy of a toy.

Elijah looks over at me. "They said you weren't speaking today."

I nod, and he squares his shoulders, hands still cradled in his lap.

"Okay," he says. "Well, I suppose I can still have this conversation. It'll just be shorter than I'd imagined."

It's been years coming, and yet the misery that follows the word *conversation* is a punishment on par with any hair shirt. A conversation that I deserve, given the way things ended.

A flash of memory: me, nearly five years ago, sitting against the wall of my living room and staring out into the inky country night beyond the window. There had been no stars that night, and no moon. Only a darkness like a palpable thing—like oil, spilling in through the window, spilling past my bare feet and under my pajama-clad ass.

Pouring down my throat.

The next morning I'd gotten in my truck and driven here for the very first time.

I realize that Elijah still hasn't spoken, he still hasn't started his conversation, which no doubt will be exactly the reckoning I dread—and have earned for myself. I broke up with him after a year of dizzying happiness, not by sitting down and talking like a rational person, but by joining a monastery.

I look over at him and find him watching me, but this time it's sans eyebrow. He's watching me with parted lips, like a man stunned, and then he gives a hard swallow, which has the knot of his Adam's apple moving up and then back down.

"You've changed," he says. And then his eyes trail down from my face to the place where my shoulders test even the generous seams of my black Benedictine habit. "A lot," he adds, in an unreadable voice.

I try to curl my shoulders in, looking down at my lap. I was vain in my former life, and that vanity still occasionally pushes its way to the surface. Like right now, when I'm remembering how I used to be a lithe Peter Pan type, slick and groomed and lean from a life that burned candles at both ends, and sometimes in the middle too.

And now I'm Brother Lumberjack. Who has to have his robes custom-tailored and who has cooked his fair skin under the sun so long that he has fine lines coming from his eyes and freckles spattering his face. And who currently has his cock in a cage because he can't stop dreaming about his ex-boyfriend.

Not that anyone else knows that last part.

So of course Elijah is startled by my appearance, of course he's shocked. I used to look fantastic, and now I look like I live with bears. Mean ones.

I keep my eyes on my hands where they curl around the papers the abbot gave me. I don't want to see Elijah's face as he processes how I look now, which is a silly vanity, I know, I know, but I can't help it. A weak part of me wants him to think I'm handsome, because he is still so gorgeous, still so breathtakingly gorgeous.

"I assume Sean told you about the farmhouse," he says after a moment.

I nod, my head down, my body rippling with awareness as he shifts, pulling one knee up onto the bench so he can turn toward me. I allow myself one look at his legs—shorts pulled taut over strong thighs, calves dusted lightly with hair, those well-formed ankles so taunting their nakedness—before I look back to my lap.

I remember what it felt like to trail my lips down his shins and up the backs of his calves. I remember kissing the firm knobs of his ankles on my way down to suck his toes. I remember those thighs pressed to the back of my own as he took his pleasure inside me.

And now we're sitting on a bench, as far apart as possible, while the wind tugs at the hem of my monk habit and flutters the edges of the papers that could take me all the way across the world.

"I couldn't keep it," Elijah explains. "I'm not cut out for cows and fences."

I nod again. He'd sold it right before I'd taken my simple vows, a year or so after I'd left. Sean had come to tell me, and that afternoon, I'd gone down to the creek and chopped wood until my hands were splintered and raw and I could barely breathe. And then, finally spent, I'd sunk to my knees and sobbed until it was time for vespers.

It made sense, of course—I'd known when I'd left it to him that he would probably sell it. Renovating the farmhouse had been my dream, not his, and his job was in the city, planning events for corporations and nonprofits at one of Kansas City's biggest event venues. Commuting practically to Lawrence and back would be a chore, even if he had wanted the farmhouse to begin with.

But the sale of it had felt so final. Its own kind of vow.

"It was the first time I understood the need to leave the past behind so thoroughly that I never had to think about it again," he says. "I would have *paid* someone to buy that thing, just so I wouldn't have to look at that goddamn key on my key ring anymore."

Of course, I know that feeling well too. But in my case, I'd had to leave the past so that I could have a future—any future—at all.

"I'm a writer now," Elijah says abruptly as the clouds cover the sun again. Shadows fall everywhere in the cloister. "Did Sean tell you?"

I shake my head. He hadn't told me. And maybe I wouldn't have believed him if he had, because Elijah had never been the "work in solitude with a big mug of tea" kind of guy. He was more like the "coolly charming his way through an art gallery event with a glass of wine" kind of guy. And of all the things I fucked up between us, perhaps this is the best evidence of my profound carelessness with the people closest to me: I'd never had any idea that he actually wanted to be a writer. None at all.

"I'm a staff writer for *Mode* now."

I know the surprise shows on my face, because he makes a dismissive noise.

"It's not as glamorous as it sounds," he says, although working for the bestselling men's magazine in the country sounds fairly glamorous to me. "There's a lot of interviewing minor celebrities. A lot of 'These Ten Belts Will Make Any Man a Man of Style.' That kind of thing."

I'm still very impressed. I swivel my head so he can see that, my pleasure for him and my pride in him. There's a lacerating sort of satisfaction in knowing that he's thriving now, without me. That I was right to leave him, to extract myself from his life.

Everyone really is better off with me here at Mount Sergius.

"Aiden," Elijah says. "I didn't actually come here to talk about the house or *Mode*."

I look at my own hands again. *Here it comes*, I think to myself. Here comes the excoriation I deserve, the accountability he's allowed to demand from me. This is its own liturgy—the liturgy of closure after heartbreak, a reconciliation not of God to human, but of man to man—and I will pray this liturgy with him. I will bow my head and nod along.

I wouldn't have been able to do that four years ago. I suppose that means this monk thing is working.

But instead of dropping into the long litany of ways I fucked up, Elijah says, in a voice that's once again cool and inscrutable:

"I'm getting married. Soon."

I suck in a breath—or at least I try to. My ribs move but nothing else seems to work the way it should. Not my throat or my lungs, not my diaphragm, and not my heart, which is stuttering in an abnormal tattoo. A stupid knot cinches my throat shut, and it aches, it *aches*, like all the misery flooding through me is snagging on one spot, the spot where voice and breath meet.

Married.

Elijah Iverson, the love of my life, the adoration of my God-pledged soul, married to someone else.

A pole-axe to the head would have hurt less.

"His name is Jamie," Elijah continues in that same voice. "We met a couple years ago at a gallery exhibition. He proposed last year, and I said yes."

I nod.

I nod and I nod and I nod, because what else can I do? I cannot speak. I cannot *speak.*

Even if I could force words past the balled clench in my throat, I'm silent today. I've already promised all my words to God, and I've worked too hard to learn how to keep promises to break one now.

Even so, I feel the words coming, piling on my tongue, crowding against my lips. I press my mouth together; I turn away. I squeeze my eyes shut and fight, fight, fight. I won't speak them, I won't utter a thing. I owe God and Elijah that much at least—my silence and my acceptance.

"I didn't think I needed to—" Elijah pauses, as if searching for the right words. "Well, the longer I thought about it, the more it didn't feel like something I could have Sean tell you. And I—ah—*fuck*, Aiden, will you look at me?"

For the first time, the composed calm of his voice falters, and his words are unsteady and rough.

I look at him. He is so beautiful, and even now, even with everything, my cock tries to swell at the sight of the muscles bunched and tense under his thin shirt, at the tempting contours of his thighs. At the bulge in his shorts I'd have to be dead not to be aware of.

He stares at me with dark amber eyes, his mouth set, his stubbled jaw tight with some emotion I can't name. "You *left*," he says in a thick, angry voice.

It's inevitable—it's even what I expected when I first sat down on this bench—but I still flinch at the words. At the accusation buried inside them.

"You left me. For this," he says. "What should I have done, Aiden? Stayed frozen in time, like a fly in amber for you? Refused to move on or live again?"

I shake my head. No. No, of course not. I left him to become a monk, I left him to marry my god, to give my heart to my god, to give my *body* to my god, and so I cannot be jealous of this Jamie now, not when I picked another lover first. That the lover was Jesus Christ seems immaterial to the situation.

The effect is the same.

He slumps back, as if all the fight has suddenly left him. "I think I had to tell you in person because otherwise I couldn't have been sure," he says quietly. "I needed to see that you were really here forever. I needed to come to terms with the fact that I am never going to know why."

I remember that night again—that window bled utterly dry of stars and moonlight. The clamminess of the newly sealed hardwoods and the flash of my phone in the dark.

Why.

Why leave a life as a millionaire? Why leave a perfect boyfriend?

Why leave family and a cute, derelict farmhouse and sex—God, why give up sex?

Because if I hadn't, that darkness spilling in through my farmhouse window would have taken me. I'd *wanted* it to take me. I was ready for it to take me.

And somehow I managed to crawl my way here instead, gasping like a drowning man who'd just clawed his way to shore. I managed to save my own life—or I managed to let God save my life.

Either way, that was the cost of surviving. My old life.

Him.

Elijah scrubs his hands over his head, his fingertips sinking into the tight curls for a moment. It's longer now; he used to wear his hair short, with crisp, immaculate edges. Another change I wasn't there to see.

I wasn't sitting on the couch with him when he rubbed his face and mused about growing a beard; I wasn't poking him out of the way with my toothbrush while he faced the mirror, posing this way and that to imagine longer hair. I wasn't there in bed with him at night, my legs tangled with his, while he complained about his job or feeling bored with his work, I wasn't there when he wrote his first article or when he submitted a portfolio to *Mode*.

I wasn't there, because I was here. Praying and chopping wood.

I wasn't there, and this Jamie person was.

Elijah stands up, facing away from me for a moment, before he turns back. The sun abruptly shafts through a break

37

in the clouds and drives back the pre-rain murk in the cloister, illuminating Elijah in a haze of gold.

If I were to make a stained-glass window displaying an image of God's creativity and capacity for beauty, it would be this. It would be Elijah with an unshaven face and in those shorts, it would be his eyes in that dark gold-brown hue, it would be his mouth, that jaw, that throat. It would be a saint in low-top sneakers with a halo of Kansas sunshine around his head.

He pulls his lower lip between his teeth for just an instant before releasing it, and then he straightens up, looking at me with an expression that defies interpretation. Only his eyes seem beyond his usual control, blazing with a heat that might be fury or grief, I can't tell.

"I loved you for a long time after you left," he says. "I thought you should know that."

He doesn't have to say the next part, because I already know; I already know he doesn't love me anymore.

And with a small nod, he turns and walks out of the cloister, the first spots of rain blooming on his shirt and his head bowed, as if in prayer.

CHAPTER FIVE

from the notebook of Elijah Iverson

Shoulders.

That was my first thought when I saw him.

The kind of shoulders that could blot out the sun, shoulders which tested the seams of his monk habit. (Which is a garment designed on purpose to be loose and shapeless, so that's…something.)

Four years of changes, and it was his shoulders I noticed first. But there were other changes too. A thick scruff on his striking jaw, calluses on his big hands. And even though those green eyes still made my heart speed, they no longer glittered with mischief and boyish joy, but something…I don't know, solemn feels like the wrong word. Secret, maybe.

And the *quiet* of him, quiet like I'd never seen from Aiden

Bell. He listened to every word I spoke as if I were uttering a prophecy, and when he did look at me and not at his hands, his gaze was so intensely *present*. Like all of him was there with me, <u>so very there</u>, like he'd existed his entire life just to look at me for thirty minutes in a cloister.

That part…it *is* like the old Aiden, and yet it isn't, not with the quiet thrown in along with it.

Why can't I stop thinking about how quiet he was?

Why can't I stop thinking about his shoulders?

I did what I went there to do. I told him about Jamie, about the wedding, I successfully instigated closure.

~~Nothing feels closed~~

~~Why can't I stop thinking about~~

CHAPTER
SIX

I'm not sure how I make it back to the hermitage. I know that I do because I'm here on the thin secondhand rug which covers most of the cracked concrete floor. And I know that it must have been raining the whole two miles back because the papers the abbot gave me are wet and limp in my hands.

I know that I'm still alive because I can feel my heart juddering inside my ribs. Because I'm crying and the tears run hot trails down my chilled, rain-slicked face.

I'm kneeling as the rain roars down around the little limestone cottage, as it drums like mad on the roof and whips against the windows. I see nothing of the world I'm in, nothing but worn rug fibers and the now-wavy picture of St. Columba's and its dark, unforgiving sea.

I see nothing but Elijah in my mind.

He's getting married. He's getting married and it's not to me.

I loved you for a long time after you left.

And I still love him.

I still love him.

The noise comes out of me like thunder comes—a slow roll, growing louder and louder until it's upon me and I'm groaning, I'm keening as I stagger to my feet and lurch through the door and into the clearing, crying back at the thunder and the god who sent it.

I drop to my knees again, quaking with the need to—I don't even know. To run maybe. To run through the trees until I'm at the top of the huge limestone swell above the abbey and then stand there until lightning burns up my stupid, miserable flesh. To run all the way to an ocean and then swim my way to the stark sanctuary of St. Columba's.

To run to the highway and hitch a ride to Kansas City and fall at Elijah's feet and beg for forgiveness.

I slump forward, throat stinging, sides heaving. The rain continues to sluice down without a care for my rage or my pain, the thunder rolls on and on, like rumbling church bells across the prairie, summoning every person within hearing to this ancient service of sky meeting earth.

I stare at my hands in the mud, at the torn grass between them.

"I love him so much," I whisper, rain running off my head and down to my lips, where the drops fall along with my words to the mud and grass below. "And it hurts and I want it to stop. Please, Lord. If you love me, make it stop."

There is no answer from God, no sweet or poignant omen I can take as a sign. No ray of sunshine, no birdsong. Nothing but mud and thunder and a green-tinted sky. Green enough that there might be sirens later, and I almost wish for them. I almost wish for a storm to blow me away.

I lift my eyes to the hills.

I press my eyes shut and wait.

The sirens never come and eventually the storm abates, leaving my creek swollen and the ground soggy. I feel soggy too as I clean up my mess and gather my clothes and sheets and towels so I can trudge back to the abbey proper. So soggy that I barely even care that my retreat has ended, that I'll be back in the dormitory with the other brothers. Back doing spreadsheet-y things and odd jobs around the printing press or brewhouse, listening to the others laugh and pray and talk.

What does it matter where I am at? Hermitage or dormitory, everywhere is empty of him.

That's okay, I try to remind myself. *You're okay.*

I'm okay. I came to the monastery to be okay and now I am, and Elijah will be happy, and I'm going to be okay.

Maybe if I say it to myself enough times, I'll start to believe it. Like a prayer.

That evening is warm and humid, the kind of sticky that almost makes you wish for a pool, even though it's not officially summer yet. I sit cross-legged under the oak that spreads its shade over the graves of long-dead monks and stare down at the crinkly, now-dried papers in my lap. Several feet away, Brother Connor runs through his katas with a fluid grace that I envy. Even before my monk-cum-lumberjack phase, I was never a graceful man. I played sports with a puppy-like enthusiasm, crashing into other players and tripping over my own feet, and later, I fumbled plastic cups of beer and bowls of nacho cheese all over my frat house.

The only place I've ever had any real smoothness was in bed, but so much of that was instinct, was hunger without thought or skill. If I wanted to kiss, I kissed, if I wanted to grab, I grabbed. And somehow it always worked. And with Elijah—

A tense heat grips my belly and thighs, and the discomfort of the cage I wore again today cautions me away from memories of him. From recalling that first time, his breath ragged in my ear as fundraiser guests laughed and drank champagne on the other side of the balcony door.

It had built and built and built, hadn't it, for years and years. My older brother's best friend. What a cliche. And yet nothing about it felt trite or threadbare when he'd brushed his lips over mine. When he'd taken my hand and brought my fingers to his mouth.

What if…

I shift automatically, trying to relieve some of the pressure on my cock, even though it's a welcome counterpoint to the pressure in my chest and throat. I can speak today, now that I've kept my promise, but I've found I hardly want to, because what can I say? What can I say other than the man I love is getting married and that I need to accept it?

I close my eyes and lean my head back against the wide trunk of the oak. Even in the days after coming here, fresh from leaving Elijah—fresh from that oil-black night in the farmhouse when there was nothing, nothing, nothing crawling along my skin until my phone flashed in the dark—even then, I wasn't as raw and restless as I am now.

Which is stupid. So stupid. I'm taking my solemn vows next year; there was never any plan to stop being a monk. There was no way Elijah and I were ending up together anyway, because I'd chosen to leave, and some choices can't be undone, and oh God, what if I want this choice to be undone?

It can't be undone. This choice is the only reason you're alive right now.

The only reason you're going to be okay.

No, I don't want to undo my choice. I'm certain of it. I came here after the bleakest night of my life; I came to somehow turn a selfish, horny millionaire into a good man, and this doubt—this selfish need for love and sex—is the proof that there is still more work to be done. I am an undone man; I am unfinished; I am so far from where I want to be, which is as close to God as a person can get.

I am so far from being a saint.

And this restlessness—maybe it's proof that I need something harder, harsher, meaner. A rigor and asceticism I can't get here from the gentle Benedictines.

A shadow comes across me, and I open my eyes to see Brother Connor's faded gi pants in front of my face. I tilt my head up to see him extending a hand.

"Thinking of your visitor?" he asks. His voice is so mild, so serene, that it doesn't feel invasive, this question. More like he's remarking on it the same way he would remark on a pretty cloud or a fox darting along the edge of the barley.

I accept his hand, still surprised at how someone so compact can shift someone of my bulk as he pulls me to my feet. "Yes," I admit, my voice rough and scratchy from my muddy lamentations yesterday. "I was."

"This visitor—he was your Elijah?"

I nod, looking off towards the graves. When I first came here, I imagined where my grave would be one day, nestled among these holy men who've lived and died here learning how to be humble and simple and close to God. But now I'm not so sure where my one-day grave will be.

I think of the papers in my hand, of the abbot's office only a short walk away.

I huff out a breath and then look back at my friend. "He's—he's getting married."

"Oh, Brother Patrick. I'm so sorry."

I wish I could shrug or smile. I wish I could turn it into a joke, laugh it off, make it a hilarious story to tell over a beer and some of Father Matthew's homemade pretzels. Before—in the Aiden-times—I was so good at faking what people wanted to hear. I was so good at making a moment feel as light and as sweet as cotton candy, at sweeping anything remotely uncomfortable under the rug until it disappeared.

I used to think I was so good at it because I had to learn how to make people love me again after I fucked up, and it turned out that was useful in all sorts of social situations, not just the ones where I needed to charm my way into forgiveness.

But I don't think that's true anymore. Or at least, it's not the entire truth.

I think the real reason I know how to divert people away from my pain or my fuck-ups is the same reason I was on the floor of my house the night before I came here. Staring out the window as my mind chanted poison to itself, like a corrupt but suspiciously comforting litany.

I know that I am very far away from that night; I understand things now that I didn't before.

One of those things is that confession isn't about sitting across from a priest and doing a moral Schedule C. It's meant to be small moments of honesty shared with those close to us, and it's not only for sins, but for confusions, hurts, and hopes too.

I confess now, to Brother Connor. "I'm still in love with him."

He nods, as if this doesn't surprise him. "You loved him deeply when you came here."

"I don't want to love him."

Brother Connor regards me. "I hope—sincerely—that you do not believe it's a sin for you to love him. You did not used to."

"It wasn't a sin for me to love him then, but I can't help but feel that it is *now*. I came here to pledge my heart to God and God alone, and so what does it say about me that there is still another object of my devotion? That no matter how much I pray and work, a hunger for someone other than my lord still gnaws at me? I would feel the same way if I were still in love with a woman after four years of being here."

"I think," Brother Connor says, "that is a very human way of seeing things. If God's love is boundless, then becoming more Christlike means growing a love that is like Christ's—without boundary or border. And a boundless love, by definition, would effortlessly encompass *many* loves, would it not?"

Shadows stretch behind the gravestones now, like long fingers reaching east toward the trees. It will be compline soon, our final prayers before night closes over the abbey.

"This life is supposed to be an offering," I say finally, gesturing toward the graves with the hand holding the details of the Trappist monasteries. "A holy and *whole* offering, and I still feel that I'm offering only in part, that I'm holding back part of my sacrifice. Maybe Elijah's coming here was a gift, because I see that now—I see how far away I am from being totally and completely God's."

"You still sound like a banker," Brother Connor says, a little sadly, as the first bells begin tolling for compline. "Like life is about closing out accounts and reallocating funds."

"I wasn't actually a ban—it doesn't matter. What matters is I'm still holding on to my past life, when I need it to be burned away, threshed away. I need *more*."

Brother Connor looks down at the papers in my hand as the bells ring again. "You've made up your mind then. About the trip."

"I have," I say, and a new energy fills me, something akin to what drove me to Mount Sergius in the first place. It's

48

something close to hope. "I'm going to go."

Brother Connor touches my arm, gently, fondly. "I'm happy for you, Brother Patrick. My only worry is that you're going now not to seek, but to flee from something. Or someone."

I shake my head. "This is what I'm supposed to do. I know it. I know it like I knew I was supposed to come here almost five years ago."

"Then I am happy for you," he says softly. "And you are certain?"

"I'm certain. I even know the three monasteries I want to visit."

We begin walking to the church, the bells insistent now and comforting in their peals.

"Then I suppose we should tell the abbot," Brother Connor says. "And get you a new passport."

CHAPTER SEVEN

Time at the abbey pours itself into basins, just as the fountain in the south cloister does, with the water in each pool rippling into a near stillness before gravity gently and inevitably pushes it onward.

We wake for vigils, and we dress in our habits, which vary in the details, but which all have a long black robe, a belt, and a length of black fabric called a scapular which hangs down both the front and the back of the body but remains open at the sides. Then we go to prayer, shuffling from our cells in the pre-dawn dark.

After we pray vigils, it's time for lectio divina—holy reading.

When I was in finance, reading was crucial—scanning, skimming, assessing, all of it as quickly as possible because time was money and any time spent taking in information was time not spent turning that information into the next pile of money. And so when I came here, I assumed that reading the

Bible would be much the same. You get through the chapters as quickly as possible so you can move on to the next thing.

But that's not how lectio works—that's not actually how being a monk works, either. Productivity is never the point, the outcome is never the point. The doing is the point.

And so too with lectio. You are not reading to get through a chapter or to accomplish a task, you are not searching for an epiphany. You are there to linger and to savor. To be snared by a single word or image and then let it waft through your thoughts like candle smoke, letting it call forth all the memories and feelings and thoughts it will.

In a way, it reminds me of sex. There is something wonderful about slow, languorous lovemaking, about tracing over someone's body with loitering fingers and lips. The kind of sex that remits revelations which might sound infinitesimal to anyone else—the existence of a small scar, perhaps, or a few crisp hairs at the top of a foot—but that are life-changing in their discovery. In its intimacy, its affection, its vulnerability, and in its capacity to haunt, evoke, tease, reward...

Yes, lectio divina is very much like sex to me.

After lectio-sex is lauds, our prayers said in the light of the now-waking sun, and breakfast, which concludes the Grand Silence for the day. After breakfast is a few hours of work, which for me is principally about being the abbey's de facto CPA, accounting for our printing press, brewhouse, and taproom, as well as any income brought in by people staying in our retreat center. I'm not exactly managing seven- and eight-figure portfolios, but careful allocation and expansion means the monastery has a healthy buffer for any potential crisis and can easily meet its needs for the coming year—the charities we support in our county and in Kansas City, funding our health insurance plan, paying for the usual utilities and business expenses, paying for our agricultural equipment and supplies.

When I'm not in the office next to the abbot's, trying to tune out the French audiobook du jour and assessing farm equipment repairs and potential grant applications, I'm helping out wherever a set of big shoulders and an uninjured back can be of use. Usually in the barn or the brewhouse—or chopping deadfall—but I'm often needed in the taproom too, wheeling in kegs and rolling the tapped ones out.

I'm grateful for it, for the work that tires my body enough that sometimes I can sleep without dreaming. I'm grateful for the honesty of the sweat and the soreness of it. I spent the first eleven years of my adult life earning money in the slickest and most oblique ways, by convincing people and companies and trusts to let me play with the money *they'd* earned. So yes, it feels nice to work with my body, and my hands. It feels nice to use whatever gifts I have for math and money to make the abbey more secure in its future and the care of its dependents.

It feels nice to do good things.

After work, there is Mass in the abbey church, lunch, and then communal prayer. We go back to work in the afternoon—some of us changing in and out of habits depending on our various jobs—and then we return to the church for vespers, our early evening prayers. Then there is lectio again, dinner, and our free time, which is usually when Brother Connor practices his katas under the oak tree and many of us treat ourselves to a cold glass of beer—or two. Thus lubricated, we're back to the church for compline, and then off to bed.

Prayer and work.

Ora et labora.

Two weeks after Elijah told me he was getting married, I'm sitting in the beer garden outside the taproom, watching the sun sink toward the horizon. Brothers Titus and Thomas are winging wet sponges at each other instead of wiping down the tables, and a visiting brother from an abbey in Italy is valiantly attempting to make conversation with our carpenter, Brother Andrew, who is not exactly known for his chitchat and who is grunting into his beer every time the Italian asks him a question.

It strikes me how different this beer-filled evening is from the evenings I spent before I came here—especially before I started dating Elijah. Working until it was definitively playtime, skipping dinner so I could get hammered or go to a strip club or both. And if for some reason I *did* get dinner, my phone was in my hand the entire time. In fact, even if I went out to drink after or to get a lap dance, my phone was still out. I have vivid memories of strippers purring in my lap while I stroked their hips with one hand and answered emails with the other.

Not so here at the abbey.

(With the phones, I mean. But the strippers too.)

A small handful of brothers have phones if their abbey

jobs require it, like our marketing director and the brothers who work with retreatants, but most of us don't own a phone and take turns using the library computers for email. So there are no screens at the table right now, no smart watches beeping with messages or alarms. There is no one fussing over the work to be done, because we will all wash the glasses together before we go to prayer, and there is no one considering sneaking back to answer one last email, because when the time for work is over, it's really, actually over.

There is only beer now and prayer later, and I think the first monks to figure out that this was the way to run a monastery were geniuses.

I also think God must love us all very much to give us Kansas sunsets and beer.

For the first time since Elijah visited, I know I'm doing okay. Right now and in this life and in whichever place I find next to deepen my relationship with God.

There was a time in my life when my favorite two words were *what if*, and as I drink deep of my cold beer and watch the sun sink behind the hill, I ask myself a question I already know the answer to.

What if this is a good life?

What if this is a very good life?

That night, after half a month of near-constant use, I take off the chastity device for good. I take it off every day, of course, to wash myself and it, but I haven't spent much functional time without it since Elijah's visit, which is how it used to be when I first came here.

Before I was a monk, I fucked nearly every day, sometimes more than once—and that's not even attempting to account for all the jerking off—and so I was terrified of getting a hard-on in my habit.

As I'm sure you know, there's only so much a flat-fronted robe can conceal.

But I'm no longer a newbie at this celibacy thing, like I was then—and also I can't deny that one of the reasons I've been wearing the cage has nothing to do with actual chastity and everything to do with feeling close to Elijah.

Feeling close to the time when denial was a game instead of a mandate.

But it's a mandate I'm content enough to obey—even though it chafes a little knowing that by official Church doctrine, queer Catholics are only considered fully Catholic if they're celibate. I'm participating in that doctrine, even if it's only incidentally, and I'm not entirely sure what to do about that. I've chosen celibacy because it's part of consecrating my entire self to the god who brought me back to life, but the idea that this is the only way a queer person can know God in this life, and after this life too, seems more about post-Reformation politics than divine inspiration to me.

But I'm not a theologian like my brother Tyler—who was a priest before he left his collar behind for his now-wife, Poppy—and I'm not a spiritual activist like my sister-in-law Zenny, who was almost a nun. I don't know how to reconcile my choices with a doctrine I know is fundamentally broken, because at the end of the day I still choose celibacy, and I still choose being a monk.

I still choose this life.

Anyway, I can stop wearing the cage again. I'm back to being okay after Elijah's visit, and also I'm almost thirty-seven. I'm past getting public boners, I think? Even though I wasn't when I was thirty-two and chasing Elijah into every empty room I could find.

A cheerless swell moves through me as I remember that someone else is chasing Elijah around right now; someone else gets to press their face into his neck and inhale the sage and saltwater smell of his skin. I've spent the last four years aching with physical need for him, and he's found someone else to kiss and watch *The Repair Shop* with.

Jamie. Jamie who probably teaches eighth-grade orchestra and volunteers in a community garden and has never been fist-bumped by a strip club security guard, not even once.

I stare at the metal cage on the ledge of my small shower stall and then make my decision. If Elijah can move on, then so can I.

God, give me strength. Make all my desire for you and no one else.

Empty me. Empty me. Empty me.

There's no ejaculate on the sheets the next morning.

Or the morning after that.

CHAPTER EIGHT

from the notebook of Elijah Iverson

I can't stop thinking about ice cream.

There was a night with him at some pretentious pop-up gallery I'd dragged him to, where despite being the pro-sports-watching, millionaire fish out of water, he'd managed to charm all of my arty friends into falling in love with him. It was something about his smile, I think, which was slightly too wide and punctuated with dimples pressed into his cheeks by a surely smitten god. Or maybe it was those eyes—a bright bottle-green, perpetually alight with playfulness or intensity or both.

Or maybe it was that Aiden Bell could always make you feel like you were his new best friend. Like he'd been waiting for you all night, and now that you were there with him, the party could really get started.

With all the crimes I can lay at his feet—recklessness, obliviousness, a sort-of Lost Boy-ness in his refusal to finish growing up—I must not forget this. Aiden Bell would make you laugh, would make you happy. Aiden Bell would make your blood rush and your skin hum and your heart pound.

Aiden Bell would make you feel like your life was waiting for you to take it with both hands.

After we'd left the gallery, my friends still choked with laughter from a story he told them about a stolen pole-vaulting mat, a grease fire, and a fire extinguisher fight, he turned to me and said, "I have a surprise."

We'd been dating for seven months by this point, and there were some things I'd had to adjust to while dating a millionaire. (I know, I know, poor me.)

But sometimes Aiden would say, "Let's get a pain au chocolat" and I would think we were going to a bakery, and instead we'd go to the airport and fly to Paris for the best pain au chocolat in the world. Or sometimes he'd tell me he'd gotten me a little thing for my apartment, and it would be a painting that would have cost me an entire year's salary, a painting that I'd mentioned liking at a gallery in New York or Montreal.

So when he said he had a surprise that night, I braced myself for some extravagance, some casually absurd display of wealth. But instead of taking me to the airport or giving me the key to a new car or something, he laced his fingers through mine, and we walked the next block over to an ice cream truck parked on the sidewalk.

I waited under a tree strung with blue-white lights as he bought our ice creams and returned to me looking as proud as if he'd taken me to a place with Michelin stars, holding his ice cream cone in one hand and a bowl for me in the other, because he knew I felt negatively about the cone experience.

We ate our ice cream on the sidewalk, city lights glittering around us, music humming from a nearby bar, traffic whooshing past.

Aiden's eyes fluttered as he licked his bubble gum ice cream cone, moans coming from his chest as if he were eating something prepared by a renowned pastry chef and not freezer-burned ice cream from a sketchy van.

But that was Aiden Bell for you.

"Elijah," Aiden said after a moment. His voice was serious. "Hold still a moment."

I held still, suddenly worried I had a bug on my shirt or something, but Aiden leaned in and gently licked a stray drop of ice cream from my lower lip.

I shivered at the touch of his tongue—cold from his own ice cream—and the warmth of his breath over my mouth. He licked again, this time his tongue tracing along the seam of my lips, until I let him inside.

He tasted like bubble gum and heaven. He tasted like impulsive decisions and lust and funny stories and the rest of my life.

And when he pulled away and gave me that too-wide grin, I suddenly couldn't imagine any other life than this one. The life before him, when he'd just been Sean's cute but off-limits younger brother. A life after, when I wouldn't have bubble gum kisses with the city sparkling around us.

I took another bite of my ice cream and then made a mock-pout, mostly to make him smile. "They never put enough sprinkles on my sundae."

"I know," he said with a smile and pulled something out of his pocket. It was a small container of sprinkles from a grocery store that he'd brought just for me. Turns out he'd been carrying those sprinkles around for weeks, just in case we went out for ice cream and they didn't give me enough.

The thing about falling in love is that by the time you realize it's happened, it's already too late. Your boyfriend already has sprinkles for you in the pocket of his Tom Ford suit. You've already had bubble gum kisses on a warm city night.

You've already let him swallow your heart.

But that's Aiden Bell for you. Or it was.

And now he spends his days without kissing, without even ice cream to take the sting out of ugly clothes and early mornings and praying to a god that doesn't exist. Why? How?

Does he miss his old life? Does he miss being himself?

~~Does he miss~~

CHAPTER NINE

On the last Friday of May, I take the path through the woods not to the hermitage, but to the base of the hill Mount Sergius is named for, where there is a labyrinth made of limestone rocks half sunk into the earth. In the middle of the labyrinth is a cluster of benches, and on those benches are scattered several monks. Others sit on the shady ground or lie on their backs with their eyes shut, stealing a few moments of sleep. One is pacing, his head down and his forehead furrowed, and someone else is humming what I'm reasonably certain is a Harry Styles song.

It is the last Friday of the month, and so it's time for Lectio Lexapro.

"Ah, Brother Patrick," Brother Matthew says. "Is that everyone?"

I scan the brothers assembled as I reach the center. Brothers Matthew, Stephen, Denis, Francis, Michael, Leander, John, Crispin, and Titus. Brother Thomas is here too, not because he's truly part of our informal little liturgy, but because he and Titus are joined at the hip and hate doing anything apart.

"I think we're missing Brother Peter," I say. "But it's still a few minutes until nine."

When I was a teenager, I no more saw myself eventually founding a support group for people living with mental illnesses than I saw myself one day founding a support group for fishing boat captains. Even after my sister died by suicide when I was in high school, there was no talk in my household about mental illness. Our focus had been on the shock of our loss and the twinned grief of learning at the same time that she'd been sexually abused by our parish priest. And then that focus had ignited into an anger at the Church that had consumed my brothers and me.

I feel flares of that anger even now. They complicate the joy I've found here, and the peace, knowing that my relationship to God and my newfound contentment are knitted indelibly with the pain of thousands and thousands.

But I also feel a sense of rightness at the abbey, like I'm meant to be here *with* my anger, like I'm meant to be driven by it.

It is often stressful, and agonizing, and I don't recommend cognitive dissonance as your next skincare routine. But it's where I feel called to be.

Lectio Lexapro is one of the fruits of my anger, I suppose. After I came here and started seeing Dr. Rosie and treating the depression that brought me to the abbey in the first place, I began to talk about what happened to Lizzy, *really* talk about it for the first time. And even though what drove me to the abbey had been something different than the memories of her death, I began to wonder if my entire family would have been better off if we'd been able to translate our hurt into language.

And when I think about what might have happened if Lizzy herself could have had that...

So after learning firsthand that many in the Church still don't admit that therapy and medication are needed alongside prayer, yes, I was angry. And I did something about it—something small, maybe, and limited in scope. But something. My little group, a space I wish someone would have made for me a long time ago.

Birds sing somewhere in the trees while we wait for our last brother, and I listen to the endless wind ruffling high up on the hill, my thoughts drifting away from Lizzy and onto what's happening right now, onto what's going to happen when I leave for my trip.

What might happen after.

If I changed orders, my familiar black habit would change. If I changed orders, I might never see these woods again, hear these birds, or listen to these brothers gossip and tease.

Would it really be worth it? Leaving behind all these tangible, *good* things and people for the mere promise of more?

I don't know yet, not for certain. That's why I have to go and see for myself, because if I can feel there the way I felt simply looking at those pictures...

Then yes. It would be worth it.

Brother Peter arrives right at nine, and we go around the

circle, speaking a little bit as to how our month has gone. Years ago, this would have been something I would have monopolized, trying to make people laugh, rambling on, talking too much. I would have left the group on a giddy socializing high, which would have crashed not thirty minutes later as I relived every cringey comment or joke in vivid, miserable detail. As I remembered exactly how foolish or unthoughtful or inappropriate or grasping or needy I had been, and then I'd be haunted by shame for days after.

And no matter how many times this talking-too-much/shame-for-talking-too-much cycle repeated itself, I could never break myself of it, I could never stop myself from plunging right into the middle of a conversation and making an ass of myself all over again.

It is easier now. St. Benedict says that monks should strive for silence—that monks should love silence—and learning to listen is one of the first things a postulant is taught here. You listen to psalms, to prayers, to Mass. You listen to the clanging of the bells or the rumble of the tractor engines or the clank of metal on glass as you wash dishes.

I have learned to listen. Or listen better at least.

And anyway, the point of Lectio Lexapro is to be totally honest about the hard parts of our days. The anxieties, the depressions, the dank and clammy fingers that tug on our habits and grasp at our thoughts. Sharing here is the point, and so I feel less selfish when I do talk, because we are all here to help each other.

Brother Matthew, our resident baking enthusiast, is

switching head meds and is struggling. Crispin has just added Wellbutrin to his rotation and is having difficulty dealing with the libido increase.

When it's finally my turn, I lie by omission and say that it's been a quiet month. It's only a partial lie, because my brain *has* been quiet on the depression and anxiety front (thank you, Lexapro, Wellbutrin, and therapy). It's only my soul that's been unquiet, and my heart, and I don't feel ready to talk to my fellow brothers about it. I don't feel ready to talk about it at all.

Unfortunately, I forget that Brother Titus and Brother Thomas witnessed part of the reason for my unquiet. "What about your visitor a few weeks ago?" Brother Titus demands, leaning forward so his blond hair falls over his lightly suntanned forehead in a very attractive way. We don't do tonsures here, but if we did, Brother Titus would be the first to need it. His vanity about his hair is palpable.

Brother Thomas, on the other hand, keeps his hair soldier-short—probably because he was in the army before he came here. "Who was he?" he asks.

"Family lawyer?" Titus follows up.

"Doctor making a house call?"

"Do you owe him money?"

"Is he a librarian coming to collect a book you never returned?"

"Was it a mystery book?"

"A cookbook?"

"One of those financial self-help books with a blond lady on the cover?"

"Gentlemen," Brother Matthew intervenes gently, folding his hands over his stomach. "Please."

"No, it's fine," I say, my face hot. "He was my boy—*ex*-boyfriend." How is it that I can forget the *ex* part after so many years of it being true?

"Oooh," Brother Thomas says, leaning forward into a sunbeam. His face, ordinarily a deep olive, begins flushing pink under the early summer sun. "What did he come back here for?"

"Closure, I suppose," I say uncomfortably. I'm not uncomfortable talking about an ex-boyfriend with the Lectio Lexapro group—they know many of the intimate details of my life, and they know I'm queer—but I *am* uncomfortable talking about Elijah specifically, because it's too close to talking about how I still feel about Elijah. How I still feel the tendrils and vines of him whispering around my ankles and snaking up my thighs.

It's gotten better since his visit, but I don't think it will be totally fixed until I leave. Until I find the monastery that can press everything out of me that's not living for God, press me like grapes being turned into wine.

"Does this have anything to do with why you're going to Europe?" Brother Crispin asks curiously.

"No," I say quickly. "That was proposed before he came."

I didn't agree until *after* his visit, but I don't say that out loud.

"Do you really want to be a Trappist?" Brother Denis asks. He's the oldest of our group, a white man with a short beard and an accent straight from a BBC documentary. "They're quite diligent, aren't they?"

Brother Francis scoffs. "I think you mean *dour.*"

"Better stock up on Welly before you become a Trappist then, so you can smile through the dourness," Brother Crispin advises, half teasing.

I smile at him. "Maybe the dourness is the point."

"Is it safe?" Brother Matthew asks after a moment, quietly. "Will it be safe for you?"

I think about this a moment. While managing depression isn't—in my experience—a recipe that stays precisely the same over time, some things make it exponentially easier. Therapy. Meds. Good community. Friendship. Meditation. While I feel certain that I'd have plenty of meditation in any monastery, I can't be sure of the other ingredients. So much depends on the abbots and priors, on the particular culture of a monastic house. "I don't know," I finally reply. "I'd have to be vigilant."

"But you're not turned off by the potential suffering?" Brother Titus asks.

I shake my head. "They're hardly wearing hair shirts or flogging themselves. They're just quieter than us, a bit more rigid. That's all."

But again, I'm not telling them the entire truth here.

I am the opposite of turned off by the potential suffering— I crave it, I crave it to the point of masochistic desire. Suffering can be good; suffering can be essential.

Paul the Apostle says that suffering produces endurance, and endurance produces character, and character produces hope, which is the Jesus-y photo-negative of Yoda's speech in the Jedi Council scene in *The Phantom Menace*.

And if I could only set my feet on the right road, if I could only follow this flickering candle all the way to its finish, then I will be better than empty by the time my life is done. I will be filled with hope.

"Anyway," I say, "it's only a visit. Nothing's decided yet."

Sort of.

Before I became a monk, I spent Saturday mornings jerking off and eating Toaster Strudels, and now I spend my Saturday mornings singing psalms and vacuuming the abbey offices. It's funny where life can take you sometimes.

I do miss the Toaster Strudels.

I'm nearly done with the individual offices, and I'm moving on to the central office area when I hear it.

A distinct *boing BOING boing BOING*.

I turn off the vacuum, verify that I am indeed hearing *boing*-ing, and walk to the office door, where I see Brothers Titus and Thomas on those big rubber bouncy balls—the kind with the handles—bouncing exuberantly down the hallway.

"Gangway for the bouncy ball parade!" Brother Titus shouts as he bounces past me, the rubber slapping against the sealed brick floor of the hallway with each landing.

"Halt the parade!" Brother Thomas says, executing a nearly perfect one hundred and eighty degree turn in a single bounce, so he can bounce back to the doorway I'm standing in.

He stops at my feet, peering up at me.

"You should have a turn," he declares, and Brother Titus moves to join him, looking thoughtful as he bounces.

"Yes, he should," Brother Titus agrees, alighting from his ball and then gesturing toward it like he's inviting me to drive an Italian sports car. "The road beckons."

"He means the hallway," Thomas says.

I hesitate for a moment. Not because I'm not finished with my work or even because it's silly, but because it's precisely the kind of thing Aiden Bell would have instigated back in the day.

Aiden Bell, the overgrown frat boy.

Aiden Bell, the fuck-up.

"No, I probably shouldn't—"

"Are you refusing my valiant steed?" Brother Titus says, pressing a hand to his heart. "My brave, noble, *valiant* steed?"

I look at them both, so much younger than me and so full of unfiltered joy, and my resolve wavers. For a moment, just for a moment, I want to be impulsive again. Impulsive and reckless and Aiden.

With a small smile and with the cheers of Brother Titus and Brother Thomas echoing in the hallway around me, I mount the rubber ball. My lumberjack frame tests the rubber for a moment—the toy compressing in protest as I get my habit tucked around my legs—but it holds. And when I give it a test bounce, it acquits itself well, launching me forward a couple feet.

"Good, good. Now again," Titus says, like he's the teacher in a training montage. "Harder this time."

"I've heard that before," I say, before I can stop myself, and both Titus and Thomas blink at me.

"Did you just make a joke?" Thomas says, letting go of his handle to press his hands to his face. "Brother Patrick made a *joke.* Brother Patrick can have fun!"

If only they knew. If only they knew that Elijah had once found me swimming in an indoor hotel fountain with a tie around my head. Or that Ryan and I once hitched a futon mattress behind a truck after a snowstorm and rode it like a sleigh through the Plaza shopping district. Or that I'd once filled Sean's Audi so full of pingpong balls that when he opened the door five million plastic balls spilled onto the ground and then rolled all over his church's parking lot.

Zenny made him pick up every single one too. Ha.

I listen to Titus though, bracing my feet on the floor, and sending myself a few good feet in the air, unable to stop the grin splitting my face as I look back to see Titus giving me a thumbs-up. I bounce again, my worn work shoes finding easy purchase on the floor, the rubber slapping hard on the brick, my habit flapping everywhere.

Soon Brother Thomas joins me, and we're racing down the hallway, ramming into each other's shoulders to knock each other off balance while Brother Titus cautions us not to land on our *balls*, and it's the most fun I've had in so long that it's almost giddying. Like a shot of Fireball—pointless and a sign of a deeper insanity—but I don't care.

"Where did you even get these?" I ask Thomas as we line up for another race.

"Titus's mom sent them to us. Told us to share. Which, no way."

"You're sharing with me. On three?"

"We're only sharing because you looked so sad pushing that vacuum around...*Go!*"

"Cheater!" I yell as he takes off without warning, the ends of his belt bouncing in the air as he charges ahead.

Brother Titus tries to coach me from the office doorway, even though I'm clearly losing. "If you lean forward as you bounce, you'll cover more ground."

"Unless you're going for height," Thomas adds over his shoulder.

"Why would he in a race, dummy?"

"Ahh, not the old height vs distance debate," says a voice from the far end of the hallway.

I look up and catch a glimpse of a raised eyebrow and whiskey eyes. I fumble my next bounce and then unintentionally come to land after a series of unbalanced, very embarrassing bounces at the feet of Elijah Iverson.

CHAPTER TEN

from Mode Magazine

I'd originally pitched this article as something about beer and anti-capitalism, and I thought it would be easy to write. After all, who doesn't want to spend a week drinking beer and pretending the Wi-Fi is too weak to get emails? Add in a dash of monastic resistance to conceptions of productivity and profit, and bam—*done*. I'd have an article and a beer-cation out of the deal too.

Little did I know that this week would launch me deep into the heart of monastic brewing and take me to hidden corners of Europe where prayers and pH testing go hand in hand. Little did I know that I'd be changed by it too, by my brush against this ancient world of faith and devotion, and by living with my guide for the duration of the trip, a broad-shouldered monk who is also my ex-boyfriend.

That's right. I have a monk ex-boyfriend. It's my only party trick.

—"The Eternal Cool of Monks: Beer and Prayer in Some of the World's Loneliest Abbeys" by Elijah Iverson

CHAPTER
ELEVEN

"Oh good!" the abbot exclaims, stepping out from behind Elijah and beaming down at me. "We were just looking for you."

Oh God. Why were they looking for me?

Why is Elijah here *again*? Why did Elijah have to find me right *now*, at the stupidest possible moment? It couldn't have been while I was vacuuming? Praying? Reading a book? Looking very serious and important? It had to be *now*?

Why why why why why—

I try to dismount my bouncy ball, which is harder than it sounds in a robe and heavy work shoes. Eventually giving up on dignity, I stand up with the ball between my legs and free my robes, until I'm finally standing like a normal person in front of my abbot and my ex-boyfriend. The embarrassment is like being shellacked with hot asphalt from the inside out—all of me is gloppy and burning with it.

And I'm not sure which is more embarrassing, that I was

bouncing on a giant toy like a child, or that my ex-boyfriend who has never been anything other than perfectly poised from the moment he was born witnessed it.

"Um," I finally say to them. "Hi."

"Why don't you give Brother Titus his rubber ball back," the abbot says, his eyes crinkling around the corners, "and come to my office for a moment."

I can't even bear to look up into Elijah's face as I pick up the ball by the handle and hand it to Brother Titus as solemnly as someone handing off a briefcase with nuclear codes inside. And then I duck my head and follow Abbot Jerome and Elijah into the freshly vacuumed office area, and then into the abbot's office itself. I see Brothers Thomas and Titus staring after us with heads tilted like curious puppies before the abbot shuts the office door and makes his way over to his seat.

"Sit down, sit down," he entreats. Out of the corner of my eye, I see Elijah sit with an easy grace that's as relaxed as it is attentive. He's casual again today, so casual, although effortlessly stylish as always—olive trousers and an olive T-shirt, the look finished by loafers and a tattoo on his left forearm.

He didn't have that when we were together.

Curiosity gnaws at me, but I can't make myself look any closer. I'm still burning with shame that he saw me being so much like the man I used to be. I'm burning with shame that I *acted* like the man I used to be.

Irresponsible and silly and cringe-inducing.

What had Elijah ever seen in me?

I sit down too—with all the grace of a man who chants ancient temple hymns for a job and chops wood as a hobby—and look at my hands. I can hardly separate the shame from the dread for why I'm here. The abbot seems to be in a good enough mood, but nothing positive can come from this little convocation. My boss and the man whose heart I broke? This is how nightmares begin.

"So can I expect lots of bouncy ball parades while I'm here?" Elijah asks, and I have such a visceral response to the low music of his voice that I'm suddenly and terribly aware that I'm not in chastity right now.

And *then* I'm suddenly and terribly aware of what he's just said.

"While you're here?" I ask, keeping my head ducked but turning it slightly to look at him again. Not completely—I don't think I can face him completely. But enough that I can see him cross his legs at the ankles. Enough that I catch a glimpse of amber eyes and a single raised eyebrow.

I look away again, my entire body in tumult.

"That's right," the abbot says amiably. "Mr. Iverson was so charmed by his visit a month back that he's coming to retreat with us for a week. He'll be writing a piece about his experience with us for *Mode*."

Elijah. Here.

For a week.

I want to flatten myself into the shape of an extinct sea creature and burrow into the seabed; I want to brick myself into an anchorage and eat nothing but crushed-up bricks until I die;

I want to crawl into a keg of beer and pickle myself—because how am I supposed to survive this? I could barely survive seeing him in the cloister for thirty minutes, how am I going to survive him being at prayers, at Mass, at mealtimes? How, literally in the hell, am I going to live through the next week?

Calm down, I try to think rationally. *You'll only have to see him during prayers and meals—communal things. You won't have to talk to him. You won't have to hear about how great and dependable his new fiancé is.*

The part of me that is already half-Cambrian sea bug doesn't care. I was barely holding on before Elijah came, and I can't see how I won't be abject with his presence now. I'm supposed to be clearing my heart and mind of everything but God, and how am I supposed to do that when Elijah Iverson is here with his eyebrow arches and that cool composure which practically begs to be inflamed and also that mouth and also that *stubble*—

"—and yes, it's not traditionally how we do things, but I thought this would make the most sense, since your duties routinely take you all over the abbey grounds in the course of a day, and with your brother being Mr. Iverson's brother-in-law and all..."

The abbot has been talking while I've been Kafka-ing into a sea bug, and it takes me a moment to catch up.

"Excuse me?" I ask hoarsely. I didn't hear the beginning of what he said, and so I must be wrong, I must be so wrong about what I think he's asking me to do. Because there's no way he can ask me to do that.

The abbot beams at me. "You'll be Mr. Iverson's host while he's here. I knew it would please you both, since you're basically family."

Right. Because my brother Sean is married to Elijah's sister Zenny, and they're currently producing squishy, dimpled babies at a rate that would make the pope himself shed an approving tear.

But while that makes us family in a sociological sense, Elijah and I are not family in any *normal* sense, unless family is being defined in extremely kinky terms these days. This is going to be less like walking around with a brother-in-law and more like walking around with...well, with a guy I want to shove against a cloister wall and kiss. Preferably while I've got my hand down his pants.

"I know that normally the guestmaster would see to Mr. Iverson," the abbot continues, still beaming. At me, at Elijah, at me again. Lots of beaming going on. "But this will be so much cozier. And since you are already acquainted, I know you'll be able to provide Mr. Iverson with the answers to any questions he has while he's researching his article. Especially about the brewery and taproom, since you work on the financial side and help with production."

Oh.

The brewery and the taproom. Right.

Now all the beaming is starting to make some kind of sense. These are the beams of a man who knows he's only a few well-written paragraphs away from free publicity on a national scale. These are the beams of someone who might sell *many* cases of artisanal, monk-made beer merely by loaning out his resident CPA-slash-lumberjack for a week.

It's smart—the businessman I used to be appreciates that—but that won't make this week any easier on me, and surely the abbot knows this. Surely Brother Connor told him that my surprise visitor last month was actually my ex; surely Brother Connor told him I'm still in love with him. But then again, maybe not…as gossipy as monks can be about abbey goings-ons, sometimes we're also really good at respecting confidences, and I could see Brother Connor doing exactly that. Which normally would be great! So wonderful!

I love what good and loyal friends I have!

But it means that I either have to blurt out the truth *right now*, or wait until I'm not with Elijah, and then find the abbot and plead my case.

And I'm so, so far away from holy, because my pride balks at both of those possibilities. It absolutely refuses to say anything now, in front of Elijah, and if I say something later, if I manage to get someone else assigned to the role of Elijah's host, then Elijah might guess the truth.

He might guess that I'm still affected by him in some kind of way, and then he might be able to guess the reason why, and I don't think I can exist with him knowing it. Not after I flounced off to become a monk—breaking his heart in the process. Not after he fell in love with someone else.

No, if he discovers I'm still in love with him, I really will have to find a beer barrel big enough to pickle myself in.

"Yes, Father Abbot," I say, nodding down at my lap.

"Whatever you need."

"Excellent!" the abbot says, probably beaming again, I don't know, I'm not looking at him. I'm looking at Elijah's feet as he uncrosses them, I'm watching the smooth, brown contours of his ankles and the barely-there dustings of hair on the tops of his sockless feet before they disappear under the tongues of his loafers. I'm watching as Elijah rubs the soles of his shoes ever so slightly on the industrial carpet, and then crosses his ankles again.

It's the only tell for restlessness or unhappiness he's never been able to shake, that crossing and uncrossing of his legs. Even cotillion lessons and a career of pretending to be interested in keynote speeches hasn't been able to rid him of it.

I'm glad.

It's a little glimpse of him, the real him, underneath the style and the distant amusement. It's a reminder that he must be feeling something too right now, and maybe that makes me a selfish monster, but I'm relieved I'm not the only one.

The abbot stands, and we stand too. "Now," he says, smiling more and gesturing in the direction of the door like any cheerful host about to have free publicity for his microbrewery. "Let's get you to the guesthouse. Brother Patrick will get you acquainted with the schedule and all that, and then when you're ready, he can start taking you around. And if you need anything at all, Brother Patrick will help you. Isn't that right, Brother Patrick?"

Chapter Fifty-Three of St. Benedict's Rule says that all guests are to be welcomed as Christ himself would be. With the caveat that even Christ would have to endure scratchy bath towels and lukewarm scrambled eggs, I suppose. But I understand the heart of the rule, the idea behind it. Anyone who comes here should be greeted warmly, with trust and kindness.

Even if you've screwed them in multiple hot tubs and still want to put your tongue in their navel sometimes.

"That's right," I say.

Out of the edge of my vision, I see Elijah look down. As if he doesn't want anyone to see what's on his face right now. I know the feeling.

Abbot Jerome guides us out of his office and then on to the hallway, where he gives a small bow and a beam for the road. "Thank you for visiting, Mr. Iverson. Looking forward to speaking with you more at dinner—and possibly in the beer garden."

Beam. Beam.

Elijah doesn't look like he knows whether he should bow back or not, so I give a slow nod toward the abbot, which he mimics. And then we step out into the covered walkway, which will lead us to the classroom building, and then onto the guesthouse via another covered walkway.

"The guesthouse is through here," I say as we walk. I still can't look at him, but I have an excuse now. I'm showing him the way around; I couldn't possibly look over at him when I have so many emergency exits and benches to gesture at. "The refectory is accessed by the walkway on the other side of the cloister there, and beyond that is the lawn where most of the walking paths start. The cloisters, paths, and refectory are shared spaces, as are the common rooms in the guesthouse. The only real food is in the refectory at mealtimes, but there's always coffee on and some fruit and stuff like that. The building we're approaching is full of classrooms for conferences and large retreats, and there are a few vending machines scattered between the floors too, if you ever need a non-fruit snack."

The first cloister is thinly populated with the usual mix of gardening monks and visitors with sticky name tags badged to their chests. Beyond, the classroom building is full of men milling around with paper cups of coffee as they chatter to each other.

The average age appears to be somewhere between fifty-nine and one hundred and twelve.

"Who were they?" Elijah asks as we emerge into the covered walkway on the other side.

"It's a Knights of Columbus conference this weekend, I believe."

I'm walking fast, I realize, my strides long enough to send my habit fluttering around my ankles. I want to get Elijah settled in the guesthouse, and then I need to—I don't even know yet. Press my face against a tree and scream.

Elijah, though an inch or two shorter than me, keeps pace easily as we get to the guesthouse door, and even reaches for the door handle before I do, pulling it open for me. I see a flash of his tattoo—an abstract collage of grids, buildings, and trees with two small words underneath—and then the subtle flex of his forearm muscles underneath it as he pulls on the handle. And then the door is open and also so is the hole in my chest. It's hard to think pure thoughts when his forearm muscles do that.

But I *chose* this life.

I chose it I chose it I chose it—

"Brother Patrick," Elijah says. We're inside the guesthouse now, in the spacious, wood-beamed lobby, and the guest services director Claudia is nowhere in sight. It's just us and I have no reason to keep us moving, no reason not to stop.

I stop. Misery and something else—something worse—churns through me. I can't look at him, I just can't, because he'll know. I can't look anywhere but straight ahead.

"Brother Patrick," he says again, quietly this time. "Aiden."

If only Claudia would come. If only Claudia would come and get him a key and some scratchy towels and then I could run away—

"Look at me."

His voice is still quiet, but it's husky too, and low. Hearing it burns a little, like drinking a peated scotch or smoking a clove cigarette. "Look at me," he repeats, and I can't take it anymore, I can't. The need for him now is stronger than any survival instinct I've ever had.

I look.

CHAPTER
TWELVE

"Is it really so awful having me here?" he asks.

I don't know if I can even speak to answer that question.

Not only because *yes*—yes, it's so fucking awful—but because all the strength to speak has left my body at the first, full sight of him. At the stylish, monochrome outfit clinging to the curves of his arms and the muscles of his thighs. At his gorgeous eyes and his mouth framed so lickably by stubble.

Abruptly, I want to tell him everything. I want to say, *here's the reason I left*, and have it mean something, have it be worth all the miserable days and weeks I caused us both. Have it clarify its own delay, because the reason I left is the same reason I couldn't tell him why I left. I was still too fucked up for a long time to face the idea of explaining things. And then even after I slowly unfucked myself, I began to feel that I didn't deserve to tell him. I didn't deserve a—I don't even know. An apologia. A rebuttal of the worst things he must have thought of me. I deserved his anger, his disgust. Even his hatred.

I maybe deserved that most of all.

But I shouldn't be thinking about what I deserve, but about what he deserves. I've been nothing but selfish and careless with him since the moment I dragged him onto a barely lit balcony at a fundraiser and pushed my mouth against his. And maybe I was careless even before that—*years* before— when I was in high school and college and romping around like a puppy, goading and teasing him whenever I saw him with Sean, desperate for him to see me as something other than Sean's little brother, for reasons I didn't entirely understand at the time.

I had been selfish with him for so long that it seemed like the only way to stop was to leave.

So what does he deserve from me now? Everything, of course, everything under the sun, but I can start with this.

"It's not awful having you here," I tell him. (It's a lie, but it's the kind of lie I think God will forgive.)

The corner of his mouth deepens, like he knows I'm lying. But he doesn't call me on it. Thank fuck. "So you'll help me this week?" he asks instead. "I don't want to make you uncomfortable."

"It's my job to be of service," I reply with a duck of my head. And then I desperately cast around for anything to say that's not related to how he makes me feel. "I'm surprised *Mode* finds monastic life interesting enough to feature," I say. "It's not very fashionable here."

Elijah lifts a shoulder, and I try to ignore the way the fabric of the T-shirt pulls around him as he does. "They do their fair share of broader feature pieces, and they were really excited about this pitch. Monks who make beer and refuse to answer emails. You know, living the dream. Oh hello," Elijah says to the woman bustling over to us.

It's Claudia, with spots of bright red high in her medium tan cheeks and her clothes spattered with water. And I'm very, very relieved, even when she scowls at us both, because I'm not sure how much longer I can listen to Elijah speak in that husky voice without needing to go find my chastity device.

"You're bringing me another guest right now?" Claudia demands. "*Right now*? On this day?"

"Yes?" I offer hesitantly, and she shakes her head hard enough that her shoulders move too.

"No, Brother Patrick, you are not. A water pipe ruptured upstairs and now half my rooms are flooded, and I've already had to move eleven Knights of Columbus over to the dormitory. So your guest is going to have to stay in the dormitory too."

AHHHHH, goes my brain.

"I…I see," is what I end up saying, in a voice that's somehow pleading and gruff all at the same time.

She narrows her eyes at me, and then clearly decides she doesn't have time for whatever my deal is. She gestures to the check-in desk behind her. "Towels and soap are behind there. Two towels, one bar of soap." She looks at Elijah. "If we get this mess fixed, you can stay in the guesthouse, but otherwise you'll be with the monks during your stay. I promise they don't bite."

"Actually, Brother Patrick used to bite me quite often,"

Elijah says with a small smile, and Claudia laughs because she thinks he's joking.

He's not joking.

"You're funny. Brother Patrick could use a funny friend. Okay, towels, soap, et cetera. Have a nice evening, gentlemen."

And then Claudia is heading back up the stairs, and we're left on our own to go to the dormitory. Together.

"So this is where the monk bedrooms are?" Elijah asks as I nod and knock on a door. I get a muffled reply back, and with a small, internal sigh, I move on to the next door, but that room is occupied too.

My dormitory is officially packed to the rafters with timeworn Knights of Columbi, and normally I wouldn't mind at all, except it's looking more and more like the only empty room left is going to be the one next to mine.

Please, God. Please don't do this to me, don't test me like this.

I'll fail, and we both know it.

"Is that what they're called?" he asks after I try another door. "Bedrooms? Or dorm rooms?"

"We call them cells, but *room* works too," I respond. "We should try the upstairs."

"And each cell has its own bathroom?"

"Yes," I say as we climb, trying to remember if there're any empty cells on my floor other than the room next to mine.

"Is that common, the private bathrooms? In monasteries?"

"Not generally," I say, trying a door next to the stairs with a soft knock. I hear a dry, wavery *hello?* and apologize to the occupant. "But there was a local parishioner in the 1990s who owned a plumbing company and donated toilets and shower stalls to the monastery—and offered to plumb them all in too. So the bathrooms were themselves a donation, of a sort. They're not very glamorous, but it's nice to have some privacy. Before that there were communal bathrooms on each floor."

There's one last room I can try before there's only the one next to mine left, and I pray as many silent prayers as I can in the twenty seconds before I reach it.

I knock.

The door opens, revealing a Knight of Columbus with a paper coffee cup still firmly in hand. "Yes?" he asks. Disappointment crashes through me, followed by fear…and something much worse.

Excitement.

"Just looking for a room for another guest," I say with a small bow. "Apologies for the interruption."

"No problem!" is the cheerful reply, and then I lead Elijah to the door next to mine, which is at the end of the hall. I knock and there's no response, so I open the door to reveal the small suite inside.

Elijah steps past me—close enough that his legs brush against my habit—and I catch the faint hint of sage and saltwater. Like he's just gotten out of the saltwater pool in my family's backyard, like he's just dried off after a long summer day lounging in the sun with Sean.

And I'm reminded of all those days I came out and bothered them as they were swimming or napping, all those times I decided I had to swim too just because they were out there, and the urge to be wherever they were was something I had no interest in fighting. Sean and Elijah were only five years older than me, but what's nothing to adults is a yawning chasm when you're a kid, and even more so when you're a teenager. The distance between my fourteen and their nineteen felt uncrossable, vast—and also seductive in a way, because it constantly begged to be bridged. I needed more than anything else to prove to Elijah that I was just as mature and worldly and interesting as he and Sean were, and I used to think doing backflips off the edge of the pool or obnoxiously changing the stations on our battered outdoor radio was the best way to do it.

It wasn't until I was well into college when I realized the fascination I had with Elijah was more complicated than the usual *I want my older brother's best friend to think I'm cool.* That all the times I'd measured the precise latitude of the low-slung waistband of his shorts, all the times I'd brought out cold cans of Coke just so I could see Elijah's throat move as he drank…all the times I'd provoked him into wrestling and horseplay so I had an excuse to touch his water-slick arms and chest…

All those times had been pointing to what I was too oblivious to understand until I made out with another boy for a fraternity dare and liked it a lot.

I wonder if it was obvious to Elijah then. Or if he thinks I was being a typical little brother, tagging along because that's what little brothers do.

Whatever's left of my pride takes some small comfort in that.

I finally manage to speak, although there are still visions of Elijah wearing board shorts sliding through my mind. "Your key is on the hook by the door," I tell him. "I'll leave you to get settled and everything. Do you need help getting your things from your car?"

He shakes his head, walking over to the window and looking out onto the cloisters below and the steep hill beyond. "It's very pretty," he murmurs to the glass.

You're so pretty, he used to tell me, in that same low, appreciative voice. Usually before I was bent over the nearest flat surface. *You're the prettiest man I've ever seen.*

I catch a glimpse of myself in the small mirror over the desk and sigh at the stubble and the plainly sewn habit. Not so pretty anymore.

"I'll leave your towels on the bed, then, and be back in about thirty minutes to get you—"

Elijah comes away from the window before I can finish, his hands outstretched to take the towels and soap I've been cradling in the crook of my elbow. I put the towels on his upturned palms, a transaction that should be as touchless as a banker's deposit drawer, but then the paper-wrapped soap threatens to slide off the top and he moves to catch it— trapping it between his hand and mine.

For the first time in years, our hands are pressed together.

And even with a wafer of homemade soap between us, even with his palm to the top of my hand and my own palm pressed against the old terrycloth, I still feel his touch like I'd feel a tongue of fire licking my skin.

I can't meet his eyes—I could barely do it before, but certainly not now, not while we're touching—and it seems like the only thing that exists in my world is the top of his hand. It is so geometrically precise, that hand, with the strong lines of his fingers, with the short, squared-off nails. The metacarpals like the hammers on a piano, held in absolute stillness. Poised to move at a second's notice.

His hand is like everything else about him. Perfect. And soon there will be a slender band of metal decorating one of those fingers and this Jamie person will get to look at it and know it's for him.

I slide my hand out from under his, and he clears his throat in the way a polite person does to cover an awkward moment, and of course my drooling over his hand was obvious, of course it was.

He deserves for you to be good for him, I remind myself. *That's the least of what you owe him.*

I take two big steps back, still not able to meet his eyes. "I'll let you get your things and get settled. I'll be back in a bit."

CHAPTER THIRTEEN

from Mode Magazine

I used to be a fairly devout Catholic, however those things can be measured. My parents were front-pew Catholics; I was an officer in the Junior Knights of Peter Claver; I flirted with the fantasy of becoming a priest after learning the Jesuit motto: ite, inflammate omnia.

Go, set the world on fire.

But then sexual abuse committed by my parish priest—which resulted in unspeakable tragedy for my best friend's family—tore our world in half. The deep friendship between my family and my best friend's family ruptured, along with my faith.

And I was getting old enough to see that there was no place for me in the Church anyway. I knew I was gay; now I also knew that the church didn't want me if I wasn't willing to embrace celibacy or an outright lie.

So I left.

That should be the end of the story...but somehow the Church keeps inveigling itself into my life. My sister, one of the smartest and best people I know, was a postulant for religious sisterhood before she began seeing the man who's now her husband. And then a year later, the love of my life left me for the cloister.

And sometimes when I ask myself what I should write about, when I ask myself where I need to use my voice, I hear Ignatius of Loyola speaking to me.

Go, set the world on fire.

—"The Eternal Cool of Monks: Beer and Prayer in Some of the World's Loneliest Abbeys" by Elijah Iverson

CHAPTER
FOURTEEN

Piano notes waft through the church, floating up to the vaults of the ceiling and echoing off the stained glass and limestone of the sanctuary. The scent of incense pervades the space; decades and decades of smoke curling up to God. Racks of votive candles flicker and dance from invisible drafts, and high above the altar, an oculus window made of clear glass reveals a circle of bright blue sky.

Sunlight slants in from the clerestory windows and bathes the life-sized figure behind the altar in light and shadow.

We walk slowly up the center of the nave, passing the dim recesses of the transepts and then stepping into the choir, where the monks stand to pray and sing. We are the only ones here—save for the brother practicing on the piano—but it feels holier for its emptiness, even more sacred somehow. There is no escaping that this place has always been the living crypt of the god who chose to die.

We stop as we get to the shallow steps leading up to the altar.

"That is"—Elijah seems to search for the right words as he looks at the sculpture hanging behind it—"very affecting."

I follow his gaze up to our crucifix, which despite the beautiful things around it, eclipses everything else in the sanctuary. No amount of candelabra or fresh flowers or gold-trimmed linens can compete with the corpus of our suffering god, because this crucifix hides nothing, softens nothing. You can see the strain in Jesus's arms and in his stomach; the muscles of his thighs are flexed with the effort of it all. His head is not bowed in surrender or death, but turned to the side in agony, struggle manifest in the tight cords of his neck and in the clench of his jaw. His eyes—half-lidded—gaze out with some wordless plea. His full lips are parted as if in a gasp.

I could look at him forever.

It's a long-buried instinct that has me turning to Elijah, greedy for his reaction, to see if he sees what I see, something so stirring and so haunting that it necessitates devotion, it necessitates a lifetime of love laid at its feet, but Elijah isn't looking at the crucifix right now.

He's looking at me.

And for a dizzy, breathless, unreal moment, I think that this is how it would feel to have the Jesus on the cross look back at me. There is the same half-lidded look, the same parted lips.

The same urge to offer up the wet flesh of my heart to be scored deep with the love of this person.

But unlike the man on the cross, there is no plea in Elijah's eyes, no supplication. I cannot decipher what's there in its place, but it is nothing so vulnerable as all that, nothing so naked. The look he's giving me is guarded and laced with something bitter and doubtful and hard.

A muscle jumps once in his jaw, and then he turns away.

"Where will I be for prayers?" he asks, distant and removed once more. "Over there?"

"Yes," I say quietly and show him where the laity sits in the nave. Far away from the crucifix. Close enough that his gaze will burn the side of my face as I sing.

Before we'd gone to the church, I'd taken Elijah to the brewery, although there hadn't been enough time to see the taproom and still get back for dinner, and then I took him around to the trailheads in case he'd like to spend some time walking this week. He had a small leather notebook and a fine point Sharpie, and he took notes the entire time, his eyes flicking from thing to thing with efficient, penetrating assessment.

It was a familiar enough sight; maybe he was taking notes for an article instead of walking through a venue before an event, but it was the same thing really. The kind of observation that missed nothing, cataloged everything. The kind of surveying gaze I spent so many of my teenage years hoping would be raked over me, and then followed with that specific elixir of older-brother's-best-friend approval.

After we finish praying compline, he still has his notebook in hand. His long fingers are wedged between the pages, his Sharpie sticking out like a cigarette from a pack. I catch him staring at the crucifix with an inscrutable expression as I file out behind my brothers through the door near the altar.

After we bow to the altar and exit the sanctuary, I loop around the front of the church and come back to the pews, weaving through the already-chattering Knights of Columbi to get to Elijah, who is still studying Christ on the cross while old men shuffle and talk around him. He is looking at the crucifix like Jesus owes him money.

Elijah taps his notebook slowly against his thigh, the rest of his body utterly still except for the subtle lifting of his shoulders as he breathes. His T-shirt—made of something silkier than ordinary jersey—clings to his body in a way that's almost greedy, as if it can't stop touching those deltoids and trapezius muscles. As if it's as enraptured with the tempting furrow of his spine as I am. And the way its hem catches on his waistband, showcasing an ass that I once spent an entire night biting...

The flare of heat low in my belly is matched by the immediate constriction between my legs, and I'm grateful I locked myself up this afternoon. The grip of the metal cage no longer feels like pain to me, only safety. Only the comforting reassurance that I'm not about to walk up to my ex in a sanctuary with a hard-on beneath my monk's robes.

I step into his pew, and he turns to me. A single eyebrow is lifted in query, but he doesn't speak, and I feel suddenly seventeen again, crashing down into the basement while Sean and Elijah were hanging out and having Elijah giving me this exact same look. A look that says, *well?*

A look that says, *tell me what you want and then I'll decide if I have the energy to react to it or not.*

I feel a flush coming on. It was hard enough to pray compline tonight knowing that Elijah was here, that he could be watching me with that detached gaze while I kept my eyes fixed on my breviary. Just the knowledge that he was in the church with me was enough to make me stumble over psalms I'd chanted hundreds of times before, it was enough to send my pulse skittering through my veins at random intervals. It was enough to make me hyper-conscious of how I did the smallest and most mundane actions. Was he watching as I turned the page of my breviary? Was he watching as I sat for the reading? As I angled my body toward the altar?

It was stupid to care how I looked when I was wearing a floor-length polyester robe, and it was even stupider when I was a monk who'd chosen a life where it didn't matter if anyone found me attractive ever again, but stupid had never stopped Aiden Bell before, I guess.

I clear my throat and try to sound unaffected by his presence. "I came to make sure you had everything you needed for the night before I went back to the dormitory."

Elijah glances at his watch, and then up at the oculus window, where the sky is still painted in the bright colors of mid-evening. "Bed already?"

"Vigils come early in the morning," I explain, understanding his confusion. Before I came here, I was an incurable night owl—although I still got up at the crack of dawn to work out and commute in to work. Functioning on three or four hours of sleep had become my norm. It had seemed so normal at the time, so *necessary*. I *had* to exercise, *had* to work ten hours a day, *had* to drink and party and fuck, there was no other choice, and no one around me was living any differently—except for maybe my older brother Tyler. But he'd been a former priest who went back to college to study theology after he unpriested, like a real weirdo. I had no interest in being like him at the time.

Except now I've definitely surpassed him in the *holy weirdo* department, and that includes going to bed with the sun, like one of Sean and Zenny's squishy babies.

"Should I plan on coming to vigils?" Elijah asks, looking back to the sky with something like wariness. As if he's already anticipating how soon dawn will come.

"Guests are invited to come to as many or as few prayers as they like," I say. "And it can vary from day to day. The only absolutes are meal-times and respecting the Grand Silence."

"Hmm." He taps his notebook against his thigh again. "I suppose I should at least go to my room and start typing up notes. I'll walk back with you."

We've been walking around the campus together for half the day, and still my heart gives an uneven stutter at the thought of walking back with him, of *being* with him, just the two of us. It's almost worse than being seventeen and having no idea my Elijah-idolatry was actually a crush, because now I know what it is. Now I know who he is. Now that crush has had years to deepen, to grow roots around my bones and through my ribs, to thicken itself into a robust devotion that surpasses nearly everything else, and is matched only for my devotion to the suffering son of the desert. It has replaced my marrow and my fascia, and now Elijah is here, and we are walking into the fading light together, shoulder to shoulder.

I remind myself to breathe. He deserves my kindness, my assistance. *Not* my torment. Nor the hunger that's barely stifled by the metal banding my sex.

We don't say anything as we walk, which is fine by me, because I don't know what I could say anyway, other than *I still love you, don't hate me, please go home.*

So near-silence it is, broken only by the sound of the fountain in the cloister and the staccato thunks of car doors closing in the parking lot—visitors leaving after a day on the trails or in the taproom.

When we get to our floor, I make sure Elijah has his key, and then step over to my door, relieved at the distance between us, but hating it too.

"I'm right here if you need anything," I say, managing to sound normal.

A brow hikes up. "Your cell is next to mine?"

I can't tell if this is unwelcome news or not. "I'm a quiet neighbor, if you're worried about noise."

"No—I. No. I'm not worried. It's fine."

It's the first hesitation I've sensed from him today, and it makes me a little miserable. Why, I don't know, since I've been nothing but hesitation all day today myself.

"Okay, then," I say as he goes back to unlocking his door, and this is so awkward. Why do they never say how awkward it is to talk to someone you used to fuck? "Good night, Elijah."

Elijah gives me a nod and then opens his door and steps inside.

I open my door—I don't lock my cell because there's nothing in here but old blankets and secondhand books—and stagger inside like I've just finished running a race. And not a spirit-race like Paul the Apostle talks about, but a terrible, pointless race where the only reward is a cold sports drink and a free T-shirt.

Except I don't even get a T-shirt. My reward for surviving the day with my ex-boyfriend is waking up and doing it all over again.

I shower quickly, clean my cage and put it back on, and pull on the faded flannel pajama pants I sometimes wear to sleep. (No, we don't wear our robes to bed.) After brushing my teeth and saying my prayers, I stretch out in bed and stare at the ceiling.

The wall between my cell and Elijah's is so thin that I can hear the faint *tap-tap-taptaptaptap* of his laptop keys. I can hear when he pushes his chair back on the wooden floor; I can hear when he heaves a giant sigh and then slides his chair back in again. *Tap-tap-tap.*

It's so wonderful to listen to that I don't even close my eyes. I want to treasure every second of this, I want to remember everything about how it felt to have him tapping and sighing and thinking on the other side of the wall.

I want to remember how it felt having him close.

But somehow, sleep comes for me anyway, tugging me

under as the muffled sighs and key taps come from the other side of the wall, and I don't wake until just before sunrise and it's time for vigils.

And once again, I wake up knowing that I've dreamed of Elijah. The memories of the dream cling and stick to me as much as my bedsheets do.

CHAPTER FIFTEEN

It's Sunday, so Mass, lunch, and daytime prayer are earlier in the day, and aside from some of the farming and brewing must-dos, there is no work in the afternoon. We are allowed to pray, read, walk, meditate, visit—or take our ex-boyfriend up to the barley fields to show him where the barley for the beer is grown. I tell him about a grant from K-State to grow a more beer-friendly strain of barley while the hot wind whips my habit around my legs and he takes notes in his notebook, and then we go down to the barn, where I introduce him to Father Nathaniel and Brother Amos, our lead farmers.

And then on to the printing room, and the bottling room. And then the taproom, which is closed to the public today, and so we have the entire echoing space to ourselves. I pour him a little flight of our different ales—a dubbel, a tripel, a farmhouse ale, and an abbey blonde.

For the first time today, Elijah looks truly interested. He sits at the bar I'm standing behind, and with the afternoon sun blaring into the taproom, he starts to taste our different beers, holding each glass up to the light before he does.

I pour the farmhouse ale for myself and lift it. "Sláinte."

"Sláinte," he repeats, and we touch the glasses together before we drink. His Adam's apple works up and then down as he swallows, and I quickly turn my attention to my own ale, gulping down a few desperate swigs before I set the glass on the bar.

He sets his down too—empty, since it was a very small pour—but doesn't pick up the next glass yet. Instead, he turns the glass on the polished wood of the bar, his eyes on the suds sliding down the inside.

"Is this it?" he asks. "Is this really it?"

I think he means the beer at first.

"The idea is to focus on a few core products—"

I stop, because there's now something in his face that tells me this isn't about the beer.

He looks at me, and his brows are drawn, knitted together like he's trying to work out a problem. "This is all that's here? There's a church for praying in, cells for sleeping in, and then places to work in? Those are the bounds of your life?"

"Ora et labora," I say, not sure if I should feel defensive or apologetic or patient or what. "The point is for my life to be bounded, Elijah. Otherwise, I wouldn't be here."

He opens his mouth like he's going to say something, and with the sun at his back, his normally amber eyes are dark and unreadable.

But then instead of speaking, he presses his lips together

and reaches for another sample of ale.

We drink the rest of our beer in silence.

Monday doesn't go much better. There's not much left to see, so I take Elijah around the grounds again so he can interview the different brothers about their tasks and trades, as well as their reasons for choosing such a strange life.

Elijah is an excellent interviewer, and he's as polite and charming as ever with everyone he talks to, but I can tell he's restless. Or bored. Or frustrated. As he listens to people talk, he uncrosses and recrosses his ankles. As we walk, he keeps looking around the monastery with something like disbelief narrowing his eyes. As he sits in the church for prayers, he stands and sits with the congregation, but he doesn't sing, and I don't think he prays either. Instead, he stares at the crucifix as if he'd like to ask God some questions, on the record, of course.

And at night, I hear so much sighing and chair-scooting from his side of the wall that I can't actually fall asleep until long after dark. There is no more soothing *tap-tap-tap* coming from his cell.

Only *tap*-SIGH-*tap*-SCOOT-*tap*-LOUDER SIGH.

And then something that sounds an awful lot like the delete key being hit over and over again.

When I meet him at breakfast Tuesday morning, he's visibly fraying a little. I'm not sure if anyone else could tell, because outwardly, he's still all cool smiles and lifted brows.

But there's a certain agitation to the way he rips the skin off his orange. A brittleness to his mouth as he looks at the dining room where we all sit silently at our trays, eating our toast and fruit and mass-made scrambled eggs.

After breakfast ends—and with it the morning silence—I ask Elijah where he'd like to go today.

He scrubs at his hair and lets out a soft laugh. "Is there anything here that I haven't seen already?"

I think he means it rhetorically, but I still answer in case he's really asking. "Have you seen the hermitage yet?"

"The hermitage? I don't think so, no."

"It's two miles down the eastward path," I say. "By the creek. I could take you there if you'd like."

He stares at me. I've gotten better about looking at him over the past three days—partially because I've let my stubble thicken and I think it hides the worst of my flushing—but when he stares at me like this, like I'm the next thing he's going to write five thousand words about, I can't handle it. I look away to the cloister, where brothers are already dead-heading roses and pulling up weeds.

"I want to see someplace that means something to you," Elijah says suddenly. "I want to see the place where you wish you could spend all your time."

"Well, then," I say. "We ought to go to the hermitage."

It's early enough that the walk is warm but not oppressively hot, and the wind has settled down enough that my habit behaves as we wend our way through the woods. I show Elijah the path that branches off toward the labyrinth at the base of Mount Sergius, and then I show him the bridges over the creek I've built since I came here. And finally we get to the hermitage itself, a small cottage made of limestone and salvaged windows with the creek burbling nearby. No one is staying here currently, and so I show Elijah the inside, which does have electricity and running water but is fairly rustic otherwise.

He stands in the middle of the small room, turning in a slow circle. "So you come here," he says carefully, "to retreat from the abbey. Which is already a retreat from the rest of the world."

"Yes."

"Doesn't that feel a little like needing a vacation from a vacation to you?"

I dare to look at him, since he's wandered over to a window and is peering out at the creek. "The original monks lived alone," I say. "Monastic life, in its original form, was utter solitude. Total deprivation. The desert fathers found God in that life."

Elijah turns back to face me. He's wearing a short-sleeve button-down shirt, and the top two buttons are unbuttoned. I can see the notch of his clavicle like this.

Fuck me.

"And that's what you want?" Elijah asks. "To live in the desert and write proverbs?"

"Yes. Well, not the desert literally," I explain at the look on his face, "but a desert in every other sense. I want to be alone with God."

"How alone do you need to be?" Elijah demands, turning all the way toward me. "God is the radiant dawn and the shepherd who finds every lost sheep—are you telling me that you can't be alone with him in your cell? Or in a farmhouse, say? He can only find you in the middle of nowhere while you're off playing Thoreau?"

It stings to hear the private hopes of my heart talked about like this. Like they're ridiculous.

"It is not about what God is capable of," I say quietly, "but what I am incapable of."

"And what about the rest of the world?"

"I'm not sure what you mean."

He stares at me, the frustration on his face plain. "So you get to just leave the world and everyone in it, because you don't feel *capable* of praying if you're not given complete freedom and latitude to live your life entirely for yourself. I'm sorry, for *God,*" he adds, when he sees me open my mouth. "Here's a question for you, Brother Patrick? *Who* gets to do this? Who gets to just opt out of living in the world? Who gets to give up on it and retreat from it all while people still suffer? Who gets to leave everyone else to their fate while they hole up and pray?"

Shame crawls up my neck. Shame I thought I was done feeling; shame I thought I'd atoned for. The shame of being selfish, thoughtless. The shame of being Aiden Bell.

"I thought—I just think it's better if I'm not in the larger world at all," I try to explain. "I'm not buying a private island to fill with coke mirrors and swimsuit models. I'm not taking anything away from anyone—I'm not in the world making it a worse place."

"Why is that the only option?" Elijah demands. "Why does you being out there mean you'll make it *worse*?"

"Because that's what I *did*!" I answer, louder than I expect.

He looks at me, his lips parted like I've surprised him into silence.

"Because that's what I did," I say again, quieter this time. "I came here to learn how to be good. How to be empty of everything but faith and devotion. And when I came here, I gave all my money away—some as a donation to Mount Sergius, but most of it went to nonprofits around the country. So me leaving *did* concretely make the world a better place, because those places all have millions of dollars they wouldn't otherwise."

"You could have made *more* better if you'd stayed," Elijah says. "You could have done *more* good. Instead of being here, where nothing you do matters outside the abbey walls."

"I should have stayed in the secular world so I could earn more money to eventually donate?" I ask, not bothering to hide my incredulity. "Is that all I'm worth? Earning money?"

"You know that's not what I meant," Elijah replies. "You know that's not what this is about."

"Do I?" I fire back, and then immediately regret it. Shame and anger are filling me like wine overfilling a cup, and I feel sour with it all. Stained. But never, even in my most masochistic fantasies, had I imagined *this*. That Elijah would see my path to survival and atonement as selfish, as silly. As shallow as an influencer's performative yoga retreats or something.

I'd never imagined that I'd be considered less than ethical for the kind of seeking that asks nothing of anyone except an empty chair at Thanksgiving.

"Opting out of the world doesn't help anyone but yourself," Elijah says, and there's a real edge to his voice now. An edge sharp enough to cut. "What is the point of all this holiness if it doesn't reach anyone else? What is the point of becoming *good* if that goodness begins and ends with you? If the only people ever touched by your *goodness* are the people who have the time or the bandwidth to make it inside your abbey walls?"

My temper flares. "I'm not hurting anyone by being in here," I say sharply.

"No, you're not," comes the cold response. "Not anymore."

I cannot believe how deeply his words slice. Even though I've expected them for years. Even though I know I deserve to hear them.

We stare at each other from across the room, our breaths coming quick and hard, and I can't speak right now; it's like every possible response I could have has knotted itself up in my throat and snagged on the flesh there, like barbed wire.

It's Elijah who speaks first anyway. "This," he says, gesturing around to the cottage that has held so many of my best and worst moments, "is a waste of privilege. A waste of a life. You have blown a hole in the hearts of everyone who loved you for absolutely fucking nothing, and I hope it was worth it. I hope *God* was worth it."

And then he pulls open the door to the hermitage and he leaves.

I don't follow.

CHAPTER
SIXTEEN

Elijah isn't at vespers or at dinner. I think he might be in his cell, but I'm not sure, because when I go into mine, there is silence from the other side of the wall. I walk to my window and stare out at the hill for a moment, and then at the cloisters soaking up the evening light, and back to the hill, which is lit with orange as the sun begins to set.

The bells for compline will toll soon.

I press my hand to the glass, as if I can touch the hill itself. *I lift my eyes to the hills.* Five years ago, I would have fought Elijah tooth and nail. I would be pounding down his door right now, demanding we either fight or fuck, the order wasn't important.

Five years ago, I would have said *you're goddamn wrong* and would have conceded the point only after an adrenaline-filled argument or a marathon fucking session.

But now, I'm not so sure he's wrong.

I'm not sure he's entirely right either though, and I

suppose if there's any gift being a monk has given me, it's that I know how to handle that feeling now, that ambiguity. In my old life, decisions had to come fast, in minutes or seconds. Opinions even faster. It suited me, enabled my naturally impulsive thinking, and truly, it felt like there was no other way to live. Everyone else around me was making a thousand decisions a day, moving fast, thinking fast, living fast. Slowing down and taking time—to listen or ruminate or be anything other than absolutely productive in the sense of churning out choice after choice—was worse than pointless. It was weak.

And now in that weakness, I've found strength.

I decide not to bother Elijah. I have no right to him anymore, no right to knock on his door when he's made it clear he's pissed at me. And honestly, I'm still feeling a hundred different things from his words, and all those feelings are stabbing around in my chest like shards of broken glass, and I don't trust myself with those shards inside me.

A waste of a life, he said.

I hope God was worth it.

The bells for compline ring, and I leave my cell, hoping the familiar songs and prayers will clear the glass out of my chest and bleed the anger from my blood.

Elijah isn't at compline either, and I feel so full of all my own feelings, not at all empty like I so want to be, and my hands shake a little as I turn the pages of my breviary.

Do not hide your face from me, we sing. And later: *Lord, make haste and answer, for my spirit fails within me.*

Make me know the way I should walk. To you, I lift up my soul.

The sun is sliding down the sky when I leave the church with my brothers, and the heat of the day has finally started to die off. The mood is high and easy, and several brothers decide on a pre-sleep pint in the picnic area, and several others go for a walk up to the barn to see the new loft Brother Amos built. There's talk of getting chickens and goats to add to our three dairy cows, and I can hear Brother Titus and Brother Thomas already making a case for why we'd need an abbey dog (or four) if we have more farm animals.

I don't go with any of them. Instead, I go to the south cloister, which is completely empty, and I find my favorite bench. I sit and I wait.

The fountain trickles gently, and a breeze finds its way through the covered walkways to tug at the flowers. The sky slowly changes overhead, from a bright blue to a pale blue to streaks of orange and pink and lavender. I can just see the first star now, winking in the sky.

My first year here, when I was nothing but a dirty sock hamper of feelings, Brother Connor told me about a book he'd read by a Gethsemani monk, who'd written about how the abbey eventually became not only the container for his thoughts, but the shapes of them too.

"One day you will wake up and realize that your thoughts are the same shape as your favorite oak tree," Brother Connor had explained. "Or that they follow the winding edges of the creek. They will echo to the tolling of the bell. They will flutter in the prairie wind."

"And this has happened to you?" I asked, a little dubiously.

"You mean, are my thoughts part of my places and are my places part of my thoughts? Do they shape each other, remember each other—recognize each other? Yes, as strange as it might sound, but that's what comes from living in a place instead of merely on it."

It had sounded like medicine for an illness I'd only just realized I'd had. "How long?" I'd asked him. "How long does that take?"

He'd smiled at me, eyes crinkling. "It's not like a 3D printer, Aiden. It's organic, and the process of existing in a place is as important as the end." Seeing the expression on my face, he took some pity. "Perhaps it will happen sooner than I think. Perhaps you only need to find your first place to be *in* instead of on."

And I did find it—entirely by accident one night, when I'd sat out in the cloister because going to bed felt impossible but walking also felt impossible and reading also felt impossible and just *everything here* felt so damn impossible. I wanted to leave. I wanted to go back to Kansas City—not to my house, because my house had been sold—but maybe to Sean's place and say *I made a mistake.*

I wanted to find Elijah and say *I'm sorry I'm sorry, I fucked up and I'm back and I'm sorry.*

And in that moment of lowness, that brink-of-tears lostness, a small light winked into the twilight from the fountain. I'd looked up in time to see another, and then another.

Fireflies.

So many of them that it almost felt impossible, like a scene in a movie. Like something from a dream.

And I'd begun to understand what Brother Connor meant about a place becoming my thoughts, and I began to see how that could be as holy as any plainchant or sacrament. Because it felt like God was using that cloister, that warm summer night, to brush his fingers across my face. As if God himself was giving me a *what if.*

What if I showed you something beautiful, what if I showed you a glimpse of my love for you?

And every summer since, in peak lightning bug season, I try to give myself a few nights here in this place. A few nights of God in the cloister, putting on a show under the stars just for me.

As the sky darkens even further, I close my eyes for a moment and pray. I've heard sometimes that it's greedy to go to God with demands and requests, like God is some kind of cosmic customer service manager, but after five years of singing the psalms day in and day out, I can say with authority that complaining to God is a very ancient tradition. Berating and wheedling and lamenting too.

And right now, I don't even know what I want from God. Comfort? A message? For the fireflies to spell out *it's okay, you didn't make a mistake coming here* with their little glowing bodies? For Elijah to leave and for July to get here sooner, so I can find some bleaker place to retreat to?

My own desert, finally?

But I don't keep my eyes closed for long. Prayer still unformed, I open my eyes so I can be sure to see the first firefly beckon, and that's when I hear the footsteps. Slow, hesitant. They pause at the entrance to the cloister just behind me, and then resume.

I don't need to look over to see that it's Elijah, but I do anyway. I'm finally brave enough to look at him...now, when he's furious with me. Go figure.

"Can I sit?" he asks in a low voice. The words are as hard and smooth as pebbles. I have no idea if he's here to continue our fight or tell me he's leaving, but it doesn't matter because I want him to sit. I want him to stay. Even if it's only to tell me things that will hurt me again.

"Yes," I say, and then I can't help it, I smile.

He looks startled by that smile, his eyebrow lifting and his eyes intense on my mouth as he sits.

"What are you thinking about?" he asks.

"Nothing," I say, ducking my head and smiling harder.

"Lying is a sin," Elijah replies. "Or at least that sounds like something I've heard before."

It must be the impending firefly show making me giddy, because I decide to say it. "I was thinking about how strange it is that I used to lick the sweat off the back of your neck, and now you have to ask if it's okay to share a bench with me."

It's dark enough that when I look back over at him, his eyes are nothing but glitter and shine. I have no idea what he's thinking, but once—just once—I see a muscle jump in his jaw.

"Why are you sitting here?" he asks finally, wisely not addressing what I said. "Isn't it bedtime?"

"I'm waiting for something, but you're welcome to wait with me, if you'd like."

His shoes shift on the flagstones beneath the bench. He's uneasy. Or unsure. "Okay," he says after a minute, and then we sit.

It is not silent—silence is never silent after all—but it is quiet. The Knights of Columbi are gone, the other brothers are either in bed or far away from the cloister. Even the slow weep of the fountain is hushed and small, halfway to slumber.

And next to me, I can hear the steady whisper of Elijah's breathing, the scuff of his shoes on the stones as he tries to stifle whatever he's feeling right now.

I wonder if the quiet is hard for him. It used to be nearly impossible for me.

The first firefly comes without warning, a soft flash from somewhere in the lavender. It takes a few minutes for the next one to show itself, and a few minutes more for the next after that, but then the lights come faster and faster, until we are surrounded by them. Until the air itself is hung with soft glimmers, until it feels like the world is hung with stars.

It is so simple a thing—fireflies in the cloister. And yet every time, I'm humbled by it. By the magic God so casually lets loose for us, by these sweet moments which are so freely given.

For nearly an hour, the air is aglow, shimmering from

between flowers and above the purling water of the fountain. For nearly an hour we sit there, not touching, not speaking, barely moving.

But yet my skin prickles with his nearness. My heart speeds. A continually thwarted erection pushes futilely at my cage.

I'm as aware of him as I would be if I were crawling over him in bed.

Slowly, the lights fade, the fireflies vanishing back into the night. I'm not sure what I expect when I look over at my ex-boyfriend, but I'm still arrested by it. Arrested by the shine of his eyes and the part of his mouth. The gentle, vulnerable awe that lingers in his expression as he turns to meet my gaze. My heart jumps again, and I very nearly reach for him, because he is lovely and because he trusted me enough to wait and because he saw what I saw too. The gorgeous, playful magic of it all.

His eyes don't leave mine, and then something changes in his face. It's something almost like…longing. Or maybe he's mirroring my expression, which I know has to betray everything. That I crave, I dream, I love—that I am a garden of him to this day.

"Aiden," he says softly, and I relish hearing my secular name from him, because it was the name that belonged to him, to his lips and thoughts and even his fingers when he was scolding or flirting over text or email.

I don't realize I'm leaning toward him until my cage presses into my thigh. I stop, because he's leaned forward too, and we are only inches apart.

What if...?

His long eyelashes flutter over his cheeks as he blinks fast, drawing in a slow breath. "You..." he murmurs, and then closes his eyes, and he's leaning in, and I'm leaning in, and I can feel his breath on my lips—

A low laugh breaks the quiet of the cloister, followed by another, and then a not-so-quiet *shhhh!*

Both Elijah and I jerk back like puppets yanked by the strings, our eyes wide as we stare at each other. I look quickly at the covered walkways to make sure no one saw, and then shudder out a relieved exhale when I see that we're still alone. The laugh is coming from the cloister just beyond—the brothers returning from their pre-bed beer, I think—and they haven't reached us yet.

My shoulders slump and I pass a shaking hand over my face. I hadn't been about to kiss Elijah, I definitely hadn't, because I took a vow never to kiss anyone again, and if I *had* been about to kiss Elijah, then what did that mean?

What did that mean about my vows?

About me?

No, we couldn't have been about to kiss. I'm imagining things in some kind of sex-starved, emotional collapse, because I've taken a vow and Elijah *is engaged to be married* and he was pissed at me today anyway and we were only leaning in to talk.

But when I drop my hand and look at Elijah, the expression on his face gives me no reassurance whatsoever.

He looks fucking shell-shocked.

"I—" I don't know what to say and my voice comes out all strangled anyway. "I think I should get to bed now. Vigils and all."

"Right," Elijah says with a swallow. "Vigils."

"Good night," I whisper, and then I stand, and then I leave.

But it's not relief I feel as I push inside the dormitory and find my way to my cell, it's something much, much more dangerous.

It's hunger.

Hot, restless hunger, and I spend the night wracked with it.

CHAPTER SEVENTEEN

from the notebook of Elijah Iverson

~~What if~~
~~What if he~~
~~What if I still~~

CHAPTER EIGHTEEN

I wake up bleary and miserable, damp with sweat and other fluids. I send up a silent prayer of thanks that we throw all our sheets down the same chute each week and so no one knows whose bed linens are whose. For now I scrub them as best as I can and then clean myself up for vigils. Despite whatever emitted from me nocturnally, my body is aching for sex in a way I haven't felt in years, and I feel nearly fevered with it. All of my thoughts are of things hot and slick and firm, and I'm so fucking tired, and it's fucking *raining* and so by the time I'm stumbling into the church to the toll of the bell, I'm all wet too.

There's supposed to be a psalm for everything, but there is no psalm for this, there's no proverb. A jeremiad *maybe*, but we're not reading Jeremiah right now, we're in Joshua, and there's nothing about being horny and wet in that whatsoever. Even the river dries up in Joshua.

In fact, in addition to there being no psalms about this, the psalms we are reading almost seem to taunt me today. *I will be watchful of my ways, for fear I should sin with my tongue.* And later: *we groan inwardly and await the redemption of our bodies.*

The verses are meant to exhort me to righteousness, which as a monk inevitably includes chastity. But now all I can think about are the sins I want to commit with my tongue.

They are many.

I make it through vigils and hopefully look merely tired and not like a monk who nearly kissed someone last night, and then after morning lectio, I return for lauds and see Elijah there. Our eyes meet—once, quickly—and I feel it like a lightning strike. I can barely breathe.

I keep my eyes on my breviary for the rest of the prayer, barely able to mumble-sing along for how fast my thoughts are racing. I'm still supposed to be his host, right? I can hardly duck out of that duty without telling the abbot what happened, and I'm…not going to do that.

Not because I'm being dishonest, of course, but because it wasn't a big deal to begin with. Even if we *had* been about to kiss, it was muscle memory more than anything, it was a habit that had never been properly broken, only fled from. Nothing to confess there.

Maybe Elijah won't want me to be his host any longer anyway. He had been angry with me, and then there was the whole muscle memory kiss thing, which even though it *wasn't* a real kiss *at all*, still probably felt icky to him on account of the whole being engaged thing.

So it'll all work itself out. He won't want to see me, and then I will lick my horny wounds in peace until I can fling myself on the mercy of the starkest monastery that will have me. And then, with an ocean between us, there will be no choice but to weed him from my heart and finally empty myself of everything but God.

But when Elijah walks up to me after breakfast, he doesn't briskly inform me that he'll be quite all right on his own, thank you very much. Instead, he kicks one foot behind the other and asks, quietly, "Can we take a walk?"

I glance outside, where rain is still streaking down in build-an-ark amounts.

"Um, in the walkways," Elijah clarifies. "Just for a moment."

"Of course," I say, although I'm suspecting once again that I might be fired as his abbey host. Which would be a good thing. The sharp pain in my chest is totally irrelevant to how much of a good thing it would be.

I lead Elijah through the office building to the north end of the campus, where most of the walkway traffic leads on to the printing room and is therefore fairly private. We come to a stop around the far end of the north cloister, and Elijah turns to face the green garth inside, his large hands gripping the wet stone of the walkway railing. He looks down, as if drawing strength for something, and I brace for impact.

But what he says is so unexpected, that I nearly stagger back with it anyway.

"I'm sorry," he says, lifting his head to look at me. A brow is lifted ever so slightly, but there's a knot above the bridge of his nose too, as if I'm some kind of puzzle he can't decipher right now.

"You're sorry?" I repeat, and it occurs to me that I should be the one apologizing—I left him years ago after all, and I was equally culpable for the muscle-memory moment last night and...

"For what I said in the hermitage yesterday afternoon," he clarifies. "I have some complicated feelings about how this kind of life relates to our responsibilities in the world, but I realize now that I hadn't untangled those from my complicated feelings about you. What I said—the way I said it—I meant it to hurt. And I'm sorry for that. You didn't deserve that. Not from me."

I huff out a short laugh—barely audible over the patter of the rain. "I think I deserve a lot more than that, Elijah. Especially from you."

He shook his head. "I don't want it to be that way between us."

I should say that there is no *between us* and there won't be. He has a few more days of research and then he'll be gone, and then eventually I'll be gone too, donning a white Trappist robe instead of my black Benedictine one, and working even harder to be a good man.

Instead, I ask, my voice low, "What way do you want it between us, Elijah?"

His lips part, just a touch, and his eyes darken. For a moment, there is only the rain and that intense stare. There are

126

only the memories of how it used to be.

Hot. Urgent. Dirty as hell.

What if...

Abruptly, he shoves himself off the railing and takes a few steps in the opposite direction. When he turns back, though, his face is composed.

"Jamie is coming to the abbey later today."

I must have heard him wrong. "Sorry, what?"

"My fiancé," Elijah says, and there's a stubborn set to his mouth now. "He's a microbrew enthusiast, and when I told him about the beer here, he was really excited, so I invited him to come up this afternoon and spend some time in the taproom. He knows who you are to me, so it's not a secret or anything."

"Ah," I say faintly. How did we go from him looking at me like *that* to Jamie coming here today? "Well, I can be present as little or as much as you'd like while he's here."

"There's no need for that," Elijah says. "I'm perfectly comfortable having you around."

Right. Because I'm not just an ex, I'm a *monk*-ex. I should be the safest ex who ever exed. And I'm definitely not swallowing down acrid thoughts right now at the prospect of meeting Jamie; I am definitely not already prickling with jealousy.

"Just let me know when he arrives, and I'll be happy to give him a tour of the brewery and bottling room before we go to the taproom." I manage to sound almost normal when I say that.

Now just to manage that normality for hours and hours while Jamie and Elijah hold hands and smile at each other in front of me.

Job from the Old Testament was tested less.

Elijah gives me a nod. "I'm going to write until he gets here, I think," he says. "But I'll see you this afternoon."

He starts to walk away, and I step forward.

"Wait," I say, and I have to say it again, because the rain drowns out my words. "Wait."

Elijah stops and turns, eyebrow arched perfectly.

"I'm glad you said the things you said," I tell him. "In the hermitage. I'll be thinking about them. Truly."

He studies me a moment longer and then gives me a slow nod.

"Okay," he says softly. And it's a long time after he disappears into the office building before I can make myself follow him. So long as I don't move, I don't have to start living the rest of my day.

The rest of my day which now includes *Jamie*.

CHAPTER NINETEEN

Elijah didn't say anything about our not-kiss in the walkway, and I can't decide what that *means*. Does that mean it's not worth talking about? That he feels the same way I do and that it was habit and muscle memory and nothing more?

Probably.

I ignore the disappointment which tugs on my stomach at the thought. It doesn't matter anyway; what difference would it make if Elijah had been as affected by our not-kiss as me? Absolutely none. None difference. And I have the polyester robes to prove it.

Since I'm on my own for the rest of the day, I catch up on emails and a few financial things, and then help out in the printing room. I'm hauling a box of ordination invitations over to the table we use for postage when I see Elijah in the doorway. His hands are at his sides, and he looks like he's just come to a sudden stop. He's staring at me like he's never seen me before.

It takes me a minute to realize why—and then I flush. Since lugging things around the printing room is usually sweaty work, I've switched out my habit for jeans and an old T-shirt. The T-shirt is one of the few things the abbot allowed me to keep when I came here, since we all need at least one or two sets of work clothes, but my body has changed enough over the last four years that it barely fits anymore. I might as well be wearing no shirt at all.

"I. Hi." Elijah blinks and looks up at my face. "Jamie is almost here. I thought I'd let you know."

I set down the box and rub at the back of my neck, noticing I'm all sweaty too. Great. Like Elijah really needed any more reminders that the svelte, hyper-groomed city boy he used to love is now a pious Neanderthal.

"Thanks," I say. "I'll clean up real fast and meet you near the parking lot, if you'd like?"

Elijah nods quickly and leaves without another word. With a sigh, I finish printing postage for the invitations, set the box on the rack of outgoing mail, and leave for my cell. So I can get ready to meet Jamie.

Yay.

The sun came out with a vengeance after the rain stopped, and so the parking lot is a furnace of Kansas-grade humidity as Elijah and I watch Jamie approach in his Jeep Rubicon. There is a bike rack mounted over the spare tire on the back. A bike rack meant for two bikes.

Elijah had never even said the word *bicycle* to me when we were dating, and now he's engaged to a man with a bike rack that can hold two bikes.

Jamie gets out of the Jeep with an easy hop and then strides toward us with a smile on his face. He's white, with sun-tanned skin and tousled hair in every shade of blond imaginable. He has a friendly smile, glasses, and slightly sticky-outy ears. Magazine-ready muscles swell under his fitted polo and shorts. He looks like he owns a kayak. He looks like he helps little old ladies cross the road.

I am trying very hard not to hate him.

He greets Elijah with a kiss to the cheek, and Elijah gives him a slow, warm smile as he pulls way. "Hey," he murmurs to Jamie in a low voice. "I've missed you."

Cells die, my blood thins. It would be easier to suck out my own bone marrow with a green Starbucks straw than to hear those three words spoken in that voice to someone else.

Jamie smiles back at Elijah, all Boy Scout-y goodness, and squeezes his fiancé's hand. Then he turns to me. "You must be Brother Patrick," he says, beaming. "It's wonderful to meet you. Thank you for letting me come."

It would be unkind to point out that hospitality has been our Benedictine bag for a millennium and a half and that I hardly have a choice in letting visitors visit, so I force out a smile. "Happy to have you here. Welcome to Mount Sergius."

I extend a hand for a welcoming handshake that is all about welcoming Jamie and not at all about getting him to let go of Elijah's hand. And I'm not at all irritated when the handshake is steady and strong. Or when he goes right back to holding his fiancé's hand after.

"Is this okay?" Jamie asks Elijah quietly, looking down at their linked hands. "While we're on the grounds?"

My reflexive dislike vanishes in the face of a reality I shared with him before monkhood—which is that safety is contingent on space, on who is in that space, and even though I am wearing the robes of the god-man who chose people from the margins to share his heart, I know that his spaces and believers have often been the least safe of all.

"You'll be with only me until we get to the taproom," I assure him. "And the brothers who are meeting us there are my friends and I…" I am out of practice with how to word such things. "I trust them," I finish.

Jamie nods, his well-muscled shoulders dropping a little from around his ears.

"Shall we start?" I ask, and then when Jamie and Elijah both look at each other—that casual checking-in glance that couples have—I slide my gaze up to the hill and breathe out a silent prayer for strength.

It's going to be a long evening.

Jamie is as friendly as his smile and glasses make him appear, and at least two times as wholesome. It turns out he doesn't run an eighth-grade orchestra—he's a librarian who focuses on senior outreach. He teaches Sunday school at an Episcopalian church and has dinner with his mom and dad every week. His hobbies are biking, baking, and camping, and the last book he read was *The Thursday Murder Club*, which he's happy to mail to me at any time!

As we make our way through the brewery tour and the bottling room, I keep glancing over at Elijah, feeling like I missed something crucial in all the years I've been around him. I'd never known him to camp or care about baking; he liked weird, experimental fiction, not cozy mysteries; and as far as the wholesomeness went, well...

The wholesomeness was new too.

Does Elijah play any *what if* games with Jamie? Jamie, who is good and earnest and who drinks from his reusable water bottle during the tour like a responsible adult and probably never forgets to wear sunscreen, even in the winter? Does Jamie ever trap Elijah against a kitchen counter and daisy-chain bites around his collarbone? Does Elijah ever text him during the day with instructions for later that night?

I don't know what's worse: Elijah sharing those kinds of games with Jamie—or them having sweet, vanilla sex with lots of eye contact and cuddling and eight hours of sleep after.

Because if they are having sweet, vanilla sex, then maybe that's what Elijah really wanted all along. Maybe I was some wild oats to sow, or worse—maybe I corrupted him.

That's a depressing thought, and I try to draw comfort from the swish of my habit around my feet as I lead them on to the taproom. At least I'm here now, where I can't corrupt anyone else, where I can't distract people from finding outdoorsy fiancés who know the difference between baking soda and baking powder.

That's got to count for something, right?

CHAPTER
TWENTY

"Okay, okay," Brother Titus says to Jamie, "now you have to try the Archangel."

"Which one is that?" Jamie asks, looking down at the flight in front of him. There's another empty flight at the edge of the table, and several empty glasses crowded around that. The eight of us at this table have been "hosting" Jamie for the last ninety minutes and have the empty glasses to show for it. A few of the glasses are mine on account of the impromptu drinking game I invented, which is called *Drink whenever watching your ex-boyfriend with his fiancé makes you feel sad.*

"The Archangel is our tripel," Brother Amos answers.

"We call it that because it could knock even the devil on his ass," Brother Thomas chimes in.

Jamie consults the paper slip he's secured under the wooden board holding his flight glasses, and then finds the tripel and holds it up to the fading sun. It's past dinner and prayer time, and with permission from the abbot, we've kept the beer garden open after compline for our guest. The lights strung above the garden are turned on now, and it won't be long until it's only them and the stars glinting off our glasses in the dark.

The table cheers as Jamie drinks and as he gives us all a rosy-cheeked grin after. "It's very good," he declares, and the table cheers again. I cheer too—trying to be good, trying to be happy that Elijah has found a nice boy who bakes bread and helps seniors find new knitting mysteries to read.

I don't think I ever baked for Elijah once. Why bake bread when you can wheedle your lover into a spontaneous trip to Paris to eat pastries by the Seine? Why bend over a hot stove when you can bend over for your hot boyfriend instead?

Doesn't Jamie know they sell bread at the store???

"You know," Jamie says, turning his tipsy grin on Elijah, who gives him a closed-mouth smile back, "this is very different from how I thought it would be."

"How did you think it would be?" Brother Crispin asks.

"I'm not sure," Jamie admits. "More monk-y, I guess."

"We are *soo* monk-y," Brother Titus says. "You just need to know more monks, is all."

"He knows us now," Brother Thomas chides him and then looks back to Jamie. "Ask us anything. As your new best monk friends, we're going to acquaint you with all things monastic."

Jamie laughs, but Elijah bumps his shoulder, the corner of his mouth tilting up. "It'll help me with my research, you know," he says.

"Oh, yes," Brother Titus agrees. "You should help him

with his research. Come on, ask us anything! How much we miss Chinese food and pizza—"

"How much we miss Netflix—"

"And Chiefs games—"

"If we wear underwear under our robes—"

"Why Brother Patrick won't show us his tattoo—"

I choke on the beer I'm drinking, coughing it down as I shake my head violently. "No. Shh. Stop."

Elijah lifts an eyebrow at me from across the table, his eyes glittering with mischief. "You haven't shown these gentlemen the masterpiece that is your tattoo?"

"This is what I'm *saying*!" Brother Titus bursts out. "The mystery is more than I can bear!"

"It's from an event in my life that I'm not proud of," I attempt to explain, and then Jamie—gentle, rosy-cheeked Jamie—says three words I'd hoped to literal God I'd never hear again.

"Ohhh," he says, his eyes round. "Is this about Flamin' Hot Aiden?"

I drop my face in my hands, slumping my shoulders in deep, bodily misery.

"I'm sorry," Jamie whispers, and he does truly sound sorry, the sweet asshole. "Sean had just called you that once at a family dinner—"

I groan. Fucking *Sean*. Of course it would be him.

"Okay, well now I have to know," Brother Crispin asks from the edge of the table. "What is Flamin' Hot Aiden?"

"A better question would be *whom*?" Elijah replies. I look

up enough from my hands to glare at him. He smiles evilly back.

"Flamin' Hot Aiden is no one," I say, a little desperately. "He's dead. He died at Rockhurst High School."

"No, he didn't," Elijah corrects. "Because I believe that you got the tattoo your freshman year of *college*."

"Ah, so we're back to the tattoo!" Brother Thomas crows.

"Look," I say, trying one last time to head this off. "It's not really an abbey appropriate story—"

This was absolutely the wrong thing to say. Everyone perks up in unison, like meerkats on the savannah, except instead of scenting a Nat Geo photographer, they're scenting a juicy story, which all monks love.

"Not-abbey-appropriate stories are our favorite kind, aren't they, Brother Titus?" Brother Thomas says.

"They are indeed, Brother Thomas," Brother Titus agrees.

"No," I say. "It's not—the abbot would kill me."

Brother Amos laughs. "The abbot wants to know about your mystery tattoo just as much of the rest of us. Come on, you know you're going to end up telling us."

"He's right, you know," Elijah says to me. "You might as well have dignity in defeat."

It's a mistake to look over and see that smile tugging at the corners of his mouth. The things I've done to see that smile…

I feel the old me surge up a little. The impulsive me. The fun-time guy who made everyone laugh with his reckless, ridiculous misadventures.

"Well, I—fine. *Fine.* I'll show you the tattoo. But first I want you all to know that I'm not proud of any of it, the tattoo or being Flamin' Hot Aiden."

"But whomst is Flamin' Hot Aiden?" Brother Titus asks. "We need to know this person in order to understand the story. We need *context*."

Context. Oh God.

I grab my glass and take a few quick swallows to fortify myself.

"In high school," I start, already regretting everything about this entire night and maybe my life in general, "I liked three things. Girls, sports, and Cheetos of the Flamin' Hot variety."

Brother Titus leans forward, propping his chin on his hands and looking at me with giant eyes. "Go on," he urges.

"And the sports made it easy to meet girls, especially from Sion."

"What's Sion?" Jamie asks.

"Sion is one of the sister schools to Rockhurst, my sweet Episcopalian," Elijah answers, his eyes staying on me. "An all-girls school companion to the all-boys school."

Jamie nods and then squeezes Elijah's hand affectionately. Part of me wants to make this story as silly and rotten as possible, just to spite all his healthy, well-adjusted goodness. The other part of me wants to jump into the bushes at the edge of the beer garden and stay there until I'm a skeleton and no one expects me to tell my most embarrassing stories in front of my ex's fiancé.

But it's too late; I've already given them too much. The

table is practically salivating with interest now.

"Anyway," I go on, "after every football game, I'd eat a bag of Flamin' Hot Cheetos. It was my thing. My happy place. But there was a party after the game, and there was a girl there, Chelsie Lynch. I could tell that things were going to end well on the making-out front that night, except…"

"Your Cheetos," Brother Titus realizes.

"Precisely," I reply. Gravely. "I had yet to eat my Flamin' Hot Cheetos. It was tradition. A superstition even. What if I didn't eat them after this game and then I never won a game again? Also I was hungry."

Brother Denis cuts in, his English accent making his dry words even drier. "And there were no breath mints around? Before the kissing?"

Elijah starts laughing. Silently but uncontrollably. "Oh, this"—he chokes out—"this is much worse than kissing."

I glare at him again.

"What can be worse than kissing someone after eating Flamin' Hot Cheetos?" Brother Thomas asks. Too innocently, in my opinion.

I glare at him too. "I just want to remind everyone that hindsight is twenty-twenty."

"Especially if you were four-twenty," Elijah teases.

"I wasn't—" I huff. "For better or worse, no drugs or alcohol were involved in this. Just hormones and a genuine love for the crunchy heat of Cheeto's brand Flamin' Hot Cheetos."

"So what happened?" Brother Denis asks. Everyone is leaning forward now, totally rapt, even Jamie. Sweet, bespectacled Jamie, who's probably never even tasted a Cheeto. He probably ate granola bars in high school, the really crumbly ones, and actually liked the way they tasted and never got the crumbs caught in his crotch and also never forgot to throw the wrappers away when he was near a trash can and shoved them in his best friend's backpack instead.

And now he's a librarian-slash-Sunday school teacher who makes the world a better place, and I'm a former millionaire who wears polyester and cries when he chops wood.

"Chelsie crawled into my lap as I was finishing up my traditional bag of spicy, cheesy victory," I continue, my voice grim now. "She didn't seem to mind the *kissing* being Flamin' Hot flavored. And I kind of forgot all about the Cheetos in the moment, because I had Chelsie Lynch in my lap, and the kissing was very excellent, and then she—" I flush, so aware of Jamie and his healthful healthiness that I could die. "She pushed my hand under her skirt." And then because the people at the picnic table aren't reacting—aside from Elijah, who is shaking with silent laughter again—I add, "My *Cheeto* hand."

Horrified silence reigns across the beer garden.

Until it explodes with laughter. Brother Thomas collapses sideways into Brother Titus, eyelashes wet with tears of joy. "And then you...you...?"

"Yes," I confirm wearily. "I knew her in the biblical sense with my Flamin' Hot Cheeto hand."

Everyone is outright howling now, even Jamie, who is laughing but also looks like he's worried about Chelsie Lynch.

(She's fine, by the way. After I attempted to finger her with

Flamin' fingers, she slapped me in the face and ran to the bathroom with her best friend, and emerged twenty minutes later clearly furious, but at least no longer in Cheeto-related discomfort.)

She's married to a dentist now. They have ninety-seven Catholic babies. They go to Sean and Zenny's church, which Tyler's best friend Father Jordan Brady pastors.

"So she told everyone about how much I sucked, and that's how I got the nickname Flamin' Hot Aiden. And I guess I leaned into it a bit."

"A bit?" Elijah asks. "You customized your license plate to say FLMNHOT."

"Just while I was in college!"

"*And* you custom-ordered T-shirts with your face printed on Chester Cheetah's body and gave them to all your friends."

"Everyone likes a free T-shirt!"

"And then there is the tattoo," Elijah points out, and I sigh, defeated.

Because yes. *Then there is the tattoo.*

The table is still laughing when I stand up and push my scapular to the side so I can unzip the zipper on my habit, which goes from my neck to my stomach. Plenty of room for me to extricate an arm and—since I'm wearing nothing but boxer briefs under the habit—show the table my bare shoulder. Show the table my shame.

"It's hideous!" Brother Thomas says with glee as he stands up to get a better look.

"Cursed," says Brother Titus.

"Brother Patrick," Brother Denis says carefully. "Is that the dove of the Holy Spirit on your shoulder?"

"And is it carrying a Flamin' Hot Cheeto in its beak?" Brother Amos asks. Everyone else joins Brother Thomas in standing up to get a better look—everyone except Elijah, who has seen it before. But just before Jamie leans in closer and blocks him from my sight, I notice that Elijah's eyes are not on my tattoo but on the exposed parts of my body. My lightly furred chest. My wood-chopping shoulders and arms.

I can't decipher his expression in time before he's blocked from view. Curiosity?

Indifference?

And then I realize what he's looking at.

The key around my neck. The key he must recognize as belonging to my cage. I clear my throat and try to tuck it under the collar of my scapular. Maybe he doesn't recognize it. Maybe he's forgotten that we used to play with chastity at all.

"That is truly spectacular," Brother Crispin says wryly. "I can't see why you don't show that off more often."

"They could make it into a stained-glass window," Brother Denis suggests. "The iconography is actually quite striking."

Because I'm a masochist, I look over to Jamie, already braced for his superior amusement. But I don't find any—either superiority or amusement. Instead he is looking at me with something like understanding…and pity. Probably all the things he's heard about me in bits and pieces are starting to make sense. Here is Aiden Bell the fuck-up, who was so famously a fuck-up that only a monastery could fix him.

I feel stupid all over again, standing there with the warm summer air kissing my shoulder, my regr-tat exposed to everyone, the idiocy of the Flamin' Hot Aiden story still making everyone erupt in giggles. My fellow brothers are looking at me like they've never met me before—which isn't *un*true given how hard I've worked to change who I am since I came here—and Elijah is looking at me with that inscrutable gaze, and Jamie is looking very sorry for me, his eyes soft behind his glasses and his free hand fiddling with his Apple Watch, which has probably already logged ten thousand steps today.

I shrug my habit back on and zip it up, smoothing my scapular back over the front of my robe before plonking myself back on the bench and shoving my head in my hands. I can't believe I just told the Flamin' Hot story to two-bicycle rack, senior outreach *Jamie*, of all people.

I close my eyes against my palms and pray someone brings me another beer. Preferably the Archangel.

"So," Jamie says as everyone settles back in their seats, "I do have a question actually. How does one become a monk?"

I recognize immediately that he's trying to be polite and helpful and shift the conversation to something less embarrassing to me. Little does he know.

"Well, if you're Brother Patrick," Brother Amos says, grinning behind his beard, "you come in through the gift shop."

The brothers all laugh; this is a perennial fave. It's the "Free Bird" of Mount Sergius stories. I usually never mind it being a favorite because it *is* funny, but now with Jamie and Elijah here—Elijah who still knows so little about why and how

I came to the abbey—it feels like agony waiting to happen.

Elijah straightens up. "Sorry, you said through the gift shop?"

"Oh yes," Brother Crispin says. "One morning, right after the gift shop opens, Brother Patrick comes staggering in."

"In his pajamas," Brother Amos adds.

"Walks right up to the counter where we keep our cash register and says to me—"

"'I'd like to become a monk, please,'" Brother Amos finishes for him.

Brothers Thomas and Titus are already cracking up.

"Maybe I should go get everyone more beer," I say, standing up. I don't need to watch Jamie and Elijah's faces while they listen to yet another tale of *Aiden Bell, Ridiculous Man*.

"Aw, come on, Brother Patrick," Brother Crispin says. "Stay and tell it yourself!"

I wave a hand. "You all tell it better than me anyway," I say with smile. "I'll be right back."

I hear him start up with the story again as I walk into the taproom and start pouring everyone a round of the Raphael— our farmhouse saison—and load the tulip glasses onto a tray. And then when I'm done, I brace my hands against the bar for a moment and close my eyes. I knew even that day that I was being so very Aiden; I knew that showing up in my pajamas and asking a gift shop employee where I could sign up for Monk School was no less impulsive or outrageous than anything else I'd done in my silly life.

But it had been different in one important way. Because after years and years of running from the slithers and whispers in my mind, I wasn't chasing sex or alcohol or money in order to drown the whispers out. I was searching for a safe place to confront them once and for all—even if I didn't entirely understand that's what I had been doing at the time.

And if I needed any more proof that God exists, it was right there in what happened that damp, desperate morning. Because as a confused Brother Crispin went to go get Father Harry, Brother Connor happened to walk in. And instead of seeming surprised that a grown-ass man in pajamas was trying to become a monk at the gift shop checkout counter, he nodded to himself, like he'd been expecting me.

"Would you like some coffee?" he'd asked gently, and then after leaving a note for Brother Crispin, took me to the south cloister and fed me breakfast. We talked—him asking compassionate, delicate questions, me as shaky as someone who'd just escaped a burning building—and afterward, he took me straight to the abbot. At the time, I had no idea how unusual this was, how many steps I was skipping. I had no idea of *anything*. The last time I'd gone to a Mass that wasn't a wedding or a baptism was for my sister's funeral, and that had been so bleak and awkward and awful that I'd never had the energy to come back for something that wasn't explicitly a happy event.

So when the abbot greeted me warmly and took me for a walk around the grounds, I assumed that was the way it was done. I assumed he would hand me some robes and a rosary and then swat me on the butt the way basketball coaches do to players before they take the court. I assumed I was in, and all I had left to do was give him the keys to my truck and figure out if I needed to learn Latin or something.

But when we got to the graveyard, and the old oak tree I would come to know as Brother Connor's tree, the abbot stopped, and instead of giving me a *you're hired* handshake, he turned and looked up at the hill, which crested above the abbey in a sweep of rock and tall, dry grass.

"I love this hill," he said. "I love watching the shadows of the clouds move over its face. I love how it breaks the wind in winter, as if it's trying to throw its arms around me. I love waking to it, each morning, like an old friend."

It was the hill that had brought me there, actually, which he'd already known from what I told him on our walk. But seeing it like this, tall and friendly and strong—a fort of nothing but wind and grass—I could *feel* the words that had brought me here. I could feel them moving over my body like the shadows of the clouds the abbot had just described.

I lift my eyes to the hills.

"But I've come to see that while this hill was an invitation to the brothers who moved here in the late nineteenth century—an invitation of shelter in winter and shade in summer—the brothers still had to build the abbey themselves, you see. They still had to build the foundations of their new life. This place could *help*, but it could not become anything other than what it was. It could not do the work for them." He paused then. "Do you understand what I am saying?"

Halfway. Enough to have felt the hope sliding out from under me like a rug. Enough for that oil-slick danger to start pooling at my feet again. "I can't stay here," I said dully.

He turned his eyes to me then. "You can," he said gently. "But not tonight. Not yet. Do you really feel called to this life, Aiden?"

I nodded. It was outlandish, absurd even, but that call was the only reason I was alive and breathing for this conversation. It was the only thing I'd felt in years stronger than the poison which swam in my mind and grasped at my thoughts.

"Then we can start today. Part of life in an abbey is obedience. Obedience to God and obedience to your superior, which would be me." The abbot pulled his hand out of his robe pocket. He was holding a business card. "Your first task is to leave here and go straight to this office, please. Once you've gone there and done as she's asked, then you may return. That might be tomorrow, it might be a week from now, but either way, the door is completely open to you when you come back. And then we will begin."

I took the card. *Rosie Campolo, LP.*

"A psychologist?" I asked.

The abbot touched my shoulder. "The abbey will help shelter you, Aiden, but you must build the foundations yourself. You must be ready in order to begin."

I know now that God was with me that day. He sent me Brother Connor and not Father Harry. He made it so I got Dr. Rosie's card, so I got *to* Dr. Rosie that day. And when I returned five days later, after a three-day in-patient stint and with a checklist of the things I'd need to do to bring my secular life to a close, the abbot welcomed me with a warm smile and open arms.

I owe my life, in the most literal sense, to him and Dr. Rosie and this abbey.

I owe my life to God.

CHAPTER
TWENTY-ONE

I carry the tray outside at precisely the right time. I can tell the story has ended because Jamie is asking another polite question, which is how do normal, non-Aiden people become monks, and Brother Denis is answering him.

I set the glasses down for everyone and sit on the bench right as Brother Amos declares, with great, beardy affection, "But we are glad you came into the gift shop that day, Brother Patrick. Who else would lift all our heavy things?"

"And who else would have started Lectio Lexapro?" Brother Titus asks, and the other brothers rumble in agreement, lifting their glasses to me.

"Lectio Lexapro?" Jamie asks. "What's that?"

I look down at my beer, letting someone else take the lead on explaining it. It feels weird to talk about my little group of friends to someone who actually does Things That Matter. All I did was find the other brothers living with fussy brain chemistry and suggest we hang out from time to time.

"Brother Patrick started it as a bible study group of sorts," Brother Denis explains. "Lectio divina is individual contemplation of scripture, but some monks practice communal lectio too. And so Lectio Lexapro started as a way to study scripture together and in conversation with our experiences of mental illnesses, but it grew into more than that. It's our time to talk about all kinds of things."

"Monastic life with a mental illness is different," Brother Titus says. "And a lot of older monks are really resistant to the idea that God can use things like therapy and head meds just as much as he can use prayer and contemplation to help."

"And so everyone in Lectio Lexapro has lived with a mental illness?" Elijah asks, and I feel his eyes slide over to me.

I keep my gaze on my beer, afraid to look up at him. Afraid he'll see—I'm not sure what. Afraid that he'll see *me*, maybe. Afraid that he'll see the truth of that night and why I left.

"Everyone," Brother Amos confirms. "I mean, we welcome anyone who wants to join. But that's our focus. Brother Patrick said when he first gathered us all up that the Bible tells us to lift our eyes to the hills, but that we should lift our eyes to each other first. And that's been our guiding vision ever since."

"I think that's wonderful," Jamie says.

Of course he does.

"Okay, it's my turn to ask questions," Brother Thomas says to Jamie. "Take a drink and then tell me the grossest thing that's ever happened to you as a librarian."

The table laughs, and the conversation swings over to

Jamie, who is gracious and gently funny as he recounts some good public library stories for us. The table is totally engaged, smiling and laughing and drinking with him, all eyes on the sweet baker with the sticky-outy ears and the button nose.

All eyes, that is, except for his fiancé's.

I look up to find Elijah watching me with narrowed eyes, his fingers tracing agitated circles on the belly of his tulip glass. He's looking at me like he's never seen me before, like I'm an utter stranger to him.

I can almost see the question in his eyes, shimmering under the beer garden lights.

What haven't you told me?

The sun vanishes completely; the fireflies come out. In the distance, fresh lightning flickers on the horizon, harkening the next summer storm to roll over our patch of prairie. We finish this round of beers, and Brother Crispin suggests one final drink of our dark ale to close out the night, and I gratefully take the opportunity to get it for everyone—and then to bus the table and start washing the glasses. Maybe if I take long enough, Jamie will be gone by the time I'm done...

But no. When I come back to collect the final round of glasses, everyone is still present and accounted for. My heart lifts for a moment when I see that they're no longer sitting, but it promptly sinks as I recognize the early stages of the Midwestern Goodbye, which means Jamie will be here for another forty-five minutes.

At any rate, I know the right thing to do is to say farewell and wish him a safe drive, so I take a deep breath and stride over to the group, mustering the closest thing to a smile I can manage as I do.

"Brother Patrick," Jamie says warmly, "thank you so much for having me visit. Elijah knows I love all things beer, and I had to see what had captivated him enough to bring him back to a monastery for an entire week."

He's shaking my hand as he says this, and there's nothing in his handshake or in his voice to indicate a deeper meaning to his words. He seems like the kind of guy who's above jealousy, who is super great at communication, who's just full of trust and reciprocated fidelity. But then when he drops my hand and steps back, there's something to the way his gaze moves back to Elijah and then to me...

And then as the Midwestern Goodbye inevitably devolves into more conversation, I catch Jamie staring at me again. At first I think I must be imagining it—that my keen awareness of him as the man who has Elijah's heart is making me hyperaware of very normal social things—but over the next fifteen minutes, it becomes so obvious that even Elijah seems to notice, his gaze flicking between me and Jamie, his brows knitted together.

I finally decide that I need to Irish Goodbye this Midwestern Goodbye, and make a polite murmur of farewell and step back—which is when my eyes meet Jamie's. And while his gray eyes aren't unkind or jealous, there is something uncomfortably scrutinizing about them, as if he's surveying me. As if he's trying to see through my clothes and skin and bones to something invisible underneath.

It's not fun to feel that kind of stare on me. It makes me feel very aware that I'm a scruffy hulk in polyester robes with a regrettable tattoo on my shoulder and an even more regrettable nickname. It makes me very aware that I was the fuck-up who broke Elijah's heart and that Jamie is the good citizen who's fixing it.

I escape by mumbling something about the glasses and then gather up everything from the picnic table, leaving the others to finish their slow goodbyes to Jamie while I wash up.

And it's while I'm washing up, my sleeves pushed to my elbows and my forearms slick with soap suds, that I realize I've seen that look before, the look Jamie was giving me outside.

It's the same look Elijah gave Jesus on the cross after his first compline here. Jamie looked at me like he needed to make sure I was staying exactly where I'd been put.

I don't go to the dormitory after the dishes are done. I know I'll pay for it tomorrow—and for that last glass of beer too—but the thought of going to bed right now makes me viscerally miserable. After seeing Jamie and Elijah hold hands and brush shoulders and pet each other as they sat on the picnic bench across from me…

No. The last place I want to be is on my hard, narrow mattress, alone, alone, alone. I know isolation is the *point*, solitude is the *point*, and I know that real loneliness—that soul-deep lack of affection and touch and love—is supposed to be assuaged by God and the other monks. By friendship and by devotion.

But sometimes, I am so lonely I could scream. And tonight I saw just how not-lonely Elijah is.

I wipe down the taproom bar, rinse all the taps and spouts, and then make sure the taps and spouts are covered. I mop behind the bar and take out the trash. I turn off the lights and lock the door and decide to take the long way back to the dorms, the way that skirts along the base of the hill. The fireflies are gone, and only a few lights are lit—two in the parking lot, and one on the doorway to the dormitory. The rest of the world is stars and shadows and restless lightning far to the west.

It's because the parking lot is lit that I see them. Elijah and Jamie, alone in the now-deserted lot, saying their own private farewell. Jamie is backed against his Jeep, his hands on Elijah's shoulders like they're middle-schoolers having their first slow dance, and there's definitely room for the Holy Spirit between them. But then Elijah leans forward, his body arcing carefully toward his fiancé's, and then they kiss. Slowly and sweetly. Like courting beaux. Elijah reaches up to cradle Jamie's face, and that's when I duck my head and start walking as fast as I can to the dormitory so I don't have to see any more. So I won't be tempted to watch any more.

It's not for me.

Elijah's not for me.

My bed is as hard and narrow as I knew it would be, and while the dormitory technically has air-conditioning, we turn it off at night to save energy. Which means even with the window open, it's hot and damp, and I'm hot and damp too, even though I skipped pajamas tonight and I'm wearing nothing but my cage.

I'm lying there in the dark, staring up at the ceiling, when I hear the key in Elijah's door, and then the door's quiet opening and closing. It's only been thirty minutes maybe, but my imagination still runs wild with what he and Jamie were doing. Thirty minutes is enough time for a lot of things if you believe in yourself. And while the parking lot of a Benedictine abbey isn't the most likely spot for an assignation, that wouldn't have stopped Elijah and me back in the day. We would have crawled into the back of the Jeep like teenagers and made it work.

The water in Elijah's room runs, and then I hear him moving around, the sharp zip of a suitcase, the squeak of his bed. No typing tonight, I suppose, which makes me a little sad. Falling asleep to the sound of him tapping away has become one of my new favorite things.

After a few minutes, though, it's silent on his side of the wall, and it's just me again. Just me in this too-warm room, utterly alone, listening through my open window for the distant rumble of thunder from miles and miles away. Sleep refuses to come, and I don't debase myself for it, trying tricks and games. I simply wait for it to come to me, like the stubborn asshole I am, and that means I'm awake to hear it.

Something that's not thunder, that's not the rustle of trees outside. Something almost rhythmic. Unhurried and even.

It's faint enough that I'm still not sure what it could be until I hear a soft, barely-there moan, so quiet that it almost feels like I imagined it.

But I know I didn't.

I sit up slowly—as not to make any noise—and then listen again. For the measured slide of skin against skin, for the short, hard breaths that come with it.

Elijah is masturbating. On the other side of the wall, he's masturbating, and I can hear him.

My organ has been swelling a while now, but it's just hit the point where the cage bites back, and I instinctively go to rub myself as I stand up, soothing the needy flesh with the pad of my thumb as I walk silently over to the window. His window isn't open, which while disappointing to me in the short-term, is probably a good thing in the long run, because then any other sleepless monk could hear what I'm hearing right now.

As it is, my cell is the only one that borders his, and so I'm the only one who gets to hear this. I'm the only one who gets to hear Elijah Iverson make himself come.

I stroke my fingers along the base of my cage as I listen, wondering why Elijah needs to jerk off. Did Jamie get him all hot and bothered, and then leave him hanging? Did they mutually agree to be grown-ups and not fuck around in the parking lot of a Catholic monastery? Or *did* they fuck around in the back seat of his Jeep, and it was so hot that Elijah can't even sleep afterward without getting off again?

Another soft groan, and I press my forehead against our shared wall, caressing myself shamelessly now. My cock strains against the bars of the cage, and my balls are trying desperately to draw up tight to my body, and I'd forgotten how *fucking good* it feels to touch myself. Even with the cage making everything tight and just a little bit miserable, it still feels so powerfully good. To stroke and fondle and squeeze.

I haven't done this in nearly five years. I've been tempted—sorely tempted—often, but I've never broken down and done it. Until tonight. Until I had to listen to the quiet stroke of Elijah's fist on his cock. Until I heard his choked-off noises of pleasure.

I want to get the key to the cage, which hangs from the post of my bed when I'm not wearing it around my neck. I want to unlock myself and wrap my entire fist around my cock. I want an orgasm like I used to have—full and uncaged.

But I don't move to get the key. If I stop, then that will be long enough for the doubt to creep in, for my *conscience* to creep in.

Monks aren't supposed to beat themselves off. Period.

And while only I would know...*I* would still know. I would know that I was weak, that I caved to a gratification that helps no one else, that doesn't even help me. The point of celibacy is to sublimate sexual energy altogether, to transform ourselves, and if we feed our lusts by masturbating every time we feel like it, then that transformation is incomplete. I don't want an incomplete transformation; I came here to be changed utterly and entirely.

But...but I've been so good. I've been so good for so long, and surely no one else could resist this right now, no one else could resist the sound of Elijah fucking his own hand and grunting softly and—

It's been so long since I've come while awake that I'm almost surprised by it. My stomach tenses; my thighs lock, and then a grunt escapes me as the orgasm crests and then breaks, ruined by metal banding my flesh. My cock tries to surge against the cage and can't, and ejaculate leaks out in slow, dripping pulses, and it's nowhere near as good as an unlocked orgasm because I'm still so desperately aroused after.

I almost feel worse than before. Hornier. Achier.

I stand there with my dick dripping, my muscles shaking, my chest tight. From the other side of the wall, I hear the sharp intake of breath which I'll recognize until my dying day. Elijah has just come too.

Into his fist? Onto his belly?

I close my eyes and imagine it for one minute. One minute before the shame and the guilt creep in, one minute before I have to clean myself up and pray and make plans to confess.

One minute where I can pretend that the only thing which separates us is the humid night air, and that we have the rest of the night for sin.

CHAPTER TWENTY-TWO

from the notebook of Elijah Iverson

The incessant quiet and the nonstop introspection are having an undesired effect on me. I am becoming self-aware. I am beginning to realize that I'm not only here for the beer and the anti-capitalism.

I keep thinking about that key around his neck. About what might be around his dick.

I can't stop. I can't stop.

~~I don't want to stop~~

Here's a thing that I don't think anyone knows but me: I have been painfully aware of Aiden Bell since he was eighteen. It crept up over time, I think, little moments of realizing he was getting tall, that he needed to shave, that his voice had deepened, but those things were fragments of observations, swimming in a sea of memories of him as he had been, which had been indelibly Sean's little brother. There had been moments—brief ones—when I caught him looking at me, when he trailed around behind us, moments that maybe any other older brother's best friend would've ascribed to an adolescent crush.

But there was no keeping Aiden Bell away from girls—from the time he was old enough to flash his dimples even—and so I thought I must be imagining it. I felt relieved at the time, grateful there wouldn't be any awkward fallout from having to gently shut down this newly-not-a-baby.

Five years. Five years between us, and I was in college by that point anyway, making up for lost Catholic time by having as much energetic sex as I could.

But here's the thing about five years: the numbers stay the same, but the equation changes. And when I went over to the Bells' one night and saw Aiden out by the pool, I realized that the equation had changed somehow, without me knowing it. Because in the year since I'd seen him, since I'd graduated college and he was about to start, he'd changed enough that five years felt like barely any years at all.

I remember I couldn't stop watching him through the glass patio door while Sean dithered about what shirt to wear and kept squirting more gel into his hair. I couldn't stop watching Aiden's body, his face, his constant motion, jumping, diving, swimming. Hauling himself out of the water with newly spread shoulders and a leanly muscled back.

He was swimming in boxers instead of swim trunks, and

they clung everywhere—to the curve of his ass, to the swell of his thighs, to his dick—and the waistband dragged down enough that I could see where the dark line of hair running down his stomach met the hair above his cock.

Water ran over the new muscles in his arms and dropped off a carved jaw. It streaked down the cords of his throat, it stuck his dark hair to his forehead and his neck. It gathered in his flat navel before spilling out.

And the way he *moved*. All of his body, all of his strength, wholly bent on whatever he did. Diving, flipping, not doing it to show off because there was no one to show off to, because he didn't know I was watching. He was doing it for himself. For the sheer joy and thrill of it.

I left the Bells' that night with a secret. A secret with a name. *Aiden.*

Aiden in my thoughts, Aiden creeping into my fantasies and reveries and *what ifs*. A crush on a best friend's straight little brother. It was almost like a joke, like the setup for a porn. It was a bad idea any way I sliced it.

He's still a bad idea.

He's still a bad idea.

He's a bad idea and a monk and he broke my fucking heart and I'm engaged to be married and so why am I sitting here in a monastery, my mind running through a thousand *what ifs*?

What if the key around his neck is for what I think it's for? What if he was about to kiss me that night in the cloister? What if he *wasn't*?

Because I've seen, haven't I? Those fireflies in the cloister?

The way he looked at them?

I thought it was impossible to reconcile that lanky, flipping freshman—that reckless millionaire, that infuriating, adorable man who carried sprinkles in his pocket just for me— with this quiet, giant man who watches fireflies dance with reverence and *patience*.

I thought it was impossible, and now I'm remembering that young college Aiden flinging himself into the pool for the sheer hell of it, for no other purpose other than living in the moment, and are they really so far apart? That careless freshman and this monk with the faintest traces of silver at his temples?

Or maybe it's not how close or how far apart those two Aidens are. Maybe it's about something else.

Maybe it's the fireflies.

What if it's the fireflies.

~~What if I went and found him right now~~

CHAPTER
TWENTY-THREE

As I expect, shame is there to greet me the minute I wake. But what I don't expect is everything else that comes along with the shame. Like smoke curling off a fire, like heat curling off a flame, there's also loneliness and stubbornness and a longing that would surpass that of a king watching a woman bathe on a rooftop.

And then there's something else, something that I can't quite name. It's there, translucent and untouchable as I pray vigils and attempt lectio and then pray lauds too. It's there as I surreptitiously watch Elijah eat his breakfast from across the refectory. As Elijah tells me after we eat that he plans to spend the day writing, and so I'm free to attend to my usual duties.

It's like I'm looking at everything through stained glass, warped and bubbled and shaded in vital, jeweled hues.

The storm is finally blowing in for real, and Brother Andrew asks me to go collect the last batch of wood I chopped, so he can stack it for seasoning before it gets soaked. I'm thankful for the chance to go out to the woods, to be alone with the creek and my thoughts, but it doesn't help with the feeling that something's strange, something's changed. It must be that I masturbated last night, for the first time in years, but it can't be *only* that. It's not the familiar anchor of guilt I feel or even the sting of unrequited love, but something altogether apart. Like I've woken up in someone else's life—but *not*, because I still feel like myself too.

I don't know. I don't know, and I don't think I can live with it. I have to forget Elijah. I have to leave my abbey and find someplace new.

I'll feel better then, I know I will.

The drizzle is fitful and easy enough to work in, but I can see the dark edge of true storm clouds rolling in. Brother Andrew already told me not to worry about making it back for our afternoon prayers if the storm got bad, and I'm almost hoping it will. I'm almost hoping I'll be stuck here today, and I won't have to be around anyone else while I'm thinking stained-glass thoughts.

Especially Elijah.

I get the wood piled into the four wheeler's little trailer and secure a tarp over it in the nick of time—right as I finish lashing the tarp down, the skies open and issue forth Noah-levels of rain. I check to make sure that the tarp is tied tight enough that the wind won't be able to rip it off, and then I trot back to the hermitage, ducking my head to keep the rain out of my eyes.

But I'm not alone when I get there. I lift my head to see

Elijah standing in the doorway, his hands braced on the frame and his face wet with rain.

I stop and stare from a few feet away, blinking water out of my eyes as he stares back at me.

For a moment, neither of us move.

And then he steps back into the hermitage. I follow him in, both of us dripping everywhere, me in my work T-shirt and jeans, him in a fitted button-down and cuffed jean shorts.

It's dark in the hermitage—even when it's sunny, not much light makes it in, and it's hardly sunny right now. I stop a few steps inside, my eyes adjusting to the shadows as I watch Elijah pace, his thumb rubbing against his fingers in agitation as he does.

He is the only thing in my world that feels real now, the only thing that I can truly see. I'm hypnotized by him.

"I came here for you," he says finally. His voice is strange.

"Here to the hermitage?" I ask. "Or to the abbey?"

"Both."

I step closer and then stop myself. I don't know what I'm doing or what I even want. I watched him make out with his fiancé in the parking lot last night; I listened to him jerk off thinking of that same fiancé. This is a man who loves someone else, and who emphatically does not love me anymore.

His face is still wet as he looks back to me with his brows drawn together and up into his forehead. "I think I just wanted to understand," he says, and it sounds like he's pleading something, like he's admitting something. "Can you blame me for that? Can anyone?"

"You wanted to understand why I left," I say over the drumming of the rain.

"I thought if I saw what you left me *for*—if I stayed here and found whatever it was that drew you here in the first place, then I'd be able to leave you alone in my mind. I'd be able to forget you."

My heart skips and stutters, feeling both too big and too small for my chest all at the same time. "Leave me alone in your mind?" I whisper. It's too much to hope for—it's too much to hope he means something *good*, something fond, when he says things like that. I am Flamin' Hot Aiden after all, hardly worth brooding over, hardly worth remembering except for all the times I made everyone else's lives harder.

He looks at me like I'm being intentionally obtuse. "Don't."

"I'm not."

"You *are*. Stop it."

The rain drones on, a relentless tapping on the roof, and then thunder rolls through the room.

"Did you find what you were looking for, at least?" I ask. I don't know if he can ever understand why I chose an abbey to run to if he doesn't know why I was running in the first place, but I'm curious to hear what he thinks.

"No," he says. And then he closes his eyes. "And yes."

"What does that mean?"

He opens his eyes. Summer in Kansas is never cold, but it *feels* cold compared to the simmering frustration in his amber gaze right now.

"At first I didn't understand it. At all. It's everything you used to hate, Aiden, like seriously everything. Waking up early, doing the same thing every day, no travel, no fun, no sex. *Praying*." He starts pacing again. "I kept thinking *how was this a better choice than me?* How? Was I that bad of a boyfriend? Was our fight that night so bad that you gave up on living a real life entirely?"

My rain-wet T-shirt is clingy and clammy, and I pluck at it as I say, "This *is* a real life, Elijah. And the fight we had before I came—" *Had nothing to do with me coming here*, I'm about to say, but Elijah keeps going as if I haven't spoken.

"And I was pissed. And hurt. And then pissed all over again, because I'm getting married this year, and I shouldn't give a shit about why my ex-boyfriend became a monk. And I—" His thumb is rubbing against his fingers again. "After we fought here in the hermitage, I was going to find you and tell you that I was leaving the abbey early, that there was nothing here for me to understand. That you'd deprived yourself of everything for nothing. But when I found you to tell you all that, you were sitting in the cloister, and then—"

He gives me an agonized look.

"The fireflies," I say. "That was the night with the fireflies."

"I thought you'd chosen the Church over me, but you didn't, did you?" he asks in a jagged voice. "You chose *God* over me, and somehow that's worse than anything else I'd ever thought of, because I can't compete with God, Aiden." He gives a short laugh which sounds like it's been punched out of him. "I can't compete with fireflies in the cloister."

I should say a million things right now. I should say that it doesn't matter—that I chose God in spite of Elijah, not *to* spite him. I should say that Elijah doesn't need to compete with anything or anyone ever again, because I've taken vows and he's engaged, and this is between more people than just the two of us now.

I should tell him that I'm sorry for all the pain I've caused and ask him how I can make sure I don't cause him any more.

But I don't. I don't say any of those things because rain has gathered in the small dent above his upper lip, making a little dish out of his philtrum, and suddenly nothing else matters, nothing at all.

I take a step closer to him, my eyes on his mouth.

"Aiden," he says hoarsely.

I catch a glimpse of gold-brown eyes, his agitated hands, and then he's against me, and I'm against him, our wet clothes pressed between us and his mouth hot on mine. I'd forgotten what a kiss was, what it felt like, what it meant to have someone taste my hunger and lick the urgency right off my lips. The shock of it nearly sends me to my knees.

His lips are warm, firm, barely yielding to the hard kiss I'm giving him as he kisses me back just as rough, just as fiercely. But I'm the one to demand entrance, to slot my lips against his and stroke against the seam of his mouth with my tongue until he lets me inside.

And then—*oh*. And *then*.

His tongue is hot, strong, slick, and the moment I feel it, all control leaves me. I'm hungry for that tongue against mine, hungry for it on my neck and in my navel and on the secret places of my body, and I have the sudden, desperate fear that I'll never be close enough to him to satisfy this need, that there's no kiss deep enough to fix me and I'll be splitting, burning, yawning open with hunger until I die.

I'm walking him back, I'm *pushing* him back, and then he's against the wall, shoving his hands up my wet T-shirt as my hands find his face and hold him still for my kiss.

"Fuck," he breathes against my mouth. His eyes aren't closed and neither are mine, like we can't stop ourselves from watching, like we have to wring every last second of pleasure from this stolen, reckless moment before we come to our senses.

His hands are so restless all over me, like he's feeling me for the first time. Like he's feeling me for the last time.

"Yeah," I say roughly, pushing my mouth against his again as my hips press against him. "Fuck." For so long, growing up, he was the older one, the *larger* one, and even when we were together, he felt that way to me. But while he's still the same leanly muscled man he was before, I'm not. And as I'm crowding him against a wall, it's clearer than ever how much bigger I am now. Big enough that my thighs can cage his, that my shoulders can curl in around him as I brace my forearms against the wall and kiss him breathless.

My cage squeezes my erection down, but it hurts so good, and it's so sensitive that I know I could get off just by rubbing against him inside my jeans, and that's even before his hands wander down to explore my hips, my stomach, my ass.

"No one kisses like you," Elijah murmurs, his eyes closing as I bite his jaw and then his neck. I can feel his dick in his shorts—hard for me, maybe even leaking at the tip for me—and it makes me ferocious. Brutal. I suck and lick around his throat, and then he presses a large palm to my groin.

"Aiden," he whispers as I kiss his neck. His stubble stings my lips. When I lift my head, I see that his pupils have dilated nearly to the edge of his irises. His mouth is parted, but his jaw is tight. "So you *are* in chastity."

"Yeah," I say, shuddering as his long fingers curl around my caged bulge. "I have to be."

"Why?" he asks breathlessly.

"I think of you too much."

We can't stop looking at each other, frozen but not actually frozen—mouths swollen and chests heaving and hips pressing—but we're not kissing and my arms are still braced against the wall on either side of his head. His hand still curls possessively over my cock.

"You think of me too much," he echoes. "*You've been thinking of me.*"

This somehow feels more dangerous than kissing—it's a more sinful sin than pressing against each other. No longer a mere violation of celibacy, but a flickering threat to my devotion to God. To what is supposed to be a singular and whole offering of my heart.

This feels like admitting my heart wasn't mine to offer God in the first place.

After a long moment, I speak.

"Yes," I say. "Not just after you came back. Since I came here."

His eyebrows lift and knit, and he looks helpless, so helpless as he leans his head back against the wall and offers me his throat again. And he sounds helpless too as he moans after I begin sucking at the warm skin there. He *feels* helpless, shifting and squirming and panting, his hand still tight over my cage, and he whispers, "Your key, where is your key?"

"In my cell," I mutter, hardly caring, because my lips are on Elijah and his hands are on me and what does anything else matter?

"But—"

"Shh," I grunt, pushing him harder against the wall and dragging my mouth over his. "Quiet."

"Fuck, you're so bossy now. And so big. *Fuck*—"

A ringtone splits the air—bright, tinny, manufactured—and after hearing nothing but thunder and rain and our own guttural words, it's jarring as hell. I half step, half stagger away from him, my skin tingling and my breath coming fast, and he fumbles for his phone in his back pocket. When he finally sees the screen, I see the realization of what we've just done slam into him.

And then it slams into me too.

"It's Jamie," he says in a voice that's awful to hear. "Shit. *Shit.*"

He looks at me and what can I say? Except that I feel the exact same way?

"Elijah," I start, but he shakes his head, raising the hand

holding the still-ringing phone to stop me from speaking.

"No," he says. "Please. Don't." And for the second time this week, he leaves through the hermitage door.

And for the second time this week, I don't follow.

CHAPTER
TWENTY-FOUR

Unlike Elijah, I don't have to live with the dread of my infidelity being discovered or have to figure out how to tell the person I betrayed. Because God already knows.

I wait out the worst of the storm and then drive the four-wheeler back in the wet twilight, wiping drizzle off my face, and trying to ignore the buzz of panic and shame everywhere in my body and mind.

But nearly bigger than the panic—than the guilt, than the still-coiling lust—is a thought that won't stop twining around my ankles and cinching around the organs in my chest.

Elijah kissed me back.

Elijah let me pin him against a wall and make out with him until we were both weak in the knees.

I can hear the bells for vespers tolling as I unload the wood into Brother Andrew's woodshed, stacking it the way he taught me so it can season properly, and then I go to shower and change into my habit, noticing that Elijah's cell door is closed when I open mine.

Is he inside? At prayer?

Walking one of the paths as he talks to Jamie on the phone?

My skin feels hotter than the shower water, like I'm boiling alive from the inside out, and all of me screams for *something*—release or punishment, I don't know. I fucked up, I know I did, but all I can think of right now is the way Elijah's throat arched so prettily for me. Of the rain slicking the dent above his upper lip.

Of how it felt to kiss him again after all these years, and to have him kiss me back.

I'm sorry, I manage to whisper to God in my head. *I'm so sorry.*

By the time I'm dressed and in the refectory for dinner, I'm feeling a fresh kind of guilt, a new layer of unhappiness over the "breaking my vows" kind I've been feeling since Elijah left the hermitage. Because if there's one thing living in an abbey has taught me, it's that we are responsible for each other—we are responsible for loving each other and caring for one another. Not in the way that would make my therapist give me a pucker-face, but in the sense that we are called to present love and help and welcome.

I didn't do that today, when I dropped my eyes to Elijah's mouth and advanced on him. I didn't do that when I kissed him, pushed him against a wall, bit his neck. I led someone I love into unfaithfulness to someone *they* love and I feel like shit about it.

I helped Elijah cheat—made him cheat even. On a Sunday school teacher who likes baking. Who does that?

A bad man, that's who.

Selfish. I'm still so selfish.

Elijah's not at dinner or at compline, and I know I have to apologize to him, I have to own up to what I did, and—and—

And it's not only contrition driving me to his cell door after prayers, I know that. I know that because while my stomach feels heavy and hollow all at once, my heart is skipping around in my chest, forgetting how to beat properly whenever I remember Elijah's mouth on mine. Whenever I remember his low, broken words. *I can't compete with fireflies in the cloister.*

Can't.

Present tense.

Like he still wants to try.

I tell myself the whole way to the dormitory that I'm not going to do anything about my skipping heart, that I won't look at his mouth, or search his dark gold eyes for answers to questions I can't ask. I'm going to apologize, sincerely, and then promise to stay away. Yes, that's what I'll do—I'll stay away from him for the rest of his visit here, and then he can promise Jamie in good faith that nothing else will happen, and—

Elijah's door is open.

Open all the way, and when I stop in the doorway, it becomes clear that he's not inside. The bathroom door is open and the bathroom is empty; the small wardrobe is bare of everything except hangers and an ironing board. The towels and blankets have been folded neatly at the edge of the bed.

Nowhere is there luggage, clothes, charging cords, an ex-boyfriend. The cell is empty.

Elijah is gone.

"He had some business back home and had to leave early," is what I'm told by the abbot.

"He tore out of here like his ass was on fire," is what Brother Andrew says.

He left without saying goodbye, and I guess I deserve that, I deserve to know how it feels, but I'm totally lost for the next day, and the day after that. I drift from prayer to prayer, from meal to meal and work to work, my thoughts everywhere and nowhere all at once.

I didn't get to apologize to Elijah.

I didn't get to see him one last time.

I confess to my confessor, Father Nathaniel, who listens with sympathy and then tells me what I already know—I have to tell the abbot.

Which is how I end up next to Abbot Jerome as we walk the path along the base of the hill he loves so much.

"Well," he says after I haltingly and awkwardly explain that I made out with my ex-boyfriend in the hermitage, "I appreciate that you've come to me with this so soon after the fact, and that you haven't tried to hold it inside. I can tell that it's affecting you."

I look over to where he's walking, his hands tucked under his scapular and his face serene. His pectoral cross glints in the sunshine. "*Affected* is a small word. The things I'm feeling are…larger."

"Yes, I suppose they would be. But I hope they are not on account of fear. I hope you know you are safe here."

I look back to the hill. The sun is blinding today, and I have to squint to make out the small path that snakes up the hill's side. "I'm not upset that I kissed a man, Father Abbot. I'm upset that I kissed *anyone* when I vowed not to. And that I led him into sinning against someone else…"

Selfish. Just like I've always been.

And fuck, what if it's how I'll always be?

"Vows are not meant to be burdens, Brother Patrick," the abbot says gently. "They are meant to clarify our lives and why we're here. Perhaps what is causing these larger feelings is not guilt that you tested the boundaries of your conversatio morum vow, but rather an invitation from God to ask yourself what you really want before you take your solemn vows. To ask yourself if you feel called, truly, to your life here."

Conversatio morum. *Fidelity to monastic life.* Meaning poverty, prayer, and, crucially, chastity. Along with a vow to stability and obedience, it composites the simple vows I made almost three years ago.

"I don't need an invitation," I say, panic rising in my throat.

I have to be a monk—I can't *not* be a monk. It's what saved my life. And if I stopped…

I don't let my thoughts drift any further than that. I can't think about what might happen to me and my stable but tentative okayness if I'm not a monk.

"I know what I want," I add as quickly as I can. "I know what I'm called to do. I'm supposed to be a monk. I just messed up is all, and it won't happen again, I'll make sure of it."

The abbot stops walking, and so do I. The look on his face is kind, but his warm brown eyes see so much that I don't want him to see, and I can hardly bear to look at him.

"Brother Patrick," he says, pressing his hand to my shoulder. "There is no shame attached to examining your heart. In fact, it's why we're here to begin with. It's why our fathers sought the desert. We are here to learn how to be faithful to God, even if the faithfulness might not look how we think. Think of your brother Tyler, after all. Didn't he learn that his call lay outside the priesthood?"

He did, but the thought doesn't reassure me at all. In fact, it panics me even more, because Tyler *proves* there are only these two paths, and that they're mutually exclusive. You can have either a life consecrated to God or a life out in the world. And while laypeople can be holy in their own way, they aren't cloistered, they aren't *dedicated,* and that's what I need. I need to live every day not only alongside God, but inside him too.

"My heart is determined, Father Abbot; I know how to be faithful and how God means for me to be faithful. I just have to do better, that's all."

I have to do better, I have to leave—

Yes. That's it. When I leave, it'll be easier to be a good

monk and a good man. I'll find someplace colder and harder than Mount Sergius with its friendly faces and cheerful creek and it will burn all the selfishness right out of me.

The abbot regards me for a moment, and I can see him coming to some conclusion as he nods to himself and starts walking again. "I think it's time we started preparing for your trip, don't you?"

"You're still going to let me go?" I ask, my voice cracking with relief. "I thought maybe you might—"

In my peripheral vision, I can see his bushy eyebrows slant down in a frown. "That I might punish you for a kiss by taking away something important to you? No. You are a man seeking God, not a teenager who took the family car without permission. But I am letting you go on a condition."

"What's that?" I ask, ready for anything. Hair shirts, fasting, a hundred rosaries a day, *anything*. I'll do it.

He nods up at the sun. "That you take God's invitation. Use your time away to ask yourself what you really want."

CHAPTER TWENTY-FIVE

THREE WEEKS LATER

"Do you have enough socks?" Brother Connor asks. "Maybe you need more."

"I'm sure they'll have a way for me to do laundry," I say, joining him to look down at my borrowed suitcase. It's currently the most boring suitcase known to humankind—black socks, black boxer briefs, black habits and scapulars. My breviary, the copy of *Summa Theologiae* that Tyler gave me for Christmas last year. Toiletries. Head meds. Passport.

Everything is ready for me to go tomorrow. And I've been ready for so long that I'd start walking to the airport *now* if they'd let me.

The abbot said I could go as long as I used the trip to examine what I wanted out of a monastic life, and I told him I would...but I already know I don't need to. And I'm eager to prove it to him—that this is the life I'm meant to live, that I'm called to be a monk, celibacy and all.

A knock on my open door announces the abbot, who joins me and Brother Connor in the now-crowded cell after I welcome him in. He comes to join us around my bed, where we are staring down at my suitcase.

"Do you think you need more socks?" the abbot asks, and Brother Connor shakes his head.

"He won't listen."

I chuff, but I don't bother answering because Brother Connor and the abbot are exchanging a look I know well. It's a pre-*Conversation* look—conversation in italics with a capital C. Dread, small but sharp, sinks a hook deep into my stomach.

"I'll see you tomorrow morning, Brother Patrick," Brother Connor says and gives me a fond smile. It's a smile that says *best of luck*, and the dread sinks even deeper into my vital places.

I turn to the abbot, who is sitting on the narrow bed beside my suitcase, his hands laced over his stomach.

"I have some news," he says, and I know, I just *know*, that he's about to tell me the trip is cancelled. That the monasteries in Europe have changed their minds about having me visit, that they don't want me. That I won't stand on the cliffs of St. Columba's after all, and that the stark, holy place I've been seeking will remain forever out of my grasp.

I slowly sit onto the chair by my desk, bracing myself to receive this news with humility and grace. Or at least the absence of a full-blown, bawling cry.

I can survive anything but this, I want to tell the abbot. I've survived my sister's death from suicide, my mother's death from cancer—I've even survived that seeping, oil-slick dark that wanted so much to swallow me whole.

I survived leaving Elijah, and I survived torching my entire life as a burnt offering to God.

But I cannot survive this being taken away from me, I just can't. I will waste away like a river in the desert. I will blow away like dust in a drought.

"Mr. Iverson has requested to accompany you on your trip," the abbot says, and I'm glad I'm already sitting down, because I'm not sure I would be able to stand. Both from relief that the trip isn't cancelled and also from utter, unfiltered shock.

"Elijah?" I ask, totally unable to modulate how stunned I sound. "On my trip?"

"Yes," the abbot replies, looking at me from under his formidable eyebrows. "For further research for his article. He asked last week, and I informed him that I would need permission from the abbots of the hosting monasteries before we could discuss the possibility. But as of this afternoon, I've heard from all of the abbots, and they have all happily consented to host him as well."

He asked last week.

So after the kiss—after Jamie called him and after he left the abbey early—he wanted to come with me to Europe.

He wants to come with me to Europe.

And oh, the thrill that zips under my skin at that. Not only at the prospect of seeing him, but at the prospect of him seeking me out, even if it's only for research.

But the thrill is followed immediately by panic. By a preemptive sort of guilt.

I want to tell the abbot that it's impossible. That I cannot do this, because the memory of raindrops gathered in the cup of his upper lip haunts me still.

I look down at my lap. "God is not supposed to test me beyond what I can bear," I say. "And neither are you."

"Is it beyond what you can bear, Brother Patrick?" the abbot asks calmly.

I mumble a "I don't know."

"Because," says the abbot, "the choice is yours. If you tell me that you do not want this, that you cannot bear it, then I will tell Mr. Iverson that he cannot come."

Still looking down, I think of the hermitage. I think of the thunder, of the rasp of stubble against my lips, of the hands sliding over my skin like there would never be enough of me to touch.

And then I think of incense and psalms and Christ staring at me heavy-lidded from the cross. I think of fireflies in the cloister.

No, a stubborn voice inside me insists. *You spent all this time learning how to make a promise and you're keeping it, dammit.*

I know living this life is what I'm supposed to do. I just have to make sure the abbot knows too.

And maybe…maybe this is an opportunity. An opportunity

wrapped in temptation, but an opportunity, nonetheless. Maybe if I can take this trip with Elijah and have no more, um, *incidents*, then I can prove to the abbot that I've taken God's invitation to explore what I want—*and* I'll have done it with the desire of my earthly heart nearby.

I will be able to prove that I'm ready for solemn vows, and that I'm ready for an entire lifetime of them.

"I can do it," I hear myself say before I've even finished forming the plan in my mind. I look up to the abbot. "He's welcome to come. For the sake of his article and all."

Abbot Jerome studies me. Not in an unkind way, but in a penetrating way that's still a little uncomfortable. "You'll probably recall that I was very excited for this article," he says after a minute. "But no article is more important to me than you. I care for you deeply, Brother Patrick. I want this to be your choice."

"Thank you," I say. My mind is now completely made up. Maybe this is Impulsive Aiden rearing his head once again, but I know this is the way to prove to everyone, including myself, that I'm meant to be a monk. "I want him to come. And it will be good for me."

And it will be. Even if it means I need to sneak my cage into my suitcase to make extra sure everything will be okay.

The reward will be all the sweeter for its difficult birth.

I will know with absolute certainty that I am doing the right thing.

BELGIUM

CHAPTER TWENTY-SIX

from Mode Magazine

At this point, I have a choice, and like many people before me who can't stop thinking about broad shoulders and fireflies, I choose total emotional recklessness. What if, I ask my editor, I go with my monk ex-boyfriend to Europe and write about the beers there too?

Fine, my editor says. Just don't get me in trouble with the pope.

—"The Eternal Cool of Monks: Beer and Prayer in Some of the World's Loneliest Abbeys" by Elijah Iverson

CHAPTER
TWENTY-SEVEN

I'm not doing the right thing.

I thought I was, but now I'm sitting in a car wending its way through the forested hills of the Ardennes in Belgium on our way from the airport and how can I be doing the right thing right now? Every time I shift in the back seat of the tiny car, my knee brushes against Elijah's. Every time we speak— short, polite small talk—the air feels like it's about to pop with electric discharge.

And he and I have only been together for the last hour, since we flew separately, and met outside customs to wait for the car from Semois Abbey. It'd been less than three weeks since I'd seen him last, but the sight of him leaning against a pillar and typing on his phone still threatened to crumple me.

No one kisses like you.

But he seemed unaffected by the sight of me, nodding coolly in greeting and then asking me the usual travel questions, like we were colleagues or acquaintances—*how was your flight, did you manage to sleep, how was the food—mine was surprisingly good*—etc, etc, until the pale, bespectacled brother from Semois arrived in a battered Renault to pick us up.

And since then, we've barely spoken, even though there are a million *million* things I'm dying to ask. If he's told Jamie about our kiss and if Elijah is angry with me for kissing him to begin with, and why he wanted to come on this trip with me. I want to ask him if he's thought of me these last couple of weeks, if he's dreaded seeing me, if he's *wanted* to see me.

If this is really about an article, or if it's about something else entirely.

Brother Xavier is friendly, but like many Trappists, not particularly given to chattiness, which makes the absence of conversation between Elijah and me all the more palpable. I'm about to burst with all the unsaid things between us when we finally pull onto a narrow tree-lined lane and I get my first glimpse of Semois.

Nestled on a tongue of land tucked into a loop of La Semois—a sedate and shallow river—Semois Abbey is a mix of medieval ruins and modern buildings, which are all made of the same butter-colored stone. Tree-covered hills rear up around either side of the river, and the campus itself is choked with thick oaks, tall beeches, and evergreens with dark emerald boughs. It's like being inside the illustration of a forest from a children's fairy-tale book.

We're led not to the dormitory, but to the guesthouse, which Brother Xavier explains is their custom even for visiting monks. He tells us it's mostly used by hikers and bicyclists making their way through the Ardennes, with the occasional serious retreatant thrown in. There's only one other guest here now—a rangy German bicyclist who nods at us on his way out the door—and we're given a photocopied handout of the monastery's daily schedule and told that our host will be back to escort us to dinner.

And then we're left alone to unpack and rest.

Elijah gives a shuddering stretch like a cat waking up from a nap as he looks around the cozy common room. The walls are stone, and the floors are made of old brick, and the furniture is made of well-worn wood and leather. But my eyes are on him and on the hem of his shirt as he stretches, which reveals the narrowest sliver of taut stomach as he does.

"I know I'm getting old when I'm tired after a flight I slept my way through," he says, more to the room than to me.

"Same," I say.

He slants a look my way. "A little different from the transatlantic flights we used to take, hmm?"

A short laugh huffs out of me. Most of our long flights were spent trying to figure out how we could fuck around on the plane without arousing suspicion from flight attendants or any nearby homophobes. But those flights were always to some fun, boozy place for fun, boozy sex. Not to a monastery filled with silent, watchful monks.

There is plenty of booze here though.

"I'll see you for dinner, I guess," Elijah says, and then he's rolling his suitcase down the hall. I try not to notice the way his stylish shorts cling to the firm curves of his ass.

I close my eyes and take a deep breath.

I want to be a monk for the rest of my life.

And he's engaged.

If I fuck up again, both of us will be miserable and heartbroken, and so my task beyond scouting out my potential future monastery is clear.

I can't fuck up.

Dinner is a cheese soup, hearty bread, and a brown beer that the monks brew only for themselves, which is almost heartier than the bread itself. Dinner is silent, which is different from home where we usually read aloud from scripture or a book about scripture while we eat.

All of it is different from before I became a monk and subsisted mainly on vodka and protein bars and also sometimes went to parties where platters of sushi were laid out on naked models instead of tables.

After we silently shuffle our dishes to the kitchen and help wash, everyone silently shuffles off to bed. Not surprising because vigils—the first prayers of the day—are at *three thirty in the morning* here. And here I thought that six in the morning at Mount Sergius was uncivilized.

And so even though the July sun is still visible above the forested hills, Elijah and I walk back to the guesthouse to retire for the night.

"Are you coming to vigils?" I ask him. We've been invited

by Brother Xavier to come to all the prayers, even the ones not normally open to the public.

He looks over at me, the evening sun catching the amber threads in his eyes. "I suppose I should," he says slowly. "For the sake of the article."

We reach the guesthouse, which is empty of the German bicyclist, and I stop in the common room before going to my room, running my hand nervously along the edge of my scapular. "I've been meaning to ask…" I say, and his whole body stills, except for his eyes, which move carefully to mine.

The entire moment feels like it's trembling on the edge of a blade. If I ask what I really want to ask—if I blurt out the things I really want to blurt—then something will happen. I don't know *what* will happen, but it feels like whatever happens will be horrible. He will be angry or wary or filled with pity. He will turn away and keep his distance, or he will do whatever version of letting a man down gently happens when the man being let down is a monk.

I swallow. "So you really needed more for your article than what you got at Mount Sergius?"

There are so many questions inside that question, but they're buried deep. A coward's gambit. I know it. I think he knows it too, although he doesn't seem to relax.

"I did," he says, his body still held perfectly motionless. "I hope I'll find what I'm looking for over the next three weeks."

"And what's that?" I ask, still a total fucking coward. I'm hoping he'll volunteer something—*anything* other than this cool reserve he's put back in place between us. Even if it's anger or something worse, I want to know. *I want to know.*

"Answers," he says quietly. "Always answers."

And I'm going to be brave, I'm going to ask if those answers are only about monastic life or if they're about me, but then his phone buzzes and he sighs as he pulls it out to look at it. Whatever he sees only deepens his reserve—his face grows more expressionless, his eyes more closed off. But his hand is shaking a little as he tries to put it back in the pocket of his shorts, and it tumbles onto the floor—thankfully onto a nubby old rug instead of the polished bricks.

I crouch to pick it up for him just as he does, and our hands brush against each other's, pinky to pinky. It's warm and wonderful, but also it feels like I've just plunged my hand into a vat of molten gold. I jerk my hand away at the same time I hear him give a sharp inhale.

Our eyes meet, and then I drop my gaze to see the pulse thrumming in his neck. It's quick and fast. Like his heart is beating as hard as mine right now.

"I'm sorry," I say, and my voice comes out all strange and hoarse. My hand is still hovering in midair, and I drop it to my side, but I'm still crouching down and so it hits the floor as I do. I feel like a total dumbass.

"Don't be," he says, and then he puts the phone in his pocket and stands, and so do I.

Our eyes meet again, and it's almost like there's a small crack in his facade, a chink in that wall of ice revealing a stormy fire within, and then he turns to look down the hall toward our bedroom doors.

"I should get to bed if I'm going to vigils in the morning," he says.

"Yeah," I whisper.

When we get to our doors, Elijah hesitates, his hand hovering over the knob, poised to turn it. I can see the tendons and bones in the back of his hand like this, tensed and ready, and I can see the curl of his long fingers.

Fingers that have curled inside my body.

"Brother Patrick," he says. "Aiden…"

"Yes?" I ask.

"About the answers. It's because every time I leave, I have more questions."

And then he adds, "And because every time I leave you, the only thing I can think about is coming back."

CHAPTER
TWENTY-EIGHT

It's hard to sleep that night. While the walls are much thicker here than they are at Mount Sergius, they might as well be made of candle smoke after Elijah said the thing he said. I am so very aware of him on the other side of the wall, and at least twice I sit up in bed, determined to go knock on his door. To apologize for the hermitage, and also to promise that it will never happen again, and also to ask if he minds saying more things about how he misses me when we're apart?

But I don't do any of that. Instead, I lie back down and manage to coax myself into a fitful sleep, which ends when I hear the bell tolling from the church for vigils. I wash up, replace the plastic chastity device I'd worn yesterday to fly with my metal one, and then walk to the church. Elijah arrives a few minutes after me, and we stand shoulder to shoulder in the pews.

The prayers are in French—which I honestly hadn't thought much about when I was thinking of picking a new monastery—and I'm surprised to look over at Elijah and see him murmuring along with the prayers in the French visitor's breviary we were given at the entrance to the sanctuary.

He catches my look and quirks an eyebrow.

I tilt my head at his breviary and then up at his mouth. *You speak French?* being the unspoken question.

The edge of his mouth turns up. *Oui*, he mouths silently and then returns to the prayers.

A typical day at Semois means there's almost no time for Elijah and me to talk. I quickly learn that Trappist life is *no joke*, and the first full day we're here, it feels like Elijah and I are brand-new freshmen in high school, scrambling to get to classes on time and ending up lost in the science hallway instead.

After vigils, there is breakfast and time for lectio or other spiritual reading, and then lauds and more lectio, and then Mass. A fun thing that Trappists do is keep the small hours— the short prayer times of terce, sext, and none in the middle of the day—which means by the time you get truly settled in doing anything—work or lunch or even lectio—it's time to get up for prayers again.

During the work hours, Brother Xavier shows us the massive brewery, which makes and exports six types of beer, and introduces us to the master brewer, Father Stefan. And then there is dinner, vespers, and compline, and suddenly the day is over, having passed in the least rush-y rush I've ever experienced.

The intense schedule is counter-weighted by the agony of

being so close to Elijah—brushing against his shoulder in the yeast lab or watching his forearm flex as he takes notes—and not being able to speak to him. At Semois, speaking is only for essential information, and in special areas designated for speaking, such as the cafe when it's open, and the main garden in the middle of the abbey grounds. It feels different from the silence back home, different from the natural quietude that fills the air there. It feels a little like being in school again. Like if you speak, someone will pop up and shush you.

And so aside from essential questions about hops and yeast and secondary fermentation, there is only silence between Elijah and me. It means the words from the night before echo all the more loudly in my mind.

The next day is much the same, and so is the day after that. Our German cyclist in the guesthouse is replaced with a group of older women retreatants who crowd the common room and whisper-talk in Walloon.

Elijah and I are never alone.

On the fifth day, I do laundry, and my tangled black habits are very, very different from the baskets of neatly folded white Trappist robes—like I'm the Hot Topic monk in a campus full of pristine angel people. And none of their white robes are spattered with beer or cheese soup or *anything*.

How???

I also wash my sheets, since the dam (a very literal metaphor in this case) burst last night, and I woke up to half-dried ejaculate everywhere.

When I emerge from the laundry room that afternoon, I

find Brother Xavier waiting for me by the guesthouse entrance.

"I must apologize," he says to me with a little bow. "Your friend asked me if he could take a walk through the woods, and then I realized I've been monopolizing your time here! I know you came here to learn beer and see Semois for yourself, but that means seeing the grounds outside Semois too. For if you come here to stay, they'll be the places you visit during your free time, no?"

I nod, although I've noticed that the free time here is, well. *Limited.*

Brother Xavier smiles. "Then tomorrow, your last day here. You should explore the woods just beyond the river and the medieval ruins too. If you stop by the kitchen, we can give you some food and beer to take with you."

I give a polite response and stifle the resistance I feel at this idea. I came here to decide if the Trappist way of life was right for me and taking a freebie day feels like cheating somehow. But after I tell Elijah on our way back from compline, and he gives me the same slow smile he used to give Sean before he did a double backflip into the pool, it suddenly hits me that I'll be alone with Elijah for the entire day tomorrow. No prayers, no tours, no flights of blonds and bruins (however delicious they may be).

Just us.

We agree to skip vigils and lauds, and so when I open my eyes, it's nearly seven a.m.—the latest I've slept in almost five years. I stretch in bed, yawning and then adjusting my cage. Thankfully my sheets aren't damp or clingy this morning, but I have an unrelenting half-boner that doesn't abate even after I take a cool shower in the shared bathroom.

Please, I tell God. *Make it stop.*

But God doesn't do anything about my tumescence or the rapid thudding of my heart as I dress and prepare for the day alone with Elijah. I know after years in a monastery that God doesn't do fast answers; that he doesn't do easy ones. I will have to choose celibacy and devotion *despite* how hard it is. Otherwise it wouldn't be a choice, it would just be the path of least resistance.

But you know what, the path of least resistance doesn't get enough good press. Because this isn't fun.

And fuck, couldn't God have stopped Elijah from wearing that tank top and those short hiking shorts? Like maybe a tiny lightning strike to light his suitcase on fire? Maybe a little flood in his room? Would that have been so hard?

But no, instead I'm presented with thighs a figure skater would be jealous of and a collarbone that screams LICK ME.

I keep my eyes studiously on his face—which is no better. The high cheekbones and squared jaw are now liberally dusted with scruff, and he's serving me the same eyebrow lift which used to give seventeen-year-old Aiden such mysterious pants-feelings.

"Are you really wearing your robes to hike?" Elijah asks dubiously, shifting a backpack on his shoulder. He's got sunglasses hanging from the collar of his tank top, and they tug the fabric down just enough to expose a scalene triangle of brown chest, and I want to die.

"I only packed one pair of street clothes, and it's khakis and a button-down, because the abbot made me," I say. But I lift my habit and show him a boot. "These will be good for hiking though."

He shakes his head, but then he smiles. "Aiden Bell not having the right outfit for the occasion. Who would have thought?"

"The habit is the right outfit for every occasion," I explain as we make our way out of the guesthouse and walk to the kitchen. "It's sturdy, easy to move in, and breezy when it gets hot."

"Uh-huh," Elijah replies. "I very much believe the full-sleeved, full-length robe made of all black material is super comfortable in July."

In the kitchen, the brother on duty silently loads us up with apples, cheese, and bread, as well as a soft cooler case full of their 5.0% blond. After he tucks in a couple reusable water bottles and shows us the shallowest part of the river to ford, we're off, ambling beneath the trees to the sound of the terce bells ringing.

We don't talk much at first. Fording the river is easy enough with how shallow it is and how many sun-baked rocks break the surface, but it does require focus, especially with our cargo making us unwieldy, and then the path up the hill is a trial of faith and will. It's steep and *mean* and by the time we get to the top of the hill an hour later, I'm wheezing. I drop the cooler case and stumble over to a large, shady oak and fall to my knees, panting like Hidalgo's horse.

(Or is Hidalgo the horse? I never saw that movie.)

Elijah is irritatingly not out of breath at all. He watches me with barely disguised amusement and then walks over to deposit his backpack next to the cooler, standing over me. His sunglasses reflect me in duplicate—twin monks on their knees with their shoulders heaving and their cheeks red over their scruff.

"Built for strength and not endurance, I see," Elijah remarks, nudging me with his hiking boot.

"That's not what the strippers used to say," I pant, and Elijah laughs so loud and so bright—so *happily*—that I feel his laugh running through my body like water. Like *fun* water, like a rippling swimming pool or turquoise ocean waves. His laugh feels like a vacation destination all in itself, and then I remember that I used to hear it often. That even though I was a flake and a jackass, I could always make him smile. I could always make him laugh.

I roll back onto my ass and wipe at my forehead with my sleeve. I would never admit it to him, but a long black robe probably isn't the best summer hiking gear. I feel like I'm being broiled alive.

"You need a beer," Elijah says, taking pity on me. He comes to sit next to me in the shade, and then he rummages through the cooler case for a pair of bottles and the opener, and then hands me an open bottle. The cooler case has done its job, and the beer is still very cold.

We both drink in silence for a moment, letting the breeze and the bright, citrusy beer cool us down, and then Elijah says, "Fuck it, let's eat too," and we unpack our lunch early.

Just beyond us is the path, and beyond that is the steep slope of the hill, slanting down to the river and then to Semois Abbey itself. From our vantage away from the edge though, the river is invisible, and so are the abbey grounds. There's only the broken upper teeth of the medieval ruins and the dark roofs of the modern buildings. And then hills upon hills upon hills.

"This is hobbit food," Elijah says, looking over our spread of bread, cheese, apples, and beer.

"We're only missing mushrooms."

"I wouldn't say I'm *missing* them," Elijah mutters, reaching for an apple slice and then sticking it between his teeth before he digs in his satchel for his notebook and a fine-point Sharpie pen. He uncaps it and scribbles something down while I make myself a tiny cheese and apple sandwich.

"You know," I say after a swig of beer. "You've been interviewing every monk you come across, but I feel like the only questions you've asked me have been purely functional, about how things work at the abbey and stuff like that."

He glances at me, an eyebrow lifted over the edge of his shiny sunglasses. "What questions should I be asking you?"

I'm suddenly uncomfortable, unsure. "I don't know. Like what I want out of being a monk. What I want out of this life."

It's so close to the things we've been avoiding—why I came to Mount Sergius, why I left him. How I feel about what happened between us in the hermitage. And I feel brave and cowardly all at once because it's just close enough to lead him to those places, but far enough away that he'll have to be the one to bridge the gap.

"Never mind," I say quickly, and then I tack on a laugh for good measure. "I wouldn't have very smart answers to those things anyway. Not the kind of answers a *Mode* reader would be interested in, anyway."

"You don't think a *Mode* reader would be interested in a queer millionaire turned Catholic monk?" Elijah asks, eyebrow even higher now.

"Well, I—"

Elijah shakes his head and settles back against the wide trunk of the tree, taking his beer and his notebook with him. "I've been meaning to properly interview you, but…" He sighs. "I guess it's hard to separate the questions I want to ask as your ex-boyfriend from the questions I want to ask as a writer."

Before I can figure out how to react to that, he straightens up a little. "Okay, actually, I do have a question."

CHAPTER
TWENTY-NINE

"What's the biggest difference between your job before and your job now?" he asks as he taps his pen on the paper. "Between managing investment portfolios and being a monk?"

"This feels like a pointless question," I say, sliding my eyes over to him.

His lips twitch. "Why is that?"

"Because *everything* is different, and that difference is so laughably apparent. I mean, you could walk into an abbey and just start pointing at random things, and every single one of them would be different. Habits, incense, candles, statues, glass cruets. *God.*"

"As opposed to what?" he probes. "A windowed office overlooking the street and decanters of whiskey nearby?"

I picture my old office in my mind. I had been so proud of it once upon a time, this office I'd felt like I'd *earned*. It hadn't been until the last two years there that the pride had started to slip away, that the feeling of *earning* had shifted into some other feeling. Awareness maybe, if awareness could be called a feeling.

"It's more than that," I say. "More than different windows and different liquors. We talked about it while we were dating, but I began to really see how few women worked there. How many white men. It was a boys' club, and it was run like one."

Elijah nods. A lot of the processing what I was seeing and naming it had been with him.

"But you stayed during all that," Elijah says, looking up from his notebook. "It didn't make you leave."

"Maybe it should have," I say. "I don't know. I've chosen to stay in this church too, and it's just as fucked up. More so, even."

Elijah's pen lifts from the page, his thoughts seeming to turn inward. "My family believes you have to stay inside something to make it better."

"Do you believe that?"

"I don't know." He looks down. "I don't know anymore. All the answers felt so clear to me when I was younger—leave, walk away, burn it down. There was a right answer and a wrong answer for everything. But something like staying or leaving…it feels more complicated to me now that I'm older, I guess. Anyway, for what it's worth, I wasn't judging you for staying at the firm. Especially because you did try to make it better while you were there."

"I guess," I say. Me and a few others pushed for a DEI consultant to be hired, and for the recruiting and hiring processes to change. I think it was fear of bad PR and potential litigation that got the top-floor people on board more than genuine conversion to the cause, but it had resulted in some small concrete changes. Not enough, though.

"It threw into stark relief how little meaning the rest of it held. The 3 a.m. phone calls to Tokyo or London. The market fluctuations, the allocations, the breakpoints. The suits and pens and planes and everything, all of it. It was so *meaningless.*"

I look out onto hills that were lifted from the earth over three hundred million years ago. Even with the newer monastery buildings nestled between them, there is something so ancient about this place, so old and yet still so vital and alive.

"It was like a theater curtain had been pulled back," I continue, looking down at the bottle cradled loosely in my hands. "And I could finally see all the props and sets and costumes for what they were: a giant game of pretend. And then I began to feel pretend too, like I was wearing a costume and showing up to speak pre-written lines, pretending I knew what real happiness and success looked like. Like I was a kid who'd put on my dad's suit and thought it made me important. It was so hollow, and so empty, and—"

I pause. This is getting too close to the real reason I came to Mount Sergius. Too close to that night in the farmhouse, when there was nothing but the flash of a phone in the dark to give me enough light to make it until dawn.

I change direction, looking up from my beer to gesture at the monastery below us.

"The biggest difference between my old job and this one?

Everything down there has meaning. Everything down there has a reason to be there and a history of being there. Even the smallest things—the smallest square of cloth, the tiniest vial, the dish for the priest to wash his hands—they *mean something*. It all means something. Yes, it all points to God, but it also points back to ourselves too. It creates the sacred for us."

Elijah writes something down as I finish my beer. "So is it safe to say that what you want out of this job is different than what you wanted from your old one?"

I snort against my beer bottle. "You haven't forgotten about the Timber Wolf, have you?"

He laughs, low and rich. "Oh my God, I *had*."

In Kansas City, we have an iconic wooden roller coaster called the Timber Wolf. It's not iconic because it's a good roller coaster—it will rattle the balls right out of your ballsack—but it's one of those things you love because of its enduring unpleasantness. It was also the first roller coaster I ever rode. My big sister Lizzy took me on it on my ninth birthday, and the photo from that ride ended up being the only picture I had after she died that was just of the two of us. I still have it in a small album in my cell in Mount Sergius.

Anyway, at some point after college, I decided that the one, singular goal of my life would be to have my ashes scattered—not near the Timber Wolf—but *via* the Timber Wolf, by someone riding it. Of course, the theme park probably has some boring rule about human remains on the property, so clearly I would need to make enough money to bribe them into allowing this. Therefore I'd been collecting together millions and millions of dollars in the form of a donation, so that by the time I died, they'd have to turn down a bananas sum of money if they didn't want to allow my ashes one final shaky ride on the coaster.

Obviously, all that Timber Wolf money was given away to much better causes when I went to Mount Sergius.

"I can't believe you were never worried about the coaster still being there by the time you died," Elijah laughs, shaking his head as he writes in his journal. "Like this whole plan depended on a *wooden* roller coaster still being there in sixty years or whatever."

I'm glad he can't see my face. I reach for another beer bottle and open it, so I don't have to answer.

So I don't have to tell him that the Aiden from before never planned on living that long.

"What about you?" I ask, setting my bottle down on the soft dirt under the tree and turning to look at him.

His brows knit over his sunglasses. "What about me?"

"You switched jobs too, didn't you? What's the biggest difference you saw between them?"

"If I were writing an article about my own job, I wouldn't be in a Belgian forest right now," Elijah says. I can't see his eyeroll behind his shades, but I know it's there all the same.

"Uh-uh. I've read *Mode* and *GQ* and *Esquire*, and all those feature pieces are always super meta with the writer breaking the fourth wall or whatever. In fact, it might be your journalistic duty to let your own insights bleed into the text."

He sucks his teeth a moment, but it's a thoughtful suck,

not a judgy one, and then he sighs. "Okay, okay," he says. "You have a point about the fourth wall thing, I guess."

"I know."

He swivels his head to give me a look from behind his sunglasses. "Don't push it, Bell."

I decide to ask what I've been wanting to ask since he first came to Mount Sergius. "Why did you leave event planning to begin with? You were so great at it."

"It actually parallels your story in a way. Hand me another beer, will you?" he says, setting his notebook on the ground and stretching out his legs. His shorts have ridden up a little on his thighs, exposing the place just above his knee where his quadriceps begin. Firm swells of muscle that beg for kisses and licks.

"Thanks," he says as I hand him an opened bottle, and then he takes a drink. "So you left," he starts, and my stomach gives an automatic twist, like it's trying to eat itself, but he keeps going before I can say anything. "And it was the first breakup I'd had that didn't feel romantic in its own way. Before you, every relationship that ended—or every time I thought my heart had been broken, even if there hadn't been a relationship *per se*—came with this romantic mourning period. It felt romantic to be heartbroken, to nurse my wounds, to decide if I'd wallow or have revenge sex or live my best life or whatever it was that felt the most cathartic at the time. But after you left…there was nothing romantic about it. Nothing at all."

Pain—aged and smoky like an Islay scotch—spikes his

voice. But again he continues before I can speak.

"Everything felt grayed out. Like a bad filter had been applied to everything in my life, and I began to see my job not in terms of how good I was at it or how much I got paid, but for what it *was*, which was planning events for mostly rich white people, and for the same group of them over and over and over again. Fundraising events, galas, receptions, pre-perfomance shit, post-performance shit—the same faces, the same self-congratulatory smiles and small talk. And then amidst all that, my boss had a chat with me about my personal social media presence." Elijah uses finger quotes, bottle and all, around the word *chat*.

"She said my social media was too political, too contentious, especially for an election year. She was worried it was coming off as 'divisive.' And that it was reflecting poorly on the venue."

"That's fucking awful," I say. "Divisive?"

"Yeah. When I'm sharing my opinion about current events, it doesn't make me informed or au courant. *Informed* is for white people, *divisive* is for me." He gives a long exhale after rubbing at his forehead with the hand holding his beer. "And you know that it wasn't actually 'current events' that set her off—she wasn't offended by my tweets about Brexit or the Panama Papers. Nope. In her eyes, it was divisive to talk about things like police brutality, like white supremacy, like nativism and voting rights and basically anything that suggested in the smallest, tiniest way that racism existed anywhere, in any form whatsoever. Somehow, to her, the *real* racist thing was talking about racism in the first place. Even if it was on *Twitter*—my personal, in-no-way-associated-with-the-goddamn-venue Twitter.

"And you know the hell of it was that I didn't push back at all when we were in the meeting? Like when I was in there, when she was giving me her concerned face, her *this is purely about the venue's reputation* face, I just nodded and agreed because I was so shocked and also she was my boss and could fire me right then and there—and mostly I just wanted it to end so I could escape. But then once it was done, and I was on my way home, I could finally process what had happened in its entirety—text and subtext, so to speak. I put in my notice the next day."

"So that's why you left," I say. "I'm sorry you had to make that choice. But I'm really glad you did and got away from there."

"Me too. And there was a silver lining, I suppose—my quitting was the final straw for *her* boss, and she was fired not long after I left. They even asked me if I'd like to apply for her job, but I said no. I was ready to move on, you know? Not just from what had happened, but from being there altogether."

The wind picks up a moment, ruffling my robe and Elijah's notebook, and he reaches over, casual as you please, to tuck the edge of my fluttering habit under my calf. His fingers graze against my skin, and I feel that graze all the way up my leg to my stomach.

"While I was figuring things out," he says, leaning back all nonchalantly like he didn't just touch my leg, "I started writing more than ever. Not just for social media and for open platform sites, but for myself as well. Journaling and essaying and all the stuff that falls away when you get too busy for it."

"And this was your major, right?" I say, my hand going to the still-tingling patch on my calf. "Creative writing?"

"Yes," he says, with the self-deprecating sigh of someone who got a liberal arts degree. "After I graduated, I was hanging out with all these writers and they were hanging out with all these artists, and then I become a gallery groupie, and I sort of tumbled into event work." He shakes his head. "At the time, it was just a job. It was only supposed to be a way to pay the bills until my writing could find its place. But by the time I met you, writing had shrunk into this little ghost of a dream, barely there enough to *boo* at me when I was bored."

"I don't remember you talking about it much," I remark, although I add, "but there was a lot I missed."

"I didn't talk about it," he says. "I never thought to. It was like a kid's dream of being a ballerina or an astronaut. That's how far away it felt."

"But it didn't feel far away after you quit."

He shakes his head again, this time with a smile. "No. In a way, I have you to thank for that. After you left, I had so much I wanted to write about, so much I *needed* to write about, that suddenly it was the only thing that mattered. I started pulling together a portfolio of writing samples and submitting to places. *Mode* was my first choice, and they took me freelance at first, until a staff position opened up. And that's how I got here today."

"Of course they took you," I say. "You're the smartest person I know."

He looks over at me, his mirrored sunglasses hiding his eyes. His throat bobs in a small swallow. "It doesn't always feel that way," he says.

I drop my eyes to my beer, not sure what he means, but it's probably not good.

He clears his throat, continuing. "At *Mode*, they send me to cover stuff I really care about too. Yes, I have to write the listicles and fluff pieces sometimes, but I've also gotten to cover protests and legislation that needs paying attention to. They love that I'm active on social media—and so many of their writers are too, which means it's not just me out there. I get to use my voice frequently. Intentionally."

"It's your vocation," I say. "Only out in the world instead of in a medieval cloister."

"It is a vocation, isn't it?" He chews on his lip a minute, his stare directed at the monastery roofs in the valley below. "And it is. It *is*. That difference between my jobs is the same one you found—I went from meaningless work to work that has meaning, at least most of the time. And I love it and want to keep doing it. But—"

He lifts the beer to his lips but doesn't drink, letting the bottle sink back into his lap instead. "But I'm tired sometimes, I guess. Of always having to have a response to whatever is happening, of always having to think about it and think *fast* and then frame those thoughts into something incisive and deep within a few hours. Sometimes I want to think slowly.

Sometimes I want the space to be wrong about something. Sometimes I just want quiet and the absence of…I don't know. Production, I suppose. I want to have meandering thoughts and conversations and words that don't go anywhere, that don't always end up having a point. And sometimes I wake up and look at my phone and I'm almost upset that it hasn't bricked itself overnight. I walk into my office, and I see my computer, and I'm angry that it hasn't had some electrical issue and caught on fire. It's been almost four years now, and I'm burned out. I want to keep writing what I write because it *matters*, it matters so fucking much, but I also don't know how I can go on like this without needing to eventually buy one of those sensory deprivation tanks for my office. Shit," he says abruptly, draining the beer and then shoving the bottle in the case, along with his first beer bottle too. "I didn't mean to lay all that on you. I'm here to interview you and the monks about your beer. Not talk about me."

"I'm glad you did," I say, also putting my bottles in the case, and then starting on the picnic leftovers.

Things packed, we both stand and, by silent agreement, start walking down the hill again, back to the monastery where we'll drop off the remnants of our lunch and then poke our way through the ruins.

"I still think monasticism is a privileged way of living," he says after a minute, his words nearly lost in the wind. "But I guess I can admit now that I'm jealous of it."

I open my mouth to say something about how being a monk isn't proprietary—not actually. The medieval period was full of people who strayed across boundaries of holy and secular, who operated outside of the Church's official designations of what made someone monastic and what didn't.

But as the words form on my tongue, something else forms in my chest. A tight knot which has something to do with this very idea, which is tied to it somehow, and I suddenly feel like if I speak about it, the knot will grow tighter and cinch something vital inside of me.

I close my mouth instead, and with only the breeze, our footsteps, and near-silent dart of a goshawk from a tree to the valley below, we walk down to the abbey.

CHAPTER
THIRTY

"Aha!" Elijah crows over the hand-drawn map. "It's this way!"

It's a few hours later, and we've relieved ourselves of the remnants of our picnic, and we've also wandered through the ruins intertwined with the modern Semois Abbey. Ruins that we learned were not actually the first Semois Abbey, but the second.

Elijah sets off and I follow him, wending between the trees. "So do you believe the story of the first abbey?" Elijah asks, finally dropping the hand holding the map to look around us.

"You mean do I believe that there was a talking bird sent by God to help a stranded Italian countess find a cave to hide in so she wouldn't have to get married? And then she dedicated a monastery here in thanks?"

"Isn't it your job now to believe in miracles?"

"I believe in miracles," I say, thinking of that night in my farmhouse and the text which had lit up my phone. "But I also believe in good medieval PR."

"This does have all the good medieval miracle tropes," Elijah replies. "Talking animal, aristocratic virgin…"

"…a magic spring," I add. In the story Brother Xavier had told us, God had been so pleased by the countess's declaration to build a monastery that he'd made his godly pleasure known by producing a spring with lots of good, clear water. The water is so good, actually, that the modern abbey still uses it in their brewing process.

"Can't forget the magic spring," Elijah says absently as he stops and bends over the map again.

"Did you know there's an entire subgenre of hagiography that's dedicated to magic springs and severed heads?"

That gets his attention. "What?"

"Severed *saints'* heads," I clarify.

He stares at me from behind his sunglasses. "Is that supposed to make it less weird? Like it's only weird if it's severed heathen heads that make magic drinking water?"

I shrug.

Elijah takes his sunglasses off and looks around the dim, cool forest surrounding us. The occasional ray of sunlight glints off the amber and copper in his eyes. "We're lost."

"We can't be lost. They said it was less than a mile away. Let me see that map."

Heaving a profound sigh, Elijah holds up the map for me to look at but doesn't let go of it. Our shoulders bump as I trace my fingers over Brother Xavier's hand-drawn landmarks and twisty paths.

Because the ruins haven't been structurally evaluated, the abbey discourages most visitors and tourists from milling around them, but Brother Xavier has invited us to explore so long as we take care around the unstable walls and the old well. It also means the path there isn't very well-trodden, and easy to lose.

"I think we need to go back to the boulder and veer left from there."

"This is *Flood Plain* all over again," Elijah grumbles. "Do you remember that?"

"Was that the art installation down by the river?" I ask as we start walking again.

"We got lost. Bit by mosquitos. Saw a dead deer. And by the time we got to actual site of the installation, all the wine was gone."

"I had a good time though," I say, as I recall that night.

Elijah scoffs. "Yeah, because I blew you in the car afterward."

"Like I said. A good time!"

The boulder is coming into view now and we curve around it. A faint ribbon of a path reveals itself through the trees, and we strike towards it. In the distance, I think I glimpse gray stone among all the swaying green leaves.

"I dragged you to a lot of random art events, didn't I?" he muses.

"You did," I reply. "What was that one where it was like a short film of people sticking safety pins into a peach or something?"

"It was *Unpinning the Pit #7*!" Elijah says, laughing. "It was an examination of the destabilizing effects of new media!"

"It was gross," I say forlornly. "That peach was fucked up by the end."

"Yeah, but how many boring corporate events did I drag you to?" Elijah asks. "That's right, none."

"No, you just planned them for your *day job* and made me listen to how the printers had gotten the cardstock wrong or something."

He's laughing hard enough now that he's scrubbing at his face, and I wish I could watch him laugh forever. I wish we could stay just like this—remembering the funny things, the good times. As if our year together was just sex and terrible local art and vacations and dirty games that ate up all our hours with sighs and sweat, and there'd been nothing hard about loving each other, nothing painful at all.

"We had fun at those work events though," he says. And then, as if he's able to read my thoughts, he says, casually, "Remember the games we used to play at them?"

What if…

"Well. We used to play games everywhere," I say, and my voice is low, a little hoarser than it should be.

"We did," he says, and his voice is low too, almost a whisper. Like we don't want to be overheard, even though we're half a mile away from the abbey and that abbey is miles and miles away from the rest of the world.

We are totally and completely alone, and we are still whispering.

"Do you ever think of them?" I ask, and I shouldn't, I shouldn't ask that. It's dangerous for *me*, it's dangerous for *him*.

We shouldn't be talking about this.

For a moment, I think Elijah isn't going to answer. His face is turned away, and as we step into the clearing filled with half-broken arches and small cloisters now choked with ferns and moss, he doesn't say anything at all.

That's good. That's a good thing. A smart thing.

Healthy, even.

And I shouldn't have even spoken the words aloud, because *do you ever think of them* is the same as *I think of them all the time,* and he doesn't need to know that, it's not fair to make him know that when he's engaged and I'm still married to Christ.

But then we're in the middle of the clearing, and the trees are moving, and there's a faint tinkling from the mossy well nearby, and he says, quietly, "I always think about them."

I turn to face him head-on, and he's closer than I thought. Close enough for me to see the small cleft in his chin under his stubble. Close enough for me to see the lighter threads of amber and dark gold in his eyes, for me to see how his pupils have blown wide in the shade of the ancient forest.

He is, simply, beautiful.

"Me too," is my even quieter reply.

His lower lip gets pulled into his mouth ever so quickly, his teeth sinking into it for just a moment. "What do you—" He clears his throat. "If we were here then. Or if we were still…"

"Still…?"

"If we were still together," he says quickly, "and we were here in these ruins, what kind of game do you think we'd play?"

My caged shaft gives an almighty kick as my pulse thunders through my veins. It's like he's just put his fingers in my mouth. Like he's just sunk to his knees.

A single question from him, and I'm undone.

I swallow, my mind already swimming with every filthy thing I've ever dreamed of doing with him, with every fantasy I've had since making my vows.

"I—I can think of a game we'd play," I say. My voice is rough and rushed, because if I don't say it all at once, right now when he's looking me like that, then I'll remember all the reasons I shouldn't say it, all the reasons I should stop this.

But it's one thing to stop when you think you're alone in wanting it, when you think you're the only one with desire scorching up your thighs and searing the inside of your skin. It's another thing entirely to stop when the man in front of you is sinking his teeth into his lip and also giving you that eyebrow. The eyebrow that says…*well then?*

"I would pretend to be a monk," I say.

His voice is pure gravel when he asks, "Yeah?"

"Yeah," I breathe. "And it would have been years and years since I'd been able to fuck. I'd be desperate."

"How desperate?" he asks. His chest is heaving, but his arms and hands are still, like he can't bear to make any movement that might break the spell.

But I'm beyond spells now, I think. I'm speaking

prophecies and parables, whispering a game I've thought of so many times. "So desperate that I can't take it anymore. Not after I see you. You're so beautiful, and I think I could ask you…"

"Ask me what?" Elijah prompts.

"If I could kiss you. If you'd let me remember what it was like to be kissed. If you'd let me touch you and hold you and then make you come."

Elijah's whiskey eyes are almost all black now, a ring of amber around a circle of onyx. "And if you did ask me, and if I said yes, what would happen then?"

"Then I'd start at the end," I say, trembling all over. "I'd start on my knees, needing to taste you. And then after you'd used me, I'd ask to be kissed. Kissed until the bells ring for prayer."

Elijah takes a short step forward and then stops himself. He looks like he's shivering too, like holding himself still takes all the willpower he has. We are both caught in the same web, strung together on the same silk.

What if…

I sink to my knees. Slowly, and with all the practice I've had doing it in a monastery for almost five years. I don't let my eyes leave his—not when my knees touch the ground, not when he takes that final step forward. Because at any moment he's going to turn away, step back, bring up Jamie and my vows and all the other reasons why we can't play this game. Why we can never play a game together again.

But he doesn't do any of those things. Instead, he reaches

out his hand—slowly, slowly—and cradles my face, his fingers pushing through my hair and his palm pressed against my jaw.

I think he might speak; his lips part like he's going to speak. And never have I felt such dread and such excitement coupled at once, pinned together on the same moment—

His lips press together, leaving whatever it was he had been about to say unsaid, and disappointment crashes through me.

Right until I see his other hand drop to the fly of his shorts.

His eyes still on my face, he unzips himself and then pops open the button of his fly. On the edge of my vision, I see him hook down the waistband of his boxer-briefs, I see him take hold of himself. He stares down at me, and with his thumb rubbing gently at my temple, he presses the head of his sex to my lips.

He's already hard, and when I open my mouth and lap at him with my tongue, I taste the slick salt taste of pre-cum. He's been hard for a while.

The realization is electric and wonderful, and I want salt and electricity forever, I want this to last years and years, so that the next time two Americans stumble through the forest, they'll find not only medieval ruins but us too, still playing our game.

He guides my head so that my mouth is pressed to the warm, thick root of him, and I kiss and lick him there too, I kiss and lick what I can around his cock—the sack beneath, drawn up tight, and the firm plane of his stomach above—and then he lets me get lower still, to kiss the hard muscles above his thighs, the same thighs I'd lusted after earlier while we ate.

When I straighten up again, he looks a little wild, like I've been teasing him on purpose, and his eyebrows are pulled together so tightly that there's a deep line between them.

I open my mouth, tongue out, like I'm ready to receive communion, and he groans, fisting himself again and pushing into my mouth with a slow but inexorable stroke. When he pulls out all the way, though, I see that his eyebrows are still knitted together, that his expression is as anguished as it is wild.

Tumbling through my lust like cold water is the memory of him and Jamie holding hands in the beer garden. Him and Jamie kissing against Jamie's Jeep.

I press my hands against the front of his thighs. "Can you?" I ask him. They're the first words we've spoken aloud since I told him the game I wanted to play, and even in a hushed tone, they feel loud, loud, loud.

He exhales, slowly, his eyebrows unknitting a little. "I can," he says softly.

Relief and curiosity and—hope?—shiver through me, but later, I'll sort through all those feelings later, and I dip my head back toward the part of him which juts proudly from his body. But before I can taste him again, he catches my chin with his fingers. "Can *you*?" he asks.

I have no choice but to look up at him then and maybe this is the actual moment that will end the game, because I can't lie. I can't answer *I can*, because we both know that this isn't actually a game, that my robes aren't pretend robes and I'm not a pretend monk.

So I answer the only way I can. "I *will*," I tell him, like a fallen angel from a Milton poem, and open my mouth for him again.

This time, he doesn't stop me. Jaw tight, he rucks up his tank top so that he can see better as I start to suck him off in earnest, taking him as deep as I can, loving the feel of him against my tongue, loving that soft velvet skin stretched over what feels like solid steel. Loving the plump head that swells whenever I trace my tongue around its flared edge, loving the little jolts and jerks of him as I lap and lick and suck hard. Feeling him *respond* is the sexiest fucking thing, and it has my cock straining at its cage, it has my thighs tight and my heart beating so fast that I'm dizzy.

I forgot about this, I think, forgot all the little details that made this into *sex* and not the mechanical act my memory had flattened it into. It's so much more than a cock in a mouth—it's the heat of his dick against my lips and the way his stomach tenses and his eyes flutter closed. It's the soft pant of his breath and the way his hand twists in my hair, at turns loving and grateful and demanding and cruel. It's that indefinable flow of pleasure, that getting hot while doing hot things to someone else, that heady sense of power and love, knowing that you're making someone else feel so good they can't stand it.

Perhaps it's a mercy that I'd forgotten, because if I'd remembered, I would have been tormented beyond what any hair shirt could ever do to me.

His pants turn into moans, and I let my hands roam all over him—cupping and sliding and gently scratching—and then I open my throat and take him all the way back, all the way in. Swallowing him down until my throat aches and my lips are all the way against him and I can smell the lingering scent of soap on his skin.

"Fuck," Elijah groans, the hand in my hair restless and gripping and releasing and then gripping again. "*Fuck.*"

Everything around us is different, from my robes to the ruins to the hot slant of the Belgian summer sun, but his voice like that, his taste on my tongue…

Familiar as anything. Familiar as breathing.

I'm going to come in my robes, cage and all. And from nothing, from basically nothing but the sound of him cresting and the feel of his hand in my hair, and how am I supposed to save my body for God when this feels so necessary, so inevitable?

So right?

My abdomen contracts, and I grunt around his cock right as I start to release the dripping, unsatisfying release of a caged orgasm. And then there's the first swelling jolt of his climax, followed by my reflexive need to swallow as he begins to pump down my throat. And the way my lips and tongue move around him, it's like a prayer, it's like chanting.

A secret, silent psalm just for us.

He whispers my secular name, and I love it, I love hearing him say it. And maybe I've been more Aiden than Brother Patrick today anyway. I've made off-color jokes and sworn up a storm and played a dirty game with Elijah the first chance I got. Maybe I was kidding myself all these years when I thought I'd changed, when I thought I'd finally learned how to keep a promise.

Maybe trying to be a holy man was a doomed experiment all along.

But when he says my name again there's too much happiness coursing through me, too much excitement and relief for guilt to find much purchase. Because anything is worth this. Anything.

He holds my head still as he finishes in my mouth, a proprietary touch that has my cock trying to stiffen in its constraints all over again, and then he gives himself a long minute after, shuddering a little as I gently lick him clean.

He stares down at me, lips parted, eyes dazed, and then the front of my habit is seized in two fists, and I'm hauled up to his mouth. I'm yanked against him for a crushing kiss, the kind of kiss that almost hurts, but it has to, it has to hurt, because anything less ferocious would be dishonest and a lie.

His tongue fucks into my mouth like my mouth was made for him to fuck with anything he wants, and I love it, I whimper at the sensation of him tasting himself as he tastes me too, and then I'm kissing him back, my hand finding the back of his neck and my other hand finding his ass, until we are pressed together so tightly that my robe flutters around his legs.

"You're wearing your cage again," he moans into my kiss, a hand sliding between us to curl around me.

"Yes," I manage to say, inhaling as he cups me. Everything is still sticky and hot, and all I want is to push him down onto the moss and then make out with him until we both die of old age.

"Please tell me you have your key," he says. "Please, please—"

"It's back at the guesthouse," I say, dropping my lips to his jaw.

"Aiden," he groans. "You're supposed to have it on you all the time." He pulls back a little and gives me an eyebrow which I think he thinks is stern, even though his lips are swollen and his eyes are still half-hooded.

"Are you giving me a lecture about safe chastity practice right now?" I laugh as I press my face into his neck.

"Yes! As your former key holder—"

"For that *one* month, and even then I barely had it on because you were too horny—"

"I am duty bound to remind you to be safe! What if we fell off the hill and they had to helicopter you into a Belgian hospital and then they had to call in firefighters to saw that thing off your dick?"

I'm laughing too hard to keep kissing his neck, and I pull back to grin at him. "Firefighters? That sounds hot."

"Oh my God, it does *not.*"

"You know it does."

"Someone has to be responsible for you, Aiden," Elijah says, exasperated. "Fuck knows you never are."

And just like that, I feel the cold gel of reality sliding over my skin.

Yes.

Yes, I am irresponsible, aren't I? Sucking off my ex-boyfriend in my habit and scapular, right in the middle of an open space where anyone could see.

"We should go so we don't miss dinner," I say, stepping

back and fixing my robes. There are some stains on my knees, but there's also enough dirt everywhere else that I can claim it was all from the hike.

"Aiden," Elijah says softly. "I didn't mean it like—"

"No, no, you're right." I force a smile. "Probably the last thirty minutes proves exactly how right you are. Are you ready?"

He looks at me like he wants to say no, like he wants to say something else. But after a minute, he just nods, his jaw tight.

"Yeah," he says. "Yeah. Let's go back."

CHAPTER THIRTY-ONE

Elijah and I don't speak until it's bedtime, and even then, it's only to exchange polite words of good night as we meet in the hallway and take turns with the shower. He looks like he wants to say more, but then a burst of impassioned Walloon makes its way from the common room, and we are reminded we are not alone.

I nod at him and go to my room.

I pray on my knees for a few minutes, my usual nightly prayers, my brain skirting around what I did that day in the clearing. The garish break from celibacy. And when I try to think of something to say to God, some apology I can genuinely speak, my tongue stays still. I feel miserable with what I did, but I know I would do it again. And again. As many times as there are chances.

And I don't know what the right prayer is for that.

My mind keeps drifting from prayer anyway. To Elijah. To Jamie. Curiosity burns at me, and I want to know *so badly* if they've broken up, but both the curiosity and excitement I feel at that idea make me feel mean and mean-hearted, and I should only want happiness for Elijah, and I shouldn't care anyway!

Disgusted with myself, I get off my knees. Given that I've already made a joke of the idea of chastity, I decide to sleep with my cage off tonight. I flick off the light and crawl into bed. Tomorrow will be an early drive to Luxembourg and then an epic journey via train to Carcassonne, where we'll be met by a monk from the next stop on our trip, Abbaye Notre Dame des Fontaines. Or Our Lady of the Fountains for the French-ly challenged, like me.

I'm packed and ready, but I already miss Semois. Or rather, I miss what happened here between Elijah and me, because surely after today, we'll behave. We know we fucked up—well, me more than him—and of course I won't actually do it again. Even if my guilt is threaded through with so much desire that it doesn't feel like guilt at all, but like something else entirely.

Like a net of heavy gold draped over my shoulders; a wine so dark and biting that even a communion wafer can't blunt the taste.

My newly freed cock is unused to so much sensation, and I have trouble finding a position in bed that doesn't stimulate it, that doesn't pull my mind to memories of pressing my body to someone else's. Memories of fucking, fast and slow and all the ways in between.

I'm nowhere near sleep when I hear the catch of my

doorknob, but maybe I'm dreaming. Maybe I've finally deprived myself of too much, broken something essential between reality and my horny brain, and now I'm having a waking dream where Elijah is opening my door at midnight. Where he's stepping inside my room and quietly closing the door behind him.

Where he's coming to my bed on bare feet, wearing nothing but loose linen pants which hang low on his hips.

He doesn't speak, but when he runs a flat, possessive palm over my bicep and shoulder, I know he's real. This is real. And I want—I *want*. After years of denial, polyester, and missing human touch so much I could cry, I *want*. Selfishly, carnally. Not for the betterment of a community or for the improvement of my immortal soul or for the rewiring of my brain.

I just…want.

I sit up and grab his arms, and he lets me. He lets me pull him down and flip him on his back, lets me straddle him and lick at his mouth until he parts his lips and gives me his tongue.

We don't say anything—we aren't alone in the guesthouse after all, and even whispers carry their own risk. I can't imagine one of those sweet old ladies telling on me, but I have to stretch my imagination to accommodate not only the danger to my vocation but the danger to myself—or more importantly, to Elijah.

But we're quiet, so quiet, even though I don't feel quiet on the inside at all. I feel loud with how much I want this, how much I need it, like my desire is a bell tolling over and over again, high peals mixed with low, bone-thrumming vibrations.

I kiss Elijah with every day of denial and every hour of chastity I've lived since I left him. And then I push down my own pajama pants, grab his hand, and guide it right to my erection, which is hanging heavy and swollen between us.

His strong fingers curl around me, and it's the first time I've felt this in so long. The tug of a hand on my unconstrained skin, the squeeze and stroke done only for pleasure, only for sex, and this—I'd forgotten this too. How fucking *good* it feels.

His hand is big and tight, and he's doing short but slow strokes, so that I feel every centimeter of his squeeze over me. I drop my forehead to his and I'm able to look down my chest and stomach to the sight of him jerking me off. And then his hand disappears to trace around my testicles, to fondle me gently and teasingly until a growl rumbles through me and I reach down to put his hand back where it belongs.

This time, I wrap my own fingers around his, and together we stroke and stroke until—in an embarrassingly short amount of time—my hips are punching forward and my muscles are quivering hard enough that I must be shaking the bed. The pleasure burns through me like a fire through kindling and spills out of my organ, a thick stripe of white all over the muscles of his stomach, followed by another and another.

The sensation is mind-blowing, incredible, awful, delicious. Unsurvivable. I can barely endure it, I can barely keep breathing. It's too much for one body to handle, and I slump onto Elijah, letting him take my weight as I breathe in the lingering scent of sage and soap on his skin.

His hands come around my hips and slide down to my ass, palming me and parting me so that air kisses my intimate skin. If this were five years ago, if we were anywhere else, I'd be doing the same to him, reaching into those overpriced linen pants and finding the places of him that were just for me.

I'd make him tell me what game he wanted to play—the needy monk whose control has finally snapped and he has to take what his visitor is offering? Or maybe the game where the monk is obligated by centuries of tradition to offer his guest *every* kind of hospitality?

Or maybe we could play the game where I make up for leaving him all those years ago. Make up for it with anything he wants.

But we aren't anywhere else. We're here in a Trappist guesthouse with a clump of gossipy, old women, we're within a stone's throw of a building full of monks who would almost certainly tell my abbot I had a man in my room if they found out.

I allow myself one last inhale against his neck, and then I peel myself free, giving him a soft kiss before I stand and walk over to the small hook where I've been hanging my towels. When I walk back to him, towel in hand, his eyes glitter at me, unreadable as ever. But his movements when he takes the towel to scrub his stomach aren't quick or agitated. He seems more thoughtful than anything else.

I wipe off my own skin and watch him as he stands and ties the string of his pants. His erection stretches all the way to his hip, but when I reach for him, he shakes his head.

"Good night, Aiden," he murmurs, and then he's out of my room with soft footfalls and the barely-there *click* of the doorknob.

I stare at the door a minute, not sure how to feel about what just happened. The chemicals in my blood tell me I'm sated and content, but my chest is still full of all the things it was before: regret and not-regret, a desire to be God's and the ache of still being Elijah's.

This is not a riddle for the dark, but that's never stopped painful riddles before in my experience. In the sunshine, under the blue sky, anxieties and miseries can feel so small. Nothing more than puddles in the road, their edges already drying, their surfaces reflecting nothing but the open sky above. But in the blear of night…that's when they like best to visit. When they can spread themselves against your ceiling as you try to sleep, when they can lean over you with clicking teeth and long, greedy fingers.

And as sleep finally, fitfully closes around me, I have the uneasy thought that I've bitten into an apple that I can't untaste today. That folding myself back into the Brother Patrick of yesterday might be impossible.

No, I think fiercely. *I learned how to live without this once.* I can do it again.

SAINT

FRANCE

CHAPTER THIRTY-TWO

from the notebook of Elijah Iverson

I don't know what I'm doing right now. What am I doing?

I was supposed to use this train ride to catch up on emails and organize my notes.

But I'm not working so much as I'm staring at the screen of my laptop, and I'm not staring at the screen so much as I'm watching Aiden out of the corner of my eye. He's sleeping with his arms folded on the table between us, his head pillowed on his arms and his eyelashes long and dark against his cheeks. If not for the monk's robes and the stray thread of silver glinting in his hair, he could be a college student stealing a nap between classes. He could be nothing but Sean's little brother again, long limbs sprawling and dangling everywhere as he sleeps on the basement couch.

Over the course of the last two months, I've essentially upended my entire life, and it's because of this big, green-eyed monk in front of me, and I don't even know if I entirely understand why. He left me, in the worst possible way, without a goodbye, without an explanation, with only a quick phone call that night to tell me that he was taking care of some things before he joined a monastery and that he was leaving me the farmhouse to keep or to sell.

He left me just as I was loving him the most, just as I'd been about to declare my love in the most romantic way I could think of.

I'm not romantic by nature; that was always Aiden. Spontaneous extravagance and then boyish preening when I'd thanked him for it.

So I'd wanted to return the favor; I'd wanted to prove to him and maybe to myself that I wasn't a silo of reserve and reproof. I'd wanted to be vulnerable and brave and poetic for him too. Isn't that half the thrill of being in love? Being vulnerable?

Anyway, with as much as we'd fucked, traveled, and spent every waking minute together, we hadn't told each other *I love you*, and I'd known that was my fault. Because I could see *I love you* in his eyes whenever he looked at me, I could hear it slipping between his words as he spoke.

He would have said it to me on that very first night if I'd let him.

But I had to be sure. I'm like that: I have to know, I have to know for certain.

(Or I used to be like that at least. Because now I don't know what I'm doing at all, I have no certainty whatsoever, and I've broken up with a good man and flown halfway across the world for what is essentially total uncertainty in the shape of a monk.)

The point was I'd finally been ready to say those three words. Even though there were times Aiden blazed too bright or winked out altogether, like a phone with a dead battery. Times when he ghosted me, times when he wouldn't show up to an event or a dinner where he was my date and then I'd get home and find him lying in the dark, like he'd decided to just hang out by himself instead of doing the thing he said he'd do.

And then there were the too-bright times, the times when he was too loud, too careless, too drunk.

None of these things happened all that often, but they happened enough to make loving Aiden like being on one of those roller coasters he loved so much. I was thrilled, dizzy, sick from loving him. I'd survive a ride, head spinning, breathless and nauseous too, but then I'd want to do it all over again.

And I was ready for that, for everything saying *I love you* would mean, and so I'd planned an elaborate dinner which I cooked myself. I dressed up, I had flowers. I would say those magic words and he would give me one of those Aiden looks, with his eyes burning and his cheeks flushing, and then I'd spend the night with him greedy and playful underneath me. And then we'd have the rest of our lives together, and I'd know that it had started with that night, with my *I love you*.

Except he didn't show up. He was hours late to dinner at his own fucking house, and when he finally walked through the door, he'd had no real reason for his absence. He'd simply forgotten.

Perhaps it would have stung less if I hadn't tried so hard to be open, to be the kind of boyfriend who did more than drag him to local art events and try to get him to read something other than *Star Wars* novels. Perhaps it would have stung less if I hadn't decided saying those words needed to be an event, if I'd just murmured them into the dark while he gave me a handjob, like a normal person.

But it didn't matter. It *had* stung. And the fight was a big one, the kind of fight that can end a relationship, although it hadn't occurred to me to end anything at the time. Why would it have? I loved him. There'd been no doubt in my mind that I'd go to bed pissed and wake up still pissed, but maybe less so, and then we'd sort it out.

And then I woke up in an empty farmhouse. No truck, no boyfriend, no explanation.

And when I did finally get an explanation, it was the last thing in the entire world I expected to hear.

A monk.

Who could expect that? And from Aiden Bell, of all fucking people? The poster boy for money and sex? Maybe there's a part of me that still can't believe it, even though I've seen the transformed Aiden with my own eyes. But how can it be true?

And why am I here?

And what am I doing with him? This vowed man, this celibate man, whom I can't seem to stop tempting—or maybe it's him tempting me.

I don't know.

I don't know.

CHAPTER
THIRTY-THREE

Somewhere after Sens, our train car empties out nearly completely, so that it's just Elijah and me sitting across a table from each other, and a young woman fast asleep at the end of the car.

We'd had a fairly easy morning, if an early one. The brothers had already been awake for vigils when it was time for us to leave and so had given us all warm, friendly handshakes as we piled into the Renault with Brother Xavier at the helm. He'd even spoken a little—a very little—as we drove, asking how we'd enjoyed our stay and the beer.

I had joked that we'd be piping his spring water into Kansas, and he'd laughed, and then he'd told us a little about the French abbey we were visiting and the honey beer they brewed there. Apparently, it had been rated one of the best beers in the world, but they refused to make more of it than they needed to pay for their needs. And so with a very constrained supply, the demand for their beer was, in a word, nutballs.

The monks only sold it at the gates of the abbey, never to nearby liquor stores or bars, and purchasers were limited to one case at a time. Orders were only opened up once every six weeks, and the orders had to be placed over the phone, like it was the olden times or something.

The phone!

There had been instances of beer enthusiasts enduring entire spiritual retreats just to drink the beer; twice in the last five years, the offsite bottling facility had been robbed not of equipment but of the brew itself. It was the rarest beer in the world, and on the beer bucket list of thousands.

Brother Xavier confessed he was jealous since he'd never had a chance to drink the Our Lady of the Fountains beer himself. We promised to smuggle him a bottle if we could, and he thanked us profusely, shaking our hands as we decanted ourselves out of the Renault and got our things.

It was a pleasant farewell to what had been a pleasant stay, but as we'd boarded the train and found places for our suitcases, Elijah had said, perceptively, "Semois isn't the one for you, is it?" and I'd answered with a reluctant nod.

Semois had been lovely: the beer was good, and the faith more than evident from all the brothers there. But there was no denying it was the mid-priced gray sedan of abbeys. An abbey too decent and well-engineered to say no to, but not the kind of thing to excite the heart. And I might as well stay at Mount Sergius with the people I already loved and my big hill and my creek if I wasn't going to fall in love with anywhere else.

Anyway, from Luxembourg to Paris we went—me

napping the whole way—and then we changed trains and headed south.

And now it was full daylight, and I could see farm fields and distant hills and dark hazes of small forests in the distance. Elijah has been writing in his laptop most of the time while I've been glued to the window like a kid, and I finally ask, "Are you working on your article?"

He finishes typing something as he shakes his head. "Emails right now. I'd pitched an article about how the work of TERF-y academics is helping fuel a wave of anti-trans legislation, and my editor said yes, but he's also assigned me a piece on a new Dior line and another one about whether or not the martini is dead, so I'm trying to plan out what I need to do when in order to get everything written on time. And also figure out whether I should drink a martini again before I decide it's dead in a national publication."

"The martini is a classic," I say.

"Vermouth is gross," he counters without looking at me, and he does have a point.

I return to staring out the window, and he continues typing.

An hour later, he abruptly shuts his laptop and looks at me.

"Why the Church?" he asks without warning. I can tell from the intensity in his voice that this has been bothering him for a while…maybe even for the last several years. "You want to change your entire life, get away from it all, find yourself, whatever, I can understand that. But why *this* way? You'd never given a single genuflecting shit about church or Mass or anything, and then bam—monk. You didn't even try going vegan first."

I don't answer right away, rubbing at the scruff on my jaw as I search for an answer that doesn't stray too closely to the full truth of that night—although I'm beginning to wonder if telling him is inevitable. I hope not. I don't want to dump all that at his feet and make it seem like I'm trying to buy my way out of his justified anger at the way I left.

And also, even after years of therapy, I don't know if I can frame the events of that night in words. That is the cruelest thing about depression: it is at the edge of speech, at the very edge of what words can shape and describe.

"I was sent a Bible verse," I finally say, dropping my hand and looking at him. "That night. From a number I didn't know. I still don't know who sent it to me, actually. Only that it came when I needed to read it the most."

When the darkness had been eating the stars as I watched through my window. As it spilled around my feet and slicked between my toes. And then there'd been a flash of bluish light.

I lift my eyes to the hills.

"You got a Bible verse," Elijah repeats. "From a mystery number. And it made you decide to be a monk."

"It had been a hard night," I say honestly.

He drums his fingertips on the top of his laptop, that normally inscrutable mouth curving into a slight frown. "I remember," he says, his voice short.

"You do?" I ask, and then a memory filters in, him in a suit, a vase of flowers in the trash.

"Ah," I say quietly. "The fight."

It had been swallowed up by the rest of the night in my mind, since it had been merely the cracked door which had let in the demons who'd been chasing me for years. It had been awful, yes, but the rest of the night had been so much worse.

Elijah works his jaw to the side. "Yes, Aiden. The fight."

"For what it's worth," I say, "I am sorry. I am still so very, very sorry."

"I'm sure you are," he says.

He'd wanted to surprise me that night. Dinner, flowers, a declaration of love. But in typical Aiden fashion, I'd shown up late and half-drunk from a dinner celebrating a new deal at work.

It wasn't unusual for me—I was late to a lot of things or I missed them altogether. I showed up a mess or I turned into a mess when I was there. Sometimes it was for easy-to-understand reasons, like a meeting running long, like oversleeping after an international flight. And sometimes they were for less easy-to-understand reasons—reasons I couldn't even articulate if I'd tried.

Like sometimes I would truly, *really* mean to remember something, but I'd get sucked into something else—work, play, whatever—and not realize that hours and hours had slipped by. Sometimes it would be because I'd get home after a long day of work and know I'd need to change to meet Elijah at some event or party, but I'd sink down onto my bed and find myself literally unable to move. And it wouldn't be that I'd forgotten that the event was important to my boyfriend, and it wouldn't even be that I didn't *want* to go, because often I did. It was more like my pilot light would suddenly go out, and there would be nothing left to animate me, no heat or energy or life at all. Like being sunk into liquid concrete, sunk into a substance where even the slightest movement required superhuman effort.

But how do you explain that to a disappointed boyfriend and not have it sound like, "I chose to stare at a wall instead of come to the thing you explicitly told me was important to you?"

You don't. You can't.

I know because I tried.

I reach out now and touch Elijah's wrist…the first time we've touched since last night. I trail my fingers up to clasp his forearm, waiting for him to meet my gaze.

When he does, whatever he sees there makes his shoulders drop the tiniest bit. And then slowly—so slowly that I think he's going to change his mind at any moment—he rolls his arm so that his palm is up and his fingers are holding my forearm too. It's not like holding hands; it feels more like we're holding each other *here*, in this place, in this moment.

He lets out a long breath and says after a minute, quietly, "I thought that's why you left."

"The fight?"

He nods and horror slides through me. I shake my head. "*No*," I say empathically. "Elijah, no. I left because *I* was fucked up, and leaving seemed like the only way to fix myself and stop hurting everyone else. If I'd known that you'd thought…"

But how could I have known? I left without a word and came back only to drop the key to the farmhouse in his hand. And even then, I was still too lost in the fires of my own mind to speak with him, to give him a proper explanation. The only goal I'd had was to disappear from the world as quickly as possible.

"No," I say again, catching his gaze. "Elijah, I didn't leave because of the fight."

There's a line between his brows again and a frown curving the sharp edges of his mouth, like maybe he doesn't entirely believe me, and I realize that I'm going to have to tell him the truth at some point. Maybe not even at some point— maybe soon.

Maybe now.

But before I can think of how to start, what to say, the train pulls to a stop, and the sleeping woman in back wakes up to leave. I reluctantly let go of Elijah and he of me, as she stands up and the half-crowded train platform comes into view.

As my fingers slide down his tattoo, I realize I'm the right direction to properly see the collage. The grid which I now recognize as the grid of streets from our neighborhood. The tree which I now see is the tree from his backyard with tiny little rungs leading up to a tiny treehouse in its branches. And the words inked in a small, typewritten font under the collage. They are in Latin, and I have enough grasp of the dead language now to know what they mean.

Quid si.

My heart flips over, once, inside my chest.

It means: *what if.*

I look up at him, and he looks back at me, and I can't tell what he's thinking. Not at all.

What if.

He'd put that on his body…why? As a remembrance? As a reminder? I open my mouth to ask, but then other people begin boarding the train and he pulls his arm off the table and clears his throat.

And I want to ask anyway—or I want to spill the truth of that night—or at least I want to touch him again, but the train is crowded again, and what I might have done without much hesitation in Paris is a different kind of calculus now, so deep in an unfamiliar countryside.

It's not until I look out the window as the train starts moving that I remember the other limit to touching him in public.

I'm in my full monk robes today, scapular, belt, and all.

CHAPTER THIRTY-FOUR

Our Lady of the Fountains reveals itself like a little brooch stuck into the folds of a scarf. Steep hills rear up everywhere, all rocks and trees, and then we are plunged into a thick ribbon of lavender. Fields and fields of it in the flat bottom of the valley, its scent filling the inside of the car immediately.

And nestled among all this green and purple is the abbey itself, a small cluster of buildings made of the same honey-colored stone the hills are made of. Between the tree-crowded slopes surrounding it, the sea of lavender, and the bright blue sky, the abbey's surroundings are a living postcard, and the abbey itself—over nine hundred years old—is just as venerable and lovely.

As the car rolls between the tall cypresses which line the drive to the campus, I feel the heavy mood from the train begin to lift. When I look over at Elijah, he's already looking back at me from behind his sunglasses, his mouth tilted in an almost smile.

And between Elijah's almost smile and the sharp scent of

lavender and wild herbs crowding along the sides of the road, I'm already in love with this place.

Which is strange, because it was *St. Columba's* my heart quickened at, it was St. Columba's that matched everything I knew I needed, not this happy Provençal retreat.

You haven't been to St. Columba's yet, I assure myself. *You'll love it the most when you get there.*

Our driver is Brother Luc, a young monk with light golden skin and a close-cropped beard, and he is much chattier than Brother Xavier was at Semois, telling us about the history of the area and of the abbey as we roll to a stop in the gravel parking lot. He helps us unload our suitcases, and then he leads us to the small guesthouse—a low-slung stone building studded with small round windows and narrow wooden doors.

"We only have one other guest at the moment," he says, "because we will start harvesting the lavender soon, and the abbey is quite different during the harvest, since we are so busy. Not good for visitors. But you are not regular visitors—and our other guest is a visiting priest—so Abbé Bernard thinks you won't mind that we will be so busy." Brother Luc's French accent turns every word into a soft melody—much different than the harder, faster French of Luxembourg or Paris. It seems to match the landscape somehow, like even the words here are sunny and happy and ready to smile.

"We won't mind at all," I tell him as he opens an unlocked door on the far end of the guesthouse, and we walk into the cool, shaded hallway. "And I'm happy to help with anything you need when it comes to the harvest."

"We may accept your offer, because there is always so much to be done," Brother Luc says. And then he adds, "How do you feel about bees?"

"Bees?" Elijah repeats warily.

"Bees," Brother Luc confirms happily as we walk. "They pollinate the lavender and then we harvest their honey and sell it. We use it in the beer too. Ah, voici! The room is all ready for you, and the one down the hall is ready as well."

I step into the cell he indicates and can't help but smile. It is furnished as sparsely as one would imagine a Trappist cell to be, with a narrow wooden bed, a small desk, and a crucifix on the wall, but somehow, it's still like the rest of Our Lady of the Fountains. Bright with sunshine pouring in, everything clean and fresh and pleasant beyond belief.

Elijah wheels his suitcase into his room and returns as Brother Luc hands us a small hand-drawn map of the abbey and points out the refectory, brewhouse, apiary, and the other outbuildings.

"The rest of the brothers are having a meeting now," Brother Luc explains, "so we won't be able to greet you properly until after dinner. And I must warn you that during the harvest, we keep the little hours on our own—stopping to pray wherever we are and then getting back to work. So I'm afraid you're visiting at a time when our daily rhythm is less..." he seems to search for the right word in English. "Traditional."

"We're very modern men," Elijah says smoothly. "Is there anything you'd like us to do before dinner? Or after?"

"You are completely free," Brother Luc says. "As are all

visitors here. I imagine Brother Patrick would like to pray the major hours with us, but they are not compulsory for guests. In fact, Abbé Bernard told me to tell you that he wishes for you to feel like a—oh, what is the word? Observer? Very new— before a postulant. And here, our observers are not expected to be so strict with their attendance; they are invited to spend their days discerning if they are meant for this place. Or rather, if this place is meant for them."

Brother Luc glances at his watch and then flashes us another wide smile. "There's plenty of beer stocked in the refectory if you'd like some to cool off with. The grounds are yours, and we'll see you in a couple hours for dinner."

Brother Luc leaves with a clasp of hands and a swish of his black scapular layered over his white Trappist robes, and then it's just me and Elijah.

"Want to explore?" he asks at the same time I say, "Want to get a beer?"

We do both, and with cold, unlabeled bottles of beer in hand, we wander out to the lavender fields. Bees buzz everywhere, fat and fuzzy, and a faint breeze nods the purple heads of the flowers as we walk down one of the unnervingly straight rows. In the distance, I see monks milling around a stone farm building that looks older than the country I'm from, and up in the hills, I see the roof of a medieval chapel built over one of the springs that Our Lady of the Fountains is named for, according to Brother Luc.

Elijah follows my gaze up to the hill, coming to stand next to me. His fingers around the neck of his beer brush against mine, and even here in the July sun, even this close to the Mediterranean Sea, I shiver.

"Were any saints beheaded up there for those springs?" Elijah asks, nodding toward the hill. "Or perhaps a singing fish led a parched hermit to the water or something?"

"Don't be ridiculous," I say. "The Virgin Mary appeared on that hill to weep over a sick child. The springs appeared as her tears fell to the ground, and the child was healed by their waters after."

"I can't imagine why I didn't guess that," Elijah says, taking a drink.

"Let's go up there," I suggest suddenly. "It doesn't look like too bad a climb, and we still have plenty of time before dinner."

"All right," Elijah agrees, which is how we find ourselves at the top of the hill twenty minutes later, panting and sweaty and also smelling of all the thyme and rosemary we crushed on our way up the hill.

But it's undeniably worth it. Guarded by a mix of umbrella pines, white oak, and a few rogue beeches, the chapel overlooks the purple seam of the valley and reveals the craggy, tree-choked hills rumpling the landscape all the way down to the sea.

And then when we go inside the chapel itself, we are greeted with a shock of cool, cool air. A well was built around the holy spring and it now burbles sweetly in the corner of the chapel, leaving the place temperate and damp even in the bright heat of summer.

There's an altar made of stone that looks like it hasn't been used in at least a hundred years, but the wooden pews are solid and untouched by rot, and set on a windowsill, there's—what else?—a small box for donations.

"You think they say Mass up here?" Elijah asks.

I watch as he runs a long finger along the edge of the altar. "No," I say absently. "It's been deconsecrated for some time. The abbey says it's simply a place for contemplation for visitors these days."

Elijah turns and looks at me, his lower lip catching between his teeth as his eyes trail down to my chest and shoulders and then back up to my face. "Do you think we have it to ourselves?" he asks softly.

I swallow. "Yeah."

I move first, but he's just as quick, and suddenly we are caught up in each other, my hands in his silk blend T-shirt, his in my scapular and then in my habit, and our mouths together, seeking and hot. And this is why I couldn't properly pray last night, this is why excitement has been thrumming under my skin all day.

Because somehow I knew this would happen.

I knew we weren't ready to stop.

Elijah sighs with something like relief the moment I lick into his mouth, like he's been waiting for my kiss his entire life, and then he's tugging on me and we're stumbling sideways until he's sitting down on a pew and pulling me down to straddle him.

"I'm too big," I murmur between kisses, but his hands are

already pushing my robe up past my thighs.

"I like it," he breathes against me. "I like you big." His hands are on the bare skin of my thighs now, sliding up to my boxer briefs. His fingertips slide between the tight fabric and my skin, and then he gently scratches his way back down, sending goose bumps pebbling everywhere under my robe.

"You're wearing your cage again," he says, as his fingertips finally graze the metal ring banding around the base of my sex.

I groan at the touch. My cock is trying *so hard* to fill, to thicken, and the exposed shaft above the rest of the cage is unbearably sensitive. And then he starts touching my testicles, teasing touches and fondles and tugs, until I break off our kiss and I'm breathing hard into his neck.

"The game we played in the ruins," he says, his experienced hands playing so skillfully under my habit. "I keep thinking about it. About that poor monk who's so desperate to fuck that he'll beg a stranger to let him suck his cock."

"Yeah?"

"I keep thinking about what else he'd do. How much he must…ache…" Elijah's fingers stray farther—deliberately, probingly—and then I feel the light brush of his fingers over my hole. Sensation tingles along the delicate skin long after his touch drifts away, sinking its way deeper and deeper into me, deep into my belly. It curls and hooks around the base of my spine, and I have to brace my hands on the back of the pew to keep from crushing him entirely as I shudder through it.

Because I do, I do ache. Despite my release last night, and the tepid, half-releases while in chastity, I'm miserable. As if all the years of celibacy are finally catching up with me all at once, swelling me and filling me. My shaft is seeking any way out of its cage; my balls are heavy, twinging with something that's between pleasure and pain.

Need.

I find his mouth again and pant against his kiss as he strokes my entrance. Nothing more than strokes, nothing more than teases. And despite the certainty in his touch, there's a kind of hesitation there too. Almost like it's the first time we're doing this. Like we're making out for real, wanting so much more, but only kissing and touching because we don't know how much further the other person will let us go.

"Can you fix it?" I breathe, my lips ghosting over his as I speak. "The ache?"

His other hand finds my hip and curls tight around it, holding me in place for his fingers to push against me. "Yeah," he rasps.

"I want you to fuck it away," I tell him, pressing my forehead to his. "I want you to fuck me until I'm empty, until I'm drained all the way dry."

That had been the idea behind my cages, once upon a time. We'd bought them as toys, thinking he'd lock me up for days and days, until I was bursting to come, and then he would fuck the denied seed right out of me. It turned out that both of us were too impatient to spend much time on delayed gratification, and so we never really finished that game. My two cages sat in a drawer until I was packing my bag for Mount Sergius, when I'd grabbed them on a whim, somehow intuiting that quitting sex cold turkey was going to require some extra help. Padlock-level help.

"Fuck, yes," Elijah groans, and we're kissing so hard now, him dragging me all the way down to his lap, where I can feel his erection swollen underneath me. Our tongues fuck the way our bodies want to, urgent and hard, and then I give up trying to keep my weight off him.

I settle onto his thighs and let my hands roam over the muscles of his arms and shoulders and over the sculpted contours of his throat and chest. I do what I once spent a year doing—what I spent all my twenties wishing I'd had the courage to do—and I trace over his perfect face with my fingers, following the rise of his cheekbones and the curve of his nose. Finding those eyebrows which show his every thought, the jaw that tenses so often around me, the corners of the mouth I was always so desperate to make smile.

And his hands are all over me too, greedy, a little desperate, and I don't know if it's the years between us, or the monk's robes currently pushed up around my thighs, or the fact that this moment is so very, very stolen and we have no idea when we'll get another, but we're touching each other like we'll have to sketch each other from memory later.

Like memory is all we'll have.

"I love sitting in your lap," I confess after a long moment of nothing but kissing. His hand has found its way back to my rim again, and he's still teasing me there, still tickling me there.

"Is that so?" he murmurs, kissing his way to bite at my stubbled jaw.

"I wish I would have done it years ago," I whisper. "All those times you were over with Sean. I wish I would have crawled right onto your lap and made you kiss me."

There's a new tension in his body when I speak, but when I pull back to see the burn in his eyes, I know it's a good tension. A hungry tension.

"I wish you would have too," he says, moving both hands to my hips and holding me down against his lap. It seems to escape neither of us that this is a position for fucking, that we're so close to it, so close after so long. His lips are parted as he looks down at where my thighs straddle him, at where his hands hold me under my habit. "I remember coming over to pick up Sean to go out for my twenty-third birthday—do you remember? You were eighteen then, and it must have been almost a year since I'd seen you, maybe more. And you were out by the pool, wearing nothing but boxer shorts because you couldn't be bothered to put your trunks on." He lets out a shaky breath. "It was the first time I saw you and realized you weren't a kid anymore, and I *wanted* you. I wanted you so suddenly and so much that nothing else mattered, not my friendship with Sean, not the schism between our families after Lizzy's death. I wanted to stalk out to that pool and push you down onto a lounge chair and kiss you until you agreed to anything I wanted."

I stare at him, stunned. "I had no idea. You noticed me that early? I thought…I thought it wasn't until the gala, until years later—"

He's already shaking his head, his mouth in a rueful twist.

"I saw you that day, and nothing was the same for me. Nothing."

"Then why didn't you say anything?"

He blows out a long breath, his hands easing a little on my hips, but his thumbs now rubbing possessive circles there. "Because as horny as I was, all those things did still matter. My friendship with Sean mattered. The shit between our families mattered. It mattered that you were eighteen and at the time, twenty-three felt like a creepy age to be wanting a college freshman. And," he says with a lifted eyebrow, "in my defense, you were in the pants of every girl your age in a five-parish radius. I thought you were straight."

I huff out a laugh. "Me too." Even after college when I'd realized that I wanted to fuck *everybody*, it was still too easy to compare every man I'd met to Elijah. No one else was as smart as him, as sophisticated as him. No one was as considerate or as dryly funny—or as clear about who he was and about what he believed.

No one else was him, period.

"I sometimes feel guilty that I didn't do things sooner. That I didn't do things the right way," I say.

"There's a right way?" he asks. We aren't really making out anymore or even groping each other, but he still has his hands on my hips and I still have mine on his shoulders. It feels like the horny version of slow dancing. It's amazing.

"I don't know," I say. "I guess I feel like I should have been Aiden Bell, Bisexual more quickly. It took me until I was in my thirties to tell my dad and my brothers, and even then I felt like I was stumbling into it."

I'll never forget the look on Sean's face that night, after he'd found Elijah at my farmhouse. He'd been stunned—and stung. Stung that he hadn't known, stung that I hadn't told him. I'd had to inform him that it wasn't actually about him and his feelings—it was about *me*, and Elijah too, in a way. It was about when I would be ready. Me. No one else.

But then Mom died.

She died without knowing about the most important person in my life, she died without knowing about a very, very important part of me, and after that...

I don't know. I guess *ready* felt different then. I told the rest of my brothers and my dad, and I started bringing Elijah to work functions and things like that. Family had been easy, work a little harder.

But Elijah had been worth any amount of hard.

I think for a moment, and then add, "I should have been braver too. Brave like you were."

Elijah looks down. Not at my thighs, but at my belt, where a small wooden rosary hangs. "It didn't feel brave," he says after a minute. "You know? Or quick. I'd known I was gay since middle school, but I waited until college to come out to my parents. I kept thinking that eventually I'd find the right words, the perfect moment to say them in. Like one day I'd wake up, and there'd be an angel of the Lord in my bedroom telling me that today was the day and not to have any fear, because the Holy Spirit would teach me the right words to say." He gives a little noise then, a small laugh. It's not bitter or cynical. It's almost affectionate, as if he wishes he could travel back twenty years and give that version of himself a hug. "In the end, I had no choice. You know my parents—a judge and chief physician at our biggest hospital? They're all over our city. They'd hear about me dating someone the minute it happened, and I knew it would be so much worse if they found out that way instead of from me."

He pulls his hand out from under my habit and takes the small crucifix of the rosary between his fingers.

"I learned then that there's so much room between a best-case scenario and a worst-case scenario. That they could listen to what I was saying, and that they could say so many of the right things back, and yet there could be so much else that was unsaid too. And so I do sometimes wish that I had waited longer. Not for the angel to appear in my bedroom, but maybe a few more months, when I was more certain of what my adult life was going to look like, and after I'd spent more time with queer friends and heard more of their stories. Maybe if I'd waited those few months, it would have been easier for me."

He gently sets the crucifix back against the fabric of my habit, looking up to meet my stare. "There's no one right way, Aiden. Even running off to become a monk isn't the wrong way."

"Maybe I just wish I hadn't wasted all that time," I say softly. "That we'd had more time together."

He doesn't reply, but he tucks his lip between his teeth and his eyes are full of things I can't quite decipher.

And I feel so full right now, so full of every feeling, and I'm not supposed to be here in my ex-boyfriend's lap with his hands all over me and my mouth chafed from his stubble, but also I can't be anywhere else, and it's a problem for later, it's a confession for later, everything else can wait. Because right now he is my pillar of flame in the desert, my light, my urgency.

Elijah's watch chimes, and he looks down at it and then closes his eyes.

"We need to go if we don't want to be late for dinner," he says, reluctance in his voice, and indeed, there's reluctance even in his hands as it takes me pulling against him for him to let me go.

I can't bring myself to assure him that we'll kiss again, or to tell him that I'm dying to play our little monk game from earlier. Speaking the sins against celibacy out loud seems worse than committing them, somehow.

So instead I straighten my robes and find our beer bottles, and by the time I'm done, he's waiting for me at the chapel door, framed in the colors of encroaching evening. He once again looks like a stained-glass saint, and it's blasphemous maybe that the sight of his beauty pushes a prayer out of my soul. A prayer of pure love, pure gratitude to God that Elijah exists. That he is here and beautiful and perfect, and God has made him so.

Like an apple tree among the trees of the forest is my beloved among the young men.

His mouth is sweetness itself; he is altogether lovely.

This is my beloved, this is my friend.

266

CHAPTER
THIRTY-FIVE

Dinner is a simple but delicious affair of bread, oil, and herbs, and a creamy seafood soup called bourride, all of it set off by the light honey beer they brew here at the abbey. (It's as delicious as Brother Xavier made it sound—crisp and floral and the perfect amount of sweet.) And while the meal is silent in theory, it's a light silence that settles easily over the room.

At Semois, there was a thickness to the quietude that made it feel watchful, almost like a sentient thing, but here the silence comes as gently as a breeze, lifted by smiles and the inevitable happy food noises that we all make as we eat. Noises that turn in *ahhh*s and excited claps when two of the brothers emerge from the kitchen with cast iron skillets of something called flaugnarde—which is a custard-y thing made of sweet batter and fresh fruit from the abbey's small grove of fruit trees.

I finish Elijah's serving for him when he can't eat it all, much to his amusement.

And then afterward, like another soft breeze, the silence

drifts away, and conversation fills it. We help clear away the meal from the long wooden trestle tables, and then Abbé Bernard invites us into the cloister for more beer and proper introductions.

The cloister is surrounded by covered walkways, all made of stone and original to the original twelfth-century abbey. Between each arch is a low but deep ledge, perfect for sitting on, and the monks quickly find spots that seem to be personal favorites, sitting cross-legged or with knees pulled up, chatting as they wait for Brother Luc to return with the beer. A fountain trickles brightly in the middle, like it wants to chat with us too.

There are only thirty monks here, which is a little surprising given how much they produce. The lavender itself accounts for several different products—soaps and essential oils and eaux de toilette—and then there is the honey, which is sold on its own and turned into candies and nougats. And of course, there is the brewing operation that creates the rarest beer in the world, the beer that people are willing to steal from literal, actual monks for.

"How do you manage with so few people?" I ask the abbot as I accept the bottle of beer Brother Luc is handing me. "Without letting work take over everything?"

Abbé Bernard thinks for a moment. He is a short, clean-shaven man with deep brown skin and faint smile lines around his eyes. He is often smiling, I notice, especially when he's looking at his little family of monks—the majority of whom are around my age or slightly above, which is shockingly young for an abbey.

"It is a challenge, I suppose," the abbot says in a deep French accent. "We are mandated to be self-sufficient, and yet our true purpose is knowing Christ through contemplation and prayer. St. Benedict says himself in the Rule that he wants nothing too harsh or too rigorous for a monastic life, but in order to earn our abbey's keep, we must work hard. But how to do this without losing sight of why we are here to begin with?" He shakes his head, as if this is a question he puzzles over often.

I think of what Brother Luc had told Elijah and me earlier, about keeping the small hours. "But you are flexible too— stopping to pray where you are in the lavender fields, for example. Surely that's a good compromise between the *ora* and the *labora* parts of our creed?"

"I hope so," he replies, and he's still smiling, but there's a certain thoughtful distance to his gaze as he surveys the cloister full of monks. "But deciding which adaptations keep our prayers at the center of our lives and which are edging us toward becoming something we are not requires discernment. Discernment which I'm concerned is overshadowed by worldly concerns."

"Adaptations are good, though, aren't they?" Elijah asks, leaning his shoulder against a wide stone column lining the edge of the cloister. "If monasteries didn't adapt, you'd still be selling wool and brewing beer in wooden tubs. And if the Church didn't adapt, women would still be covering their hair in church while they listened to a Latin Mass."

The abbot nods, but his eyes are on the monks lounging and drinking beer. "In nearly every other environment, a word like *compromise* is a very good word indeed. And truthfully, there is much that I wish Rome was willing to change about itself today—my English is not so good that I can speak of the subtle differences between words like *compromise* and *adapt* without changing to French—but I can say that I see changes meant to open the arms of the Church very differently from changes which open our time with God to concerns like money and capital improvement schemes.

"To paraphrase—what will it profit us to repair the bell tower or invest in a new fermenting tank, if the real cost is our communion with God? Because it is so very easy to let that communion be nibbled away at, bit by bit. A prayer here, a period of lectio divina there, all to get a little further in our work, all to finish one last task. But tasks must make time for our souls, I think. Not the other way around. Even when your tasks are bound very tightly to your soul." Abbé Bernard's smile deepens a little as he turns to look at Elijah. "You are a journalist, n'est-ce pas? I think you must understand this too."

Elijah nods, and even though his demeanor is all polite sophistication, I can see that the abbot has made him consider something. Maybe something about me, because his eyes slide over to my face as he answers. "I'm beginning to."

"Now," the abbot says, straightening up and clapping once like a party host who's realized they've neglected something. "Abbot Jerome told me you're here to write an article. You can see how bad we are at staying silent like good Trappists—you must go interview my brothers and then their idle words will still serve some good in this lifetime!"

Elijah, who has been carrying his little leather notebook with him, drains the last of his beer and nods. "Yes, yes, definitely. Thank you."

I extend my hand for his empty bottle—a habit left over from the year of being his date to every arty and pretentious event in the city—and the abbot seems to notice, his eyes dipping to where our fingers brush as Elijah hands me the bottle and then starts searching out monks to talk with.

A zing of defiant panic fries up my nervous system to my brain and then back out to my nerves again, and I have to remind myself that I didn't do anything too telling. We just passed a bottle between us, we just accidentally brushed fingers, nothing more. And I'd checked my jaw and neck for love bites after the chapel, and I'm certain no one else had been up there with us...

But the abbot merely deepens his smile and nods over at the cart. "You may put it there if you like. We'll send it out for sanitizing and then reuse it."

I do as he asks, and he's waiting where I left him when I return. There's nothing in his face to make me think that he's cataloguing the way Elijah and I had touched, and I clamp down on the urge to say something about it. Something like *he's family* or *we've known each other since I was born* or *I was really worried he wouldn't recycle that bottle.* Even though the last thing would one hundred percent be a lie—Elijah always recycles, even the really annoying-to-recycle things like plastic bubble mailers and printer cartridges—and the other two options feel too shitty to even think about saying, even if they're technically true. It feels too close to denying Elijah, and even though we aren't together and can never be together again, I can't bring myself to do it.

"Brother Luc tells me you've offered to help with the harvest tomorrow," the abbot says, and I relax infinitesimally. Maybe he didn't think anything was too familiar or habitual about that bottle hand-off at all. Maybe I'm overthinking this.

"Yes," I reply, trying very hard not to look over at Elijah now, even though I can hear him speaking flawless French to a monk sitting on the edge of the fountain. At least, I assume it's flawless French—aside from this trip, my experience with French was mostly limited to Lumiere from *Beauty and the Beast* and the weird guy from the Matrix sequels.

"This is very good," the abbot says. "I know you are here to get a sense of our abbey life and what it's like to live here, and the harvest is our life in a microcosm, I suppose. Hard work, and yet also striving for intimacy with God."

"That's what I want," I respond, although when I speak the words, my mind doesn't conjure up images of flickering candles and stained glass. Instead, I think of Elijah's hand under my habit. I think of kissing him in the Semois ruins, kissing him so hard it hurt. I exhale quickly, trying to clear my mind. "It's what I want more than anything else."

"Abbot Jerome said as much. That you were looking for a life more austere than what you had at Mount Sergius. I have to warn you that while we keep our prayers and silences, there is too much of God's joy here for true asceticism. For the kind of stark austerity that so many people seek."

I'd guessed as much, hadn't I, when I'd leafed through the

information about the abbeys I was visiting? That only St. Columba's could awaken me entirely, that it had to be that bleak and rocky place where I lost the last of myself?

But what if I was wrong? What if I'm better suited to lavender and olive trees and sunshine?

I think of the chapel and of Elijah's hands on the forbidden places of my body.

What if I'm not suited for this at all?

Elijah doesn't come to my room that night and I don't go to his, although it's all I can think about, all I can imagine and dream of. Brother Luc tells us that the other guest—an American priest—has been coming and going all week, sometimes sleeping outside under the stars, the way Brother Connor likes to do.

"A mystic," Brother Luc had confided as he showed us the communal bathrooms and where our towels would be. "You know the type. Seeing angels, hearing God. Il est dans la lune. I suppose he'll wander back to the abbey once he gets hungry, although I wouldn't be surprised if he was living off locusts and wild honey like Saint-Jean-Baptiste."

But despite how restlessly I sleep, morning comes fast, and with it come vigils and breakfast. Elijah is there for both, looking as composed as ever, and not at all like we spent yesterday afternoon making out and talking about him fucking me. Not at all like one of our *what if* games is hanging in the air like a summer storm.

We'll have time to talk later today, I tell myself. Although I know the reason I'm already tightening my thighs in anticipation is not because I'm thinking of talking. It's because I want more. I want kisses and touches and sex.

Sex.

I want it. I want it at the same time I'm praying lauds, at the same time I'm finding my breviary and letting Brother Luc and a stout Gallic monk named Dom Francis lead me out to the lavender fields. I want it as they're explaining the harvesting process to me—a by-hand method, since the bridge into the valley is too narrow for harvesting equipment.

And I definitely want it as I'm scanning the fields and watching the monks begin to unload bundles of green netting from a truck. "Have you seen Elijah?" I ask Brother Luc. "I didn't have a chance to ask him at breakfast if he was coming out with us."

Dom Francis, who understands English but who doesn't speak it, says something in French to Brother Luc, who nods as he listens.

"He says your friend went to Cavaillon with Brother Jean to pick up some copper pots we've had re-tinned."

"Oh," is my reply, which comes out sadder than I mean it to. But the disappointment which rolls through me is elemental in its force. It's not like I planned on making out with him in the lavender fields or anything, but after a week of being together all the time, being without him already feels painful, like we've had to be unstitched in order to be apart, and that's a bad feeling, that's very bad, because that's how I'm supposed to feel about God. That's how I *do* feel about God.

But if I'm stitched to God, then I can't be stitched to anyone else. That's the rule, that's been the basis of western monasticism for nearly two thousand years.

Give your life to God and to no one else. Give your life to God and don't count the minutes until you can sneak off with the hot journalist again.

And I have to wonder as I help Brother Luc and Dom Francis roll the netting down the long rows of bare earth between lavender plants if there's a way to do both, if anyone has ever found a way to do both. To live their life in prayer and silence and also with their heart beating inside someone else's chest at the same time.

"Vous allez avoir chaud," Dom Francis tells me, and I manage to scrape enough high school French together in my brain to realize he's telling me I'm going to get hot in my black Benedictine robes while working in the sun.

In fact, now that I look, I'm the only one in robes at all. Everyone else is wearing the same kind of thing we wear at Mount Sergius for work like this—old T-shirts and jeans.

"You can take the habit off," Brother Luc tells me. "The abbey isn't open to the public during the harvest."

I make a face. "I only have underwear on under this."

Both monks stare back at me, like *and?*

"Like I don't have pants or a shirt on under my habit," I explain.

Dom Francis seems not to understand at all, but it seems to dawn on Brother Luc. "I forget you are American," he says.

"You will be fine in your underthings."

"Or maybe I'll be fine in the robes," I mumble, thinking of how short my boxer briefs are. At least the cage is discreet enough that I'm not worried about it being obvious, but you know what's really not discreet? A big tattoo of a dove with a Flamin' Hot Cheeto in its mouth.

Dom Francis shakes his head with a grin and hands me another bundle of netting as he mutters something in French.

"He says that you'll be cooked like a duck in its own fat if you remain so stubborn. Even Bernard of Clairvaux would admit defeat to the July heat."

I take the netting and start unrolling it, taking care to tuck its edges under the tufts of lavender so it can catch all the harvested flowers. "I'll take that under consideration."

"L'humilité est une vertu," Dom Francis mutters, "surtout l'humilité pour *le soleil*."

Six hours later and the robes are long gone, folded in a pile next to the small electric truck the monks use to haul the lavender to their distillery. I'm in nothing but boxer briefs, sweaty all over and flocked with lavender petals, and I'm happier than I can remember being in a long time. Yes, my back and shoulders ache from trimming the lavender flowers with the handheld gas-powered trimmer, and yes, it's so fucking hot out here that I keep sweating off the sunscreen Dom Francis handed me early on (along with a series of untranslatable jokes about my tattoo). But deep breezes plunge through the valley often enough to cool us down, and the scent of freshly cut lavender is everywhere, and all around me, the brothers in their own lavender rows sing and talk and laugh.

Three times the bells have rung, and three times we have all stopped where we were to pray the small hours. We murmured psalms and sung hymns, and though we were all scattered apart, we were together too. There was something about it, keeping the small hours in this way, that felt more natural than it had at Semois, where you could barely start something before it was time to march back to the church. Here the tasks are made to make room for the soul, just as Abbé Bernard wished, here the soul is first. But here at Our Lady of the Fountains, the soul can come first anywhere. Here the soul can sing in a valley of lavender just as loud as it can in a room made for singing, and I wonder—can I know God differently here than I can anywhere else? Is this feeling between me and God right now as I'm singing the psalms in the lavender a feeling I can only have *here*? If I did this exact same thing at Mount Sergius or Semois, would it feel the same?

Will it be the same at St. Columba's, the abbey I have my heart set on?

But as I cut more flowers and help the other monks carry armloads of them to the truck, I think for the very first time that maybe I was wrong, maybe St. Columba's isn't for me at all. Maybe I was made for a place like this, where the tasks make room for the soul and where the chapels are filled with kisses...

Stop. That's hardly a trait of Our Lady of the Fountains.

That would hardly be my future if I stayed here. And anyway, I can't let myself think that way. I can't let myself think of it all. Because thinking about it means I'll have to name it to myself, name all the ways my chastity is falling apart in my hands, and if my chastity is falling apart, then so is my obedience, so is my honesty. So is my devotion to God.

And so therefore, is my future taking solemn vows and living ascetically ever after on a cold sea cliff.

I drop an armful of lavender into the bed of the little truck and then turn to see Elijah standing there, sunglasses on, looking like he just strolled off some Parisian magazine shoot in his black-and-white striped T-shirt, dark jeans, and white, low-top sneakers. The strap of his leather satchel pulls diagonally across his chest, highlighting the toned muscles underneath.

He's standing there, staring at me from behind his sunglasses, and I can see nothing of his expression really, just that his mouth is pressed together and that a single eyebrow lifts above the frame of his shades. Like he's looking at something ridiculous, and I *am* ridiculous, so I give him a giant grin.

"So on the scale of Aiden Bell, where does this rank?" I ask.

"You mean, where does nearly naked and covered in flower petals rank against jumping into a fountain with a tie around your head?"

Man, a fountain swim sounds really nice right now. "Yes."

He shakes his head, the corner of his mouth pressing in, like he can't decide whether to smile or pity me. "I'm not sure. You, um. Are you going to put your habit on again?"

My grin fades a little. And then a lot. Because the times we've been together in the past week have been in the dark—or I've been fully dressed—and this is the first time he's really seen me in almost five years, the first time he's seen my body since it's changed. There's dark hair covering my chest now, and my stomach—a stomach that is no longer flat and rippling with muscle but is now solid and undeniably convex.

Perhaps I wouldn't be self-conscious if it weren't *so* different from my old body. My vodka-and-protein-shake body. And right now, with the way Elijah is looking at me, with the way his question hangs in the air—as if he's trying to save me from embarrassing myself—I feel like a caveman. Big and clumsy and hairy, and so far away from the man I used to be, and I'm reaching for my habit before I even fully digest this feeling. And I shouldn't care anyway, because it *doesn't matter*. The bigness and wideness of it not mattering can't be measured in miles or kilometers, but in vows of the soul and pledges of the heart. Not in distance and decisions, but in fireflies in the cloister.

But even with it not mattering, it matters, and my face burns a little as I pull my habit over my head and zip it up to my throat.

"Bien," Brother Luc says to me, as he walks up with another monk whose name I can't remember. "You are ready to head back."

"Back for what?" Elijah asks.

"Naps, of course!" Brother Luc says with a laugh. "Best part of the day."

"I'll need to shower before I do anything," I say as the two monks climb into the little truck. "I'm gross and covered in petals."

"If you don't want to nap," Brother Luc says, "you should see the grotto behind the chapel. Many pilgrims come to visit it—it's said the shrine there is where the Virgin first cried her tears for the sick child."

"C'était d'abord un sanctuaire païen, mais on ne le dit pas aux visiteurs," the other monk says and Elijah laughs.

"It was a pagan shrine first, but we don't tell the visitors that," Elijah translates for me.

"And maybe you will find our missing American priest while you're up there, hm?" Brother Luc says before starting the truck. "Tell him to come down and eat something other than locusts."

With a wave, they drive off, and I look to Elijah. "Grotto after I shower?" I ask.

"I thought you'd never ask."

CHAPTER
THIRTY-SIX

The grotto is old, pretty, and also very creepy. It's the entrance to a small cave, flooded with water from a spring inside, and guarded by weathered stone statues of the Virgin and some other saints, which stare at us with sightless eyes as we approach.

I don't know as much about pagans and history as my brother Tyler does, but even based on my limited knowledge, the place has a super pagan vibe to me. The water swirling at the Virgin's feet; the gnarled trees interrupted by upthrust crags of limestone and clumps of yellow-flowered woad.

Elijah takes his sunglasses off and tucks them into the collar of his shirt, squatting down to dip his fingertips in the water. His jeans pull tight around his thighs and ass as he does, and I vividly remember how it felt to crowd him against the wall in the hermitage, and I want it. I want it again. Him and me, touching, and then he lifts his head to look at me, and I know he sees the wanting all over my face.

His lips part, and he slowly stands up, and maybe he

doesn't mind my new body so much, because he steps toward me with dark, hungry eyes.

And then his phone rings.

My first thought is *really? Reception up here on Pagan Water Hill?*

My second thought is *who would be calling us now?* It's got to be balls early back home.

"Is it Sean?" I ask. "Or Zenny? Are they up with the babies? Answer it and make them show us the babies on FaceTime—"

Elijah shakes his head slowly as he holds the phone in his hand like it's a live grenade. "It's not Sean or Zenny," he says. "It's Jamie."

"Oh," I say. And then it hits me even deeper. "Oh."

Eyes on his screen, Elijah lets out a long, trembling exhale. And then he silences the call.

"Elijah," I say, not sure what I want to tell him, but knowing I need to say *something*. Apart from telling me that it was okay to blow him in the ruins at Semois, he hasn't breathed a word about him and Jamie, or about the engagement, and I suddenly wonder why, why he hasn't brought it up, and maybe it's because I've assumed wrong, and he and Jamie are actually still together...

Elijah looks up at me, and whatever he sees there makes him exhale again. "We ended our engagement," he says after a minute. "If that's what you're wondering."

I just blink at him. It's what I've hoped, and hated myself for hoping, for all sorts of reasons, and even in the middle of my relief and the murky guilt spawned by that relief, I feel doubt too, because a broken engagement doesn't necessarily mean a broken relationship, or broken love. He might still be *with* Jamie, even if they're not getting married. He might still love him.

And I have no right to care, but goddammit, I do.

Elijah laces his fingers behind his neck and walks away from the grotto, and then back toward it, his satchel bumping against his thigh as he turns.

"*I* ended the engagement," Elijah clarifies. "I came home from Mount Sergius, and I told him what happened, and he wanted—he was ready to—"

He stops pacing and drops his hands to his sides.

"He was ready to forgive me," he says dully. "He thought it was just an understandable lapse. An innocent mistake. Like there's something understandable about cheating on your fiancé. Like there was anything innocent about how we kissed that day."

The apology I need to say—what I should have said that day and every day since—crowds against my lips and tumbles out. "Elijah, I'm so sorry," I say. The wind threatens to blow my words away before they can reach him, and I step forward, coming close enough to touch him. "I'm so, so sorry for what happened that day. For what happened between you and Jamie."

"I know," he says.

And I finally speak aloud the fear I've felt since he told me *I can* at Semois. "But you can't choose me," I whisper. "You can't choose me. Because I can't choose you back."

His eyes glitter in the sunlight—liquid shadows ringed with dark, dark gold.

"I know," he says again.

But then his hands are in my habit and scapular, yanking me close, yanking me to his mouth, which is hot and angry against mine, and then we are kissing, fumbling for each other, and Elijah says, "I know," again, in a breathless rush against my lips, and then I say the magic words. The ones he'd inked on his arm in Latin.

"What if…?"

He pulls away, mouth wet and pupils blown wide. "Yes," he says, not even waiting for me to finish the sentence. "Yes."

He grabs my wrist and he's hauling me off somewhere—to the chapel, I realize as we pass back into the woods—and we're both rushing now, practically jogging, until we crash through the wooden door of the empty chapel and we're all over each other again, his hands yanking impatiently at my habit as I'm trying to pop open the button of his jeans.

"You're desperate for it," Elijah whispers, pulling me deeper and deeper into the cool shadows of the chapel. "You'll do anything for it."

Yes, yes, this is the game, this is the *what if.* I'm a monk who's aching, dying, pleading. He's the stranger wicked enough to take advantage of it. It's the only game I want to play for the rest of my life, this one where I'm shoving my hands down the front of his pants and he is dropping his satchel to the floor so he can shove me back against the stone altar.

"I'll do anything," I beg, rubbing my face against his jaw, his neck. He smells like sage and soap and Elijah, and his scruff chafes against my lips and cheeks. He smells like how I hope God smells. Clean and botanical and real.

I find the stiff length of him behind his zipper, and he gives a ragged groan that has my toes curling in my shoes.

"Anything," I mumble against his neck, my breath practically punched out of me by lust, because he's so huge and hot in my hand, so alive, so necessary. "I'll do anything."

"Oh, I fucking know you will," he replies. A little coldly like a stranger would, but also like maybe an ex-boyfriend would, because of course this game is not a game at all, it's the raw and unvarnished truth. I spent years denying myself out of a convert's zeal, out of a need to atone, and now here I am, my cock straining in its cage and my entire body trembling with that sweet, sick misery which is unsatisfied lust. I'm brought absolutely low with it, and I don't care, I don't care that I'm begging, that I'm forsaking, that I'm nothing more than flesh craving flesh, a mortal heart craving another very mortal heart, and that I'm surrendering something more vital than my body right now.

The vows I made, the promises I made, the life I swore to lead…they are gone now, blown away in the dry, pagan wind whispering outside the chapel. They've been blowing away since Semois, since that day in the hermitage.

Maybe even since the day I saw Elijah sitting in the cloister, waiting to tell me that he was getting married.

Elijah takes my jaw in his hand and gives me a deep, searching kiss, the kind where his tongue fucks ruthlessly against mine, and then he just as ruthlessly spins me around and shoves me back into the altar.

"Bend over," he rasps, pushing my habit up to my hips and then pulling my boxer briefs down past the curve of my backside. He runs an appreciative palm over one cheek and then tugs the briefs down my legs and then off one foot so he can kick my feet apart. "This fucking thing," he says, sounding pissed as his fingers find my cage and the tumescent flesh inside it. But he presses his naked organ to my ass as he says it, and so I know that he's at least as turned on as he is angry, maybe more so.

"I can come in it," I pant, closing my eyes against the feel of his erection moving against me, shaking with the need to rock back into him. "You can make me come in it."

"Is that what you need, Brother Patrick?" he murmurs. "Someone to milk this cock until you don't have to be hard during your prayers anymore?"

"Yes," I say miserably, my head hanging between my shoulders, my breath juddering in and out. My cock is dripping now, the clear pre-cum that would taste like salt if either of us could taste it, like the actual salt of the earth.

"You'd have to be careful," he says, his voice low in my ear. "Maybe you'd need it again. And again. Maybe you'd need it every day. Maybe you wouldn't be able to last a single night without having all this lust fucked right out of you."

"It's too late to be careful," I mumble between inhales, and I mean that in every possible way it can be meant. It's too late, it's too late, it's too late. There's only this, only now, only his fingers running up the center of me to find the place where I open. They are rough, insistent, just like a careless stranger's— or an angry ex-boyfriend's—would be.

"You're goddamn right about that," he says, his voice as rough as his touch. "Hold still."

I do as he says, too shivery and hot to care that I'm bent over a medieval altar with my habit up around my waist. Too inflamed to worry about how ridiculous I must look with my boots still on, my feet planted apart and my hands planted on the stone in front of me. Nothing matters, nothing at all, it's too late, it's too late, thank fucking God it's too late for anything else to matter.

He returns with a firm, possessive grip of my ass and then with slick fingertips. Slick and cool.

Lubricant.

I look back over my shoulder at him. He has a condom packet clenched between his teeth, and his eyes are heavy-lidded when he looks back at me.

"How did you…?"

"What did you think I went into town for?" he mutters around the condom, his fingers finding the heart of me again. "It wasn't to help with the copper pots."

Knowing that he planned this—that he walked up to the grotto with his satchel, prepared to fuck me—makes it all the more wonderfully unbearable. "So this whole day…"

"Yeah," he says, tearing open the condom packet with his teeth and then rolling it over his cock, which juts out from between the zipper of his jeans. "This whole day."

A fingertip presses in, and I shiver so hard that I feel like I'm going to shiver myself into a pile of atoms at the foot of this altar, and then I hear the click of a bottle and everything gets slicker, cooler. My body clenches around him, but it welcomes him too, welcomes the gorgeous invasion that was familiar once upon a time and now feels new all over again.

I press my face against the cool stone, breathing heavily as he pushes a second finger inside. And then both fingers move, grazing against something deep, something vital, and I groan into the altar.

Elijah's voice is low and triumphant when he speaks. "I knew you needed it. I could tell the moment I saw you. Luckily for you, I wouldn't refuse a monk. It's the least I can do for a man of God, don't you think?"

I nod against the altar, making a noise of shameless assent as he fists his cock and presses the slippery, latex-covered head against me. It's huge, vast, bigger than grace and larger than sin, and as it begins to breach me, I forget how to think. I forget how to breathe. The only thing I can remember is him, is the heavy need of him slowly pushing inside. Impaling me. Pinning me. Nailing me to a cross I built myself five years ago out of loneliness and despair and hope.

I feel stretched open and for a single moment, there is more pain than pleasure, but it is pleasure too, this pain. A flogging, a cilice around the arm, a cord below the knee, kneeling for hours on a stone floor with only the Host for company—this is the same. This is dying to the self, this is sanctifying, this is salvation and baptism, and he is the one giving it to me.

"Please," I say, sucking in a breath. "I need—"

"I know what you need," he says, and then with a slow drag out, he pushes in again, all the way, until his hips are flush with the curves of my backside. We stay still like that a moment, and then he splays a hand between my shoulder blades and presses me down. "Stay still, and I'll help. You'll see how good I can help."

I close my eyes. "Please," I whisper. "Let me feel you."

He does, with more slow strokes and another drizzle of lube, moving his hands to my ass to spread me apart. "Look at you," he says in a rough voice. "Look at how good you take me."

I nod against the stone, electricity zapping through me, up my spine and back down again. Every time he moves, his shaft drags against my prostate and soon I'm to that place where my shivers have become shudders and the shudders have become uncontrollable tremors all over my body. My belly quivers. My thighs shake.

"Yes," Elijah murmurs, his hands still holding me apart. "That's it. Doesn't that feel better? Aren't you so glad you asked me to help?"

I'm beyond speaking now, rocking back into him, and then he slides a hand under my throat and lifts me so that I'm nearly upright. He finds my jaw and turns my head for a kiss, and it's brief and sharply angled and it's more meeting lips and exchanging breath than a true kiss, but it's enough because it's him, it's Elijah, and we're playing one of our games, and even if this never happens again, it's happening *now*, and I will have this memory forever. His chest against my back and his hand on my throat and pleasure scissoring its way up my thighs to my groin until it threatens to saw me right in half.

"Elijah," I grunt. "Elijah."

And then it takes me. Like ecstasy, like being pierced with

angelic spears of love, like being run through with swords of light. I understand so much in this moment, I think I might understand everything, every mystery of creation, even why God made love for him and sex so close together, and right as the first wave shreds its way down my belly, I open my eyes and see the white and green hills on the other side of the valley through the open chapel door. I smell the lavender and see the wind playing with the leaves and feel the faint fingers of the sun stretching in toward the altar. And it's those hills I pin my gaze on as the release takes me, takes my body and offers it up to Elijah, to God, to myself. As the difference between the three of us shrinks to nothing, and we are all bound together in this moment, one spirit, one flesh, together, together, together. Evil exorcised with the salt of our sweat, joy anointed with seed.

Joined and incarnated and *here*. Alive.

I lift my eyes to the hills.

I'm an empty vessel after this orgasm, a chalice holding nothing but the memory of wine, and Elijah lets me slump over the altar as he reaches down to fondle me. He finds where I'm slick with dripping semen.

"Yes," he hisses, his strokes changing. Turning hard and using and rutting. "I knew it. I knew you needed this. And you're going to keep needing it, aren't you? It can be our secret, you know, what you need me to do to you. No one else needs to know how you ache under that pious little habit of yours."

"I am," I manage to say between his vicious thrusts. "I am going to need it. Please don't stop. Please don't stop—"

Behind me, he stiffens, and I hear a sharp gasp. And then

he plants his hands on the edge of the altar and begins pumping the condom full in short, full jerks that I can feel inside me.

It takes him a long time, as if even his body doesn't want this to end, and when he finally, finally goes still, he doesn't seem to want to pull out.

I don't want him to either.

But biology dictates it, and he slides free of my body after a moment, as slowly as possible. "Stay here," he commands, and then I hear the sounds of him rustling through the satchel. When he returns, he turns me around and then urges me to sit on the altar with my habit still up to my waist.

For some reason, this is the thing that makes me hesitate, even though I know this altar has been deconsecrated, and even though I just had my hands braced on it so my ex-boyfriend could rail me into Judgement Day. But putting my ass on an altar just feels wrong somehow.

Once I see what's dangling from Elijah's long fingers, however, my objections vanish.

It's the key to my cage.

"You got it from my room," I breathe.

Elijah gives me a look that's all heat, irritation, and lust together. "I've thought of nothing but this game all fucking day, the whole time I was in Cavaillon making excuses so I could sneak off to find les presérvatifs. And then I come back to the abbey to find you practically fucking naked and grinning at me like you used to do, like you were daring me, and Jesus, how I've missed being dared. And I knew if you were in this cage one minute longer, I was going to lose my goddamn mind, so I got your key while you were taking your shower."

I spread my legs as he takes the small padlock of my cage between his fingers and fits the key inside. "I thought maybe when you saw me this afternoon—" I stop. It feels too stupid to say out loud.

"You thought what?" Elijah asks, eyes on my cage as he turns the key and the lock clicks open. "Tell me."

"I thought that maybe you were turned off," I confess. "Since my body is so different."

He straightens up, his expression incredulous. "You what?"

"You know," I say, feeling my face burn along with my chest. "Because I'm different now. Hairier. My stomach—"

He grabs my hand and drags it to his cock, which has been de-condomed but not put away. It's already getting hard again.

"The daddy monk body works for me. *A lot.* And I want…" He leans forward to press his lips to my jaw, my ear. "I want you like this so much that sometimes I can't even look at you, because once I do, I can't think straight until I can escape somewhere to get off."

He pulls back and eases my sore flesh free of the chastity device, and then with a bite of pain and a swell of primitive pleasure, my cock fills between my thighs, lengthening between us.

"I want more *what ifs*," I say.

He looks down at my sex and then back up to my face. One eyebrow is lifted, but I don't know if it's in agreement or disagreement until he speaks.

"Me too," he says finally.

"I don't—I can't give you—"

"I know, Aiden."

He gets to his knees, his eyes on mine, and then he parts those perfect lips and lowers his head. His mouth envelops me, hot and silky and soft too, and it only takes one suck.

One suck, and I erupt again, fully this time, my hands finding his face to hold him close as the hard, delicious contractions quake through my thighs and cock and spurt a full release onto his tongue, a full release that has me stunned after it pulses its way to a long, ball-draining finish. His eyes are still looking up at me, his lips stretched around my flesh, and this is perfect, this is so perfect.

I will have to confess eventually, I will have to stop and find my way to celibacy again, but wasn't it Abbot Jerome's idea that I should use this trip to truly ask myself what I wanted, what *God* wanted? That this was an invitation to examine if I was meant for solemn vows and the rest of my life in a monastery? And I *know* I am, I know I'm supposed to be a monk and spend the rest of my life alone with God…but surely it can't hurt to take the invitation up to its fullest? Just for this trip? Just for the next couple of weeks? What are a few weeks in a lifetime of devotion, when you think about it? What are a few stolen hours when the rest of the day is prayer and work?

What are a few *what ifs* when the rest of my life is set in stone?

CHAPTER
THIRTY-SEVEN

As we slowly clean up and gather our things—both of us dragging our feet, reluctant to leave our little sex-chapel—I confront the other barrier between us.

Jamie. The broken engagement.

"You don't have to talk about this if you don't want to," I say carefully, picking up part of the condom wrapper from the floor and tucking it into the satchel, "But not a day goes by that I'm not sorry for what happened in the hermitage, what I made you do—"

"You didn't make me do anything," he cuts in. "You felt me against you that day. I wanted every bit of it and more. And don't act like you didn't have as much to lose."

"But I—if I hadn't kissed you, then you and Jamie might still be—"

"No, Aiden," he says. "We wouldn't."

We stare at each other from across the altar. From the corner of the chapel, the well burbles on, unperturbed by the small griefs and miseries of men.

Elijah sighs and passes a slow hand over his face. "We wouldn't," he says again, finally. "We wouldn't still be together, because I cared about him too much to fake a life where I wasn't still in love with you."

Still in love with you.

The words roll over me like a wave, they crush me like deep water. I can't breathe and my chest is collapsing, and I love him back, I've loved him all these years, and *he's still in love with me...*

"Elijah," I whisper, stepping forward, and he holds up a hand, stopping me.

"No," he says, eyebrows lifted, and he looks pained right now, like he's in so much pain. "Please don't. I already know. I already know everything you're going to say, and so you don't have to say it. You're a monk. You're going to stay a monk. Whatever we have here is going to end when we get back home."

I draw a breath to speak, but then I stop. Because that's not what I was going to say...but also he's not wrong either. He's not wrong about the monk part.

And the ending part.

"I love you too," is what I do say. It had been what I was planning to say anyway, but there's no missing what is unsaid now. There's no missing that it's an *I love you but...*

He certainly doesn't miss it, because his mouth tilts into a sad smile. "Do you?"

"You must know," I say. "I'm not that good an actor. You must have known the moment you saw me again. You must have realized that I'd never stopped loving you."

He shakes his head. "You left, Aiden. Why would I have thought you still loved me?"

The knowledge that I'm going to have to tell him about that night—about all of it, even the parts that feel impossible to put into words—flaps its wings inside me like a restless bird. But he saves me from myself by speaking again, and I'm granted a reprieve.

For now.

"I thought I had stopped loving you," he says bluntly. "I threw all my energy into trying. And I thought since I began to love someone else that I'd succeeded in doing it, that I'd buried the part of myself that loved hopeless, careless millionaires. And then I saw you walking into that cloister, and I'd realized that all the work I'd put into un-loving you had been for nothing. And maybe it would've always been for nothing anyway, but especially because you were different. You'd changed, and I was just as vulnerable to this new version of you as I had been to the old." He passes a hand over his face again. "Maybe more so, if I'm honest."

"I didn't need to see you again to know I still loved you," I say softly. "Elijah, this whole time…" I don't finish. I can't finish. It feels both too obvious and too important to shove into a few small words.

He meets my gaze, and his eyes are soft and open.

"Then maybe this was supposed to happen," he says. "Maybe we were always meant to end up here, together. Maybe God wanted that for us."

"But God also wants you to be happy and have what you need," I say, stepping all the way to the altar so that I can put my hand next to his. My thumb brushes against his pinky, and it's so warm compared to the cool stone of the altar that I sigh. "I feel like I've stolen something from you."

He shakes his head at my words. "That's what I'm trying to tell you. You haven't stolen anything. After our kiss in the hermitage, I…"

He rubs his pinky slowly along my thumb, his eyes on our hands as he does. "I've built a life for myself where everything has a point and a meaning, where every minute is filled with doing, and all that doing always has a reason. There are no abrupt road trips to see a bison herd you saw on the internet. There are no two a.m. picnics under the stars. No random days off so we can spend the day watching superhero movies in chronological order. And I'd thought—I'd thought, okay. All of those things are whimsical and silly and that's what I loved about them, and since you were a monk, all the whimsy would have been austerity-ed right out of you, and therefore what I loved about you would be gone too. But I was wrong." He looks up at me. "You're as intoxicating quiet as you are laughing. And you're as beautiful serious as you are silly. And you are altogether more potent like this, more powerful, more stirring, and maybe it's because silliness and contemplation are so much the same thing. Maybe it's because no matter what you're doing, you're reminding me that I'm here and alive and that there's more to living than work. That sometimes we can sleep in or play or pray and have nothing to show for it."

I come around the altar, not able to stand the separation between us any longer. "You've made me want to be better because you are so smart and self-possessed, and when I'm with you, I want to eat up life with great big bites, I want to feed life to you until you're full. There's never been anyone like you, and all I've ever wanted was to give you everything."

And knowing I couldn't—realizing viscerally that I would let him down over and over again—had been so much of what had broken me that night.

Elijah lets me cup his jaw in my hands, and his eyes shut, his thick eyelashes resting against the crests of his cheeks.

"I'd rather have you for three weeks in Europe than spend the rest of my life wishing I'd kissed you one last time," he whispers.

Yes. Yes.

"I love you," I tell him, the thrill of being able to say the words almost enough to blunt the pain waiting for us after our trip is over.

He opens his eyes and kisses my palm. "And I love you," he says roughly, but I see the knot between his brows as he says it, I feel the tension in his jaw.

Funny how *I love you* could be enough for any other couple in the world. The beginning of a happily ever after.

But for us, it's like vinegar instead of wine—it stings and it sours and it only makes us thirstier for something we can never, ever have.

I worry that perhaps all of this shows on our faces as we sit at dinner. The *I love you*s, the sex. Especially the sex. Surely there must be something different about me, about my face, about my voice. Surely the way Elijah and I move around each other—careful not to look too much, speak too much—must give it away.

I *feel* different, and not helping matters is my unbound sex beneath my habit, and even tucked into my boxer briefs, the amount of stimulation that comes merely from the constant press and friction of the fabric is so much more than I've had on this trip. And then I move a certain way and feel the ache of where Elijah penetrated me, and my body threatens to awaken all over again.

I feel like I did when we'd just started fucking, and it was all I'd wanted to do. I'd beg him to take days off work, I'd keep him up all hours of the night, like I could make up for all the time I'd missed having sex with him if I tried hard enough.

I feel that way now. And when I catch him looking at me in the refectory with a quick but unguarded smolder, I think he might feel the same way. A plan forms in my mind.

When we walk into the guesthouse after compline—the mysterious priest still unreturned from whatever sojourn he's on—I close the door behind us and turn to Elijah in the stone corridor.

"What if…" I say and his eyes immediately grow heavy-lidded.

"Yes."

"You're spending the night," I whisper. "With Sean."

His eyes hood even more. This isn't a new game; it's one of our favorites. The older brother's best friend game.

"And he's asleep and you're asleep in the guest room, but I can't sleep. And I come into your room without knocking."

He swallows. "Yeah," he says, his voice sounding dry. "I like that game."

And about an hour later, we're each in our own cells, cleaned up and ostensibly trying to sleep, me waiting until I absolutely can't stand it anymore, and then I finally push out of bed and open the wooden door to the corridor.

In a way, despite the medieval stone and the empty cells, it feels like sneaking through my childhood home while everyone else is asleep. I'm in nothing but my underwear, and so if I'm caught, I'll have to pretend I was on my way to the bathroom or something. And while I highly doubt getting caught will be an issue, since it doesn't seem likely any of the monks here would be fussing around the guesthouse during the precious hours of sleep between compline and vigils, it's a possibility I still brace for as I pad down the hall to Elijah's cell, walking on the balls of my feet in order to be as quiet as possible.

I might as well be creeping past Sean's and Tyler's rooms in order to get to the guest room; I might as well be cursing my own breathing for being too loud as I find the handle for his door and slowly turn it.

It's unlocked.

The dim light from the hall spills into his room as I quietly open the door and slip inside. Elijah is on his back on the bed, one muscular leg drawn up and one arm flung over his face. He's wearing nothing but his boxer briefs, and it's warm enough that the sheet has been kicked down to where it tangles around his waist, revealing the etched expanse of his abdomen and chest.

He's breathing too quickly to be asleep, or even close to asleep, but I still act like he is, as I close the door behind me and step into the room. And then I creep to the side of his bed, my own breath catching, like I really am a teenager sneaking into an older crush's room. Like I really hadn't been able to sleep knowing he was so close.

In the moonlight pouring in through the high window, I watch his chest contract and expand, I watch the faint lifts and lowers of his stomach. I let my eyes linger on his navel and on the narrow line of hair that leads down into the sheet.

We've played this game so many different ways—subtler ways, slower ways—but if we only have the next two weeks, I don't want subtle or slow. I want everything, as dirty as we've ever made it. I want the memories to be worth the sins.

I silently get to my knees, and carefully, oh so carefully, lift the sheet that's resting over his bottom half. Just a little. Just enough so I can see the unmistakable ridge of him in the shadows.

I sip in a long breath as I see it, my own body already swollen in response, my heart beating faster. God, how often my thoughts had turned to his body when I was that age, how much I wanted to see it. His thighs, his stomach. His dick. My thoughts and fantasies had never really gotten past the *seeing*—

if I had seen him, I don't know what I would have done. I didn't even know enough to know what possibilities there were.

But I wonder what would have happened that time he came over when I was a college freshman, what would have happened if I'd crept into his room after he and Sean had taxied back from the bars and I'd satisfied my curiosity at last.

I lift the sheet even higher, wanting to see more of him, and that's when I notice him looking at me from underneath his arm, eyes shining in the half-darkness.

"What are you doing, Aiden?" he murmurs.

I quickly drop the sheet, fake-searching for an excuse. "I, uh. I couldn't sleep."

Elijah gives a long stretch, the kind that makes his stomach and thighs flex and quiver, and then tucks his arm behind his head so he can look at me better.

"It's hard to sleep when it's so warm," he says. "Isn't it?"

"Yeah," I whisper. "It is."

His other hand runs up his stomach and then back down again. Slow, idle strokes. I watch the progress of his hand as he watches me.

"You know," he says after a moment. "There's something that helps me sleep when I'm having trouble. Can you guess what it is?" His hand strays lower now, brushing against the edge of the sheet.

My cock is threatening to push free of the waistband of my briefs now, stretching out to my hip and sending hot currents of need through the center of my body. "I think so," I mumble. "I do it a lot."

Elijah chuckles, his nimble fingers plucking easily at the sheet, lowering it bit by agonizing bit. "I did it a lot in college too. It made dorm life a little awkward."

I might as well be eighteen again as I watch him hook the sheet the rest of the way down with his thumb and then press the heel of his palm to his erection over his underwear. I don't feel like I'm in my thirties, like a man who's done far kinkier shit than watching his crush touch himself; I feel young and new all over again, standing at the edge of something too exciting to fully understand or name.

"You could show me too, you know," he says, too casually. "What it looks like when you do it. I'd like to see."

I drag in a long breath and then push the waistband of my underwear down, raising up on my knees so he can see it better.

"Oh Aiden," he says. "That's really good. That's really, really good."

My organ jumps at his words, and he licks his lower lip as I fist myself and give myself a few lust-clumsy strokes. Slowly—too slowly for my liking—he pulls the waistband of his boxer briefs down and reveals the thick, slightly curved length of him. A plump vein meanders up the underside; the crown is so swollen that the skin there is stretched and shiny. Already a small pearl of clear seed beads at his tip.

My mouth goes dry as I watch him wrap his long fingers around his length and then drag his hand up to the top and then back down again. The slow shuttle of his hand on himself is framed by his naked stomach and chest, set off by the way his eyes hood as he watches my hand move on myself.

"Have you done this with someone else before?" he asks. We've played this game all sorts of ways, where I've answered *no* or *yes* or *yes but never like this, yes but never with another guy.* Tonight, I answer with his favorite answer, the one that usually spins the game off into the dirtiest possible direction.

"No," I say. "You're the first one."

Lust flares in his eyes, and I can tell from the way he stops stroking himself that he's too close to the edge and wants to make this last. He starts running his hand along his stomach again instead.

"All the way to college and you've never masturbated with anyone before?" he says softly. "I can't tell if I'm educating you or corrupting you."

"I'm plenty corrupt," I protest, my hand still working myself. "I just haven't had a chance to practice very much yet."

He lifts a sexy eyebrow. "And just how corrupt are you? Do I need to be worried about Sean's little brother getting into trouble?"

I answer exactly how an eighteen-year-old Aiden would have answered. "It depends on the trouble."

"Maybe I should be worried about you corrupting me," he sighs, stretching again, his cock bobbing against his stomach as he does. "After all, you're the one who snuck in here while I was sleeping."

"I know I shouldn't have," I whisper. "But I wanted to see you. I think about seeing you all the time."

He regards me, still with that arm propped behind his

head. "You want to touch me?"

My hand stills on my shaft. "You'll let me?"

"Yeah. What Sean doesn't know won't hurt him."

He reaches out and takes my hand, and then he guides it to where he's throbbing and hot. It's my left hand, so I don't have to pretend to make my grip clumsy for the sake of the game.

"Sorry," I murmur. "I've never done this before."

"It's okay," he says. "You'll get the hang of it." But his kind, faux-off-handed tone is betrayed by the flex of his thighs, by the slow scrape of his feet against the sheets as I stroke him. His nipples are bunched into tight points, and there's more clear seed at his tip than ever. "Ah, Aiden," he breathes as I tighten my grip and work him faster. "That feels so good. So fucking good."

The orgasm snaking through my groin is pulling tighter now, coming closer, and I feel my rhythm get jerky and unpredictable.

"I'm think I'm gonna," I mumble.

"You could do it on me," he says. "Would you like to do it on me?"

I stare at him. "Is that a real question?"

He grins, looking wicked as hell. "Climb up here and find out."

The narrow bed is not made for two people, and it's definitely not made for a giant lumberjack-y monk straddling someone, but I manage somehow, my knees on either side of his hips and one hand braced against the wall as I grip myself and start working my dick again. Elijah watches me with frank interest, his hands sanding up my hair-dusted thighs and back down again as I rub myself in front of him.

"I might have to spend the night more often," he murmurs, eyes on my erection. "Fuck, Aiden. That's it. Show me how you come, I want to see it. Show me show me—"

My balls draw up tight, my stomach clenches, and with a grunt, the climax erupts out of me with thick ropes of release all over his own erection and his stomach.

He tenses as he watches it, his jaw tight and his mouth open, his eyes darting everywhere like he doesn't want to miss a second of it, not my face, not my body, not the release itself painting him all over. And it's not until I'm totally finished that he growls and finds my hand, putting it back on his shaft, which is now slick with my seed.

"Finish what you started," he says, and I do, I fist him and stroke, and his hips try in vain to fuck up into my touch, but my bulk holds him down, and all of him is tense, damp, straining, and with an abrupt inhale and his eyes on mine in the moonlight, he spills all over my hand, all over my fingers and everywhere until we're coated in each other, until everything is shivering, slippery relief.

He reaches up, and I duck my head down, allowing him to curl his fingers around the back of my neck and pull me down for a long, searching kiss. His lips are so warm and so firm, and I hate that they're not mine to kiss always, I hate that we're on borrowed time.

I hate that the time has to be borrowed at all, but it does, I know it does.

I can't live without prayers and ordered days and quiet cloisters. I know because I tried once.

I ended up on my farmhouse floor.

"Just a minute," I whisper into his kiss and then climb off the bed. One furtive dart into the bathroom later, and I'm back with some damp washcloths to clean us off. And then after we're finished, I sit on the edge of the bed and cradle his hand in my lap.

"I wish I could lie down here with you," I say, running my fingers along his palm.

He makes a little purring noise and then adjusts himself so that his arm is all the way in my lap, so I can run my fingertips over it as well. He always did love to be petted after sex.

"We could fit," he says, sounding drowsy.

"I don't think so. You'd have to lie down on top of me."

"No complaints here."

I keep tickle-stroking his arm, not sure what the protocol is for a monk scheduling a hookup. "Tomorrow afternoon, after I'm done helping with the lavender harvest…"

"Yes," he says. "Yes."

CHAPTER THIRTY-EIGHT

"So explain celibacy to me then," Elijah says.

We're on a hike to find the final spring that inspired the location and the name of the abbey, and even though my muscles ache from another long day helping with the lavender, and even though my stomach is growling and my uncaged cock is fussing at me for attention, I can't remember being this happy in…well, in a very long time. I've been content at Mount Sergius, I've been at peace, and I've felt joy that cleaves me right down to the bone, but just the simple happiness of hard work and a sunny day and a hot guy?

It's been so long that it feels brand new to me. A new feeling that's been invented just now in these stony hills under this hot Mediterranean sun.

"Well," I say as we pass through the narrow cleft of rock that's supposed to lead to the spring, "when a man and God love each other very much…"

"Ha," Elijah says dryly. "Ha ha."

"There's not much to explain," I tell him. "It's exactly what it seems like. When you become a priest or a monastic, you give yourself to God. All of yourself, including your body and bodily desires."

"But why?" Elijah asks, stopping to look at me. "Why do you have to give up sex to devote your life to God?"

"The Church says that—"

"I can Google what the Church says," Elijah replies impatiently. "I want to know why *you* agreed to do it. Why you did it until we came here. What value you found in it."

This stops me. Not because I haven't thought about it, but because I've never had to talk about it with a non-monastic before. The only person I really could talk about it with is my older brother Tyler, but since he lives on the East Coast, we generally only talk over the phone, and talking about celibacy while I'm on the abbey phone in the common room is the literal last thing I want to do.

And anyway, Tyler Bell isn't exactly a role model for well-executed celibacy.

I take a minute, turning Elijah's words over in my mind. "I think," I say, "when it's done right, it's a way to be present for other people in a really full way. I've heard some people talk about it like it sublimates sexual energy into emotional and social energy, and others like it fosters relationships by ensuring that sex can't ever be a factor. But for me, it was more about focus. I spent my entire adult life chasing sex, loving sex, having it whenever I could, and so really for the first time, I was putting all of my energy into the parts of life that weren't about sex. It was less about what my body was doing than where my mind was. Not in denial of my body, but fully in it, fully participating *with* it to turn my entire being towards loving God and his creations."

I give Elijah a rueful grin as we start walking again. "Of course, that's the theory. In reality, so much of my mind—my heart—was still with you. It felt like you were inside me the whole time...not only my desire for you, but my love for you too. And while I felt sometimes that I'd managed *sexual* celibacy well enough, I never felt like I'd managed true celibacy. Emotional celibacy."

He doesn't speak for a moment, and then we emerge from the rocks into a deep-set ravine made of white rock and dotted with bright turquoise pools. We find the sloping edge of one of these pools and set down our things on the bed of dried pine needles there—Elijah's satchel and a blanket and a cooler of the beer Brother Luc had given on us when he learned we were heading out to the abbey's deepest spring.

And it isn't until we're settled on the blanket and Elijah has handed us each a beer, that he says, "I shouldn't like that so much."

"Shouldn't like what so much?

"Knowing I was the reason you struggled with celibacy."

I smile.

"And I think I understand what you're saying, but like— okay. Why does focus on God have to exclude sex? If we are called to love God with our entire bodies, then why can't we love God sexually too?"

I smile even bigger. "That's pretty kinky."

He gives me an impatient look. "I'm serious, Aiden. And this can't be spliced away from the reality that the Catholic Church is more concerned about celibacy from some people than it is from others. Queer people are only theologically justified if they are celibate. The Church literally canonizes women for being virgins, and only for that reason. It's one thing for an allosexual person to choose celibacy, I guess, but it feels like you're retconning reasons that are about personal choice rather than organizational control."

"Maybe," I say. "But does that make a choice less valid?"

"It depends on how informed the choice is. And I feel like you're dodging the question."

"Maybe a little." I toss a clump of pine needles into the nearby pool. "But only because the answer is so messy, and because it's the kind of answer that changes day to day, sometimes even hour to hour. Yes, the Church is obsessed with sexual control, and yes, it's directed mainly at queer people and women. I think there are some queer Catholics and women Catholics who feel like your parents did about staying in the Church after Lizzy's death—that it's better to stay and to have your voice heard, and if you have to follow the rules in order to have your voice heard, then so be it."

"You sound like you don't agree with that."

"Well, sometimes I do. But celibacy is different depending on the life you lead, isn't it? Because for the priesthood or for a religious life as a brother or sister, celibacy is required of *everyone*. A vowed life is the only place in the Church where everyone is asked to give up the same thing—unlike in the laity, where only queer believers are asked to be celibate and where sexual policing is typically only directed at women. It felt like as a monastic, I wasn't being asked to give anything more than my straight brothers and sisters were."

"But it's still not the same," Elijah argues. "What looks functionally the same can be entirely different because of context, and the context of queer celibacy in Catholicism is always going to be about control."

"I agree to a point," I reply. "But only to a point, because the Church has to be bigger than Rome, has to be bigger than its dogmas and doctrines. The Church is mine. God is mine. And what if we all started believing that? What if we all started acting like it? Like the Church is ours? Not the priests', not the bishops', but ours."

"That sounds amazing, but it also sounds like a way to manipulate yourself into staying in a broken system."

"Elijah," I say, setting my beer down and looking at him.

"Yes?"

"You're not wrong. But also if we're going to argue about what the Catholic Church does to control its faithful versus what is the choice of said faithful, we will be here arguing until we have gray pubes, and I have things I'd like to do to you before my pubes are gray."

He shakes his head, but he laughs. "Things like what?"

I turn to face him completely. "What if we played a monk game again?"

The laughter turns to something else around his mouth.

Something hungry.

"Oh yeah?"

"Yeah," I say. "But different this time."

His eyes are molten now. He licks his lips again.

"Different."

"I've just found you out here," I say. "I'm making sure you're settling into the abbey okay."

"And I tell you that I am," he says quietly. "I ask you if it's normal for a monk to check up on each guest like this."

"It's sort of normal," I say. "Usually I would let you enjoy your afternoon in peace, but I wanted to make sure you weren't lonely."

"I'm not lonely now," Elijah says, his voice low and graveled. "I suppose it must get lonely for you, though. Here. With only God for company."

I put my hand down on the blanket, next to his, our fingertips brushing in a way that could be accidental.

"I have been lonely," I admit, one of those things that's true both inside the game and outside of it. "Although they say that God comes to us in the form of strangers."

"Do they now?" Elijah replies. His hand shifts on the blanket the tiniest amount, and now our fingers are touching. "How strange. I was thinking that God must be using his faithful to speak to me while I'm here. That maybe God would come to me in the form of a monk."

"Maybe we could be God for each other," I say as I lean forward. "Just for a little while."

His lips when they meet mine are warm and slightly sweet

from the honey beer, and he holds still for me as I plunder his mouth, like it's been years since we've kissed rather than hours. Like I really am a lonely monk looking for God in the body of a stranger.

He lets me push him down to the blanket, lets me pin him in place with my hands on his wrists while I hunt over his throat and jaw and face for places to kiss. While I browse for new sage-scented hollows and sweat-dampened nooks.

This was so much of our year together, I remember, as I lick a spot on his throat and he tenses beautifully underneath me. Him allowing me to crawl all over him and learn his body. Him teaching me, him letting me learn. Maybe it is a strange thing that a lover can be a teacher too—especially since I'd been thirty-one at the time and fairly certain I had nothing left to learn—but it had been exhilarating too. Sexy.

His legs fall open as I suck on his neck, and I insert myself easily between them, pinning his hips down to the blanket with my own. My uncaged erection surges as I press against him, as I find *his* erection and grind down as we kiss.

"Yes," I breathe. "That's it, that's it. God, it's been so fucking long."

"How long has it been?"

"Years and years," I say, pressing my face into his neck and breathing him in. It doesn't even feel like I'm pretending for the sake of the game; it might as well be the truth. "It feels like it's been my entire life."

I realize that I'm holding him to the blanket with most of my weight, and I make to readjust so that I'm not pinning him down like some kind of sex villain.

"Wait," he says quickly, breathing fast. "Wait. You can— you don't have to move."

I look down at him, searching his face. When we'd been together, it had been easy to let him take charge, because he was older than me, and experienced, and I was generally easygoing and horny enough to go along with whatever meant I got to have sex.

Which isn't to say that our games didn't encompass all sorts of fantasies and power handoffs, but only that in a lot of ways, I'd defaulted to him, looked to his lead physically and emotionally. I'd been so scared of fucking things up with him, of fucking things up altogether, that I'd never asked myself if he'd wanted to hand off power more often—or more emphatically.

I turn this over in my mind for a second, and then ask, "You like how we are right now?"

"You mean do I like it when you're Mean Daddy Monk?" he asks, and he sounds amused and horny at the same time, which is no small feat. "Yes, Aiden."

Well. No complaints here. "Snap your fingers if it gets to be too much," I tell him, leaning back down to kiss his neck. He nods as I give his collarbone a long, lingering suck.

"I will," he says, and I'm already lost in our game, already letting my kisses turn less grateful and more selfish. I press my hips harder against him as I retake his mouth, and he responds almost immediately, arching up against me, panting.

"You're so beautiful. It's like you're so beautiful for me,

just for me," I tell him, reaching between us to find the button of his shorts, the zipper underneath. I want to see him, feel him, I want all of him available to me, and I grunt with satisfaction once I find the thick heat of him inside his shorts. "No underwear," I remark in a low voice, my fingertips exploring the taut, silky skin of his erection. "It's almost like you came out here expecting this."

"Maybe I did. Maybe I've seen you looking at me during prayers," Elijah says, his hips straining against my touch. "Maybe I've hoped…"

I get to my knees and pull up my habit enough to bare myself to the air, using my left hand to stroke myself while I reach for the satchel and pull it closer. Condoms and a small bottle of lubricant are right at the very top.

"Looks like you did more than hope," I say, tearing off a condom one-handed.

"God helps those who help themselves," Elijah murmurs, his throat working.

"Or maybe he's helping me right now. You know how long it's been since I had a proper fuck?" I ask, my voice more growl than speech now. "And now you're here, all stretched out for me with your cock out and your mouth looking so pretty. It's enough to break a man."

Elijah slowly shakes his head on the blanket. "Maybe I want to see you break."

I tear open the condom packet. Once upon a time, I could do this one-handed in the dark while I steered my old Lexus through post-game stadium traffic, but I'm out of practice. It takes me a minute to see which way it's rolled and then to get it properly pinched and ready. But Elijah doesn't seem to mind; his stare is hooded and sultry as he watches me, and his hips move restlessly between my knees as I work the latex down my dusky erection in preparation for fucking him.

Soon I'm sheathed, the clear latex making my cock shiny in the sun, and I don't even care that I must look ridiculous in my habit and scapular with my cock out, I don't even care that a monk's habit is the furthest thing from sexy, because I'm breaking, I'm already broken. If I wasn't already in love with this man, if I hadn't already fractured my vows, I would be reaching for the bottle in the satchel anyway. I would be growling at him to flip over for me.

With a noise that sounds helpless and surprised both, Elijah does, moving to his stomach while I'm still straddling him, and he places his head on his arms, his face down in the blanket.

Rolling to his stomach has hiked his stylish tank top up to his shoulder blades and his shorts are already pulled down to his thighs. For a moment, I simply savor the sight. The dark sepia stretch of his back—layered with slender muscles and beveled with the strong reach of his spine—and the firm rounds of his ass, curved in perfect Fibonacci curves.

I run my hands over those curves now, feeling the way goose bumps raise under my touch, even with the Provençal sun blazing overhead. I part the muscled cheeks of his backside and look down at the soft, velvety place I'm about to fuck.

"This is so good," I say, touching the pleated rim of his

entrance and pressing in. "This is so good, and I can't wait any longer. You're going to give it to me, aren't you? You're going to give it to me, because you were hoping I'd do this, weren't you? You were hoping the big, quiet monk would pin you down and make you feel how much he's needed it."

"Yes," he mumbles into the blanket, his hips lifting against my touch. "God, *yes.*"

I reach for the bottle of lube and click it open, pouring a generous amount on my fingers and painting his hole with it. "You've been driving me wild the whole time you've been here," I say, pushing a finger inside. He moans. "That pretty mouth. This perfect ass. You think I don't notice? That I'm superhuman? Made of stone? That I haven't seen you looking at me, that I haven't seen you staring at my hands like you want them all over you? That I haven't seen you staring at my habit like you want to know what's underneath?"

He's blistering hot and a mind-breaking combination of tight and soft inside. I continually check his hands, keep my hearing alert for snaps of his fingers, but most of my attention is on what I'm doing to him right now. To where I'm drizzling more lube and then sliding a second finger in and pressing until I find the lust-swollen spot inside him and start stroking.

He is restless as I do, his hips moving against the blanket like a teenager fucking his own bed because he's so horny, and noises begin to come out of his mouth. Pleading noises, urgent noises, sweeter than any psalm or canticle.

"Yeah," I say, my erection aching inside the latex as I watch him fuck himself back against my slick fingers. "That's what I thought. You need it as badly as I do. Maybe God really did send you to me. Maybe I'm ministering to you right now. Helping a poor stranger in need."

He moans something into the blanket, something barely intelligible. It contains my religious name though and is followed by another shameless squirm of his hips, and so I think he's still digging the daddy monk game, which. Good. Me too.

I slide my hands free to the sound of whimpering protests and slick my erection up with more lube before wedging it against the opening I've just been fingering. I push one cheek aside and use my other hand to tease at his rim with my crown.

Goose bumps stipple his skin, and I can feel him trembling underneath me as I breach him, moving past his tightest, narrowest barrier and into the hot heaven beyond.

"I wish you could see yourself right now," I tell him. "How gorgeous you look while you're taking me."

I get an incoherent mumble in response, but there's no snapping of fingers and the mumbling sounds moan-y in a good way, so I push in deeper, shivering as more and more of me is squeezed and then caressed by his silky, hot sheath. It's been years since I've felt the clutch of a lover's body around me, and yet it's so instinctive still to move, to take, to push, and to fuck.

And then I'm all the way inside, deep enough that I can feel my hips press into his backside. I stroke my fingers up his spine and then lean down to brace my forearm on his back, draping myself entirely over him.

"God, you feel good," I breathe in his ear, giving an experimental thrust and then grunting at how good it feels. Hotter than a furnace, hotter than the fires of hell. The kind of heat you dream about alone in bed at night. The kind of heat you'd pay any price to heaven for.

"You feel…big," he mumbles.

I withdraw and push back in as I pet his side, his hip. "Maybe it's that you're so tight. Jesus Christ. It's like fucking a fist." I punch my hips forward with a groan and then take his wrist and push his hand underneath his hips to his cock.

"Didn't expect…you to care…" he says, sounding drunk, as his arm begins to move. "Big mean monk like you."

"You thought I'd just use you and be done?" I rasp as I start rutting into him harder, a little rougher. "You thought maybe I'd just want a hot little hole for the afternoon? Maybe I like watching you getting off underneath me. Maybe I want you so limp from coming that I can fuck you again and again while you lay dazed on the blanket. Maybe I want you at prayers every day thinking of how hard you come when I'm on top of you."

He mutters a curse into the blanket, rolling his head along his forearm as I hold him down and fuck. I drive into him without mercy, my exhales harsh, my muscles hard and straining, my habit everywhere, somehow making everything all the more obscene. The monk who snapped, who broke at the first man to offer himself. The monk, who after years of denial, simply had to *take*.

"Aiden," Elijah chokes out, his arm moving faster. "Aiden,

I'm—" He turns his face toward me as he goes taut, and then with a sudden inhale, he shudders so hard that I have to ride him to stay inside.

And more than the satiny heat around my sex, more than his gorgeous ass moving against me as he rides out his climax against the blanket, it's his face that tips me over. The flutter of his eyelashes and the cut of his jaw and the helpless, helpless part of his lips against the onslaught of his pleasure.

It makes me want to fuck him seventeen times a day just to see that expression on his face as often as possible.

The orgasm grips me hard, snapping me clean in two as I stroke into him, relentlessly chasing every last throb, every last drop, etching every last bit of it to memory. The stretch of his body around my swollen length, the heat, the slick, soft kiss of him. The sweat dappling his back as he slumps limply forward, the sweat dripping off my own face now. The rasp of my thighs moving against the expensive fabric of his shorts, the drape of my habit and scapular everywhere, the ripple of the springs nearby.

The beauty of the sun along his face and the shadows hidden along the perfect shell of his ear and the heartbreakingly raw sound of his voice as he murmurs my name. My real name.

I come and come, loving it and hating it, because each pulse filling the condom is that much closer to the moment ending. This perfect moment which feels holier than prayer and deeper than contemplation.

And then finally, I am emptied out into him.

I pull free, cleaning us both quickly enough that he's still floppy and dazed when I'm done, and then I lie down and pull him into my arms and kiss him until we're both hard again and reaching for the satchel.

"Maybe I'm not the best one to explain celibacy to you," I say as he rolls a condom back over my cock, and he's still laughing even after he climbs over me and sinks his way home.

CHAPTER THIRTY-NINE

from the notebook of Elijah Iverson

Honesty, no matter how late it comes, is always best.

I'm reminding myself of this since I've just gotten off the phone with Jamie, and the consequences of my honesty feel very, very hard to bear right now, even though the call was about mundane matters like arranging for my things to be moved out of his little Westside house.

I loved Jamie. I love him still, maybe. But I couldn't marry him, and I shouldn't have said yes when he proposed. Even then I think I knew it, but I wouldn't admit it to myself, because admitting it to myself would also mean admitting why.

Admitting that nearly five years hadn't undone my feelings for a man who left me without saying goodbye.

I keep asking myself what I want. What I want from this, knowing that it will end, and it will hurt more than the first time it ended—but somehow the question has stopped mattering here. The air smells like lavender and rosemary, and there's an unlimited supply of the rarest beer in the world, and as I write this under the shade of an old oak tree, I can watch a shirtless Aiden move through the rows of lavender as he harvests the lavender flowers with the other monks.

I think I could watch him forever, simply watch him be a monk. The work, the prayer, the singing, the silence.

Maybe I don't understand, maybe I'll never understand, but when I watch him, it feels like I don't have to. It feels like simply being with him is enough. ~~For however short a time.~~

CHAPTER FORTY

I discover in lavender-scented Provence the reason the Church tries so hard to keep monastics away from sex, and it's not because sex pollutes prayer and it's not because sex is the opposite of prayer either.

It's because sex and prayer fit each other so well that splitting them apart feels like the real sin. Like bread and wine, like gold and incense, they are made for one another, both liturgies of body and soul.

Every morning, I wake and dress and go to vigils. There I sing and chant my way into wakefulness. Sometimes Elijah is there, a couple mornings he isn't, having stayed up the night before to write. And then I go back to my room and do lectio, savoring over *Song of Songs* and letting the words linger in my mind like wine. And then lauds, and then the lavender fields, where I sweat and laugh with the other brothers, where I stop to pray the little hours, feeling God's words on my tongue as his winds whisper around me.

And then under the pretense of tourist-y exploration, Elijah and I disappear into the hills and worship each other until we are deliciously wasted like heathen cities in the face of God's wrath. And then there is touring the brewhouse and more prayer and scripture until night comes, and with it, a deep, peaceful sleep that I've never known before now.

There is no hitch in my thoughts as they wander from the memory of Elijah's mouth to the word of the Lord. There is no veil between the memory of him surging into me and the surge of gratitude I feel as Dom Francis places the host on my tongue. I feel fully and deeply and completely alive. Human. Incarnated entirely.

With him and God together.

And yet.

And yet.

I have to hide my joy; I have to pretend my smiles and serenity are from fervent dedication to prayer and nothing more. We have to keep wary, keep careful, as we go into the hills and as we creep into each other's rooms.

And the same sun which breaks over me to find me more replete and alive than ever also signals the passing of time with each dawning day. Soon we will leave here for St. Columba's, and then after a week there, it's back home.

Soon this trip will be over.

Soon this will end.

We have one day left here at Our Lady when Elijah's

phone rings from his satchel.

He's fast asleep on a blanket near the shady grotto, napping the nap of the well-fucked, and I go to silence the phone so it doesn't wake him up, which is when I see that it's my brother Sean calling.

I haven't handled an iPhone in almost five years, but I manage to answer and then realize it's a FaceTime call from a computer, which is amazing because then I get to see—

"A *baby!*" I exclaim, wishing I could scrunch myself through the screen and eat the baby's giant cheeks and tickle his big pot belly. The baby blinks at me with long baby eyelashes and then shoves a chubby fist into his mouth and starts gnawing industriously on it.

The man holding the baby on his lap narrows his eyes at me. "You're not Elijah," my brother says.

"So what? This is my nephew," I say as I make a funny face at the baby. The baby regards me impassively, still chewing on his fist.

"He's Elijah's nephew too," Sean says impatiently. "Can I talk to my best friend and the best uncle of my children please?"

"*I'm* the best uncle, and anyway, Elijah's sleeping," I say, making another face at the baby. Joseph Anthony Bell—or Josie for short—pauses chewing a moment…and then decides I'm still not worthy of a smile.

"He's sleeping?" Sean asks. "I thought he was going to be watching you pray all day for an article or something. And you can't be the best uncle, because in case you haven't noticed, you're a monk."

"We'll see what Josie says when he's old enough to appreciate my delicious monk beer. And why don't you want to talk to me? Your own baby brother?"

Sean heaves a giant sigh. "I guess I can talk to you. That's fine. But for the record, Ryan is the baby brother."

That's true enough. Ryan *is* the baby. He's just gotten his bachelor's degree—barely—after a college career that makes my pre-monk life look downright saintly by comparison.

"How's Ryan doing?" I ask.

"Bad and gross," Sean says with the weary air of The Oldest Brother. "I went to pick him up for lunch last week, and he's living like how you used to before you joined a monastery."

I think back. "Making millions of dollars and planning an epic Timber Wolf funeral?"

"No. Like spiked Gatorade is a food group. No offense."

"None taken. Maybe he should join a monastery too."

Sean huffs. "What is it with my brothers all joining the Church? Am I a medieval landowner? Am I an Italian merchant in the nineteenth century? My family has to join the Church because I can give them no living and the king is fighting no wars?"

"It's not just us. Your wife was about to join the Church too," I point out. Elijah's little sister had been about to take her vows as a member of a religious order when Sean happened to her.

Or maybe she happened to Sean. I'm still not exactly sure how it all went down.

"Yes, well." Sean plants a kiss onto Josie's soft, dark curls. "I'm grateful every day that she changed her mind."

He's in his home office, and behind him is a wall of pictures: him and Zenny and their four babies in a mix of candid shots and those photoshoot-y pictures that are always taken in fields for some reason.

Once upon a time, my older brother had been sinning his way through our city with a vengeance and doing it with such cool sophistication that all I'd ever wanted was to be like him, arrogant and charming and grabbing all the good things in life while the grabbing was good. And now he's sitting here dandying a baby on his knee during what used to be the sacrosanct hours of a money-earning workday, surrounded by pictures of the love of his life and the giant family they've made with each other.

"You changed your mind about things too, you know," I say softly, which is right when his second oldest, Mary Amanirenas, charges into view and drops an empty plastic bowl onto Sean's desk with a significant look. She's only three, but like the queen she's named for, she often looks ready to symbolically behead someone.

"Goldfish all gone, Daddy," Amani tells Sean in an imperious tone.

"One second, angel," Sean says, adjusting the baby on his lap to open up a desk drawer.

"Do you have Goldfish *in* your desk?" I ask.

He gives me a critical glance. "Have you ever tried to watch four children at once while taking a work call, Aiden? I

dare you not to have Goldfish in your desk in those times, sir."
He deftly keeps Josie balanced on one knee while one-
handedly refilling the Goldfish bowl, and then leans down to
give Amani a kiss right between her pigtail puffs.

Amani accepts the kiss with great toddler dignity, takes
the bowl, and looks up at me. "Hi, Uncle Brother," she says,
because at some point she heard someone calling me Brother
Patrick and so now I'm Uncle Brother forever.

"Hi, Amani. Where are Caro and Martina?" That's her
older and younger sisters, respectively.

"Taking naps," she replies.

"How come you're not taking a nap?"

She gives me a look that reminds me of Elijah—one baby
eyebrow lifting into her forehead. "Don't like naps," she says,
as if this should be obvious, and she takes her Goldfish back
out of frame.

"Shouldn't Josie be taking a nap too?" I ask as I hear the
faint sounds of *Sesame Street* playing from a tablet somewhere.

"A of all, have you ever tried to get four people to nap at
the same time?"

"It happens every day at the monastery," I tell him, but he
ignores me.

"B of all, he's teething. If he's not nursing or being held,
he's pissed. Aren't you?" he asks the baby, kissing his curls
again. "Aren't you pissed off when we're not holding you?"

Josie pauses chewing on his drool-covered fist to give his
daddy a big, gummy grin.

"Aww, how come I don't get a smile?"

"We've been over this. You're not best uncle. But," he adds with a dramatic exhale, "I guess I could ask you how your trip is going anyway."

I look around the clearing at the ancient grotto and the big trees and the naked man sprawled on a blanket with his head pillowed on his arms and one knee drawn up.

"It's going great," I say honestly.

"And you're really thinking of moving to Europe?" Sean asks doubtfully. "To become a Europe monk or something?"

"I'm thinking of switching orders, and I'm looking at some monasteries of that order here in Europe, yes."

He stares at me a moment, and I stare back. Bell brothers come in two varieties—blond-haired and blue-eyed, or dark-haired and green-eyed. Sean's the former, and I'm the latter. But we all came out of the same Bell factory and so sometimes looking at Sean is like looking at an older, blonder mirror of myself, especially when we're both making an *are you serious right now?* face at each other.

"You know as a medieval landowner hoping to preserve Josie's inheritance that I support you being a monk. But do you have to be a monk so far away? I barely see you when you're a monk in *Kansas*. And now you're thinking about joining an abbey in Liechtenstein or something?"

"Ha. The one in Ireland is the one I'm interested in, if you're wondering."

"Ireland," Sean says, bouncing Josie a little. "Our family's from Ireland. I don't know if you knew that."

"Somehow that hasn't escaped me after two decades of

watching you and Dad get drunk at the local Irish festival while listening to very loud, very bagpipe-y cover bands."

"Oh, like you're better than IrishFest. Like you're better than the Red Hot Chilli Pipers. Who are *Scottish* by the way, so I don't even know what point you're trying to prove."

"Also you can come and visit me, you know," I say. "Stop impregnating your wife for half a minute and then come out to my Irish sea cliffs."

"Elijah sent me pictures of that place," Sean says, looking down at something on his desk. I realize it's a pair of video baby monitors. Satisfied by what he sees, which is presumably two sleeping children, he looks back up at me. "It looked *very* depressing."

"It's not depressing!" I protest. "It's starkly poetic."

"Poetic is a synonym for depressing, and you know it. Even poets know it. What about where you're at now? Is that an olive grove behind you? Aren't you really close to the sea that people pay lots of money to vacation near? What's so wrong with this place that you'd rather go to the depressing abbey instead?"

I look around the clearing again, my mouth folding into a fond smile as I watch Elijah sleep in the sunshine. With him on his stomach and his leg hiked up like that, there's a deep wedge of shadow between his legs that invites exploration, but also there's something so sweet about his face like this. There's no restraint, no doubt, no puzzling things out. Just the face of a man who hates being tickled awake and who secretly loves superhero movies even though he pretends he only likes sad indie documentaries and who will always, always chase after a stray dog and take it to a rescue shelter.

He fits in here, under the bright sun and with the wind that smells like crushed herbs, and then I think of the abbey in the valley below. Of the lavender and the chatting monks in the cloister and the sweet beer and how it feels to pray with Elijah's kisses still stinging my lips.

"Nothing," I say quietly. "There's nothing wrong with this place at all."

Sean looks at me like he wants to ask something more but decides not to. "You look good," he says, with obvious reluctance. "You seem happier than when I saw you last."

He'd visited me at Mount Sergius right after Josie's birth. "That was in February. No one looks happy in February," I say.

"No." He shakes his head. "It's something different. You're more like the old you, maybe."

That sends a ping of alarm through me. I don't want to be like the old me. But also I think he's right—I'm more the old Aiden Bell than ever. I'm fucking around, cursing up a storm, spending time I should be using to discern my future to screw my ex-boyfriend, and maybe that means...

No.

I'm just taking up God on his invitation, that's all. I'm using this trip to figure out what I really want, which of course will be to stay with God at one of his abbeys, to pledge my future to him. Of course.

"Anyway," Sean says, "Tyler will be happy to know you're doing well. He was asking about you."

"Is he doing okay?"

"He's fine," Sean says, sounding bored. "Blah, blah, he and Poppy are so very in love, blah, blah, he wants to make sure you're happy in your chosen vocation and frets about you all the time whenever we talk. The usual. Show me more of this pretty French place you're at. I want to take Zenny somewhere special, but we'll bring the babies too, of course. She wouldn't stand for leaving them for any real length of time."

He cuddles Josie tighter as he says it though, and I suspect it's not only Zenny who would be miserable leaving the children behind.

"Okay," I say, relieved not to have to respond to the part about Tyler worrying about me. Even though he'd be the most natural choice to talk to about what's going on with me and Elijah, I have the sneaking suspicion he'll ask me hard questions and expect hard answers, and I don't want that. No one wants to be pastored by their own brother.

I'd much rather talk to the brother who's just going to show me chunky babies and give me sarcastic updates on the rest of the family.

"Okay," I say again, getting to my feet and squinting down at the iPhone screen. "I can turn this around, right? I want to show you this grotto thing—"

I manage to find the button that flips the screen, careful to move the phone so that Sean can't see his best friend naked and napping behind me, except then it takes too long to flip, and I hit the button again, and then it's flipped back to me while I've got it raised in the air.

Too late I realize that I'm not showing Sean the grotto at all, but a perfectly framed view of the best uncle's ass.

Shit shit shit—

I get the screen flipped around again but it's too late. Sean's mouth has dropped into a giant round *O*.

"That is a butt!" he hisses. I'm guessing he doesn't want Amani to hear. "*Aiden*! Why is there a butt behind you?"

"I…" I hate lying, but also I have to lie, don't I?

But Sean knows me too well, and before I can say anything, he's guessed the truth anyway.

"Aiden Bell!" he whispers angrily. "I know you are not fucking around with my best friend on your 'maybe I want to be an Irish monk' trip!"

"Wait," I whisper back, aggrieved. "Aren't you supposed to be on *my* side? Aren't you supposed to be going all big brother on your best friend instead?"

"Well, maybe I would if my little brother hadn't already broken my best friend's heart!"

I glare at him.

He glares back at me.

"I'm not going to break his heart," I whisper furiously. "We both know this is just a…an interlude."

"You're a monk! You're not allowed to have interludes!"

"Well, you're an asshole! You're not allowed to have opinions!"

He covers Josie's ears. "There are babies in here! Don't call me an asshole in front of my babies, you shithead!"

We glare at each other again.

335

Finally, Sean reaches for his ace in the hole. "I'm telling Tyler," he says. A little smugly.

I feel myself pale. "No, don't. *Sean.*"

Now that our mom has died, this is endgame. The ultimate tattletale.

He gives me a sad shake of his head. "I'm telling him. I'm telling him you fell off the dick wagon so hard you left a dent in the road. And then he'll call you and he'll yell at you and then maybe you will *leave my poor friend alone* in your quest for 'interludes.'"

"I'm not—" My voice has gotten louder, and I force myself to whisper again so I don't wake Elijah. "I'm not collecting interludes in some kind of interlude harvest, okay? I've been good—I've been living exactly the way I'm supposed to. And then Elijah joined me on this trip and there were medieval ruins and it all just *happened.*"

"And so it's just going to magically stop happening once you get back home and away from medieval ruins? Is that what I'm hearing?" Sean asks.

"Yes, obviously. He won't be at Mount Sergius, and I'll probably be moving to Europe anyway, and so it'll have to stop happening."

Sean scowls at me. "I swear, if you fuck with his heart again, I am bricking you into an anchorage so you can never be near him again."

"I'm surprised you know what an anchorage is."

"I'm surprised you think it's totally fine spiritually or whatever that distance is the only reason you're going to be able to stop. You know I don't give a shit about sin, but I do give a shit about Elijah, and I guess"—another giant sigh—"a shit about you too."

"Thanks, I think."

"And when you joined the monk-hood, I thought it was a fluke, I really did. I thought it was just a bigger version of that time you said you were going to help me move a couch and then you went to Belize instead."

"Well, Jessica sent me an invitation to a festival thing and it was happening that week—"

"*But*," Sean goes on as if I haven't spoken, "it wasn't a fluke. You stayed. You stayed even when it was hard, and they made you wear a cheap robe and wake up before dawn. You worked hard and you prayed hard, and for the first time in your entire life, you shut up and let other people talk. For the first time, I saw you dedicate yourself to something, I saw you lose yourself in something that wasn't about money or sex or fun. I saw you make God a promise and I saw you keep it."

His expression is now something much, much worse than angry or smug.

It's gentle.

"This life means something to you," he says. "And if I'm learning anything by going to church, it's that we have to keep our promises even when it's hard to do. Especially when it's hard to do."

I don't answer for a moment. I don't know if I can through the ball of shame in my throat. Because I haven't been keeping very many promises lately.

I say weakly, "You're learning at *church*? Who are you and what have you done with Sean Bell?"

"Yeah, well," Sean says. "Father Jordan has his work cut out for him. But he still tries, which is very sweet of him, in my opinion."

I've only met Father Jordan once or twice in passing—he married Sean and Zenny and has performed all the baptisms for their babies—but his church is one of the youngest and most thriving in the city, and maybe if anyone can reform a sinner like Sean, it's him.

"Aiden," Sean says, his blue eyes still uncomfortably kind. "All I want is for you to have what *you* want. You know that, right?"

"Yeah," I say heavily. "I know."

I hear the sound of another call coming through, and then Sean makes a face. "It's Ryan. Probably woke up in a pile of cheerleaders and apple bongs again. I should make sure he's okay."

"Yeah. You should," I say. "And I'll tell the best uncle you called."

"You do that. Also tell him that I already promised to brick you into a hole if you fuck him over."

"Yeah, yeah." I wave at Josie—who *finally* smiles at me around his fist—and then we end the call, my stomach all heavy and unsettled as we do.

I put the phone back in the satchel and go sit next to Elijah, who's now snoring handsomely, which I didn't even know was possible before now, and I think about what Sean said. I'm glad, as silly as it sounds, that he's so protective of Elijah, because I am too, and the last thing I want to do is hurt him again. And I'm glad Sean wants for me to have what I want.

But what I actually want is getting hazier and hazier these days. I want it *all*—kisses *and* prayers, sex *and* contemplation— I want Elijah *and* God. I want the right to hunger and to crave, but I also want to be a monk, to find those crisp, keen moments of joy that can only be cracked open through the fires of showing up, day after day after day. From denial and effort and rejecting all else that isn't a holy life.

Why can't I have both? All?

Why do I have to choose?

CHAPTER FORTY-ONE

"Ahh, it is so good we are having a little celebration in the cloister for your last night with us," Brother Luc says, "because our prodigal mystic has returned!"

I turn to face the French monk after drying my plate and setting it on the stack in the cupboard. "Really?" I've become pretty curious about the missing priest over the week, wondering if he really is some kind of John the Baptist type, living like a hermit and looking like Robin Williams in *Jumanji* after he was stuck in the game-jungle for twenty years.

"Yes, now. How much beer should we bring out?" Then the monk grins at me. "Trick question, as you Americans say. We bring all of it!"

Fifteen minutes later, and we are wheeling the old wooden cart into the cloister and handing out bottles. The mood is high with the harvest going well and with it being a day of rest tomorrow. I'm laughing as the monks try to replicate Elijah's trick of opening a beer bottle with another beer bottle and fail spectacularly, fizzing beer everywhere, and that's when I hear it. A voice like a melody, a voice made for singing old, ancient words.

"May I have one?"

I turn to see the missing American priest standing in front of me, and he's not John the Baptist or Robin Williams.

He's someone I know. Someone I've spoken with.

Sean and Zenny's parish priest, Father Jordan.

I blink at him.

"Hello, Brother Patrick," he says. The evening sun burnishes his pale gold skin and dark gold hair and shimmers from the depths of his dark, dark eyes. Far from looking like he's been eating locusts and honey, he's in a crisply pressed black shirt and stark white clerical collar. His square jaw is cleanly shaven, and his black shoes gleam against the medieval stones. He looks like he just came from a runway show where all the models are priests.

"We all thought you were doing Anthony the Great cosplay in the hills or something," I say, faintly.

"Not quite," Father Jordan says. "I was in Avignon meeting with a group of ISM leaders."

"ISM?" Elijah asks, coming up to us and handing the priest the beer I'd been too surprised to fork over. "And it's good to see you, Father."

I look at Elijah. "You know him?"

Elijah lifts a brow. "I go to all the baptisms too, Aiden. Now, what's an ISM again?"

"Independent Sacramental Movement," Father Jordan says.

"Churches who've broken off from Rome or Constantinople—or even Canterbury—and seek to preserve traditional liturgy while they follow their conscience on theology."

"I'm sorry," I say. "Are we just ignoring the fact that you're here at the same time as us? *Here*? At this tiny abbey in this tiny valley so boring even the Romans didn't bother colonizing it?"

"*I* don't think the valley is boring," Elijah says, in a voice that sounds like he's apologizing for me.

"Like what are the odds?" I ask Father Jordan. "To run into an American here is already nuts, and then for it to be an American from our city! And then for it to be you!"

"It's a remarkable coincidence," the priest agrees mildly.

I feel like no one is reacting to this as much as they should be. "I was *just* talking about you with Sean! And now you're here! You've been here this whole time!"

"Do they have a bottle opener?" Father Jordan asks Elijah.

"No, but I know a trick," Elijah starts but Father Jordan is already lifting the bottle to his sculpted mouth and opening the beer with his teeth. And then he flips the cap with his tongue and drops it expertly onto his waiting palm.

"I think that's bad for your enamel," Elijah says after a minute.

"But why are you *here*?" I ask as Father Jordan takes a swallow of beer and then looks around the cloister of cheerful, sun-burned monks. "If the ISM thing was in Avignon, or whatever?"

"I've been following Abbé Bernard's writings on the future

of monasticism for a while, and when I decided to take a sabbatical, I thought I'd come stay here. The ISM meeting was a fortunate coincidence."

"That seems to happen a lot with you," I say suspiciously. "Coincidences, I mean."

"Mm," is his noncommittal reply.

"Has it been a good sabbatical?" Elijah asks politely, redirecting the conversation. "The abbey here is lovely."

"It is," Father Jordan agrees. "And it has been a very good sabbatical, I think. I came here to look for clarity, and so of course, all I've found are more questions. Which I find encouraging."

I feel my brow furrow. "You do?"

It seems like it should be the opposite. I came to Mount Sergius because I felt like I was choking on questions, and all I wanted was clarity. All I wanted was one simple answer that would cut through my life like an icy wind and blow all the indecision away.

Father Jordan gives me a small smile. On such an eerily beautiful face, the tiny expression is staggering.

"I find that fixed and unambiguous thinking is the mother of many sins," he explains. "We forget that Christ was heterodox and radical. He was not safe, in his ideas or his passions or his presence, and he demanded everything of his followers, not the least their certainty that they knew all the shapes of right and wrong in their world. And so when I'm searching for my way forward, naively hunting for certainty, I've found that God nudges me back to where God wants me.

Which is in the middle of questions that feel unanswerable. I believe it is there—in the fire and friction of things I've been told don't belong together, of things that I've been taught can't be done—that the true answers lie."

"What were you searching for when you came here?" I ask.

"If you don't mind sharing," my etiquette-minded journalist adds politely.

"I never mind sharing," Father Jordan replies, and he does give that impression, I think. That all you have to do is ask and he'd crack open his chest to show you his beating heart, his ruby red lungs. As if to him there's no meaningful difference between sharing what he thought of his eggs at breakfast and the most intimate and tangled question he asks his god.

"Once upon a time," Father Jordan says, "there were as many ways to be holy as there were people, and the space between secular and monastic, between laity and clergy, was filled with all sorts of strange nooks and crannies. You could have visions, dream dreams, you could be a monastic from the four walls of your own house or you could wander the country barefoot and begging. But we've lost much of that over the centuries. The path to God has become binary: you find God as a monastic or as clergy, or you find God as a layperson. There is precious little in between. Oblation comes close but is still only one thread when there used to be an entire tapestry." He frowns a little at the stones he's standing on. "This rigid dichotomy of holy and profane, of vowed and unvowed...it sterilizes us. Not everyone fits into those boxes to begin with, almost no one fits entirely into them, and then there are those of us who experience God so differently from what is sanctioned and prescribed that even the mere idea of boxes is..." He looks like he's searching for the right word here. "Limiting."

And there's something in the way he says the last part which makes me think that he's no longer talking in the abstract. That he's talking about himself.

"So this tapestry that you want to bring back," Elijah asks. "Is that related in any way to the Independent Sacramental Movement meeting? Are you thinking of leaving the Roman Church?"

Father Jordan looks at us both, his dark eyes like wells to his very soul, and it's a soul that's both beautiful and uncomfortable to behold. I have spent the last several years trying to live like a saint. But I think right now I'm standing in front of one.

"It is one of many questions laid at my feet," the priest says finally.

There's a strange pressure in my chest now. A pressure that shouldn't be there.

There used to be an entire tapestry.

Does that mean Father Jordan wants to find new ways for people to live a holy life? Ways that are neither entirely monastic nor entirely non-monastic?

Is that possible?

"Elijah!" one of the abbey monks calls from near the fountain. "Venez ici et ouvrez notre bière!" With an apologetic glance at me and Father Jordan, Elijah strides into the cloister to much monk-y fanfare and accepts the challenge of showing them the beer opening trick again.

"You should show them the thing you do with your teeth," I tell Father Jordan, and once again, his full mouth hints at a smile.

"It does make me very popular at wedding receptions," he says. His stare alights on Elijah with the others, and then he looks over to me. "You are blessed to have such a good friend as your traveling companion," he says.

I meet his eyes, but I can't read whatever thoughts are hidden there. "Yes," I say carefully. "I am very blessed."

"I would think," Father Jordan says, his voice as inscrutable as his gaze, "that such a blessing would need to be deeply received. Even when it's uncomfortable."

I'm nervous enough that I don't even want to make a joke about *deeply receiving*. "I would think you're right," I say, not sure how to steer away from this conversation, but knowing I need to. "He's a good friend."

I hate the words as soon as I say them. Obviously, I can't let Father Jordan know what's going on, and yet hiding it feels weird too. Slippery and wrong. Hiding our—I can't even call it a relationship because it's so temporary—*liaison*, I guess, because I'm a monk feels too close to hiding it for other reasons. And I had too long a road to being openly queer to easily dismiss how hiding feels now. The discomfort in my chest doesn't care if it's because of the habit or because of something else. Hiding feels like hiding, period.

But strangely, Father Jordan seems to sense this.

He says, simply, "I know what Elijah is to you."

I don't answer, and he doesn't make me. He merely nods toward the man I love, who is in a throng of people understandably enchanted by him, and says, quietly, "And there's nothing to be gained by keeping secrets."

"Easy for you to say," I mumble into my beer.

A distant expression passes over his face. "Perhaps not as easy as you think." But before I can respond to that, he turns to the cart and sets his half-empty bottle down on the shelf reserved for used bottles. "But I'm not speaking of secrets from your abbot or even your family, although those are important too. I'm speaking of secrets from the one you love. Elijah."

"Him? But I don't have any secrets from him."

Father Jordan doesn't elaborate; instead he looks at his watch. "I'm supposed to call my bishop before compline," he says. "I should go. But I hope to see you back in Kansas City. I think we could have much to talk about."

"*Wait*," I say. "Father, please. What secrets? Why would you say that? Can we—"

But he's already making his way down the covered walkway to the guesthouse, already out of earshot, his stride graceful and determined, like that of a man who's just completed what was asked of him.

Shit.

What did he mean by secrets? And how does he know about me and Elijah? I run through his words again, trying to figure out what he could know that would make him say such things. Trying to judge whether or not Tyler was pulling my leg all those years ago when he told me he thought his seminary friend could speak to angels.

I'm speaking of secrets from the one you love. Elijah.

It's not until that night, as I'm trying to sleep and watching the darkness gather on the windowsill, that it comes to me. Slowly and by degrees.

Somehow, Father Jordan knew—or could guess—the only thing I still haven't told Elijah.

The full story of the night I decided to become a monk.

CHAPTER
FORTY-TWO

The lovely thing about staying in a Trappist monastery is that no matter how early you leave, the monks are usually awake to see you off, and the *double* lovely thing about Trappists is that the Grand Silence of the morning is totally sacred, so there are no Midwestern Goodbyes. Just fond handshakes and hugs and several bottles of beer for the road, and then Brother Luc is driving us to the train station at Cavaillon, where we'll begin our patchwork trip to London, and then on to Dublin, where we'll drive a rented car to the west coast and St. Columba's.

The breaking dawn is cheerful and sweet-smelling, but I'm too preoccupied with Father Jordan's words to enjoy my last glimpses of the hills and the valley carpeted with freshly shorn lavender. It's only once we're out of the valley that I realize what I've done, and I twist around in the back seat to look, but it's too late. The place where Elijah and I spent afternoons in a dreamy, lust-sweet haze is already behind me. The place where prayer and sex scented the air in equal measure, where loving God and Elijah both didn't feel like a betrayal of either, is falling farther and farther away, and now it's on to the last stop. On to Ireland.

Somewhere near Lyon, I spill a giant coffee all over my scapular and habit, and because I'd bought myself a big, sweet coffee-milkshake-thing instead of a grown-up coffee, there's no doubt that very soon I will be a sticky monk, and not in a kinky way. I find my suitcase and change in the small, swaying bathroom of the train, my shoulders bumping noisily against the walls, and then I emerge in the one pair of street clothes I brought.

Elijah raises his eyebrows. "Khakis and a button-down? For me? Be still my heart."

"Very funny," I say. "This outfit was on top in the suitcase and the bathroom was too small for me to open everything up to find a new robe." I fit my bulk between the table and the seat and sit down across from him.

He looks out the window, his brows still digging into his forehead, and I wonder if he's trying to spy one of the little villages which are tucked into the hills here, but then I realize he's looking at our reflection in the window. The reflection where we're sitting together and I'm not in a monk's habit and we could just be any two men. We could be anyone.

"What if…" I say, looking at him in the reflection, and a slow, excited smile breaks across his face.

"Yes," he says. "What if."

It's evening when we get to London, but London evenings have long legs in the summer, and so there's still light kissing the tops of the buildings when Elijah and I walk hand in hand into the Tate Modern. We show the tickets we bought earlier during our train ride to the employees at the stiles, and then we're inside the belly of the forbidding modern art beast. There's a clump of young people near the entrance, all dressed in the painfully curated way which comes with trying to broadcast *this is me* with clothes and accessories. Two of them—both young men—are making out against the wall while the group deliberates over their next move.

It makes me feel nostalgic for those days, when all that mattered was the next spot you were going to, the next drink you were getting, the next mouth you could kiss. But it also reminds me that I'm here, *now*, with the man I love in a big foreign city and I'm not wearing monk robes and we are on a date. Unbelievably, impossibly, on a date.

I lace my fingers through Elijah's and squeeze.

"So," he says as we walk into the big central hall of the museum. "What would you like to see while we're here? Dali? Rothko? Warhol?"

"I don't care," I say honestly, looking at him. "I just want to be with you."

In the strange, shadowy light of the Turbine Hall, Elijah looks back at me, his eyes dark and glimmering with the reflection of the narrow, artificial lights of the space. There's something almost pained to the angle of his eyebrows, to the notch that's carved itself between them, and instinctively I reach out to rub at that notch with my thumb.

"Don't look so sad," I whisper, my heart twisting. "I'll pretend really hard to like Rothko, I promise."

He lets me rub at the space between his brows right there in the middle of the museum. It's so much like how it used to be before I became a monk, when the city was ours, when we went to every exhibition and opening and reading because Elijah wanted to and because he was too handsome for me to refuse even though I don't understand any art that's not a bowl of fruit.

"I'm not sad," Elijah says finally, looking at me from underneath my hand. "How can I be sad when you're saying shit like that?"

Satisfied that the line between his brows is erased, I drop my hand and find his again. I bring it to my mouth and kiss his knuckles. Softly.

In the light of the hall, every rise and hollow of his perfect face is sketched in light and shadow. Light at the ridge of his nose and the square of his jaw, light along his cheeks and touching the sharp peaks and edges of his mouth. Shadows in the faint, stubble-covered cleft of his chin and under his eyelashes.

He shivers as I kiss his knuckles, and then he says after I finish, "I think this might be my favorite *what if* game."

I smile at him, but maybe it's my turn to look sad now,

because this *what if* game is one of the simplest we've ever played, it's the closest to not a game at all.

What if we were together?

Lovers, boyfriends, partners, spouses—we didn't specify, and I'm glad, because the way Elijah handled getting the Oyster cards for the Tube while I held his iced coffee and satchel felt very spouse-y, and yet the way he preened a little after I glared and practically snarled at the docent just inside the door who was definitely flirting with him? That felt very new boyfriend-y.

Almost as if we can have a taste of our entire past and our entire future here in this one night. Newness and oldness both, the thrill of the chase and the deep passion for a heart that I've felt beat against my own for months and months.

We are husbands as I hold his things while he takes pictures with his phone; we are brand new lovers as I fumble for the right responses to the paintings and sculptures so he'll think I'm sophisticated and cerebral; and when we pass through an empty exhibit room with a convenient half-wall and I push him into the corner and shove my tongue in his mouth, then we are just Aiden and Elijah.

I do the kissing the rest of the night, actually. On the rooftop bar at the Tate, in another rooftop bar Elijah finds near the Globe, against the railing of the Millennium Bridge as the Thames washes quietly below us. Every chance I get, I press my mouth to his and taste inside, and he lets me, he slides his hands into the cheap fabric of my button-down and holds me close as I nibble gently at his mouth, as I kiss his upper lip and then his lower, and then slowly search out every last secret in between.

We're kissing on the bridge, when I think, dizzily, *this is what we could've had.* If I hadn't left, if I'd found some other way to slay my demons. If I'd stayed. In that alternate timeline, we might be kissing on this very same bridge, listening to this very same city churn indifferently around us. We might be here as boyfriends still or even as husbands, and I would be Elijah's to kiss and use as an iced coffee holder whenever he wanted. Any time. All the time. Always.

My feet are planted on the outside of Elijah's, my hands braced on the railing on either side of him, and when I pull back a little to catch my breath and check that we're safe, I'm close enough to feel him panting too. To see the pupils of his dark whiskey eyes blown wide with lust, to see how he searches my face like he wants to commit every eyelash to memory.

He looks so beautiful like this, with the wide river behind him and the moonlight gleaming on his chiseled features, and with all the smart things he said at the Tate still lingering in my mind and with all the funny things he said at the bar lingering too. He is the kind of man you give your entire heart to, the kind of man you ache for, the kind of man you buy a house with and adopt a dog with and the kind of man you marry.

And I left him.

And suddenly, I don't want Father Jordan's words to be true anymore, I don't want there to be any secrets between us. I want to explain to him why I left, about what really happened that night so he can understand that it was never, ever about him, that it was all my fault, and that I didn't see any other way to stay alive and stop hurting him at the same time.

I want him to know, even if he despises me after, because I don't want there to be anything about me that he doesn't know. I want him to know me as well as God knows me, to know my sittings and my risings, to find me at the farthest reaches of the sea.

I want to be entirely his, even if it's only for one night by the Thames.

I lean in to kiss him again, seeking courage from his lips, pulling strength from his mouth.

"You're kissing me like you're already saying goodbye," he murmurs, and I lift my head a little to look at him.

I need to tell him. I want to tell him, give him this one last burnt offering under the moon.

"Elijah," I say, not sure how to begin, but he must hear the difference in my voice, he must see something on my face, because he shakes his head decisively and presses a long finger to my mouth.

"No," he says, and I think he means to say it firmly, but there's a catch in his voice on the *o* part of the word, like he can't push the word out fast enough. "No. Not tonight."

"You don't even know what I was going to—"

"Please," he pleads, and his other hand fists even harder in my shirt. It breaks my heart a little. "Whatever it is, it can wait. It can wait until we're cold and gloomy tomorrow, it can even wait until we get home. But tonight I just want our what if. Tonight I just want—I want—"

His voice breaks again, and I don't have the stomach to force him to finish. "Hey, it's okay," I say, leaning in to kiss his face with soft, soothing kisses. "It's okay. I won't say it. Tonight will just be *what if*. I promise, I promise." And I keep layering his cheeks and mouth and jaw with kisses; I kiss the corners of his eyes and the shallow depressions of his temples; I kiss him until his hips are restless and searching against mine and the only thing we can do is stumble back to our hotel, where I get to my knees and start sucking him the minute we get inside his hotel room.

The only thing we can do is kiss and peel each other out of our clothes, and fuck more than once, fuck again and again, on the bed and in the shower and against the big window overlooking the street below. The only thing we can do is hold each other as we fall asleep together for the first time in almost five years, and when I feel the slow, wet leak of Elijah's tears on my naked chest, the only thing I can do is hold him even tighter. Because I love him and I would play the *what if* game forever if I could, but I can't, I can't. I built my life around being a monk—I built my *mind* around being a monk. I can't surrender what saved me.

Even for the sweetest *what if* I've ever known.

Right?

CHAPTER FORTY-THREE

from the notebook of Elijah Iverson

Franciscan friar Richard Rohr says that there are two kinds of time, at least according to the ancient Greeks. There is chronos—or chronological, ordered time—and then there is kairos.

Kairos is subjective, qualitative. Deep Time is what Rohr calls it. A fullness, he says. The moments when the dots of our lives connect.

I've been living in Deep Time these last two weeks, in medieval monasteries where monks sing prayers thousands of years old and where Aiden looks at me like I'm a human hymn. For a handful of days, I have been suspended with him, and maybe even with God, inside that fullness, all my dots connecting, hovering, shimmering.

My inbox didn't matter, deadlines didn't matter. Even the relentless notifications on my phone fell away as the shitty monastery wi-fi flickered in and out. The *ping ping* of DMs, emails, news alerts, and more news alerts—the heartbeats of my day—simply stopped. And when the wi-fi *did* work and my phone came to hectic life at last, that insistent glass rectangle felt as gaudy and cheap as a slot machine in my hand.

So what did matter in that fullness?

His fingers laced in mine.

The wind on our faces, the echo of voices against stone.

Honey beer on my tongue and stillness, stillness, stillness inside.

My eyes hurt today, and I wish I could say it's from the dry air of the airplane as we whoosh our way to Dublin, but instead it's because I spent the night crying on the chest of my monk ex-boyfriend. We left the kairos behind for the very real, very frenetic chronos of London, and it was dazzling, dizzying, being in the real world with Aiden Bell. But.

But.

I just want to be with you, he said in the Tate Modern, but we were in real time again, in chronological time. Time measured in hours and minutes—time that passed so fucking fast that before I knew it, it was gone.

Outside the Tate, there'd been two young men kissing against a wall, and I remember thinking, *where did our time go?* Not the time of this trip, but the time of *us*—maybe even the time before us. I don't feel any different from those young people inside, I don't wake up thinking *act like you're in your forties now*, but I am different, aren't I? Every kiss, every arm around a waist, every brush of our pinkies, I checked around us. Even in London, even in the Tate, I checked.

It's habit, necessary habit. Look, glance, turn. Check, check, safe.

Is that generational? Or is it age?

Experience?

Will those two men do the same in twenty years?

I hope not. I hope they have the kairos of a kiss on a summer night without real time, without bitter, biting reality scraping its claws over their skin.

It's not that I wish I were young again; it's not innocence I crave, and it's not the months and years they have stretching out before them.

No, it's those moments of fullness that I want, always those moments.

And these moments with Aiden are slipping away faster than I can hold on to them. Because as he pointed out in Semois, his vocation is there, in that world of kairos and God, and my vocation is here.

It would be easy to say that I'm only a visitor in his life, but truly, this patient, petulant, vulnerable man is only a visitor in mine.

IRELAND

CHAPTER
FORTY-FOUR

The first thing Elijah does when we step outside the terminal at the Dublin airport is heave a giant sigh.

The next thing he does is take the sunglasses he'd pulled out of his satchel and put them back inside his satchel. And then he hunts for a cardigan he'd shoved in there during the flight instead. I look up at the gray sky and then around at all the slick, gray concrete. A wind blows chilly and wet in front of the terminal. It's hard to think of a place more different than the sunny, herb-scented valley where we've spent the last week.

"Shall we?" Elijah sighs, and we step out into the gray drizzle and start rolling our way to the rental car place.

Thirty minutes later, and we are on the road. Traveling on a monastery's dime means that funds are hugely limited, and we're taking the cheapest car they have, which is a tiny, tiny stick.

I have to drive, because Elijah doesn't know how to drive a manual, which means I'm currently sitting with my knees around the steering wheel, my habit pulled up to my thighs because the hem keeps snagging on my boot when I work the clutch, trying to figure out how to shift with my left hand while a very stressed-out Elijah tries to navigate.

It gets easier as we emerge from the cluster of Dublin and get onto the M4 and then onto the M6, which will take us right across the middle of the island to the west coast, where the poetic-slash-depressing sea cliffs await us. The sky doesn't get any less gray, but soon there are pretty fields lining the highway, dotted with clumps of trees and then cows and the occasional tractor. If not for the vibrant green grass and low stone walls, we could be in Kansas.

"Okay," Elijah says, somewhere after Athlone. We've both relaxed a little now that I've taught my left hand how to shift and we're on a highway I can't drive down the wrong side of because there's a dividing rail. He pulls out his notebook and rests it on the dash while he digs for his pen and his iPad. "I have a list of questions for the article—can I ask them while we drive?"

"Fire away," I tell him.

Most of the questions are perfunctory—what's the difference between a leather belt or a cloth one; where do the monks too old or infirm to live at the abbey stay; how are abbots appointed and is there some kind of Church HR process for a bad abbot?

Some of them are slightly more complicated, as I discover when we're sitting in a parking lot with Supermac's balanced on our laps and he asks me about the priesthood.

"Why are some monks priests and others aren't?" he asks, eating a French fry. There's a lingering grain of salt on his lower lip, and I want to lunge across the car and lick it off. "Is it a choice? Is it decided by the abbot? Some kind of priest vetting committee?"

"It's a personal choice," I say, reluctantly tearing my eyes from his mouth. "When you join a monastic community, you're a monk first, and any other calling is secondary. There used to be a sort of class system about it—monks who would go on to be priests were called choir monks, and they were more educated, their days revolved around liturgy and contemplation, et cetera. And then there were the monks called brothers, who were often less educated and whose days revolved around the material needs of the abbey. The work and the manual labor and stuff. I think that's changing, at least at Mount Sergius, because there's not a division of abbey work along choir-monk-slash-brother lines, and there's definitely not any weird, classist talk about how the brothers' natural aptitude for cleaning toilets frees up the educated, more sensitive souls for contemplation." I think for a minute, chewing a fry. "Okay, well, I've heard some talk like that, I suppose, but mainly from the olds. And the random people who want to be Carthusians."

Elijah looks over at me. "And you didn't have this calling?" he asks. "You wanted to be a brother?"

My entire body prickles with how much I don't want to be a priest. "I know it's surprising maybe, given that Tyler went into the priesthood, but it's never been something I wanted.

Religious priests—that is, priests in a monastic order—don't have the same breadth of pastoral care that secular or diocesan priests do, but they are still supposed to pastor their monastic communities. They still need to shepherd a flock, even if it's a well-behaved monastic flock with lots of shepherds already. They still need to hear confessions and perform sacraments."

"And you didn't want to do that?" Elijah gives me a rueful smile. "I thought every Catholic kid grew up wanting to change wine into blood."

"I think even as a kid I knew that wasn't for me. I wasn't good enough for it." I huff out a laugh. "And I'm definitely not good enough for it now."

Elijah's voice is curious. "And so that's why you've chosen not to be ordained? Because you think you're not good enough to turn wine into blood?"

I look out the windshield, struggling for a way to put how I feel about it into words. "Not in an internalized monastic class system way—because I had no idea that hierarchy was even a thing until I came to Mount Sergius—but yes, I guess. And not necessarily with performing the sacraments so much as the pastoring. I mean, who am I to hear anyone's sins? Who am I to hand out penitence or advice or…or…wisdom nuggets?"

Elijah pauses with a fry halfway to his mouth. "Wisdom nuggets?"

"You know," I say, gesturing vaguely. "When someone old and wise gives you the perfect soundbite that eventually solves everything? A nugget of wisdom?"

"Ah."

"Anyway, I'm not qualified for that! I was a catastrophe of a person until I became a monk, and I still barely know which way is up, morally speaking."

"You weren't a catastrophe of a person," he says. Softly. I look over at him, and he stares back at me. And even though we are in a gas station parking lot with fast food wrappers everywhere, we could be at a candlelit dinner with the way he's looking at me now.

"I loved the person you were," he continues. "And I think I might love you even more now, which I wouldn't have thought possible before, but here we are."

"Elijah," I start, but he shakes his head at me and keeps speaking.

"In case you need to hear it again, you weren't a catastrophe. You were human. Impulsive and a flake perhaps, but maybe that makes you more qualified to give out those nuggets of wisdom than someone who's been sensible and well-behaved his entire life. And even though I think that you should do whatever you want to do with your life—whether it's to be a brother or a priest or anything else—I want you to know that the idea of deserving something you want is only ever going to be an incomplete qualification. You're far more likely to remember the reasons you shouldn't have something you want than the reasons you should, and you're far more likely to let shame steer you than joy. Maybe we can talk about what is good and healthy for you and the people around you, but *deserving*? That sounds like Catholic nonsense to me, and I should know."

I touch his knee. "Elijah?" I say.

"Yes?"

"That was a wisdom nugget."

He throws a fry at me.

Ireland doesn't look big, but it takes longer to get places inside it than you'd think, which I discover as we hit Galway and turn north-ish to follow the coast along a series of ever-narrowing roads.

Soon the sea is in view, a dark reach leading out to the gray horizon, and everywhere are emerald cliffs and black rocks and tiny, hidden inlets carpeted with oat-colored sand. The rain returns as a mist, which veils the world and even the nearby sea, and then there's only the road—narrow as a crepe paper party streamer—and the stone walls which stitch the island into a quilt of green, brown, and gray.

The rain picks up, making everything smeary through the windshield, and I slow down to a crawl, worried I'm going to drive us off a cliff.

"So this is the Bell motherland," Elijah says, checking the directions on his phone for the umpteenth time to make sure this is actually the way to the abbey and not to the middle of the ocean. I brake the car as a sheep steps onto the road, shits a giant shit, and then meanders across to an open field.

"Charming," says Elijah.

"That's probably the Bell family crest," I reply. "A sheep shitting in the rain."

That earns me a laugh as I roll over the dung and along we go, ribboning over hills and down into bright green vales lined with stone walls and dotted with more sheep. Sometimes in the distance, we catch glimpses of shadows on the sea. Small islands.

At one point, I look over at him, and my heart feels like someone's slid a tuning fork into an atrium and struck it. I wish, desperately, that I had a phone of my own, so I could take a picture and have this image of him forever.

His long legs are bent like mine in order to fit in the tiny car, but while I look like someone tried to trick the Hulk into driving a go-kart, he looks like he's in an indie music video. Bare feet, fitted trousers, leather satchel. One knee now pulled up as he stares out the window, the top of his pen between his teeth as he watches the land reveal itself, bit by stony, green bit.

He glances back at me, and that tuning fork strikes again, vibrating everything through my chest and bones and strumming the fibers of my muscles and fascia like an eolian harp left outside in the wind. With the world reduced to gray and green around us, the dark, dark bronze of his eyes beckons me in.

In the flash before I tear my eyes back to the road, I see his hand flex on his knee, and I think about how it felt to hold his hand last night at the Tate, about his mouth against mine on the bridge, about the warm slick of tears on my chest as he cried.

I think of the fact that we will get to St. Columba's today, which is a Monday, and then we will leave first thing Saturday morning for Dublin, where we will have separate flights back home.

I think of all I haven't told him.

I think of how much I love him and how much I love being a monk and it's not fair that I can't be a garden of my god and Elijah at the same time—

I look back to the road as I open my mouth to say some of this, any of this, but right as I start to say his name, his phone breaks into the noise of the rain with its chipper voice.

"In a quarter of a mile, turn left at the fork," and even as the phone says it, we see it. A sweep of stern hills with a cluster of medieval stone buildings roosting proudly at their base. The sea heaves below, and even through the rain, I can make out the foam and churn of the water.

As we pull down the narrow lane to the abbey, a bell tolls from below. A call to prayer that I feel as keenly in my soul as I felt the tuning fork in my heart.

CHAPTER
FORTY-FIVE

It's not the abbey like something out of a children's history book, all damp gray rock weathered by centuries of wind and salt. It's not the probably haunted graveyard full of winding paths and crooked stones.

It's not even the sea, which rolls against the broken edge of the world with a ceaseless fury, or the wind, which never truly stops, but only abates into grazes and whispers.

It is none of this that makes me fall in love with St. Columba's—or rather, it's none of this alone. Instead it is the absolute, undeniable certainty that this is a place where hearts are tested. This is a place where everything but God is stripped away.

They say that Irish monks are different, special—that it was in these stark green fringes that Christianity survived the nastiness of the Early Middle Ages. That it was Irish monks who saved history, literacy, art, and faith for this part of the world.

I'm sure the actual history is more nuanced than that, but right now, I'd believe it. I'd believe every word of it. Looking at this place, being shown around by a rail-thin monk with a pale, wind-lined face and a beard the color of fire, hearing the bells against the matching song of the wind…

Yes, I'd believe it. If you found God in a place like this, you'd never lose him again.

Though the rain never leaves, the day is more than long enough for Father Finbarr (whom I've privately been calling Father Firebeard) to show Elijah and me around the relevant parts of the abbey.

St. Columba's has a very traditional layout that probably hasn't changed much since the days of Brian Boru. A square is made, with one side being the church stretching west to east, another side comprising the dormitory and former scriptorium, and yet another making up the refectory and former malthouse. The final stretch is the library, tea rooms, and gift shop, the latter two of which are only open for a few hours each day and are closed when we see them now. Set to the south is a low-slung stone building that houses their small but popular brewery, a cottage that functions as their hermitage, the parking lot, and trailheads for the visitors to take up to the cliffs or down to the sheltered beach below.

Father Finbarr talks very little, even compared to the other Trappists we've been staying with. His tone is polite, warm even, but he gives only the most perfunctory of explanations as we walk from place to place, ducking his head as we walk through the drizzle, unbothered by the way his glasses fog up when we walk back indoors.

The only meal the brothers share is lunch, he explains to us, and all other meals are taken alone when a brother chooses. A stricter silence is kept than at Our Lady or even at Semois, and typically the only conversation that doesn't directly pertain to work or prayer happens at their weekly chapter meetings, when they discuss affairs of the abbey. They are allowed to talk to visitors as needed, but Father Finbarr says most visitors seem to embrace the atmosphere of silence when they come and don't require much conversation.

Tomorrow, we will be shown the brewery and be allowed to talk to the master brewer, who is a layperson named something so Irish that I make a mental note to ask Father Finbarr for help pronouncing it later. And unlike at Semois or Our Lady, there are no assurances that prayers are optional when we are handed the prayer schedule. Our host doesn't say that they are *mandatory*, nor do I get the impression that he would scold us if we were absent. But there is something about the way his light blue eyes flicker to mine when he asks me if it's true I'm considering becoming a Trappist that I think he would mark my absence if I were gone.

He seems to assume that I'm here because I want to be here. That I'm here seeking exactly what St. Columba's has to offer—that elemental experience of belonging to God in the unique way of the Trappist monk—and that while I'm here, I'll drink deeply of it.

He's right.

That is what I'm seeking, that is why I'm here, and I will drink as deeply as I'm able. It's just that there's something else I want to drink deeply of too. *Someone* else. Because I only have five days left with him before we return to the real world and our real lives, and I feel those five days like I'm a Disney princess trapped in a villain's giant hourglass. Like the passing time is a physical thing, slowly burying me alive.

That feeling gets no easier when we pick up our bags from where we left them at the visitor's entrance near the gift shop and are shown to our accommodations. The abbey is too small to have a proper guesthouse, and so we are staying in the dormitory with the monks.

Our rooms are separated by several cells which I suspect are actively inhabited by brothers, and while the flagstone floor could possibly hide the sound of soft footsteps in the night, the doors are made of wood so creaky and old that I suspect they predate the invention of the telephone.

Elijah's eyes meet mine for a brief instant before he wheels his suitcase to his room, and I know he's thinking the same thing as me. There's no way we'll be able to meet at night without Father Firebeard and his fellow monks knowing.

I feel like a teenager as we deposit our things and then follow Father Finbarr to the refectory to serve ourselves a quick dinner before compline, because I find myself trying to triangulate breaks in the schedule and locations from our tour where I think Elijah and I could spend a few minutes alone, but it's far harder here than it was at the other two abbeys.

Perhaps I can make a case to Father Finbarr that I'd like to explore the grounds a little, perhaps there will be a day nice enough for that, or perhaps we can linger in separate spots after compline and wait until everyone has gone to bed…

No, this feels worse than being a teenager, I think, as Elijah and I help ourselves to soft bread and warm stew and a dark St. Columba's beer. This feels like cheating, like infidelity. Not the thrill of the adolescent chase, but the reckless urge of the unfaithful.

But what's my alternative? Not find time with Elijah this week? During our last week together?

Impossible.

I will find a way, and as we take our seats to eat and the rain patters on the thin glass of the windows, I tell myself explicitly what I've known since Semois, maybe even since the hermitage.

I'd rather the sting of repentance than the anguish of wishing. Wishing for the rest of my life that I'd used every hour of these last days with Elijah.

The refectory was clearly built during the times when every second son joined the Church, because the room and its long trestle tables could easily seat a hundred people. Since St. Columba's only has twenty monks now, the chairs are spaced far apart—far enough to make conversation impossible, even if we felt brave enough to break the taboo on talking. We eat in silence, and then it's time for compline, which is beautiful and haunting and also in English, which feels like a gift after two weeks of muddling through prayers in French.

And then it's bedtime, where there will be no chance of sneaking out, and as I fall asleep, I pray to myself, murmuring in my mind the words that brought me here to the Bell homeland, to the sea and the wind and the sheep.

I lift my eyes to the hills…

The next day is no better. Prayers come early, and lectio divina is strictly observed either in one's cell or in the library, and the squarish layout of the abbey makes it difficult to disguise where you're going. Plus in all the silence, there's no way to pull Elijah to the side and demand he plot a sex-heist with me.

After a breakfast of eggs and thick slabs of toast, Elijah and I are led by Father Firebeard to the master brewer, a pleasant, red-cheeked man named Oisín, and in between the nonstop trips back to the church to sing the little hours, we are given a full tour of the brewery and allowed to sample the very good beer.

"We only make two beers here," Oisín explains as he cracks open a bottle right there next to one of the big copper kettles. "A blonde ale and a dark ale, same as they made here for centuries."

Elijah and I each accept a small tasting glass of the blonde, and I sip the beer while Oisín explains the unique position St. Columba's is in. The beer is extremely popular with the locals, and indeed, the majority of the abbey's sales are to the nearby pubs and bars, but it's growing in popularity with beer enthusiasts and there's lots of international interest.

"But it's hard to expand," Oisín explains as he opens a bottle of the dark ale for us. It's the same ale we had last night for dinner, but neither of us turn down a glass of it now, because it's so damn good. With hints of dried fruit and chocolate, it tastes a little like Christmas. "The Trappist daily routine isn't favorable to scaling up production, you see, and the monks here are aging faster than younger men are signing up. I'm not sure if there will even be a St. Columba's at all in thirty years, and neither is the abbot. Which makes it hard to invest in the equipment to brew more beer."

"But surely it would still be worth it in the short-term?" I ask. My money brain is whirring as I look down the short row of kettles and pipes. "There's the physical space here to double production, and if demand is like you say, then I have to imagine there's enough coming in to justify hiring two or three more laypeople as brewers. They wouldn't be constrained by the prayer schedule, but the monks could still supervise and keep the beer a certifiable Trappist product."

Oisín tips his glass to me. "You're speaking my very own thoughts, Brother Patrick, and thoughts that I've told the abbot many times. But I think he worries about sinking too much into the future when the present already looks uncertain. But I think if there were a young monk like you here to help, to push the abbey into the future, then perhaps he might change his mind."

Elijah and I once again go to bed without having kissed or

even spoken privately, and when I wake up Wednesday with a swollen cock and an aching chest, I know I won't be able to last another day. I don't care if we fuck or not—okay, well, I care a *little*—but I just need to be alone with him. To hold his hand and kiss him.

After breakfast, I follow Father Finbarr to the library, where he works as the abbey librarian, mostly shipping off books borrowed through interlibrary loans and receiving loans which are coming back to the library.

"If you don't have any plans for me this morning, I wondered if I might explore a little? Maybe poke around the graveyard or take the paths along the cliffs?"

Father Finbarr blinks behind his glasses, as if it truly hadn't occurred to him that I would want to see the outdoors, but then he smiles the first smile I've seen on him yet. "Oh yes, you should do that. God's glory is present in all of his creation, but especially here at St. Columba's, I think. In fact, our most recent postulant applied precisely because of this location. But terce…"

I am prepared for this. I hold up my breviary. "I'll pray on my own, of course, if the circumstance arises."

"Wonderful!" he says, like he's never heard of such ingenuity, and then with another smile, he turns back to his pile of returned books. "We shall see you at lunch then?"

Trying to hide my excitement, I agree and promise to be back for lunch, and then I go to find Elijah.

It's only a few hours that I've stolen for us, but they are our hours, and I plan to make very good use of them.

CHAPTER
FORTY-SIX

"And the scapular?" Elijah asks. He's sitting against the trunk of one of the few trees at the abbey, and the only tree that looks like an actual tree and not a wind-gnarled bush older than God. It's sunny today—or sunny-ish—and warm enough that we've taken off our shoes to feel the soft graveyard grass on our toes.

The yew we're sitting underneath is tucked behind a sharp slope inside the graveyard—sharp enough that there are old, lichen-covered stairs set into the earth in order to navigate it. Here the graveyard levels off for a bit and then ends with a low stone fence. The fence is broken by gate posts which no longer have a gate.

Because the best views are from the cliffs, I've made the gamble that we'd have some privacy from visitors, and it was a good gamble. We haven't seen another soul since we came down here, and since we're tucked against the far side of the tree and also against the slope, we can't be seen unless someone literally climbs down the stone steps and circles the corded trunk we're sitting by.

We are in our own little world, and I've already pounced on Elijah once, not even waiting for him to sit before I fell to my knees and tore his pants open to take him in my mouth. And now he's sitting with hooded eyes and a smiling mouth, his pants still unbuttoned and his feet bare and his long fingers curled loosely around his notebook.

"You really want to ask me about the particulars of my habit now?" I say as I stroke the smooth knot of his ankle below the hem of his trousers.

He gives a short laugh, low and rich. "Shouldn't I at least pretend to be working while we're out here?"

I lean down to kiss his ankle. "As you wish," I murmur against his skin. "What do you want to know?"

"Are they like the brown ones we were given as kids?"

"Sort of," I say, trailing my fingertips under the cuff of his trousers and stroking his calf. "The monastic scapular came first—it started as a sort of work apron for brothers and sisters and then eventually became part of the habit. Over time, oblates and tertiaries began wearing smaller versions of the scapular to signal their devotion to the orders they were pledged to, and then *those* scapulars turned into the devotional scapulars laypeople wear today."

He shivers as I gently scrape my fingernails down his leg and then meet their progress with my mouth. "Wasn't there something about wearing them? The devotional scapulars?" he asks. "Like if you died wearing one, you wouldn't go to hell?"

"Wearing one of the devotional scapulars is an act of faith," I say, settling up on my knees and sizing up the man in front of me. An unsatisfied erection makes an obscene tent in the front of my own scapular right now. "The act itself is worship, is devotion, and it's that continuing act of worship that sanctifies the wearer of the scapular. But that's a promise specific to the Brown Scapular, and not necessarily the case with the monastic apron. Mine more so is a reminder of my obedience, both to my order and to God." I smile at Elijah. "I like to steal a little of the devotional scapular theology for myself though. I like to imagine that it's a way for me to feel my devotion in front of me and behind me." I take his hand, the one holding his pen, and press it to my chest. "To feel it on either side of my heart."

The ocean is quieter here, more shush than roar, and so I can hear the catch in his breath as my heart pounds against his palm. And then he's reaching for me, and somehow we end up tangled together on the ground, him on top and yanking up my habit, and me on the bottom, trying to kiss him and wrap my legs around his waist.

He finds the rigid, aching need under my scapular, and with the taste of his lips on mine and the shush of the waves in the distance, we show each other our own kind of devotion until the bells toll down the hill.

I right myself and say terce with my breviary while Elijah claims to write in his notebook but instead mostly just stares at me with his arm wedged behind his head and his mouth curved in a fond smile.

It should be distracting, and maybe it is, but it's wonderful too, like praying next to brightly colored stained glass or in a twisting curl of incense smoke. It makes the prayers deeper and sweeter and even older somehow, like I'm praying something beyond the words of the psalms, like I'm praying what it means to be human in the first place.

And when I finish, the moment is so perfect, like something out of a dream, with soft grass and soft sunlight and Elijah's eyes, that I know I have to tell him about that night. I don't think I'll be able to bear the perfection of this memory otherwise, knowing there was this final, unspoken truth between us.

I set my breviary in the grass and turn so that I'm facing the same direction as Elijah—toward the gateless gate and the stream beyond it. On the other side of the stream is a hill covered in green grass and yellow gorse and gray rocks, and it couldn't be more different from my Mount Sergius hill, but it still calls to me.

Maybe I'll find God in every hill I see for the rest of my life.

"That night," I say after a moment, wondering where I can even begin. "That night was more than I've made it sound. With the fight and the text and everything."

I look over at Elijah, and a new tension has seeped into him. He comes to a sitting position, his legs folded and his back against a thick root of the yew tree.

I take that as my signal to continue, to tell the entire story, and so I do.

I take a deep breath and I start from the beginning.

CHAPTER
FORTY-SEVEN

It.

The first time I met it, I wasn't in a graveyard or at a funeral. I wasn't watching a movie or a stupid early internet video or listening to my classmates make awful jokes.

I wasn't even alone.

I was in my kitchen, rummaging through the fridge for the millionth time that day, looking for something to eat, and having discovered some lasagna leftovers from last night, I took the whole pan for myself. I didn't even bother scooping the leftovers out; I just got a fork and stood at the counter staring out the window into the backyard, eating cold lasagna as mindlessly as a dog gnaws on a bone.

Which is when I heard the voices from the living room.

It had been a year after Lizzy's death, and we'd gone to the graveyard earlier that day with my uncle Colin and my aunt Trish and laid flowers at Lizzy's grave, and the adults and Tyler had cried. Sean had scowled at the cross on the headstone like he could beam a middle finger right to Jesus if he tried hard enough, and Ryan was sad too, but also he was only nine or ten at the time, and so five minutes of graveside sadness was about all he could tolerate before the fidgeting set in.

I'd wanted to scowl and be cool like Sean, but Uncle Colin had snuck me several sips of Southern Comfort from his flask before we came, and mostly I just felt floaty and apart from everything around me, like I was an audience member dragged onto a stage while the real actors acted the play around me. It felt like a good thing at the time.

Anyway, the SoCo had worn off by the time I was eating the lasagna, and so I was sober as I heard Aunt Trish say from the living room, "Of course, it's so common when people get in that mindset that they think the world will be better off without them."

I remember freezing with a lasagna-laden fork halfway to my mouth, the words etching themselves onto my mind, scratching themselves deep.

Before that moment, I'd thought all suicides were like Lizzy's, and I thought Lizzy's must have been as simple as it seemed to me, a teenage boy who'd mostly fought with her over the remote and the remaining Toaster Strudels in the freezer and who had never been privy to her inner life in any form. Lizzy was sad, and therefore she killed herself, and that was all there was to it.

And so when the beleaguered high school counselor sat me down in his cramped office and asked if I felt sad, if I knew that I could tell other people about being sad, and gave me a brochure about the warning signs of teen suicide that was definitely made for parents and not teenagers, I didn't have much to say. Yes, I felt sad that Lizzy was dead, but mostly I felt angry about the priest and what he'd done to her. No, I didn't have any of the warning signs. Yes, I knew I could talk to my parents and the counselor if the sadness ever happened to me.

But the day I heard Aunt Trish's voice from the living room, I understood something I hadn't before, and it was that the word *sad* was a word people sometimes used for something else. Something I'd felt my own thoughts brush against in the dark, which was not a darkness like how adults were afraid of teenagers finding darkness...but a darkness like the darkness beyond the event horizon of a black hole. A darkness that was an *un*-light, an emptiness, but an emptiness with hunger, an emptiness with a voice.

Better off.

I looked down at the lasagna I was scraping straight from the pan, and I thought of the shitty joke about my own mom that I'd made the night before in order to make a group of friends laugh. I thought of the rumors I'd spread about a track teammate, I thought of the last two papers for American Lit which I hadn't actually written but paid a kid in study hall to write for me. I thought of all the service hours I had fudged on my high school service hours log, all the lies I'd told, all the fights I'd started and then finished.

I thought of that feeling I had sometimes, of being full of worms, of being full of slithers and dirt. I thought of the other feeling I had sometimes, the un-feeling, which only went away when I drank or fought or fooled around.

Better off.

I set the fork down as something got up and stretched in my mind. It paced for a minute, and then sat.

It was like the smoke off an oil fire—silky and poisonous and thick; it wore my face; it spoke with my voice.

"Hello," it said. "I've been waiting for you."

At first, knowing it felt like a secret, like the kind of secret that made you wiser and more interesting than the people around you. I finished high school and started college that way, thinking I understood songs on the radio and poems in class better than any of these other carefree kids, thinking that I alone was marked, like a romantic Cain, to wander with it stamped on my forehead for the people who knew how to see.

As college went on, however, it began to feel less like a secret and more like a…like a witness. A witness to the worst things I did, the worst thoughts I had, and then it started whispering its surveillances back to me. It would remind me at odd hours, during long car drives or long college lectures, of everything bad I'd done. It would make little cuts in me and then lick up whatever oozed out.

And by the time I graduated college, it no longer felt deep

or romantic. Instead, I felt like it was my only real friend.

My other friends thought they liked me, but they liked a lie—a bright, laughing guy always in search of the next party, the next drink, the next bump of coke. They were friendly, flattering; they had no idea who I really was, because they didn't know me like *it* knew me, and they would never be honest with me like it was honest with me. It told me the truth always; it told me how empty I was, how pointless, how I wasted air and time and food. And whenever I tried to escape it and the un-feeling it brought—with drugs, with alcohol, with sex—it would always be waiting for me at the end, inexorable and inevitable.

There was death, taxes, and *it*, always it.

And it was so patient, so very patient. Sometimes it would melt away for months at a time, a mere memory of itself, and I would think: *it's gone*. I told it to go and it went, just like a demon into a herd of swine, and I was free forever now.

But it always came back, and when it came back, I would realize it had never left, for it had continued to witness everything I'd done in its absence, and it would begin again its sinister litany. The people I'd hurt or annoyed, the conversations I'd ruined or unfairly dominated, the harms great and small that I sowed being Aiden Bell, eternal fuck-up.

Better off… it would remind me, seductively.

When my mother died, a year before That Night, it told me all sorts of things, all sorts of awful, unrepeatable things. But the thing it told me the most often was that no one would miss me like people missed my mother. My brothers were wrecked, my dad was wrecked, all of her big circle of friends and coworkers were wrecked with the death of Carolyn Bell, but if I died…?

And I missed Mom. I'd missed Lizzy too, as much as my young heart was capable, but I missed my mother like an adult, with an adult's heart, and even though I'd always weathered its whispers alone, when she died, I suddenly felt stranded and solitary in a way I'd never felt before. As if a secret part of me had always thought if it grew too loud, if I was in too much danger of doing what it wanted me to do, I could go to my mom and she would make it better. She'd make me not alone, she would make it go away. Maybe we all think that, deep down, about our mothers, that they will make the monsters under our bed go away. But Carolyn Bell took that sense of safety with her when she died, and now, I was truly alone in its grip.

Elijah was the brightness, of course. The sweetness, the sex, the comfort. A gift I didn't deserve. I think without him That Night would have come faster, although it eventually weaponized him too.

This good man, what are you doing with him? Embarrassing him at events, at dinners with his parents? You know they only tolerate you because they like Sean, right? You know he's going to break up with you, right? Why would he stay? Why should he stay?

Anything good or right I did was never enough to weigh against the sagging scales of my selfishness, and the more power it had to paralyze me, the more selfish I would feel, as if the paralyses were my fault. Those times when I couldn't make my body move to leave the house…it would ask me in tones of deep concern if I knew how much I was letting my boyfriend down? How much worse I was making his life with every disappointment?

Better off…

For fifteen years, I'd been its pet, its unhappy companion. Perhaps it was surprising that I'd lasted as long as I did—for that I can only credit my family and Elijah. But after years and years of it, I was tired. I agreed with it now, with whatever it said. Why wouldn't I, when it spoke with my voice and wore my face?

And then That Night—when I came home and found dinner in the trash and Elijah sitting in the living room—it didn't even have to speak. As Elijah and I fought, and I realized how much my carelessness had hurt him—how much more this time had hurt him than the others—and by the time he'd pulled away as we were changing for bed and muttered, *we'll talk about it in the morning,* I already knew what it would say.

I didn't deserve to talk about the fight in the morning. I didn't deserve forgiveness, because I'd just need it again and again and again, and who has the energy to forgive someone that many times? Who can give someone that many fresh starts? And even if someone could, why on earth *should* they?

I didn't follow Elijah to bed. I should have, maybe. Because maybe if I'd climbed into bed, Elijah would have sighed and rolled over and let his foot touch my foot under the blankets. Maybe he would have let me press my face into his arm. Maybe we would have fucked and the un-feeling it always brought with it would have disappeared for a while.

But none of that happened. I went downstairs, first sitting on the couch and staring at the wall, and then somehow ending up on the floor, looking out of the farmhouse window to the moonless night beyond.

It joined me there, on the floor, and it congratulated me on my self-awareness, on my unflinching honesty.

"Shall we do the litany together?" it asked.

"Yes," I said, and I let it begin, an unending spool of reasons why I should listen to its kindly meant suggestions. It only cared about the people I loved, just like I did. It only wanted to make the world a better place—didn't I want that too?

After fifteen years, I was familiar with its greatest hits, its favorite horrors to dredge out of my memories and torment me with, its temptations and its judgements and its soft, ingratiating malice. Perhaps there shouldn't have been anything different enough about That Night to make it *the* night, but maybe in the end, that was exactly the reason why it became the night.

Because I'd lived through so many years of it being in my mind, and when I stared out the window, I could see all the years of it yet to live through, and it was suddenly too exhausting to contemplate.

It would never stop, it would never end. This would always be my life, and what was I even fighting for? The right to keep letting people down? The capacity to prey on their energy and patience until I'd bled them dry?

In Brendan Fraser's 1998 film *The Mummy*—which is the number one mummy-based action movie of all time—there is a holy city called Hamunaptra, and in that city is a temple, and in that temple is where the ragtag team finally defeats the mummy, who by that stage is very hunky and bald. (The hunky part isn't important to the story, but I just thought you should know about it.) Anyway, after the mummy is fatally wounded, he staggers back into what looks like a stone bathtub full of the souls of the dead. The water is slick and black and rippling, and as the mummy sinks into its depths, the darkness climbs up his legs and torso and then up to his face, and I remember watching that even as a kid and thinking that darkness could do that, it could cling to your skin and crawl up your body. It could reach and search and wither anything it touched. It would never stay where it should. Not when it knew your name and was waiting for you.

And so I watched as the darkness spilled in through my window and slicked toward my outstretched feet, understanding how that hunky mummy must have felt, knowing that death was coming, death was here. Maybe the mummy was afraid, but strangely enough, I wasn't. I felt nothing at all.

"I'll help you," it said kindly. "Just listen to me, and I'll help you."

"Okay," I said back. I would listen. It would help. I'd write Elijah a note to explain that it wasn't his fault, and then I'd make sure everything was turned off upstairs because he hated when I left the lights on and wasted electricity, even when it was just the bathroom light so I didn't stub my toe in the middle of the night.

It was time.

I felt the certainty of that like I'd never felt anything before. It was time. I'd pretended long enough, and the less pretending had worked, the harder I'd pretended, and now it was time.

But something happened then, as I made to stand. Something that took me a minute to understand. My phone, sitting on the floor next to me, lit up with a text notification.

At three thirty in the morning.

In the dark, it felt like a searing brightness, a klieg light, a bluish sun dawning right there in the shadows. And when I reached for it out of sheer habit and opened it up, it glowed as bright as the inside of the Ark of the Covenant.

It was from a number I didn't have in my contacts or even recognize—a number that I'd never even exchanged texts with before. There was only the one text, the one line, with no context whatsoever.

I lift my eyes to the hills.

Why did that sound familiar? And who would be texting me at three in the morning with something as cryptic as this? Since dating Elijah, I'd stopped with the hardcore party crowd…and even if one of those douchebags was going to text me this late, it would definitely be a video of him stumbling home drunk and singing in the middle of the street. Not a…was this a *verse*? It felt familiar like a verse would. Like a poem we'd read in school, or…

I pulled up the browser on my phone and typed in the words, which immediately returned with Psalm 121.

I lift up my eyes to the hills—
from where will my help come?

My help comes from the Lord,
who made heaven and earth…

He will not let your foot be moved;
he who keeps you will not slumber…

The Lord will keep your going out and your coming in
from this time on and forevermore.

The words bled through me—no, they *burned* through me. Like fire. Like light.

I lift my eyes to the hills…

I switched back to the text message and replied **who is this?**

But there was no answer—in fact, there hasn't been an answer for five years. To this day, I still don't know who texted me the first verse of a psalm at three thirty in the morning.

To this day, I still don't know who saved my life.

I lift my eyes to the hills…

Those words sent something through me that was not darkness, that was not un-feeling. I felt…comforted. Like the need I'd had for my mother to chase away the monsters under the bed could still be met, like someone could still do that for me, and it was this god who never slumbered or slept, this god who cared about my goings out and my comings in. This lord who would *keep* me, even if I didn't deserve to be kept. He could keep my life, he *would* keep my life, and soon it wasn't enough to see the verses on the screen, I needed to see them on paper. I went over to the bookshelves by the fireplace, which mostly held video games and every year's edition of the *Guinness Book of World Records* and found the small leather bible my grandparents had given me at my confirmation.

And there it was printed plain as day: this god would never sleep, he would help me. If I lifted my eyes to the hills, even in the darkest hours of night, he would be there.

Maybe…

Maybe it, with its silky, smoky voice, was wrong. Maybe it had been wrong for a long time.

And that was enough to push me away from what I had been about to do. Not certainty and not logic and not even a happy feeling to counterweight the heaviness of its seduction—but the sudden revelation that my thoughts, my hollowness, its whispers were somehow not the entire story.

There was something more. To me. To life.

Later, as I pulled myself through those early days of my novitiate, I would listen to the end of that Corinthians reading that people love for weddings and hear what had happened to me that night.

For we know in part…but when the complete comes, the partial will come to an end.

Then I will know fully, even as I have been fully known.

I thought I understood everything perfectly. That I was everything it whispered to me I was, and that there was no other truth that mattered. But I'd been wrong; there was so much else that mattered, so much else I hadn't seen or known, and that night I could only barely apprehend the vastness of it, I could only sense that there was an infinity of something that wasn't nothing, and that if I wanted, it could be my infinity too. This infinity was shared between all of us, it was webbed between all of us, and there were many doors and many gates, and I had found but one of them.

That was okay. This was my gate; it had called to me; and so it was the gate I wanted for that reason. I found my laptop and sat down at the kitchen table and Googled "Catholic Church near me" thinking that would be a nice starting point, and then let out a *huh* when Google came back with too many results to properly parse. I guessed that the closest one would be the one I should click on, but then I saw it.

A limestone church set in front of a tall hill, the sun breaking over the hill's crown.

Mount Sergius Abbey, the result said next to it. It was only an hour's drive from here.

I clicked the link, which opened to a picture of monks in their black habits, heads bowed in prayer. But there they were grinning around glasses of beer…walking in pairs or trios beneath the shadow of the hill with their hands behind their backs…sitting in the cloister while the hill peeked over the roofs of the buildings around it.

They looked so serene, so steady, with the kind of steadiness that spoke of hope, love, and safety. They looked like they knew this god that didn't sleep and watched over them, and I wanted to know this god too—more than anything, I wanted to know him.

I needed to know him.

And maybe—maybe this was the answer to everything, because I could still fix so many problems. The way I hurt Elijah and kept hurting him, the way I made money and then used it for absurd, meaningless shit, the way I was just in general a rich, selfish asshole who gave nothing to nobody and kept it all for himself.

The men in these pictures gave up *everything.* And looked so happy that they'd done it.

That could be me.

I closed the laptop and went to find my shoes. And then I went upstairs to see Elijah asleep in bed.

He hadn't formally moved in yet, but after a year together, his things had accreted in the farmhouse, and so his end-table was stacked with a half-finished crossword and the dog-eared Cortázar he was reading and another book that looked even harder to read underneath that and an eye mask and a bottle of unscented hand lotion. And I knew, somehow, that this would be the last time I would ever see his sweet, nerdy clutter. The last time I would ever see his face like this, relaxed in sleep, eyelashes long on his cheeks and his lips slightly parted and his eyebrows unfurrowed, unraised.

I pressed a last kiss to his sleeping lips, and he didn't stir.

Which felt like a sign.

"Goodbye," I whispered to him, and then I left the farmhouse as the sun pushed up over the horizon, at last beating back the night and illuminating a world I hoped would still have me.

A world of dark asphalt and green pastures and well-ordered fields, and eventually in the distance, the grass-covered surfs of the Flint Hills, where my future would begin.

CHAPTER
FORTY-EIGHT

When I finish, Elijah has his head in his hands. I touch his shoulder, and he looks up, his face haunted. "Why didn't you tell me?" he whispers.

I search for the right words to explain something that's fundamentally unexplainable. "I wasn't capable of presenting it verbally then, in some kind of logical order. I didn't tell you because I *couldn't* have told you."

Elijah searches my face. "But you can tell me now."

"It's taken a lot of therapy to get to this point," I explain. "And meds. Those too."

"And," he asks carefully, "being a monk?"

"Yes," I say, looking down through the gravestones to the stream and then the hills. We're sitting in a place where centuries of holy men have been buried, a testament of crooked stones and round Celtic crosses, a testament to entire lives lived on one patch of land. "The work of my day and the work of my mind mirrored each other in my first years as a monk—new routines, new kinds of sleep hygiene, spending time outside, contemplation—it created a kind of positive feedback loop, I think. They fed each other. And faith—"

I stop, not sure how to say this without making it clear that God works just as much through SSRIs and therapy as he does through prayers and hymns. "It's been the awakening of my spirit," I finally say. "And without my spirit, I don't think my life would be what it is now. Fully here. Fully present."

"But then why switch orders?" Elijah asks. "Why come here looking for something more when Mount Sergius has already done so much for you?"

"It's *because* this life has done so much for me," I say, turning to face him. "I owe God and my brothers so much, for the last five years, and yet I cannot finish the one task that is asked of me, which is to make my heart a heart for God and my community and those two things alone."

I find his hand and press it to my scapular, to my chest, just like I did earlier. "The truth is that I wear two of these, Elijah, one for God, and another one that no one else can see. For you."

We stare at each other a moment, my heart beating against his palm, his shoulders moving with heavy breaths. I don't know what I should say next—I don't even know what I would want him to say in return—only that I want him to know how true it is. How inconveniently, wonderfully, powerfully true.

A tiny alarm goes off on his watch before either of us can say anything, and with a quiet curse, he glances down at its face and silences it.

"We need to head back for lunch," he says.

"Okay," I say, and I reluctantly let his hand drop from my chest.

We put on our shoes and right our clothes and make sure there's no obvious grass or dirt stains. And then before we climb the stairs to the upper graveyard and the path back to the abbey, I fist my hands in his thin sweater and pull him to my mouth.

He tastes faintly of coffee but mostly of himself, and the inside of his mouth is silky and warm, and his lips are just a touch cool from the breeze. And this kiss is perfect and he is perfect, and I'd say twelve rosaries a day, scrub every sanctuary floor, chop up all the deadfall there ever was in order to keep him right here against me.

But the bells for sext start chiming, and I have no choice.

We break the kiss, both of us staring at each other with things we have no time to say, and then we hurry back to the abbey.

"Tomorrow," I say as we stride through the graveyard and in the direction of the church, where we'll sing sext and then move to the refectory for lunch, "I think I can get away again. In the morning."

"Okay," he says, and even though he gives a decisive enough nod, his steps stutter a little as he does, as if he wants to shift his feet and can't. But there's no time to ask about it, because we're coming up on the church now.

Tomorrow.

We'll have tomorrow.

The rest of the day is beautiful, inside and out. A playful sun peeps between clouds, emerging and then retreating and leaving pretty summer shadows to slide across the abbey rooms.

I help Father Finbarr in the library for part of the afternoon, and then spend some time with a monk named Father Louis working in the brewhouse. St. Columba's has older tuns than either Mount Sergius or Semois, and the spent grain must be removed by shoving it out the manway on the side by hand. Father Louis eyes my broad shoulders with undisguised glee as he hands me the shovel, and by the time none rolls around, I'm sweaty as hell and I smell like a brewhouse. I shower and change into a fresh habit after prayers, and then spend some time in lectio divina, still working my way through *Song of Songs*.

Set me as a seal upon your heart...

for love is as strong as death...

I stare at the bright, summery world out my cell window. It faces out towards the hills, and I think of the ten thousand particular things that had to happen in a very certain order for me to be here, right now, as a monk traveling with the man he's still in love with.

I think of Abbot Jerome and his idea of God's invitation; I think of all that I've gained in this life as a monk and then all that I would lose by remaining in it. I ask God, *is this what you really mean for me? A life here?*

I wish he would speak, that the hills would crack open and reveal a divine fire, but there is only silence and Irish sunshine, and then it is time for vespers, my questions yet unanswered.

How is it possible, I wonder through prayers and through a silent but tasty dinner, that after this week I'll never kiss Elijah again? Never again feel his lips against mine or feel the way he catches his breath when I find his hand with my own and lace my fingers through his?

That I'll never walk with him through a museum again or hold his coffee while he looks for something, that I'll never again get to watch him scribble in his notebook or listen to him tap on his keyboard while he sighs like a freshman in a boring college lecture?

That every night, my body will ache not only for sex with him, but for the those touches which are more mundane and yet somehow more intimate than sex? The way he rolls over and purrs as I stroke his back or the way he lets me use him as a body pillow or the way I used to wake up to find he'd big-spooned me while we were both asleep?

I was so certain, after Provence, that the finite edge of our *interlude* would remain finite. That it would hurt, maybe even unbearably so, but that there would be no doubt in my mind, no indecision in my soul, when it came time for us to take our separate planes back to Kansas City. Of course I would stay a monk and continue in the life that had allowed me to rebuild myself. Of course Elijah would return to his own life and eventually move on. The question didn't even bear thinking about.

Did it?

Except it's all I can think about tonight; it's crowding my thoughts as we sing compline together in the old church. Elijah has come, is sitting in the pews, and I can't keep myself from watching him as he sings, acquitting himself rather well through the plainchanting, his long fingers holding open the battered breviary and his eyebrows furrowed with concentration as he does.

What would happen, I suddenly ask myself, if I left? If I flew back home, went to Abbot Jerome's office and said, *I'm sorry but I think I'm meant to be with him?*

I'm sorry that you sunk so much money and effort into a trip to help me find my future and it turns out my future wasn't monastic all along?

It would be hard, I know that. It would be embarrassing even, when I've spent so many years trying never to be embarrassed again. It would look impulsive—it would *be* impulsive.

But I can't ignore what my intuition tells me. I can't ignore the gut-deep truth that if five years of ruthless weeding and burning in the garden of my heart couldn't eradicate Elijah, then nothing else will. I will go to my grave loving him. And I know he loves me back.

So why am I denying us?

I can give this life up, right? The plainsong, the nature, the lectio-sex. The bond that only comes through shared denial, shared toil, shared bleary mornings with jaw-cracking yawns when the abbot isn't looking.

I could give it up for him, couldn't I? Because the reward is...well, it's *him*.

And I can still remain devoted to God as a layperson—people do that, don't they? I could do that. Tyler did.

We're far enough north that the sun is already lightening the night sky when I wake for vigils. And like the sky outside, I feel lighter, clearer. Illuminated.

I'm going to leave the Church.

I choose Elijah.

Maybe it was finally telling my story yesterday, or maybe it's been the slow accretion of the last two and a half weeks, but I feel abruptly free of the need to pin my future to this one way. Maybe I needed the Church to untangle my life and my mind—maybe I needed these last five years to become the kind of man who was healthy and mature enough for a long-term relationship. The kind of man worthy of Elijah's love. I don't know.

But I can't stay.

Not when the price is losing him.

CHAPTER FORTY-NINE

We claim another morning for ourselves under the pretense of walking the cliff paths.

It's only when we get past several undulations of the path that I see the small, crumbling ruin from the pictures of St. Columba's. An old fishing cottage, I think, with walls of stone and a missing roof. I call to Elijah that I'm going to check it out, and then he joins me, ducking through the intact doorway to stand next to me inside.

"And to think, this would go for a mere million pounds in London," he says, looking at the fireplace which has weeds growing inside. But there's no trash tangled in the weeds, which as a former teenage (and adult-age) troublemaker makes me think that the little cottage is too remote for people to use as a party-spot or trysting place. The grass that's grown on what used to be a dirt floor is soft and thick and comes up past my ankles, which makes me think it's not walked on or grazed very often.

Perfect.

While Elijah is giving this place an Elijah eyebrow, I lift his satchel from his shoulder and set it in a corner.

"What are you…?" He turns to look at me, and I take his face in my hands. I want to be looking at him when I tell him. I want to see the happiness and relief dancing in his eyes as I do.

His expression changes when he sees mine, a flare of interest in his eyes as he licks his lower lip. "Is this a *what if*?" he asks in a husky voice.

"Obviously," I say, brushing my mouth over his and then slowly backing him against the wall. Without a roof, there's plenty of light for me to see his pupils dilating as I pin him against the stone with my hips, pinning him hard enough that he can feel my need even through the fabric of my robes.

"Shit," he whispers, his eyelids fluttering as I use him to grind against, shoving one of my hands up his shirt to scrape a gentle fingernail over his nipple. "What game this time?"

Excitement surges through me, a bolt of adrenaline-laced joy. I find his hands with my own and then pull them up between us.

"What if," I say, looking into his eyes, "what if…I left?" I take a deep breath. "What if I left for you?"

Elijah's lips part. He blinks twice. "Left being a monk?"

I can't help the grin that blooms on my face. "Yeah."

"Is this a game?" he asks, his brow furrowing, and I'm grinning even harder, shaking my head.

"No game," I say eagerly. "We'll fly home and then I'll tell

Abbot Jerome and then…then I can be yours, Elijah. No more habits, no more sneaking around between prayers. I'll be yours completely."

He stares at me, his eyes sharp and inquiring as they pore over my face.

"You mean this," he says slowly. "You really mean this."

"I realized yesterday that I can't live another day without you," I say, squeezing his hands. "I tried. All this time, I've tried, and it did me a lot of good, I think, because that version of Aiden wasn't ready to be a full partner for anyone. But I want to try again. And most of all, I just want to *love* you. Without inhibition, without guilt. Without a divided heart."

"And God?" he asks. "Will you not still have a divided heart for him?"

I lean in to kiss Elijah's cheek. "There are lots of devoted laypeople. I'll be one of them. I'll go to Father Jordan's church or something."

"You said that finding God was like having your spirit awakened," Elijah says. "And I've seen you these past weeks, Aiden. The prayers, the work, the early mornings. You *love* this."

"I love *you*," I say, nuzzling his cheek and then pulling back to smile at him. "Don't you see? We can be together now…"

I feel my smile fade as a small gremlin of doubt crawls around my stomach. "Unless you don't want to be? Unless you don't love me like that?"

Elijah touches my face, his own impossibly tender, his eyebrows lifted high and drawn together at the same time. "I do love you like that. And I love you like this. Aiden, I—" He lets out a long breath, and then a laugh that sounds more pained than happy. "Aiden, I love you like everything."

My heart quickens; my stomach jumps. Every kind of happiness hormone is coursing through me, and I want to have his words tattooed across my chest.

I love you like everything.

"I love you like everything too," I breathe. "Spending these last few weeks with you in the places I thought I wanted above anything else has shown me what I really want. I'm so blessed you came with me, because if you hadn't—" It's my turn to give a short laugh now, although it's not pained like his was. Why would it be? I'm within sight of my New Jerusalem, within reaching distance of my beloved. "If you hadn't—if I'd visited here alone and all I'd had was the sea and the graveyard and the beer to guide my decisions, then I might have decided to come here to live after all."

I can feel the long breath he pulls in after I say that. I assume it's because he's so relieved right now, because he's overwhelmed by how romantic I am. But I want to make sure, because as excited as I am, as *certain* as I am, I've learned in the last five years that listening is the most important job a person can do.

"Are you—is this okay with you?" I ask, lifting his hand to my mouth and kissing his knuckles.

"I love you like everything," he repeats, and then suddenly it's *my* face in his hands, it's *me* turned and pressed against the wall. He's kissing me so deeply, so thoroughly, that I feel it in my belly and in my groin. He might as well be licking his way down from my navel; he might as well be flicking his tongue along my cock; he might as well have two fingers inside me, stroking places that have never seen the light.

My hips roll mindlessly against his, and he doesn't seem to be in the mood to deny us anything, not today, because instead of rucking up my habit like we normally do, he pulls back and carefully—reverently—pulls my scapular over my head. He folds it and sets it on the grass, and then comes my leather belt, slowly unfastened and tugged free. He coils it in a loop around his wide palm before he sets it in a neat circle on top of the scapular.

Finally comes my habit, which he unzips from the throat down to my sternum, his eyes following his progress as he does. The sliver of hairy chest that's exposed has him breathing harder, faster, but he doesn't rush this. He doesn't rush pulling my habit over my head or folding it; he doesn't rush kneeling down to untie my boots and peel off my socks; he doesn't rush inching my boxer briefs down my hips to my thighs, and then off altogether.

Soon, I'm entirely naked, entirely exposed. Though the day is mostly cloudy, it's warm enough that it's not unpleasant, and the walls of the abandoned cottage keep the wind off. Not that it matters, maybe. I'm already covered with goose bumps, my nipples are already pulled taut under his stare.

He runs a trembling hand from my hip and up the solid drum of my belly to my chest, and there he presses his palm right over the hidden muscle behind my ribs. The muscle which beats so wildly for him.

"See?" I whisper. "I'm still wearing that second scapular. I'm still wearing you wherever I go."

He sucks in a shuddering breath and then pushes me to my knees in front of him, unzipping his pants as he does. He cups the back of my head with one hand and frees his cock with the other, guiding his swollen organ into my mouth. "It's so good," he mutters as I seal my lips around him. "How is it still so good? As good as the first time you sucked me?"

I make an *mm* noise as I remember. Our first night—the gala. Glances stolen across the foyer of the venue, through the forest of tippling millionaires and schmoozing donors. I'd been floored by how sexy he looked in his tuxedo, a flute of champagne dangling from his fingers as he ranged around the space, making sure everything was going according to plan. And suddenly years of lust and worship from afar crystallized into a blade.

And that blade cut through everything.

You look incredible tonight. What are you doing after this?

Aiden, are you flirting with me?

He'd had a few minutes; a place in the venue we could "catch up," and I still don't know how we both knew that we weren't going into the empty opera auditorium to catch up, but we did, we did know. The minute the door had closed behind us, we were kissing, kissing, and then he'd brought his fingers to my mouth and pushed them inside. His eyes had darkened as he watched me suck on them.

I shouldn't be doing this with my best friend's little brother…

409

It's just fucking around, I'd assured him.

Like a game?

I'd reached for the button of his tuxedo jacket then, popping it open. *Well, I like games. Don't you?*

I do. I have an idea for one now, in fact, he'd said, his hand sliding down the tuxedo shirt covering my chest. *What if I'm your older brother's best friend, and one night we run into each other at a gala, and then you and I decide to make each other feel good?*

I'd felt how *good* he was already feeling. And even though I'd never done it before, I was horny enough to be brave because fortune favors the bold and all that, and I'd dropped to my knees in front of him.

I like the sound of that what if, I'd whispered, right before I'd reached for the button of his tuxedo trousers.

And he's right—even now, years later, with so many games played between us—it's still so good. Tasting him, feeling the rigid contours of him with my tongue as I suck, it still feels brand new—but better than brand new, because it feels like coming home too.

Elijah pulls off his T-shirt, exposing acres and acres of leanly etched muscle, and then he holds me on his cock as he tugs his jeans and boxer briefs all the way down. It's only when he kicks off his shoes that he lets me go, and then once his shoes are off, he's bending down to lick inside my mouth, to shove his hands through my hair and scrape his fingers through my short beard.

With the same kind of ruthless reverence he's had since he

started undressing me, Elijah pushes me onto my back on the cool grass, grabbing his satchel and setting it nearby while he kneels between my thighs.

My cock aches beyond anything, hot against the air and weeping pre-cum all over my bare belly, and he gives it a fond caress as he razes his way up and down my body with that scorching stare. "I want to remember how you look forever," he murmurs, his free hand already inside the satchel, searching for what he needs.

I laugh at him—although the laugh turns into a moan as he caresses me again. "You'll have forever to see how I look," I say, my hips lifting to chase his touch. And then a little tide of insecurity comes in. "If you want it. The forever, I mean."

He gives me a look like I'm the worst pupil in the class. "There's nothing I want more," he says, and maybe there's some heaviness in his voice when he says it, but maybe there's not, and also he's doing that thing where he tears open a condom packet with his teeth, and I'm distracted. I'm distracted as he paints my entrance with lube and slowly works me open for him, I'm distracted as he presses his thick erection to the muscles he's just worked into welcoming pliancy, I'm distracted as he breaches me and drives the breath right from my body.

It should be one of our lovely, filthy games right now. Outside, theoretically where someone could find us. Memories of our first night swirling in our minds.

But it's not a game at all, and there's something so sweetly intimate about all our bare skin sliding together, about the hair on his thighs rasping against my own. About the way his eyes burn all over my body, as if he really is trying to remember the way I look forever.

And it's not the thrill of maybe being caught that penetrates my mind as Elijah strokes deeply into me. It's the thunder of the ocean and the playful soughing of the wind around the corners of our refuge, it's the silver clouds and the soft grass and the far-off calls of the sea birds. The way all of God's creation feels pressed into this one moment, like a flower between the pages of a book.

"Aiden," Elijah murmurs as I arch between us, wrapping my legs around his hips. He bends to kiss me, his tongue in a slow, exploring rhythm, just like his hips, and then I feel the tightness spreading all over me, not just in my belly and my groin, but in my chest and toes and lips too as I pant his name.

"Aiden," he murmurs again, like my name is more than my name, like my name is his *selah*, meant to punctuate his prayers. I writhe under him, all while my legs tighten around him, and his kisses turn soothing, calming. "I know," he says. "I know. I'm here."

It comes like a flame catching a wick—bright and fast and soaring up into a full-bodied tongue of fire that wants nothing more than to consume. My cock is trapped between our two bellies, and it jerks in time with the pulses tearing through my body from deep inside, and I cry out against Elijah's lips as it spurts hot semen between us, coating both our torsos in it and creating a slick, pressurized slide that drives my orgasm on and on and on, my entire body a being of joyous fire and dancing flames.

Elijah follows me—a quick breath like he's suddenly fallen from a great height, and then I feel his heavy pulses inside my body, his forehead dropping down to roll against mine as he uses the grip of my body to pleasure the last of his orgasm out of himself.

And then gradually, we both become still, arms and legs tangled, his breath deep and shivery on my lips.

Outside, the ocean continues its endless rush and boom, the clouds continue to thicken, the birds continue to call.

Elijah moves his head enough to look at his watch.

"We have time still," he says, lifting up to take care of the usual necessities and then draping himself back over my body. "What if we used up every last minute before we have to go back?"

"What if I said no shit, Sherlock?"

He laughs, kissing my nose as he slides his hands under my shoulders and then drops his lips to my throat, and then to my chest, kissing the place over my heart where his hand was earlier. And all I can do is smile up at the Irish sky as his hand replaces his lips and his lips drift farther and farther down until I'm all rekindled flame.

Set me as a seal upon your heart, the Song of Songs goes. *For love is strong as death.*

Its arrows are arrows of fire, flames of the divine.

And I burn with those flames for every minute that we're allowed.

413

CHAPTER
FIFTY

I can be forgiven, I think, for my joy. Even for my ebullience, although I know I do a good job modulating it once we get back to St. Columba's. I don't plan on sauntering in and announcing that I'm no longer going to be a monk before striding off with Elijah over my shoulder like a kidnapped princess. No, I owe it to Abbot Jerome not to cause a scandal while on his dime. And I owe this conversation to him within a framework of respect and decorum—or as much decorum as I can summon up, given the circumstances.

But it still feels impossible not to hold Elijah's hand, not to stare fondly at him, not to shadow him everywhere for the rest of the day, even when he goes to his cell to work. And during prayers, I just want to pull him into my lap and kiss his neck while he sings, I want to be inside him while we pray.

I don't do any of that, of course, and I manage to give him a really casual good-night nod after compline, even though he's talking with Father Finbarr and I think I could ingratiate myself into their conversation and therefore get to spend a few extra moments with Elijah before the annoying wedge of night comes to separate us.

But I don't, I behave, reminding myself that vigils will come sooner than I think, and I'll be able to spend another morning with my beloved, my Elijah. It's funny—when I was committed entirely to being a monk, even seeing Elijah for thirty minutes in a cloister was unbearable. And when I thought this interlude would end Saturday, I managed to keep myself under control. But now that I know we have forever? That forever is ours the moment I get back to Mount Sergius to put in my monk-ly two weeks' notice?

Now every moment apart feels like torture.

I sleep though, dreaming dreams sweeter than candy, waking to the early glow that comes so soon in the morning at this latitude. I quickly wash and ready myself for the day, smiling back at Elijah's closed door. The after-breakfast hours can't come soon enough.

Except Elijah's not at breakfast.

I search the refectory as I hurriedly chew through some eggs and toast, trying not to panic. There isn't *really* a set hour for breakfast here, so it's possible that he's sleeping in or working, and sometimes people miss things, even things as important as breakfast. Hell, I haven't even seen Father Finbarr yet.

But as much as I've worked to build my patience in these last few years, I barely last fifteen minutes before I'm washing my dishes and going back to the dormitory to find Elijah. I'll wake him if I have to, I'll tease him away from work, but I need him, even if it's just for a short walk to the graveyard, even if it's just so I can listen to him ponder whether the transepts of the church have been rebuilt or whether anyone's done a podcast about the history here yet.

But when I get to his door, it's already open.

Open to an empty room.

There's a slow, sinking feeling moving through me—not like my heart or my stomach sinking, but like my entire body. Like my entire body is sinking right through the floor, right into the cool stone and even lower still.

Not again, I think numbly, staring at the empty room and thinking of the one in Mount Sergius. Of the day exactly like this when Elijah left me without saying goodbye.

Not again.

A brother I've only met in passing joins me at the door. "I heard your friend went with Father Finbarr to Galway today," the monk says cheerfully. He passes me to move into the room, where he starts industriously stripping the bed. "I hope Father Finbarr stops along the way to show him some of the sights. No point in coming out to this end of the world if you aren't going to make the most of it!"

Everything sounds both lovely and wise in this monk's Irish accent, but I register almost none of it. I'm too numb.

"Excuse me," I murmur. "I've just forgotten something."

I don't hear what he says in reply, but it doesn't matter, I'm already striding as quickly as I can to my room, shutting the door and leaning back against it as I fight for breath, as I fight not to cry.

Elijah could have gone to Galway for anything; he could be planning on coming back. So what that his room is being stripped, cleaned, presumably readied for the next guest? That doesn't have to mean he isn't coming back here...

But I think I know the truth even before I open my burning eyes to see the letter on my pillow. Before I go to it and unfold it and read the words written there.

It's torn from the pages of a small notebook and written in Sharpie pen. The hand is neat, precise, not looking at all like it was written in a hurry. Which means it was probably written last night.

Aiden, it begins.

I debated whether or not to leave without saying goodbye. I prayed about it even. It is ironic that I've spent so many years hurting over the way you left without a proper explanation, and yet here I am leaving you for the second time without giving you one. If I didn't understand after you told me your story, I think I'd understand even better now that I'm faced with the same choice myself.

Except I am going to give you an explanation now—or at least the best one I can, given the circumstances.

My explanation is also a confession: every time I came to you, from the time I told you about my engagement to the time I boarded a plane to Luxembourg, I came with doubts. Not healthy, emotionally capacious doubts, you see, but cynical ones, hard and narrow and sharp. In a way, it was doubt that kept me returning, almost as much as the hunger to be near you. It's an ugly thing to admit, but there it is. I've been pressing my fingers into your wounds over and over again, because belief felt impossible. How could the Aiden I'd known and loved be this same man who chanted psalms and listened intently to every word everyone around him spoke? How could this former millionaire who rarely wore the same suit twice stand nearly naked in a field of lavender and grin at me with sore muscles and petals stuck to his sweaty skin as if he'd never been happier?

How could it be the same you? The you I knew?

And how could this be the work of the same Church I have such complicated feelings about? The Church at its most esoteric, its most privileged, and its most exclusive?

But even Thomas eventually believed, and now so do I. It took weeks of wrestling with it, weeks of coming back and leaving and coming back again. It took me to strange rivers and mountains and finally to the edge of the world with you, where there's nothing but wind and salt and graves so old they have more graves on top of them. It took more than watching—I think if I'd only watched, I never would have understood. It took praying the prayers with you, spending the days tethered between the work of the world and the work of the spirit, pulling my life away from the chimes and pop-ups and crashing deadlines and hot takes. Cloistering. That's what it took. I cloistered with you.

And I understood.

I understand.

I understand why you came, and why you stayed, and why

you saw a future for yourself like this. And that is why I cannot take it from you.

I will never regret spending these days with you—I don't think I'm capable of it, actually. An hour with you is like the fullness of years anywhere else, and maybe it was worth living an entire life just to have those hours alone. Which is why I can't tarnish them this way—by having them be the reason you leave a life that has given you yourself and given you your god.

I love you too much to do that, and I love myself too much to do it either, because what I said in the hermitage is still true, Aiden. I can't compete with fireflies in the cloister.

Please don't make me try.

I wanted to tell you all of this in person, but I chose not to for two reasons. The first being that if I'm leaving so that you can still have part of this trip—this pilgrimage—to yourself, it hardly makes sense to start a discussion that I know will go on for days and swallow up your time here.

The second reason is that I didn't want you to feel like you needed to prove to me that you really want to leave the Church by doing something irreversible and rash. You don't need to prove it to me, Aiden, I know you would leave. I know you would leap off a cliff or swim in gross grotto water if I asked, and so I don't need proof. All I need, all I'll ever need, is for you to keep living this life that means so much to you. To keep on as if I'd never come knocking at your cloister door, demanding to put my fingers in every wound you had. I need to know that you are full of all the joy and calm that you've earned over the years; that you are living like a saint. Maybe that means there's hope for the rest of us to become saints too, in our own ways.

Goodbye, Brother Patrick.

I love you like that. I love you like this.

I love you like everything.

—Elijah

I've somehow found my way up to the cliffs, his letter clutched in my hand and my breviary left back in my cell. His letter is my breviary now, my little hours. And in between reading the words again and again, I remember with clawing unhappiness the way he dodged my questions yesterday with such dexterity that I didn't even notice.

Is this okay with you?

I love you like everything.

Elijah was wrong about one thing. I'm not such a good listener after all.

The wind is strong today, and heavy clouds bring with them spatterings of drizzle, but I don't care. I sit hunched on the grass, staring out at the point where the gray sky meets the gray sea, Elijah's letter flapping in my hand, my mind as open and rough as the landscape around me. Funny how I wanted an abbey that would empty me out, a geography that would carve out everything that wasn't my love for God, and here I am. Completely empty. Hollow—a chalice without wine. A monstrance without a host.

Even my tears feel empty, pushed out of my eyes by

SAINT

biology and little else, because what I'm feeling is so beyond the scope of tears, so beyond what my body can hold for me.

Only God can hold it.

I lift my eyes to the hills.

But there are no hills in front of me now. From this direction, I can only see the sea.

CHAPTER FIFTY-ONE

My last two days at St. Columba's are filled with rain and a wordlessness that feels like it's sunk into my bone marrow and made a home there.

I can't speak, even when silence isn't required, and I have no desire to. There is no word I can produce, no sound I can utter, that will give adequate shape to what I feel inside. Which is elemental, which is tectonic. I have the feeling that if I speak, I will scream, and if I scream, I will never stop screaming.

I've practiced listening and silence for so long—long enough that it's become easy and natural and pleasant. But this is the first time it's ever felt *necessary*.

I *can* pray though. I don't feel soothed or elucidated by it or anything like that, but I still do it anyway. The liturgy—the psalms, the hymns, the Eucharist in the morning before breakfast—is the container that can hold anything, the real holy grail. Into it, I can pour fury and despair and a loneliness so sharp it slices through bone with no effort whatsoever, and the liturgy holds it all. It holds it all effortlessly.

It doesn't ask me to contextualize or extrapolate or analyze. It doesn't ask me to locate *precisely* my feelings and locate *precisely* my boundaries and what boundaries other people are allowed to have with me.

All liturgy asks is that I stand and sit and kneel. That I sing the words already printed out for me to read. All liturgy asks, essentially, is that I show up and breathe.

And right now, that's all I can do.

CHAPTER FIFTY-TWO

There are benefits to traveling in monk robes, and one of them is that no one is put off by my silence as I return the rental car and check in for my flight. I have a little left in my travel budget, and I wander to the airport bookstore, where I make an unnecessary splurge on the two issues of *Mode* they have in the magazine stand. I go to the airport bar, where I see not one, but two priests, and then the bartender gives me my Smithwick's on the house with a smile and a nod.

I muster a smile back and then thankfully the good man leaves me to stalk my ex-boyfriend's work in peace.

Both issues have articles by Elijah—one about a former boy band star who's been cast in a Hallmark-esque Christmas movie, one about an MIT scientist exposing bias in computer algorithms—both are so insightful and so dryly funny that I can hear his voice in both of them. It's the kind of hurt that I could keep hurting myself with for the rest of my life.

The rest of the magazines show me a world that was once

familiar and now utterly alien—the Egypt where I came from, as the Old Testament says. Expensive clothes, shoes, watches. Music retrospectives and movie reviews. A world of style and sophistication, and if I'd ever felt too intellectually clumsy or shallow for Elijah's world before I became a monk, I definitely feel that way now. I wear robes instead of mock turtlenecks and the newest song at the abbey is "Here I Am, Lord" and I don't even know what the men's jewelry renaissance *is*, much less whether or not it's a good fit for most casual events or not.

A slow doubt creeps in with the voiceless pain, and it grows like weeds around my feet as I board the plane, the *Mode* issues on my lap instead of my bible or *Summa Theologiae*.

Maybe…maybe it was never meant to be, me and him. Maybe he knew that. Maybe he knew I'd never fit into his life because I barely fit into it before. Not like Jamie probably did. Shit.

Over the ocean, I reread his letter again. I reread it so many times that I have it memorized. And as perversely good as it feels to pretend this is about me being unsophisticated or not fitting into his life, I can't ignore what he so plainly told me. A plea that can't be bypassed no matter what strategies or contingencies I think of.

I can't compete with fireflies in the cloister.

Please don't make me try.

And there it is. If I find him the minute my plane lands— if I wait a week, if I wait a year—it will always be the same problem, won't it? He'll always feel like my ex-boyfriend is there too, and when an ex-boyfriend is God, that's a problem.

There has never been a more captivating mistress than the carpenter from Galilee.

Elijah will always worry about measuring up to what I left behind, because I'll have left it behind for *him*, and he'll worry about me regretting the choice I made, and maybe he'll even worry that I'll go back. He'll fear that the loop of history between us is too strong, too pre-ordained even, and that I'll once again seek the silence of the cloister.

This is the beating heart of the problem: if I leave, then I'm asking him to trust that I won't make him compete with literal infinity, to trust that I'm leaving because I *want* to leave.

But…if it weren't for him, I wouldn't leave at all.

And that's the undeniable truth.

"You don't have to tell me about it if you don't want to," Brother Connor says, bowing at the beginning of a kata before moving into its salutation. The shade of the graveyard's oak tree spreads over us both, but the evening is hot, and I'm restless and sweaty under my robes. "But it's been a week and you haven't spoken to anyone. I've been formally asked to informally poke you about it. No pressure."

I make a noise of acknowledgment, watching him sink effortlessly into his stances, his steps sure, his strikes clean. He told me once that he started karate as a young man in his twenties, which means he's been doing these same forms for over forty years now, and it's incredible to watch. Soothing. There is no wasted movement, no struggle. Even missteps or mistakes are immediately folded into the flow, swallowed back into the motion. I know this from what he's told me—I'd never be able to spot a mistake in his katas even if I knew how they were supposed to go, because I suspect the mistakes are as graceful as the accuracy.

"When I went to Europe," I hear myself say, "I wanted a place where my past could be burned away. And I feel like I'm the one who caught on fire instead."

Brother Connor doesn't stop moving, but he tilts his head toward me as he strikes to show that he's listening.

"I felt so sure," I go on, finding that it feels good to talk about it, in an air-out-the-wound kind of way. "I felt so sure that I would prove the abbot wrong, that God wasn't asking me to reconsider my vocation as a monk. I knew exactly what I wanted, and it was this life, but more of it. Harder, stricter, quieter. Because more of those things would equal more of God, right? The more I emptied myself, the more of him I could hold."

I look down at my lap. I'm sitting cross-legged and my scapular has rucked up into a pool of fabric. I think of the careful way Elijah folded it in the Irish cottage after undressing me.

"But it didn't happen like that," I finally say.

I haven't confessed the particulars of the trip to anyone yet—not because I am trying to hide my sins, but because I miss them too much to speak them aloud. But I think the abbot and Brother Connor have already guessed.

"What happened was that I loved God and I loved Elijah

at the same time, and I felt more full of each the more I loved them. In France, I—" I close my eyes and think of how it felt to move from prayer to sex and then back again. From worship to worship. "I had both. God and him. And it felt better than anything."

I open my eyes to see that Brother Connor is watching me with kindness as he begins another kata.

"I would have left for him," I say slowly, the words coming out softer than I mean them to. "I offered to leave for him. He refused."

"But not because he doesn't love you," Brother Connor says.

"Worse. Because he does love me. And he knows I love this life."

"Do you, though?"

I glance sharply at the older monk, and he gives me a smile before dipping into a low stance with a series of hand strikes. "I'm not doubting you, Brother Patrick, nor your devotion to God. But is it possible that you love this life because it is the closest one you've found to the one you truly need?"

"I don't…" I shake my head. "I'm not looking for some unique path. I'm looking for the right one."

Brother Connor finishes and then walks over to me, lowering himself with grace to the ground and beginning to stretch. He's not winded in the least. "It's difficult to see it now, because it is so well-trod, but this?" Brother Connor gestures to the abbey campus, which at this hour is crawling with robed monks and agricultural students and visitors. "This was once unheard of. Strange. The roots of our story are radical ones, ones sought by people continually searching out the right way, the best way. Why else did the Cistercians feel the need to reform, and then the Trappists after them? Why are there active orders, contemplative orders, ruins of monasteries flaking off bits of damp plaster while foundations for new ones are being poured? And if it's that way just inside of our one sphere, can you imagine how many ways there must be outside of it?"

"Many gates," I murmur. It's what I said to Elijah when I was telling him the story of that night. That there are many gates, but this was the one I chose.

"Many gates," Brother Connor echoes. He makes a fist with his right hand and then brings it against his left palm. One of the opening gestures of his salutations. He looks down at his hands. "I often think that if I'd kept my school, if I'd kept my life the life of a martial artist, that I would probably be the same soul I am today. Practice is practice, whether it's psalms or stances. There are many gates, as you say. Many ways to the well."

Done stretching, he stands up and finds his habit to pull on over the T-shirt and old gi pants he's wearing.

"Do you regret it?" I ask after a minute. "Leaving the school behind? Leaving the person you loved behind?"

Brother Connor gives me a kind look. "If I didn't miss my old life, then the choice to come here would hardly have any meaning, would it? But regret is only part of the equation—an equation so long and so complicated that it will never stop being written as long as you're alive. It is fruitless to reduce everything into a category of regret or un-regret—sometimes the best and most creative decisions we make will forever hold seeds of regret inside. Sometimes our deepest happinesses start with regret, growing over it the way a pearl grows over grit."

I think about this for a minute, trapped between two regrets, as it were.

"I'm worried that if I leave for him, he still won't have me," I say. "And if I stay, my spirit will always hunger for him anyway."

Brother Connor reaches down to touch my shoulder. "Many ways to the well, Brother Patrick," he repeats. "And here you've named only two."

It's so close to what Father Jordan said to me in France— so close to his searching for something beyond the binary of vowed and unvowed—that the hair stands up on my arms. It's like I'm hearing a bible verse I've never heard before, something so indelibly true that there's no possibility of denying it.

But when I try to connect that truth to anything else—to my broken heart, to my future, to staying or leaving—nothing happens. It's like there's a wall between me and knowing what to do next.

"Come," Brother Connor says, offering me a hand as the bells toll for vespers. "The well will wait."

CHAPTER
FIFTY-THREE

Three weeks later, and I've made my confessions. But the abbot has still not asked to meet with me, which would be typical for a monk who's misbehaved as badly as I have.

I find that I don't dread the meeting the way I would've before my trip. Partly it's because the abbot seems to be just as pleasant and affectionate with me as ever and he talks to me often as I resume my duties in the office. (He's especially affectionate after I debrief him on my brewing espionage and tell him how robust Mount Sergius's operation is compared to the abbeys I visited.)

But also I don't dread it because everything seems inconsequential compared to the grinding and shifting inside my soul. I feel pressed between two millstones, which are pestling me into wet, pulpy paste. Into atoms. Into nothing.

I can't compete with fireflies in the cloister. Please don't make me try.

But why can't I have both, the fireflies and the cute

journalist? Why is *compete* the only verb possible?

And why hasn't he called? Or written? Or visited?

Why must I be ground into nothing alone?

"Brother Paaaaatrick," Brother Titus calls from my office doorway that morning. "You have a visitor!" He drops his voice conspiratorially. "And he's *handsome*."

Elijah.

I don't have the presence of mind to give him a quelling look; my entire being leaps into stuttering life with excitement—joy—lust. But then dread comes sneaking through my veins too.

As I stand and follow Brother Titus to the cloister, my thoughts crowd into my mind faster than they have in days, fueled by panic and desire both.

Okay, be quiet, be calm, I coach myself as I walk. *Be a better listener than you were last time. But convince him that you love him, that you want a future together, that you can do this—*

I come to a stop so fast at the entrance to the cloister that the hem of my habit swings around my feet.

It's not Elijah.

It's not Elijah sitting there on the bench, his arm across the back and his eyebrow arched.

It's *Jamie*. Of all the fucking people. With his back perfectly straight and his hands wrapped around some kind of Tupperware-looking thing.

I don't know what pushes me forward to the bench and has me sitting down. It may be Benedictine hospitality or morbid curiosity or a mixture of both, but somehow I find myself sitting next to Elijah's ex-fiancé.

"Muffin?" Jamie asks, holding up a container I'm certain is made from bamboo fibers or something equally responsible. The container is full of delicious-looking muffins. "I made them this morning."

I feel like it would be rude to say no, even though eating a muffin Jamie made feels like eating the manifestation of all the ways he's a better person than me. I take the muffin and hold it between my fingertips on my lap.

"Jamie, it's lovely to have you here," I say.

And I guess…I guess it's not all the way a lie. He is very nice, and he did bring me muffins even though I kind of stole his fiancé. "But I have to wonder why you want to see me, after everything that happened."

"I debated coming," Jamie admits, pushing his glasses up the bridge of his nose. They're that sort of "vaguely unhip which makes them even hipper" style of frames, and they look great on him because of course they do. "But the only real barrier to coming was my pride, and that seemed like a really weak reason at the end of the day."

"Pride might not be the best reason for doing or not doing things, but it's hardly ever weak," I say.

"Even so, I knew I'd regret not coming to see you later, and it's better to act in a way now that doesn't cause regret later, I think."

That's very emotionally healthy and wise, and obviously not the way I've ever lived. "I'll take your word for it."

He laughs, like I'm joking. I force a smile back, but as

Jamie carefully replaces the lid of his muffin container and bends down to set it next to his feet, I think about what Brother Connor said a few weeks ago. *Sometimes our deepest happinesses start with regret.*

I've been in a holding pattern these last few weeks—not making plans to leave for a new abbey *or* for a secular life. Just staying here with my hill and my creek and letting my loneliness expand to fill the halls of the church every time we pray. And even though Jamie made an active—and arguably brave—decision in coming to visit me here, maybe I've been acting more like him lately than I think. Maybe I've been trying to avoid regret more than I've been trying to reach for the right future.

Jamie straightens back up and when he does, he has something in his hand. A thick, glossy magazine. *Mode.*

"I wasn't sure if you got this here," he says, "or if someone would have mailed it to you already. But I think you should have this issue."

He hands the magazine to me. The cover story is a profile about an older actor, but on the side of the actor's grizzled but handsome face, I see it.

The Eternal Cool of Monks: Beer and Prayer in Some of the World's Loneliest Abbeys

I'm already flipping through the pages to find Elijah's article when Jamie speaks. "I thought after reading it when it came out this week…well, given the circumstances of how we ended our engagement…"

I stop flipping and look up at the friendly librarian.

He looks back at me with a look that's curious but a little guarded too. "I was surprised to learn that you're not together, is all."

I drop my eyes down to the magazine, feeling a sharp stabbing at the back of my eyelids. *Not for lack of trying, Jamie,* I want to say.

"The article…well, you'll see when you read it, I suppose." He clears his throat. "I wanted to—that is—ah, this is awkward to say. But I wanted to make sure it wasn't because of me. That you weren't holding back with him because of me."

There's no amount of monk training that can stop the incredulous noise I make at that. "I break up your engagement, and you're coming here to check on my feelings? Jamie, I celebrate saints every day, but have you ever considered that maybe you're too good of a person?"

He laughs. "I suppose I haven't." But then his look turns serious. "I hope you don't blame yourself for what happened between me and Elijah."

"Should I not?"

Jamie shakes his head, his eyes moving over to the fountain in front of us. "If I'm honest, I think I always knew that Elijah wasn't going to marry me in the end. I was the one who pushed to move in together, to get engaged, to set a date. And despite what you might think, he never made a secret of you and the number you did on him when you left."

I flinch, but Jamie is still looking at the fountain.

"I knew he was still in love with you, but I thought it was in the way we always romanticize our pasts, you know? That it

437

wasn't *you* he was still in love with, but that version of himself and that time in his life. But then when I came to visit, and I saw the way he looked at you…" Jamie sighs. "I knew then that it was more than the usual nostalgia. So I wasn't surprised when he came back and told me that you two had kissed. It still hurt like hell, but I wasn't surprised."

"Jamie, I'm so sorry," I say, "and I know that isn't enough, but I am still so sorry."

He looks over at me. "Thank you for your apology," he says evenly. "It doesn't change that it was an awful thing to go through."

"I know."

He blows out a breath. "My point is that no matter how much I loved him—and no matter how much he loved me back, because I know that he did—his heart was always elsewhere. Inside someone else's chest. Even after all that time."

I swallow as I look down at my hands and the perfect muffin cradled between them. I ache for Jamie's clear-eyed assessment of the truth, and of the pain it must have brought knowing it. I ache knowing that during all the years I'd been lamenting my traitorous heart, Elijah had been struggling with the same thing.

Both of us had found new devotions and new loves, but we'd been unable to surrender the old.

"So you see now," Jamie says after a minute. "I thought when he ended things that meant the two of you would be together. But then I find out from some mutual friends that it's not true, and then I call and learn that you're still here, and I think to myself, what's the point in all three of us being unhappy?"

That is some bleak stuff right there. "I don't want you to be unhappy either," I tell him. "Even though you're aggressively pleasant and handsome, and it makes me feel like a gargoyle."

He laughs again. "If you really were a gargoyle, it would've made the last two years of my life a lot easier."

"Unless I was a sexy gargoyle. Like from the show *Gargoyles.*"

He squints at me. "Wasn't that a cartoon?"

"Are cartoons not sexy?" I ask. "The hottest Robin Hood is a cartoon," I add.

"He's also a fox," Jamie says doubtfully. "And again, it feels strange to sexualize what's essentially a drawing."

"You're very pure," I tell him.

"I think you're the truly pure one, being a monk and all," he says, reaching for the muffin container at his feet.

I am definitely not the truly pure one.

And I'm suddenly very sad.

"I meant what I said," I say awkwardly. "I don't want this to be a situation where the only outcome is unhappiness for you no matter what."

Jamie gives me another smile, but it's coupled with a frank look. "The man I wanted to marry didn't want to marry me because he loved someone else more. It hurt, and I can't lie about that. But I'm going to be okay."

I look up at him as he stands up.

"Will you really?" I ask, needing to know. When I'd told Elijah that I'd leave a monastic life for him, I hadn't been thinking of Jamie. But I'm thinking of him now. I can't undo anything that's happened, but I can be aware of him and what he's lost and what he's felt and make sure he's okay.

"I will," he affirms. "It hurts now, but it would have hurt much more three years from now when this would've driven us apart anyway. And honestly?" he adds, handing the container of muffins to me, which I take. "I'm a lot more emotionally healthy than the two of you. I'm going to be fine a long time before you are."

Well. That's fair.

"I hope you read the article, Brother Patrick. And the muffins are for all the brothers. Also the container can't go in the dishwasher."

Of course it can't.

I stand to say goodbye, giving him a shallow bow as he leaves the cloister, and then I sit right back down and set my muffin and the container to the side, picking up the issue of *Mode* instead.

The entire article is good enough to hurt me as I read it. The vivid imagery of the Belgian forests. The lavender fields of Provence and the tall, dark cliffs of St. Columba's. I can practically taste the beer as he describes it, and all the personal moments in the article are beyond bittersweet to read. The moments I was there to witness too because I was by his side.

It's the last paragraph of the article that I reread over and over again, there in the cloister with the fountain burbling and the hot August sun moving overhead.

There was a moment at St. Columba's. Father Finbarr had graciously let me work in the library while my ex went to talk to their master brewer. It was raining, and I could still taste the communion wine on my tongue, and I was surrounded by books that have been collected over centuries and centuries with the faith that someone in the future would be there to read them, even there at the edge of the world. Through the veil of the rain outside, I could just barely make out the sea cliffs. It was impossible, in that lonely place, not to think of the faith this life requires. Monks pray, sing, sleep, work, brew beer, build libraries, and dig graves all for a love that they will never see consummated in this lifetime, for a beloved that they cannot see or touch, except by metaphor alone. It is impossible not to be affected by that, not to be humbled by the patience and the trust it requires, and so it is with the idea of patience that I leave you now. Patience is what makes good beer and good love both, and it is what I believe has now given me the greatest gift I'll ever receive. (And no, it isn't a case of the honey beer from Our Lady of the Fountains.)

The greatest gift he'll ever receive.
I take the muffins into the refectory, and then I ask the

abbot for permission to spend the next two days in the hermitage, which he grants.

I spend the days praying and chopping wood and thinking.

And this time, I have the patience to let the answers come to me instead of the other way around.

"This is Tyler Bell," the voice answers on the other end of the phone.

"I don't want to be a monk anymore," I say. I glance around—I'm in my office and it's a Saturday, so no one else would be in here, but still. This is a private conversation. Just me and my brother who also failed out of celibacy school.

"Well, I see we're getting right to it," Tyler says, and then I hear the sound of a door and the abrupt cease of a breezy, bug-filled outdoors. He's probably at the cabin he borrows from Poppy's family when he's writing. (Okay, well, it's less *cabin* than *very expensive forest retreat*, but that's how the Danforths roll.)

"Can I just start from the beginning?" I say. "Like the beginning-beginning?"

"Would that be the time you called me before you went to the monastery?"

The day I'd returned to Mount Sergius—no longer in crisis and with my life actually prepared for me to leave it—I'd called Tyler from the abbey parking lot.

Am I doing the right thing? I'd asked him. I hadn't told him about That Night; I hadn't really told him anything, aside from that I'd visited the abbey once and knew I wanted to be a monk.

Well, he'd answered slowly. *I don't know all of your reasons, Aiden. The reasons you go can be anything. But the reasons you stay? They need to be everything.*

Looking back, maybe I hadn't listened well enough. Seems to be a theme with me.

"Before that," I say heavily. "Much, much before that."

"Okay then," Tyler says, and so I begin.

I tell him about meeting *it* after Lizzy died, about living with it for all those years. I tell him about That Night as gently as I can, because I know it's hard stuff to hear, and I tell him about the text message and how it led me to the abbey. And then I tell him about the trip, about Elijah, about how certain I was that I needed a more ascetic life, and how I ended up having an interlude instead.

After I finish, I hear Tyler take in a long breath. For a moment, he doesn't say anything at all, but then he says, softly, "I had no idea. You always seemed the happiest out of all of us. The readiest for fun. I would never have guessed…"

No, most people don't guess, do they? That sometimes the people who laugh the loudest and reach for life the hardest are the ones closest to darkness.

"I'm okay now," I reassure him. "I'll have the brain I have my entire life, but I also have so many tools I didn't have before, and also Dr. Rosie, God bless her."

"Does Elijah know you're okay?" Tyler asks.

I think back to the conversation about Lectio Lexapro, about our talk in the Irish graveyard. "I'm pretty sure, yeah."

"Even without the monastic life? Because if I were him, and you told me about how integral being at Mount Sergius was to you rebuilding yourself, I don't know that I'd be willing to risk you leaving."

I look out the window of my office. I see a vegetable garden, and beyond it, my hill.

It's taken a lot of therapy to get to this point. And meds. Those too.

And...being a monk?

Yes.

"Do you think that's why he didn't want me to leave?"

"I think that's part of the reason. Along with what he explicitly told you—no one can compete with God, Aiden. You know that's not fair."

"I am so tired," I say, looking at the hill, "of everything being defined in opposition. God *or* Elijah. Monk *or* not monk."

"You sound like Jordan," Tyler says, sounding faintly amused. "It's all he ever talks about these days. The rigidity of a holy life, when it should be anything but rigid. Jordan thinks that if we forget that our tradition is a living thing—if it ossifies—it will slowly die. Maybe it already has."

"I feel like *I'm* dying," I say, and it's only half an exaggeration, because the grinding, pressing, crushing feeling certainly feels like a kind of death. "And I keep getting stuck in this loop—if I leave, Elijah won't have me. If I stay, I can't have Elijah."

"When I was thinking about leaving the priesthood," Tyler says, "Jordan asked me if I would still want to leave, even if I wasn't going to be with Poppy. I had to know if I wanted to leave for her or for myself."

I can see where he's going with this, and I sigh with impatient understanding. "That's the problem, Tyler. Saying I'm *not* leaving for him is disingenuous to the point of being an outright lie. If it weren't for him, I would stay. I wouldn't give up my communion with God."

"You're the one who was just railing against oppositional thinking," Tyler says. "Don't you think it's possible to have communion with God outside of a monastery?"

"Ugh," I groan, slumping in my chair. "On paper, yes. But the liturgy is communal. If I leave, I leave that behind."

But even as I say the words, I hear Brother Connor's from earlier.

Many ways to the well, and here you've named only two.

I'm not a creative person; I'm not a visionary. It's never occurred to me to try to forge a new way forward, to build something where before there was nothing. But as I look up at my hill, I have to wonder if that's what's being asked of me. If like the desert fathers, I'm being asked to plant my heart into unfamiliar soil and trust the harvest will come.

To have patience, like Elijah said in his article.

"It's fortunate that you weren't caught," Tyler is saying as I'm thinking all this. "With as much as you were sneaking off, it wouldn't have been surprising."

I know he's not saying it judgmentally, since his relationship with Poppy had gone catastrophically public back in the day. "No," I say, "it wouldn't have been surprising at all." But it makes sense to me, with a kind of God-logic. If we'd been caught, my hand would have been forced in many ways—it would have been easy to default into choosing what to do next.

I think God wants me to make this decision myself. And I think it's the only way Elijah would know for certain that this was what I really wanted.

And then I see the abbot walking alone on the path along the base of the hill, his hands tucked under his scapular and his face serene.

"Tyler," I say, "thank you for talking to me, but I think I have to go."

"Already?" Tyler asks. "But—"

"You were great. A-plus pastoring," I tell him. "Love you and tell Poppy hi for me and also goodbye!" I say as I stand up, and then I hear a small, *okay goodbye I guess*—as I hang up the phone and rush out of the office.

When I get to the abbot, I'm out of breath and already sweating a little under the hot sun. The breeze ruffles the abbot's eyebrows as he looks at me. "Well, Brother Patrick?" he asks pleasantly.

"I was wondering if we could talk," I manage to say between breaths. "I mean, if you have time."

"I always have time for my Brother Lumberjack," he says in a fond tone. "And I've been expecting this conversation. Come, let's find some shade, shall we?"

And together we walk toward the woods.

CHAPTER FIFTY-FOUR

Two Months Later

I wake up to see the walls of my teenage bedroom, which my mom had turned into a craft room after I left for college and which my dad has only recently gotten around to boxing up, even though she died six years ago. The walls are bare, and the bed is a twin that's a little too short, but I've opted to sleep in here instead of the guest room because this has a window that faces the slight hill at the end of our street. I like to look at it when I'm in here praying or doing lectio.

Also it's not like I really have anywhere else to go.

As a plumber, Dad keeps early hours too, and so by the time I'm done praying vigils, he's already stirring. When he comes into the kitchen, I've made coffee for us both, and we sit at the table in silence, watching dawn break over the backyard, a backyard lush with autumn reds and yellows.

"You know," he says after a minute, "you are welcome to stay here. Like really stay. Pick a better room and all that."

"I know," I tell him. I think he's a little lonely here sometimes, although he's been slowly dating his way through the front-desk ladies at his plumbing company.

"Sean being a good boss?" he asks. "I'll kick his ass for you if he's not."

When I left Mount Sergius, Sean offered me a part-time job managing the micro-lending arm of his nonprofit. I took it because it's flexible enough to allow me to pray all the hours, go to Mass at Father Jordan's church every day, and also it gets me health insurance while I figure out what to do next.

While I find my new way to the well.

It also means I get my old phone number back from Ryan. Back in the day, Bossy Sean had set up a family plan for us Bells in the area, and when I left for Mount Sergius, Ryan had inherited mine. But Bossy Sean is currently irritated with the high levels of wastrel-ness from the Baby Bell, so he's cutting some purse strings. When means I've inherited the number back.

I've bought a new phone for myself, but since the number is the same one Ryan's had through college, I keep getting random text messages asking if I know where to find weed.

Also I get lots of memes which I've spent too many years chopping wood to understand.

After coffee and a small breakfast, I take the bus downtown to Sean's nonprofit office, where I do some work until he gets there with his polo team of babies, and then I play with the babies on the floor while he works at his desk. Currently Josie is crawling over my legs while Amani is jumping onto my stomach over and over again as Caro and Martina laugh and laugh.

"Is today the day?" Sean asks, using the break to quickly tap out some emails with both hands for a change.

"Friday—*OOF*—" Caro has just jumped onto my stomach too, knees first.

"What's so special about Friday again?" Sean asks, still typing and seemingly unaware his children are trying to pop my internal organs like squishy balloons.

"Friday is *your* gala, you muppet. And it's at the same venue where Elijah and I first—"

"LA LA LA," Sean says, eyes on his computer screen. "Can't hear my little brother talk about banging my best friend at a gala right now!"

"We didn't bang," I tell him, moving to my knees so I could knee-walk over to the desk and whisper, "I blew him in the opera hall. Then *after* the gala, we banged."

Sean's head drops back as he squeezes his eyes together. "I didn't need to know that, I didn't need to know that, I didn't need to know that."

I wait for him to finish his little tantrum, and then I say, with forced casualness. "How is he doing, by the way?"

"How is he doing, my best friend whose heart you broke years ago and then rebroke again in Europe for some reason? That best friend? Is that the one you're asking about?"

I've explained to Sean *so* many times that Elijah was the

449

one who broke *my* heart in Europe, but it never makes any difference. He is firmly Team Best Friend, and will be until Judgement Day, I guess. And then probably even on Judgement Day, he'll berate Jesus into agreeing with him that I'm some kind of best friend seducer.

"He's miserable, thanks for asking," Sean says, going back to his email. "He also does the whole 'hey, not that I care about the person I'm desperately in love with, but how is he doing' thing. It's less subtle than you think."

I feel a flush of excitement that Elijah's asking about me. "Do you think he's miserable because I haven't talked to him yet? Since leaving the monastery?"

Sean apparently decides to give up on the email and turns to face me with a sigh. "Yes, okay? Yes. I think he wants to see you so badly that he would harvest his own kidney in order to do it, and it wouldn't feel like too high a price. But I think he's also miserable that you left, because he feels guilty and he thinks it's his fault and that he's stolen your Jesus-binky or whatever."

"Sean, I know you're around babies all day, but please don't say Jesus-binky again."

My brother keeps going, undeterred. "But I also think he will be very excited to see you on Friday."

God, I hope so. The minute I left Mount Sergius nearly two months ago, all I wanted to do was go to him. Drive straight to his apartment and pound on the door and then kiss him until the world ended.

But I'm doing things a little differently on this new path to the well. I'm doing things with patience—patience that I've learned at the abbey, patience that I've deepened with him and God both.

Old Aiden Bell could never.

Which reminds me, I need to get on my way if I'm going to make it to Father Jordan's church before he gets ready for Mass.

I kiss all the babies, give Martina one last toss into the air, and then get my phone.

"I wish you'd let me buy you some suits," Sean sighs as he watches me. Neither he nor Dad have anything that matches my shoulder measurements, so I've been piece-mealing together business outfits from Dad's nicer pants and button-down shirts from Kohl's.

"I don't know how long I'll be doing this," I remind him. This job is really just a stepping stone until I begin carving out my new vocation here in the world. "And also I let you rent me a tux for Friday, remember?"

"Ugh, fine. Go. Get me lunch on the way back, will you? Zenny packed me something called a superfood bowl, so I need you to bring me back a sandwich with cheese in it. Or bacon."

"I'll see what I can do," I say, and then I leave, closing the door behind me to keep the babies from escaping to have an office building adventure. And then I start my walk to Jordan's church.

It's a gorgeous fall day, the kind that used to make me think of hard cider and woodsmoke and football, but now makes me think of the crisp air in the beer garden, of the way the bright trees looked from the hermitage window. Of raking around the taproom and sharing a bottle with the other monks while the leaves burned in a smoky pile.

Ordinary time is what the Church calls it. The time strung between the liturgically heavy seasons of Lent and Advent.

But there is nothing ordinary about it. It is perfect.

The five block walk to the church is still disorienting to me, even though I've made it almost every weekday for the last month. The bustle of cars rushing past, the people darting in and out of buildings, the litter, the signs, the restless inhalations and exhalations of a downtown during business hours.

Where is everyone going, I wonder, and in such a hurry? No one even stops when the wind blows ruby-red leaves down the street, like so much autumn confetti. No one ever seems to breathe.

No one is ever silent.

I have to remind myself often of what Brother Connor said, about regret. Because I feel regret often.

I miss Mount Sergius so much it hurts.

I make it to Jordan's church, a tall edifice made of stone and stained glass, over a century old, and then I let myself inside one of the wooden doors.

I think I might have to hunt for him, but when I come inside, he's standing at the front of the sanctuary, looking up at the crucifix with his hands laced behind his back. The crucifix is a copy of the one we have at Mount Sergius, and so I could easily stare at it for hours too. I join him.

"I know the woman who makes these," Father Jordan says as I come to stand next to him.

"The crucifixes?"

He nods. "She's a sculptor here in the area. Very sensitive, very reclusive. But with a ferocious gift, wouldn't you agree?"

I do agree, and then I say, "You don't seem surprised to see me."

He looks at me, the shadows of the sanctuary making his eyes seem even darker. "I'm not, Aiden. I was expecting you."

"You were?"

He nods and then turns, gesturing to a pew in the front row. We both sit, and I say, fumbling a little, "I wanted to talk to you about something, but I've made myself wait a while before I did it, which is a new thing for me. I'm trying to be patient with things now instead of flinging myself headlong into them."

"I understand. And I'm happy to listen."

I take a breath. "I've been struggling this year with opposites. With exclusions. I know it will make me sound greedy, but I don't understand why loving someone has to exclude me from a liturgical life. I've petitioned to be an oblate at Mount Sergius, but that essentially means I'll just be visiting there occasionally, and imitating monastic life as best I can here. It's a good start and I'm grateful that I'll still be connected to my former home, but I want more."

Father Jordan nods, like of course I do. Of course it's natural to want more.

It makes me feel less greedy. And whiny.

Encouraged, I say, "I remember in Provence you said that you were trying to rediscover the tapestry that used to exist. That you wanted to make more room between vowed and unvowed, more ways to God. I'm not—look. I'm not like you or Tyler or Zenny. I've never felt like I'm the kind of person who can make new things. All I've been good at as a Catholic is doing the things someone settled on several centuries ago. But I think…I think I'm supposed to do this. At the very least, I feel driven to do this. Because I don't understand what's lost in my devotion if I'm also having sex. Sex makes my prayer *better*, not worse. And I understand that there will always be value in celibacy for some, but there's not for me. I don't see why that should exclude me from everything else." I look over at him. "I want to be a part of helping you figure it out."

"Okay," he says simply.

"I can be?"

"Yes."

"Will it be welcome to queer people?"

"Yes."

"Will it cause problems with the Church?"

"Almost certainly," is the reply, but the priest doesn't seem anxious as he says it, only thoughtful. "But I think you'll find many saints caused problems with the Church. Saints who the same Church venerates now."

"I'm not a saint though," I say.

He regards me. "Are you not?"

But before I can laugh at him or think of a response that's not scoffing or sarcastic, his eyes flick to the window, gauging the light. I feel it too, that internal sense of time, a result of years and years of praying at certain hours of the day. It's almost time for Mass.

He stands up and pulls his cell phone out of his pocket as he does. "Would you like to exchange numbers before I start preparing for Mass?"

"Oh yes," I say, standing too and getting my phone out. "What's your number? I'll text you."

He reads me his number and I punch it in, and then type out a **hi, this is aiden** and then hit send.

"There," I say, looking for the place on the text message screen to input a name for Father Jordan's number. "Now you have mine…"

But my voice trails off as I realize that the text I just sent is not the only text in our history. There's a text above it, sent years ago. Five years ago, in fact.

Sent at 3:28 a.m.

"Father Jordan," I say slowly, looking up from my phone to find Father Jordan already walking down the aisle toward the sacristy. "I've gotten a text message from this number before. Years ago."

Father Jordan stops and looks over at me. "What a coincidence," he says mildly.

And then he resumes his walk to the sacristy, leaving me there alone in the sanctuary with my phone in my hand, the screen still open to show the text message that saved my life.

I lift my eyes to the hills.

CHAPTER FIFTY-FIVE

Sean shamelessly leverages all his friends and acquaintances and former coworkers to come to his nonprofit benefit thing, and when I arrive an hour or so after it's started, the space is teeming with people too rich for their own good.

The four-story glass curtain wall of the Kauffman Center looks out onto a dark sky and a brightly lit city underneath it. From my vantage by the glass, I can see the way the city churns up into a hill, capped with the pale spire of the Liberty Memorial. It looks like a buttress for the sky.

Please, God, I say silently in the direction of the hill. *Please. Be with me tonight.*

Prayer said, I discreetly use my reflection in the glass to make sure I look okay—the tux fits fine, but I feel silly wearing it, and I've shaved and the sight of my naked jaw is strange—and that's when I see him.

Standing in the middle of the space with a flute of barely touched champagne, listening to guests chatter eagerly to his sister.

I turn to see him better, and my breath catches. Seeing in a glass darkly indeed—the reality as compared to the reflection is staggering. Even with the tense set of his jaw and the listless look to his eyes, he is gorgeous. His tuxedo makes the most of his long legs and his narrow hips, and the jacket accentuates the lean length of his torso and firmness of his chest. He is all geometry tonight, with the crisp seams of the jacket making a precise slope from the bottom of his neck to the ends of his shoulders, with the sharp peaks of his upper lip and the edges of his mouth in a straight line. Even the casual quirk of his eyebrow as he listens could have been drawn with a scale and compass.

Seeming to have had enough of whatever inane conversation he's listening to, he lifts his champagne to his mouth. And that's when he sees me.

He freezes like that, the glass rim set to his lower lip, his dark eyes wide as they lock with mine.

I send up one last prayer to God, and then I cut through the crowd in his direction, maneuvering as gracefully as I can when I'm the size of an armoire. I reach him, and then because he still seems frozen, I lift my hand and gently take the flute from his fingertips.

He lets me, swallowing a little as our fingers brush against each other's. Swallowing more when I press the same part of the rim that had just been against his mouth against mine and take a long drink.

"Hi, Elijah," I say, leaning in so the people around us can't hear. Zenny gives me a quick wink and then launches into a new conversational tangent about her birthing center which has everyone's attention. "You look incredible tonight. What are you doing after this?"

I see the bob of his Adam's apple and the flick of his eyes as he searches my face. And then he says, quietly, almost hesitantly, "Aiden, are you flirting with me?"

I do the same thing I did that night we came together six years ago. I grin at him.

And up and down that Adam's apple moves again, right over the perfectly tied bow tie at the base of his throat. "I have a few minutes," he says. "I know a place where we could catch up."

"I love catching up," I say, and so just like that night, we wend our way through the lobby and up one of the walkways to the balcony entrances. The door hasn't even closed behind us before I have him against the wall, my mouth slanting hot and urgent over his.

He makes a low noise into our kiss—a noise that usually comes with bite marks and tangled sheets—and wraps his hands around the lapels of my tux to pull me harder against him.

As if I need the encouragement. I've already got my dress shoes around his, my hips to his, my hands planted on either side of his head. I lick at his upper lip until he opens his mouth for me, and then I pillage inside, seeking him with the heat of weeks and months and years. And he kisses me back with the same heat, his desire palpable though the layers of our clothes, and all I want to do is suck him off right now, all the things unsaid between us be damned, all the pain between us be damned. I just want him panting and tensing and cursing under his breath; I just want our separation, our apartness, to be dissolved, obliterated with the kind of connection that can't be ignored.

Patience, I remind myself. If the past five years gave me anything other than God, they gave me that, and I need to use it. And anyway, this was never where Elijah and I struggled. Everything always made perfect sense when we were hard and shuddering with pleasure.

It was the other parts that needed fixing. Maturing, maybe, like wine.

I break our kiss slowly, so slowly that I myself doubt I'm actually going to do it, but somehow I manage to lift my mouth off his. It's physically painful, and my entire body keens for him again, reminding me with every beat of my heart how close he is, how handsome he is in the dim auditorium, how good his stubble feels against my lips and teeth when I kiss and nip at his jaw.

He lifts a shaking hand to my face. "You left the abbey," he whispers.

"Yes."

"For me?"

I can see the hope and the dread in his eyes, and I understand, I understand both.

"What you wrote in your article," I say, instead of answering. "At the end, about how patience had given you the greatest gift you'll ever receive…"

He bites the corner of his mouth. "I meant our trip, Aiden. I meant our time together when I thought we'd never have any time together ever again. I never thought—I didn't write that thinking that you would leave—I didn't want you to leave for me—"

I can feel the panic spilling through him, and I lean down to kiss his cheek, the smooth, warm rise of it above the line of his scruff. "Shh," I soothe, "shh. That's not what I mean. I'm telling you that I read your words and they made me see that I could have a great gift too, if I could practice patience."

He stills a little, but his thick brows are drawn together and there's a deep line between them, which I also kiss.

"Aiden, I..." He trails off, his eyes pinned to mine and glassy with emotion. "I feel so trapped. I meant what I said about competing with God, but I also can't refuse you. If you're here, then I can't...I'm not noble enough to push you away again. And when I'd heard you'd left the abbey...you can't imagine how hard it was not to come to you immediately. Beg you to forgive me and kiss me again, and every day that I didn't felt a hundred years long."

I like hearing that, and I tell him so, murmuring it low against his ear before I gently bite his lobe. I pull back and trace the line of his troubled mouth with my thumb. "There was a reason I didn't come to you right away, and it was so I could stand here and tell you this: I'm still healthy and well after nearly eight weeks outside of the abbey, and I'm under Dr. Rosie's strict supervision to make sure I stay that way. I'm helping Father Jordan explore a way for monastic life and liturgy to be available for everyone, and so I have a vocation out here too. And most importantly, you don't have to compete with God. I'm so sorry that I ever let you think that was the case, and I'm sorry I couldn't articulate the truth to you earlier. But you could never compete with God, because the two of you magnify each other in my heart. I know God and I feel God more keenly and more deeply because of you."

I find his hand and press it over my heart, over the invisible scapular I'll always wear for him. The glassy sheen in his eyes has started spilling over now, and tears are racing down his perfect cheeks.

"You bring me closer to God, Elijah," I tell him softly. "Simply by existing."

He ducks his head, his fingers scrunching a little against my tuxedo jacket, as if he wishes he could press through my skin and muscle to touch the organ that even now beats so fervently for him.

"It's everything I wanted to hear," he confesses, still not looking at me. "How do I know it's real? How do I know it will last?"

"Patience," I say. "*You* were the one who wrote about that."

He finally looks up, tears still tracking down his face and sliding down his jaw. "It feels too good to be true. Like a spring of water coming from a severed head. How can something beautiful come from the mess we've made?"

I kiss away one of his tears, and then I press my fingers under his chin and lift his face to mine. I rub my thumb against the subtle cleft there, as I give him my best Aiden Bell grin— the one that used to get me everything I wanted, everything in the entire world.

"I have an idea," I say mischievously, relishing the catch in Elijah's breath at my boxer-dropping smile. "What if we played a game?"

"A game," he whispers, the first hint of a smile returning to his mouth.

"A game," I confirm. "What if…what if we leave here together tonight?"

"I like the sound of that," he says, his tone cautious but his smile growing.

"And then, what if we decided to try again, the two of us? Knowing that it might take time, that we might be scared, that parts of it will be hard, but knowing we've been through harder?"

"I like the sound of that game a lot," he says softly.

"And," I say, keeping my fingers under his chin to hold him still for the sweetest, slowest kiss I'm capable of, "what if we loved each other until we were old and gray?"

He presses his hand harder against my chest. Against my heart.

"Okay, Aiden Bell, former monk," he says. "I have a *what if* for you too."

"And what's that?"

He gives me a smile that makes me very glad I've given up wearing my cage. His hand begins drifting south, down to my zipper, as he asks, "What if we started right now?"

EPILOGUE

from Mode Magazine

We got married on a rainy day in October—the kind of rainy day that makes you want to be in a college library or tucked into a big chair with a hot apple cider and a thick book. Of course, it mostly reminded me of the Irish abbey where I realized that I wasn't just in love with my ex, but *unconditionally and sacrificially* in love with him. And so it felt like a piece of that fateful trip was with us as we said our vows and pledged to love each other forever, with patience above all.

His brother—a former priest (yes, you might say some things run in this family)—led the ceremony, which we held in the same place where we came together the first and the final time. My husband chose it because he wanted to see the hills in the distance as he said his vows to me. I agreed because I can't deny him anything, and also because I got a very good discount on the rental fee.

My sister and his brother were there with their babies, which now number five. My parents were there too, and my father cried so hard that my mother had to sneak him a tissue during the service.

All of the usual friends and colleagues were there, and perhaps most surprising was the entire section of monks who'd driven up from Mount Sergius to see their Brother Lumberjack take some final vows at last. I think of all the weddings in this city, I can safely say that mine had the most Benedictine monks. They all cried harder than my father did.

When you marry an ex-monk, you learn to expect certain things: that he will pray at all hours of the day and what most people would term the night, that he'll crave being outside even when it's sweltering or bitterly cold, that no amount of deprivation or frustration makes him flinch (except when it comes to me—then the smallest sliver of deprivation has him whining like a puppy until I'm back in his arms).

You learn that his devotion to you will be breathtaking and fierce. You learn that the sacred you've held at arm's length ever since you became an adult has been waiting patiently for you all this time, and that it's used the man you love to speak in its small, quiet voice once more.

Of course, marrying is the easy part, *staying* married is usually where most of us find ourselves in trouble, but after a love story that's encompassed breviaries and vows and a European beer-tasting trip and actual, literal God, I think we can be forgiven for having hope. And anyway, I already love him like how forever feels.

I already love him like eternity is in the rearview mirror.

I love him like everything.

—"Vows After Vows: My Wedding to an Ex-Monk" by Elijah Iverson

AUTHOR'S NOTE

All of my books are excavated from inside my messy brain, but *Saint* is a very intimate book in that it engages with the effects of depression and suicidal ideation. If you or someone you know is experiencing thoughts of self-harm or suicide, please visit the National Suicide Prevention Lifeline website for a 24-hour help chat or resources, or call 1-800-273-8255, which is a 24-hour line staffed with people ready to listen.

I hope that *Saint* shows what I've learned, which is that no darkness lasts forever, and that we are so much more than brain chemistry, we are spirits and hearts too. And to my friends who've experienced anything related to what Aiden's lived with: we need you in the world. We need your voice and your eyes, your bodies and your souls.

You're beautiful, and I'm honored to share this earth with you.

Like *Priest* and *Sinner*, *Saint*'s settings are inspired by real locations but are all products of my imagination. Mount Sergius is loosely informed by the Benedictine abbeys we have here in the Midwest—Conception, St. Benedict's, and Saint Meinrad's among them—and is situated vaguely at the edge of the Flint Hills. Semois is a combination of Orval and Rochefort, and Our Lady of the Fountains is basically an alternate-universe version of the Abbaye de Sénanque, but with fresh-water springs and honey beer. Although the story of the world's rarest beer doesn't belong to my pretty-but-fake lavender monastery, but instead to Saint-Sixtus Abbey and its infamous Westvleteren Blond, 8, and 12.

St. Columba's, however, is entirely a fantasy, since most contemporary Irish monasteries are rudely not perched on a sea cliff.

There are a couple other small things the abbey-enthusiasts out there might notice: the Major and Minor Hours of the Daily Office are occasionally called different things at different abbeys, according to their own abbey-level or order-level traditions. I've chosen to call them by their most traditional Latin names for the very important reason that those names are the coolest to me. Likewise, I've taken some liberties with the degrees of silence observed at Trappist monasteries, since the silence isn't total anyway (Trappist monks are always allowed to speak to their abbots and priors and are usually allowed to communicate about work) and also since my research indicated that there are plenty of exceptions to observing silence, particularly when visitors (like Aiden and Elijah) are present. There are a few other things, like meat consumption, that I've been free with—in that case so I could give a better sense of a region's cuisine.

Sharp-eyed readers will also notice there are some timeline discrepancies between *Saint* and the first two books in the series. This is for selfish creative reasons—I wanted Aiden to be closer to taking his solemn vows, which would mean a six-year chronological gap between *Saint* and *Sinner,* when *Sinner* actually came out only three years before this book's release.

And finally, I'm hugely indebted to several works of nonfiction, including:

The Cloister Walk by Kathleen Norris

How to Do Nothing by Jenny Odell

In Praise of the Useless Life by Paul Quenon, O.C.S.O.

Monasticism by Stephen J. Davis

A Monk in the World by Wayne Teasdale

Radical Love by Father Patrick S. Cheng

The Seven Storey Mountain by Thomas Merton

Trappist Beer Travels by Caroline Wallace, Sarah Wood, and Jessica Deahl

And yes, if you were wondering, Father Jordan will get his own story!

(And maybe Ryan too…)

ACKNOWLEDGMENTS

Two voices were immeasurably helpful in midwifing this very long and angsty book. Thank you with all my heart to Tessa Gratton and Erica Russikoff for their insights into character, narrative, and mental health. This book would not be what it is without their generosity, instinct, and facility with story.

I owe another profound thank you to C. G. Burnette, Lexi Roark, and TJ Turner for their collective help with everything ranging from Bible translations to Elijah's journalistic vision to which parts were the most agonizing emotional to read. Thank you from the bottom of my forever-NIV-loving heart!

Thank you to Michele Ficht for her sharp eye, to Cait Greer for a gorgeous paperback, and to photographer Stevan Reyes and designer Hang Le for giving Aiden the perfect cover.

Eternal gratitude to Candi Kane, Serena McDonald, Melissa Gaston, and Ashley Lindemann for their constant help and cheerleading and publicity acumen. Additionally, I owe a huge debt to Kenya Goree-Bell for being my vampire sprinting buddy for the duration of this book!

Writing a book this intimate meant there was a *lot* of wailing to friends, and I'm indebted to Julie Murphy, Nana Malone, and Ashley Lindemann for bearing the brunt of my Type 4/INFP artist angst. I also have to credit the wonderful and creatively nourishing friendships of Natalie Parker, Tessa Gratton, Kenya Goree-Bell, Becca Mysoor, Kennedy Ryan, C.G. Burnette, Jean Siska, Skye Warren, Katee Robert, Kayti McGee, Kyla Linde, Giana Darling, Adriana Herrera, Joanna Shupe, Eva Leigh, Nicola Davidson, and anyone else who's listened to me whine for the last few months about how bad I am at my job.

I'm also very happy that Louisa Whitfield-Smith once told me a story about monks hopping around on giant bouncy balls while she was on a retreat! The happy, friendly, and thoughtful monks of Mount Sergius are inspired by her retreat stories, and by her own happiness, friendliness, and thoughtfulness.

To my forever romance hero, Mr. Simone, thank you for your unqualified support, encouragement, and oxytocin-inducing hugs, and thank you to the rest of my family for never batting an eye at my wacky books—and also for letting me go to barbecues, fireworks displays and family reunions with a laptop forever balanced on my lap.

I've been mulling over how to write *Saint* since I finished *Sinner* in 2018, which…has not been a short amount of time. So my last debt is owed to you, my friends. Thank you for your patience in letting me find just the right story for Aiden and Elijah, and for letting me take the time to find the spiritual necessity for yet another naughty Bell brother.

Thank you for traveling to the monasteries with me. I love you like that. I love you like this.

I love you like everything!

ALSO BY
SIERRA SIMONE

The Priest Series:

Priest

Midnight Mass: A Priest Novella

Sinner

Saint

Thornchapel:

A Lesson in Thorns

Feast of Sparks

Harvest of Sighs

Door of Bruises

Misadventures:

Misadventures with a Professor

Misadventures of a Curvy Girl

Misadventures in Blue

The New Camelot Trilogy:

American Queen

American Prince

American King

The Moon (Merlin's Novella)

American Squire (A Thornchapel and New Camelot Crossover)

Co-Written with Laurelin Paige

Porn Star

Hot Cop

The Markham Hall Series:

The Awakening of Ivy Leavold

The Education of Ivy Leavold

The Punishment of Ivy Leavold

The Reclaiming of Ivy Leavold

The London Lovers:

The Seduction of Molly O'Flaherty

The Persuasion of Molly O'Flaherty

The Wedding of Molly O'Flaherty

ABOUT THE AUTHOR

Sierra Simone is a USA Today bestselling former librarian who spent too much time reading romance novels at the information desk. She lives with her husband and family in Kansas City.

Sign up for her newsletter to be notified of releases, books going on sale, events, and other news!

www.thesierrasimone.com
thesierrasimone@gmail.com

9 781949 364170